EL FILIBUSTERISMO

José Rizal
The last studio portrait, Madrid 1890, aged 29.

Cover design by Joanne de León

ISBN 971-569-236-2 pbk

Published by The Bookmark, Inc.
264-A Pablo Ocampo Sr. Ave.
San Antonio Village
Makati City, Philippines 1203
☎ 895-80-61 to 65
E-mail: bookmark@globelines.com.ph
Website: www.bookmark.com.ph

Printed in the Philippines by St. Faustina Press

The National Library of the Philippines CIP Data

Recommended entry:

Locsin, Ma. Soledad L.
      Jose Rizal : El Filibusterismo :
subversion : a sequel to Noli Me
Tangere / translated by Ma. Soledad
Lacson-Locsin ; edited by Raul L.
Locsin. – Makati City : Bookmark,
c1996
      xviii, 448 p

      1. Rizal y Alonzo, Jose, 1861-
1896. El Filibusterismo. I. Locsin,
Raul L. II. Title. III. Title: El
Filibusterismo : subversion.

PL6058.4 899.21'03 1996 P964000278
ISBN 971-569-236-2
ISBN 971-569-235-4 (cb.)

10 09 08 9 8 7 6 5 4 3 2 1
0708

JOSÉ RIZAL

EL FILIBUSTERISMO

SUBVERSION

A Sequel to Noli Me Tangere

Translated by Ma. Soledad Lacson-Locsin

Edited by Raul L. Locsin

Bookmark

Easy it is to assume that a filibuster has bewitched in secret the league of friars and reactionaries, so that following unconsciously his inspirations they would favor and promote that policy which only aspires to one aim: to spread the ideas of subversion throughout the entire country and to convince the last Filipino that no other salvation exists outside of separation from the Motherland.

Ferdinand Blumentritt
GENT,
BOEKDRUKKERIJ F. MEYER VAN LOO,
VISANDERENSTRAAT, 66
1891

To the Filipino People and their Government

So often have we been haunted by the specter of subversion which, with some fostering, has come to be a positive and real being, whose very name steals our serenity and makes us commit the greatest blunders. Setting aside, therefore, the old custom of respecting myths in order not to encounter the dreaded reality, we look at it face to face instead of fleeing, and with assertive though inexpert hand, we raise the shroud in order to uncover before the multitude the structure of the skeleton.

If at the sight, our country and her government reflect, we would consider ourselves happy. It matters not if they censure our audacity; it matters not if we must pay for our boldness, as did the young student of Sais who wished to penetrate the secret of priestly deceit.

On the other hand, if before the reality, instead of changing, the fear of one is increased, and the confusion of the other exacerbated, then they may have to be left in the hands of time, which teaches the children, and in the hands of fate, which weaves the destinies of peoples and governments with their deficiencies and the mistakes which they commit each day.

The Author
Europe, 1891

To the Memory

of the priests:

Don Mariano Gomez (85 years old),
Don Jose Burgos (30 years old),
and Don Jacinto Zamora (35 years old).

Executed on the scaffold at Bagumbayan

on February 28, 1872.

The Church, in refusing to degrade you, has placed in doubt the crime imputed to you; the Government, in shrouding your cause with mystery and obscurities, creates belief in some error committed in critical moments, and the whole Philippines, in venerating your memory and calling you martyrs, in no way acknowledges your guilt.

As long therefore as your participation in the Cavite uprising is not clearly shown, whether or not you were patriots, whether or not you nourished sentiments of justice and liberty, I have the right to dedicate my work to you, as to victims of the evil that I am trying to fight. And while we wait for Spain to reinstate you and make herself jointly culpable for your death, let these pages serve as a belated wreath of dried leaves laid on your unknown graves; and may your blood be upon the hands of those who, without sufficient proof, assail your memory!

J. RIZAL

Introduction

A sequel to the *Noli Me Tangere*, the *El Filibusterismo* is a book for all seasons for peoples existing under oppressive regimes. It begins where the *Noli* leaves off, where love, romance, heroism, idealism and tragedy turn to hate, bitterness, anger, disillusionment and vengeance.

Unlike the *Noli*, which is largely a narration of events and the softer emotions, the *Fili* is dominated by dialogue, ideology and the angrier passions. How to capture the nuances of a language of almost a century gone by, in today's English and with the same rage, is itself a story.

The *Fili*, according to the preface of the centenary edition published by the National Historical Commission, was written after Rizal returned to Europe in February 1888. He was then somewhat disappointed at the reaction of his fellow Filipinos as well as of the Peninsulars to what he had written in the *Noli*. For Rizal, as Retana said, "wrote not only for the Filipinos but also for the Spaniards, not only for the colony but also for the Peninsula as well," to call attention to the abuses of the government so that they might see these defects. It was his belief that his book would open the eyes of the Filipinos and at the same time awaken the national conscience of the Spaniards. It was also an appeal to both to improve strained relations which, if not enhanced, would redound to national failure.

In a way the author identified himself with Ibarra, who desired to reconcile the situation and to harmonize conflicting interests. However, he noted that if something had been achieved, at least in part, by what he was proposing to his countrymen, it had produced a counter-productive effect among the Peninsulars. Rizal began to see the futility of expecting a change in the system of government, and wrote his second novel, *El Filibusterismo* (The Subversion), which sees the savage mutation of the ambivalence of Ibarra, or Rizal, in the *Noli*.

Simoun in the *Fili* is Ibarra transformed into a revolutionary, ruthless and implacable, radical and vengeful, as seen in his words: "...Today I have returned to destroy this system, precipitate its corruption, push it to the abyss where it runs insensate, even if I have to spill torrents of blood and tears...It has condemned itself and I do not wish to die without seeing it dashed to pieces at the bottom of the precipice!...Summoned by the vices of those who rule, I have returned to these islands...With my wealth I have opened the way and wherever I have been, greed in the most execrable forms, now hypocritical, now shameless, now cruel, feeds on a dead organism like a vulture devouring a cadaver. And I have asked myself: why does the poison not ferment in its guts, the toxin, the venom of the graves, kill the loathsome bird? The corpse is left destroyed, the vulture is satiated with flesh, and since it is not possible for me to give it life so that it would turn against its executioner, and since corruption sets in gradually, I have incited greed; I have favored it; I have multiplied the injustices and the abuses; I have fomented crime, acts of cruelty to accustom the people to the prospect of death; I have encouraged anxiety so that flight from it would lead to any solution whatever... driven the vulture itself to degrade the same cadaver that gives it life and corrupts it...I am the Judge come to punish a social system through its own crimes...."

The *Fili* is just another story to tell, but in its intensity lie the thoughts and the soul of a people, their hopes and their future, the sweep and shape of their destiny, forming part of the parcel of a national heritage. But then, the reader must judge for himself, like Simoun, whether indeed the ends justify the means, and finally agonize like Shakespeare's Casca that the fault may "...not be in our stars but in ourselves, that we are underlings."

As in the *Noli*, the dilemma confronted me: to hew closely to the original, the way Rizal wrote it, or freely and more closely to the semantics of today? I wrote then that "Spanish is a beautiful language; but translated into English literally, it becomes florid and clumsy with its long periodic sentences, shifting tenses and wandering modifiers and, therefore, less comprehensible. On the other hand, the sparse clarity of English often robs translated Spanish of its original ambience and precision." In both translations, the decision of how to structure the sentences was controlled by the thought that, after all, I was doing a translation of Rizal's own version of his work, and not my own version of Rizal. But Rizal also has to be understood in English.

Thus, I have again taken the "liberty of cutting the

long sentences by just converting them into more, but shorter ones; and of rearranging some of the adjectives and adverbs to bring them closer to the words they modify; of adding or cutting words here and there but taking care not to enlarge or diminish the original, while attempting to preserve the cadence of Spanish in the English translation. Again, I must apologize to the reader if I have inadvertently made some slips in this balancing act."

Also, some words in the *Fili* "have their modern equivalents in English but do not have connotations similar to those endowed them by the social and political structures then. I have retained some of these in the original Spanish. Many of these words are still used in the Philippine national language with the same gist. For those who have but a faint recollection of Philippine history, some of the annotations of the *Fili* as compiled by the National Historical Commission from various sources and editions already published are appended and, at times, elaborated upon."

The Translator

Contents

- 1 -

On Deck

Sic itur ad astra.

This way to the stars.

One December morning the steamship TABO was arduously sailing upstream through the winding course of the Pasig, carrying numerous passengers to the province of Laguna. It was a ship of heavy build, almost round like the *tabú* or water-dipper from which she derives her name, rather dirty despite her pretensions to whiteness, majestic and solemn in her slow calm.[1] For all that, the region had a certain fondness for her, perhaps for her Tagalog name, or for exuding a character peculiar to things native, something akin to a triumph over progress—a steamship that was not quite a steamship, a changeless entity, imperfect but indisputable, which when she wanted to pass herself off as progressive was proudly content with a new coat of paint.

And yes indeed, the lucky steamship was genuinely Filipino! With a little bit of goodwill she could be taken for the Ship of State, constructed under the supervision of the Most Reverend and Illustrious personages.[2]

Bathed by the morning sun, which makes the ripples of the river throb and the wind sing through the swaying reeds flourishing on both banks, there goes her white silhouette, waving a black plume of smoke; they say the Ship of State smokes much, too! Her whistle wails at every moment, raucous and imposing like a tyrant who seeks to rule by shouting; so much so that no one aboard understands himself. She threatens everything in her way, now seeming about to crush the *salambaw*,[3] scraggy fishing contraptions which in their movements are not unlike skeletons saluting an antediluvian turtle; now running straight against the bamboo brushes or against the floating eating places or *kárihan*,[4] which, among gumamelas and other flowers, seem like indecisive bathers, their feet already in the water but still undecided on plunging in. Sometimes, following a certain bearing marked on the river with bamboo poles, the steamship moves very surely, but suddenly a shock jolts the travelers, making them lose their balance; she has struck low-lying mud which nobody suspected.

And if her similarity to the Ship of State still seems incomplete, look at the array of passengers. From below deck loom brown faces and black heads, all types of *Indios*, Chinese and half-breeds, jammed among merchandise and trunks, while up there on deck, under a tarpaulin that protects them from the sun are seated on comfortable armchairs a few passengers dressed like Europeans, friars, and office workers, smoking cigars and contemplating the countryside, seemingly without perceiving the skipper's and the sailors' efforts to negotiate the difficulties of the river.

The skipper is a man of benevolent aspect, somewhat advanced in years, an old sailor who in his youth sailed much wider seas and in faster vessels; and now in his old age has to exert greater effort, care and vigilance to avoid lesser perils.[5] ...And they are the same difficulties all the days: the same mud-bars, the same bulk of a vessel stuck in the same curves, like a fat woman in a crushing crowd. That is why the good man, moment by moment, has to stop, to reverse, to go half speed ahead, ordering now to port and then to starboard five sailors provided with long poles or *tikines* to accentuate the turns indicated by the helm.[6] He is like a veteran who, after leading men in hazardous campaigns, has become in his old age mentor to a wayward child, disobedient and bone-idle.

And Doña Victorina, the only woman seated among the European group, is able to say if the Tabo is idle, disobedient and wayward.[7] Doña Victorina, always high-strung, hurls invectives against ships, bancas, coconut rafts, boats, *Indios* who travel, and even against laundresses and bathers who upset her with their merriment and din. Yes, the Tabo would go very well if there were no *Indios* in the river, *Indios* in the country, yes, and if there were not a single *Indio* in the world, not noticing that the helmsmen were *Indios*; the crewmen, *Indios*; the engineers, *Indios*; ninety-nine per cent of the passengers, *Indios*; and, she herself, *Indio*, if her make-up were scraped off and her showy gown shed.

That morning Doña Victorina was harder to bear than ever because the passengers in the group did not pay her any attention, and with good reason. Consider: there you could meet three friars convinced that the whole world

would go backwards on the day they moved to the right;
an indefatigable Don Custodio who sleeps peacefully,
pleased with his projects; a prolific writer like Ben Zayb,
(anagram of Ibañez) who believes that in Manila they think
because he, Ben Zayb, thinks; a canon like Padre Irene
who gives luster to the clergy with his ruddy, well-shaved
face, from which rises a beautiful Jewish nose, and his silk
soutane of elegant cut and tiny buttons; and a very rich
jeweler like Simoun who is said to be the consultant and
source of inspiration for all the acts of His Excellency, the
Capitan General.[8] Consider that finding all these pillars
sine quibus non of the country huddled in pleasant talk,
and having little sympathy for a renegade Filipina who
dyes her hair blonde—is this not enough to stretch the
patience of a female Job, an appellation Doña Victorina
always applies to herself whenever aggrieved with
someone?

And the lady's ill humor increased every time the
skipper yelled *baporb! estriborp!* and the crew rapidly took
hold of their long *tikines* and pushed now against this
bank, now against the other, keeping, with the exertion of
their legs and shoulders, the boat from hitting the banks.
Seen thus, the Ship of State could be said to transform
from turtle to crab every time danger approached.

"But, Capitan, why does your stupid helmsman veer
towards that side?" asked the lady angrily.

"Because there it is very shallow Señora," replied the
skipper very measuredly, winking slowly.

The skipper had acquired this little habit as if to warn
the words he let out: "Slowly! Very slowly."

"Half speed, come, half speed all the time!"
disdainfully protested Doña Victorina; "Why not full
speed?"

"Because we would be sailing over those rice fields, Señora," he replied unruffled, pointing with his lips to the rice fields and slowly making two winks.

This Doña Victorina was very well-known in the country for her extravagance and fancies. She frequented social gatherings, which readily tolerated her when she presented herself with her niece, Paulita Gomez, a very beautiful and rich young woman, orphaned of both mother and father, and to whom Doña Victorina was a kind of guardian. At a very late age, she had married a hapless wretch named Don Tiburcio de Espadaña,[9] and in these moments we see her after fifteen years of marriage, wigs and semi-European attire. Because all her aspiration had been to Europeanize herself since that unfortunate day of her marriage, thanks to reprehensible efforts she gradually succeeded little by little in transforming herself in such a way that now Quatrefages and Virchow together would not have known how to classify her among the known races.[10]

At the end of so many years of marriage, her husband, who had suffered with the resignation of a fakir, submitting himself to all her impositions, had on one inspired day known a fatal quarter of an hour in which he administered to her a magnificent wallop with his cripple's crutch. The surprise of Señora Job at such inconsistency of character was so great that she did not immediately perceive its effects, and only when she had recovered from her fright and her husband had escaped, did she notice the pain, keeping to bed for some days to the great joy of Paulita, who loved to laugh and make fun of her aunt.

As for the husband, terrified at his own daring, which to him smacked of horrible parricide, and pursued by the matrimonial furies (the two little dogs and a parrot in the house) he took flight as quickly as his lameness would allow. He climbed into the first carriage he encountered, boarded the first banca he saw on the river and, a Filipino Ulysses, wandered from town to town, from province to province, from island to island, followed and hounded by his Calypso with pince-nez, who bores those who have the misfortune to travel with her. She had news that he could be found in the province of Laguna, hiding in a town, and there she was going now, to seduce him with her dyed curls.

Her fellow passengers had taken to defending themselves by sustaining an animated conversation, discussing whatever matter. At that moment the turns and twists of the river lead them to talk about straightening it out and, consequently, of port projects.

Ben Zayb, the writer who looked like a friar, was discussing with a young religious who, in turn, had the looks of a gunner. Both were shouting, gesticulating, raising their arms, throwing up their hands, stamping their feet, as they discussed water levels, fishponds, the San Mateo river, ship hulls, *Indios* and so forth to the great satisfaction of the others who were listening, and the manifest displeasure of an older Franciscan, extraordinarily thin and emaciated, and that of a handsome Dominican who bore the trace of a mocking smile on his lips.

The thin Franciscan, who comprehended the Dominican's smile, wanted to cut the argument by intervening. Doubtless they must have held him in high respect because at a wave of his hand both stopped at the point when the friar-gunner was talking about experience and the writer-friar, of men of science.

"The men of science, Ben Zayb, do you know what they are?" the gaunt Franciscan said in a sepulchral voice, without moving from his seat and hardly gesturing with his withered hands. "There you have in the province the Puente del Capricho,[11] bridge of caprice built by one of our brothers, and which was not finished because the men of science, citing their own theories, criticized it as frail and unsafe, and look, it is a bridge that has withstood all the floods and earthquakes!"

"That is it, *puñales!* that is precisely what I was going to say!" exclaimed the friar-gunner banging his fist against his cane chair. "That is it, the Puente del Capricho and the men of science! that is what I was going to say, Padre Salvi, *puñales!*"

Ben Zayb remained silent, half-smiling, perhaps out of respect or because he did not know what answer to give, despite his being the only thinking head in the Philippines! Padre Irene nodded in approval, rubbing his nose.

Padre Salvi, that gaunt and emaciated religious, as if pleased with such submission, continued amid the silence:

"But this does not mean that you are not as right as Padre Camorra (that was what the friar-gunner was called); the trouble lies in the lake itself!"

"It is because there are no decent lakes in this country," interpolated Doña Victorina, thoroughly indignant, and preparing herself for another vigorous assault on the debate.

The beleaguered looked at each other with apprehension and, with the keenness of a general, the jeweler Simoun came to the rescue.

"The remedy is very simple," he said with a strange accent, a mixture of English and Latin American, "and, really, I don't know why no one has thought of it before."

All turned to give him undivided attention, including

the Dominican. The jeweler was a lean, tall, sinewy man, deeply tanned, dressed in the English fashion, and wearing a helmet of *tinsin*.[12] What called attention to him was his long hair—completely white in contrast to the black beard, which was sparse, denoting a *mestizo* origin. To avoid the light of the sun, he always wore a pair of enormous blue-tinted glasses which completely covered his eyes and part of his cheeks, giving him the aspect of a blind man or one of defective eyesight. He stood with legs apart, as if to maintain his balance, hands thrust into the pockets of his jacket.

"The remedy is so simple," he repeated, "and it would not cost a *cuarto*."

The interest intensified. It was bruited about in Manila circles that this man had a great influence over the Capitan-General, and everyone was already seeing the remedy on its way to execution. Don Custodio himself turned around.

"Dig a canal straight from the entrance of the river to its exit passing by Manila, that is: make a new river channel and close up the old Pasig. Land will be saved, distances shortened and the formation of shoals impeded."[13]

The proposal left almost all in a daze, accustomed as they were to palliative measures.

"That's a Yankee plan!" remarked Ben Zayb, who wanted to please Simoun. The jeweler had stayed in North America a long time.

All thought it was a grand project, and indicated their approval by their head movements. Only Don Custodio, the liberal Don Custodio, because of his independent position and his high offices, believed it his duty to criticize a program that had not come from him—that was a usurpation. He cleared his throat, stroked his moustache and, with an important voice as if he were in full session at the *ayuntamiento*, said:

"I beg your pardon, Señor Simoun, my esteemed friend, if I have not the same opinion as yours. It would cost a lot of money, and perhaps we would have to raze villages."

"Then raze them!" Simoun coolly replied.

"And the money with which to pay the laborers...?"

"They do not need to be paid. With the convicts and those detained..."

"Oh no, there are not enough, Señor Simoun!"

"Well, if there are not enough, then let all the villagers, the old men, the youth, the children, work, instead of the fifteen obligatory days, for three, four, five months for the State with the added obligation to each bring his own food and his tools."[14]

Shocked, Don Custodio turned to see if there was an *Indio* within hearing. Fortunately, those who were there were peasants, and the two steersmen appeared to be greatly occupied with the turns of the river.

"But Señor Simoun..."

"Disabuse yourself, Don Custodio," said Simoun dryly. "Only in that manner are great projects executed with little means. Thus were carried out to completion the Pyramids, the Lake of Moeris and the Coliseum of Rome. Entire provinces came from the desert carrying onions for their food; old, young and even children worked, hauling stones, cutting them and carrying them on their shoulders under the direction of the official whip; and afterwards those who survived returned to their villages or perished in the sands of the desert. Then, in turn, those from other provinces came, and others after them to continue the task throughout the years. The work was finished and now we admire it. We travel, we go to Egypt and Rome, we praise the Pharaohs, the family Antoninus...Do not deceive yourself: the dead remain dead; and only the strong are given credit by posterity."

"But, Señor Simoun, such measures may provoke disturbances," remarked Don Custodio, who had become uneasy at the turn the conversation was taking.

"Disturbances ha, ha! Did the Egyptians rebel even once? Did the Jewish prisoners rebel against the pious Titus? Man, I thought you were more knowledgeable about history!"

Obviously Simoun was either highly presumptuous or had no manners. To tell Don Custodio to his face that he did not know history was enough to provoke one to lose his temper. And indeed Don Custodio forgot himself and retorted:

"But you are not among the Egyptians or the Jews!"

"And these people have rebelled more than once," added the Dominican with a certain hesitation, "when they were obliged to haul huge trees for the building of ships. If it were not for the religious..."

"Those days are far away," answered Simoun, laughing more dryly than usual. "These islands will not rebel again no matter what labors or taxes they may have...And," he added, turning to the thin Franciscan, "were you not extolling to me, Padre Salvi, the house and hospital of Los Baños where his Excellency is staying?"

Padre Salvi nodded and looked surprised at the question.

"Didn't you tell me yourself that both buildings had been constructed by obliging the townspeople to work under the whip of a lay brother?[15] The Puente del Capricho was probably constructed in the same way! And tell me, did these people rebel?"

"The fact is that they rose once before," remarked the Dominican: "*y ab actu ad posse valet illatio* (what happened before can happen again)!"

"No no! far from it!" said Simoun, preparing to go down the hatchway to the lounge. "What I have said, I have said. And you, Padre Sibyla, speak no Latinisms or nonsense. What are you friars for if the people can rise in revolt?"[16]

And, without heeding further protests or replies, Simoun went down the small staircase leading to the interior, muttering contemptuously: "Well, well!"

Padre Sibyla blanched.[17] It was the first time that to him, Vice-Rector of the University, nonsense had been attributed. Don Custodio was green with rage. Never at any meeting he had attended, had he met the likes of such an adversary. That was too much!

"An American mulatto!" he muttered growling.

"A British Indian!" retorted Ben Zayb in a low voice.

"American, I tell you. Don't I know it?" replied Don Custodio in foul humor. "His Excellency has told me. He is a jeweler he met in Havana and who, I suspect, provided him his destiny by lending him money. That is why, in order to pay him back, his Excellency let him come here to do what he likes, augment his fortune by selling diamonds...fakes, who knows! And he is so ungrateful that after pocketing the *Indio's* money he even wants to....Pfft!"

And he ended the sentence with a very significant gesture of the hand.

No one dared make common cause with those diatribes; Don Custodio could fall out of favor with his Excellency if he wanted to, but neither Ben Zayb, nor Padre Irene, nor Padre Salvi, nor the offended Padre Sibyla, had confidence in the discretion of the others.

"The trouble is that this señor, being an American, undoubtedly believes we are dealing with Redskins... Talking about those matters in a steamship! Compelling, forcing people!...And it is he who suggested the expedition to the Caroline Islands,[18] and the Mindanao campaign that is going to ruin us shamefully ...It is he who offered to intervene in the construction of a cruiser. And, I say, what does a jeweler, no matter how rich and cultured, know of naval constructions?"

Don Custodio was saying all these things in a guttural voice to his neighbor Ben Zayb, gesturing and shrugging his shoulders, consulting every now and then with his eyes the rest who were making ambiguous movements with their heads. The canon Irene allowed a rather equivocal smile to play on his lips, half-concealed by his hand stroking his nose.

"I tell you, Ben Zayb," Don Custodio continued, shaking the writer's arm, "all the trouble here lies in the fact that persons of long residence are not consulted. A high-sounding project and, above all, one involving a great deal of expenditure, expenditure in nice round figures, fascinates and is immediately accepted...because of this!"

Don Custodio rubbed the tip of his thumb against his index and middle fingers.

"There is something to that, something indeed," Ben Zayb thought it his duty to reply; with his standing as a journalist he was supposed to be well-informed about everything.

"Look! before these port works, I presented a project, original, simple, useful, economical and workable: to clear the sandbars of Laguna. It was not accepted because it could not give this." And he repeated the same gestures with his fingertips, shrugged his shoulders, looked at his listeners as if telling them: "Have you ever seen such an outrage?"

"And may we know what the plan consisted of? ...Come now!" exclaimed one, with the others nearing and pressing together to hear. Don Custodio's projects were as famous as a quack doctor's prescriptions.

Don Custodio was at the point of not telling what his plan consisted of, resentful because he had not found partisans during his diatribes against Simoun. "When there is no danger involved you want me to talk, eh, and when there is, you keep silent," he was about to say, but that was to lose a good opportunity, and the project, now that it could not be realized, at least could be known and admired.

After two or three puffs of smoke, some coughing and spitting out of a corner of his mouth, he asked Ben Zayb, giving him a slap on the thigh:

"You have seen ducks?"

"I think so...we have hunted them in the lake," replied Ben Zayb, somewhat surprised.

"No, no! I am not talking of wild ducks, I mean the domesticated ones, those that are bred in Pateros and in Pasig. And do you know what they feed on?"

Ben Zayb, the only thinking head, did not know—he had not dedicated time to that industry.

"Man! they feed on little snails! on snails!" replied Padre Camorra; "One does not have to be an *Indio* to know; it is enough to have eyes."

"Exactly, they feed on snails," repeated Don Custodio gesturing with his index finger. "And do you know where they can be obtained?"

The thinking head did not know either.

"Well, if you had my years in the country, you would know that they are gathered from the sandbars, where they abound in the sands."

"What about your project?"

"I'm coming to that. I would oblige all the inhabitants of the surrounding towns near the sandbars, to breed ducks, and you will see that by themselves they will deepen the river by gathering snails. It is as simple as that, no more, no less."

And Don Custodio flung his arms wide, joyfully contemplating the amazement of his listeners. Such a rare idea had never occurred to anyone.

"Will you allow me to write an article on the subject?" asked Ben Zayb. "In this country there is so little thinking done...."

"But, Don Custodio!" said Doña Victorina with pouts and grimaces, "if everyone were to breed ducks there would be an excess of *balut* eggs.[19] Ugh! how disgusting! Leave the sandbars alone!"

- 2 -

Below Deck

B elow deck, other scenes are taking place.

Seated on benches and small wooden stools, among suitcases, boxes, baskets and *tampipi*s,[1] two paces away from the machine, the heat of the boilers, amid human stench and the pestilent odor of oil are the majority of passengers.

Some silently contemplate the varied landscape on the bank; some play cards or converse in the midst of the clatter of paddle-wheels, the noise of the machine, the hissing of the escaping steam, the roar of moving waters, the hooting of the horn. In a corner, piled up like corpses, sleeping or trying to sleep, are some Chinese peddlers, seasick, wan, slobbering with half-opened lips and bathed in the thick sweat oozing from all their pores. Only some young people, students for the greater part, easily recognizable by their spotless white attire and their well-groomed appearance, dare to circulate from bow to stern, jumping over boxes and baskets, happy with the prospect of the coming holidays. Now they are discussing the movements of the machine, trying to remember their forgotten notions of Physics, as they mill around a young *colegiala*, and the crimson-lipped *buyera*[2] with necklaces of *sampagas*, whispering into their ears words that make them smile or cover their faces with painted fans.

There are two, however, who instead of occupying themselves with those passing gallantries, are discussing at the prow with a gentleman advanced in years but still erect and arrogant. Both must have been well-known and esteemed, judging by the deferential attitude of the rest towards them. As a matter of fact, the older of the two, the one completely attired in black, is a student of medicine, Basilio, known for his successful and impressive treatments. The other, the bigger and more robust but younger, is Isagani, one of the poets, or at least a writer of verses, produced that year by the Ateneo, a student with an original character, ordinarily uncommunicative and somewhat taciturn. The gentleman talking with them is the rich Capitan Basilio, returning from a shopping trip to Manila.[3]

"Capitan Tiago is as usual; no improvement, yes Señor!" the student said, shaking his head. "He will not submit to any treatment....On *someone's* advice, he is sending me to San Diego[4] on the pretext of visiting the house, but it is to leave him to smoke opium with total freedom."

The student, when he said *someone*, gave to understand that it was Padre Irene, a great friend and adviser of Capitan Tiago in his last days.

"Opium is one of the plagues of our modern times," replied Capitan Basilio with the contempt and indignation of a Roman senator. "The ancients were acquainted with it, but they never abused it. While the study of the classics was popular (note this well, young men), opium was only a medicine. Otherwise tell me who smokes the most opium? The Chinese, the Chinese who do not know a word of Latin! Ah, if only Capitan Tiago had dedicated himself to Cicero..."

And the most classic loathing was displayed on the well-shaven Epicurean face. Isagani regarded him attentively—this señor suffered a nostalgia for antiquity.

"But going back to this Academy of Spanish," continued Capitan Basilio, "I assure you that you will not realize it...."

"Yes Señor, from day to day we expect the permit," Isagani answered. "Padre Irene, whom you must have seen up on deck, and whom we gifted with a pair of chestnut horses, has promised us. He will go and see the Capitan General."

"It does not matter! Padre Sibyla opposes it!"

"Let him oppose it! That is why he comes to ... in Los Baños, before the General."

And the student Basilio mimed what he meant by striking one of his fists against the other.

"Understood!" remarked Capitan Basilio laughing. "But even if you get the permit, where will you get the funds?"

"We have it, Señor; each student contributes a *real*."

"But ... and the professors?"

"We have them; half of them Filipinos, and half *peninsulares*."

"And the building?"

"Macaraig, the rich Macaraig, is letting us have one of his houses."

Capitan Basilio had to concede defeat: those young

men had everything ready.

"As far as it goes," he said, shrugging his shoulders, "the idea is not entirely bad, it is not a bad idea, and since you cannot master Latin, let them at least learn Spanish. Here, *tocayo*, is proof of how we are deteriorating. In our times we learned Latin because our books were written in Latin. Today you are learning it a little, but there are no books written in Latin. On the other hand, your books are in Spanish and the teaching is not in Spanish: *Aetas parentum pejor avis tulit nos nequiores!* as Horace used to say. The age of our fathers, worse than that of their fathers, has bred us even worse than them!"

And having said this he moved majestically away like a Roman emperor. The two young men smiled.

"These men of the past," remarked Isagani, "they find difficulties for everything; you propose to them one thing and instead of seeing the advantages they notice only the inconveniences. They want everything to come out smooth and round as a billiard ball."

"With your uncle he feels at home," observed Basilio, "talking of their ancient times...By the way, what does your uncle say about Paulita?"

Isagani blushed.

"My uncle gave me a sermon on the choice of a wife ... I answered him that in Manila there is no one like her, lovely, well-educated, an orphan..."

"Rich, elegant, witty, without any defects except a ridiculous aunt," added Basilio laughing.

Isagani laughed in turn.

"Talking of the aunt—do you know that she has asked me to look for her husband?"

"Doña Victorina? And you must have promised so that you can keep your sweetheart?"

"Naturally! but the problem is that the husband is hiding precisely ... in my uncle's house!"

Both roared with laughter.

"And that is why," continued Isagani, "my uncle, who is very conscientious, did not want to go to the lounge, apprehensive that Doña Victorina might ask him about Don Tiburcio. Imagine! Doña Victorina, when she learned I was a deck passenger, regarded me with contempt!"

Simoun just then was going down, and upon seeing the two young men said, "Hello, Don Basilio," in the tone of a protector. "Are you going on a holiday? Is the gentleman a townmate of yours?"

Basilio introduced Isagani to Simoun, and said they were not from the same town, but that their towns were not far from each other. Isagani lived by the side of the lake on the opposite shore.

Simoun examined Isagani with such attention that the latter, irritated, turned to look at him face to face with a certain provocative air.

"And how is the province?" asked Simoun turning to Basilio.

"Why! Are you not familiar with it?"

"How the devil should I know it when I have never set foot in it? I have been told it is very poor and does not buy jewelry."

"We do not buy jewels because we do not need them," Isagani answered curtly, his provincial pride piqued.

A smile was etched on Simoun's pale lips.

"Don't be offended, young man," he replied. "I had no evil intentions, but since I have been assured that almost all the parishes are in the hands of *Indio* clerics, I said to myself: the friars would die for a parish, and the Franciscans are content with the poorest ones, so that when

one or the other is ceded to the seculars, it must be because
there the king's profile will never be known.[5] Come,
gentlemen, have a drink of beer with me and we will toast
the prosperity of your province!"

The young men thanked him and excused themselves,
saying they did not drink beer.

"You do wrong!" answered Simoun, visibly peeved.
"Beer is a good thing, and I heard Padre Camorra say this
morning that the lack of energy noted in this country is
due to the inhabitants drinking so much water."

Isagani, almost as tall as the jeweler, drew himself
up.

"Well, you can tell Padre Camorra," Basilio hastened
to intervene, nudging Isagani with his elbow
surreptitiously, "tell him, if he drank water instead of wine
or beer, perhaps we would all profit from it and not be so
much given to gossip..."

"You can tell him," Isagani added, ignoring his friend's
nudging, "that water is very sweet and can be drunk, but
it can drown out wine and beer and put out fires; when
heated it becomes steam; when disturbed it becomes an
ocean that once destroyed humanity and shook the world
to its foundations!"

Simoun raised his head, and although his eyes could
not be read behind his blue-tinted glasses, from the rest of
his features it was apparent that he was surprised.

"Beautiful answer," he said, "but I fear Padre Camorra
will take it as a joke and ask me when the water will
convert into steam and when into an ocean. Padre Camorra
is somewhat incredulous, and a wag!"

"When fire heats it, when the small rivers which now
are found spread in their steep basins, impelled by fate,
come together in the abyss that men are digging," replied
Isagani.

"No, Señor Simoun," added Basilio in a jesting tone. "Better, quote these verses of my friend Isagani:

> *Water we are, and you fire, you say;*
> Since you wish it, let it be so!
> Let us live then together
> And fire ne'er see us encounter!
> But united by wise science,
> In the boilers of the ardent bosom,
> Without anger, without violence,
> Let us form steam, the fifth element,
> Progress, life, light and movement![6]"

"Utopia, utopia!" Simoun wryly replied. "The engine is about to collide...In the meantime I take my beer."

And without farewell he left the two friends.

"But what is the matter with you today that you are in a fighting mood?" asked Basilio.

"Nothing, I don't know, but that man incites in me horror, almost fear."

"I was nudging you with my elbow. Don't you know that they call that one the Brown Cardinal?"

"Cardinal Brown?"

"Or Black Eminence, if you wish."

"I don't understand you!"

"Richelieu had a Capuchin adviser who was called the Grey Eminence. Well this one is, to the Capitan-General..."

"Really?"

"As I have heard from *someone*...who always talks against him behind his back and flatters him to his face."

"Does he also call on Capitan Tiago?"

"Since the first day of his arrival, and for certain, *a certain someone* considers him a rival...for the inheritance...I

believe he is going to see the General about the teaching
of Spanish."

At that moment a manservant came to tell Isagani
that his uncle was calling him.

On one of the benches astern, together with other
passengers, was seated a cleric gazing at the view which
unrolled before him. His neighbors made room for him,
people when they passed nearby raised their hats, and the
gamblers dared not put up their tables near where he
was. The priest said little, and did not smoke or assume
arrogant airs. He did not disdain to mingle with other
folks, and he returned their greetings with finesse and
grace as if he felt very much honored and very grateful.
He was quite old, his hair almost all white, but he still
seemed to be in good health; even while seated, he kept
his body erect and his head straight, but without pride or
arrogance.

He differed from the ordinary run of *Indio* priests,
few as they were, who in that epoch served merely as
coadjutores, assistants, or provisionally administered other
parishes, in the air of self-possession and gravity of one
conscious of the dignity of his person and the holiness of
his office. A quick glance at his facade, if not at his grey
hair, showed at once that he belonged to a different epoch,
or another generation, when the best young men did not
fear to hazard their dignity by becoming priests; when the
secular priests looked upon whatever friar as an equal;
and when their calling, not yet defamed and reviled,
attracted free men, not slaves, superior intelligences, not
subservient wills.[7] In his sad and sober features could be
read a tranquility of soul fortified by study and meditation
and perchance put to test by intimate moral sufferings.
That priest was Padre Florentino, Isagani's uncle, and his

history can be told briefly.[8]

The son of a very rich and well-connected Manila family, possessed of great charm and the happy disposition to shine in the world, he had never felt a priestly vocation, but his mother, because of some promises or vows, compelled him to enter the seminary after long quarrels and violent discussions. She had a great friendship with the archbishop, was of an iron will, and inexorable as are all devout women who believe themselves interpreters of the will of God. In vain did the young Florentino oppose her; in vain he pleaded, in vain he prevented it with his amours and provoked scandals. A priest he had to be, and at the age of twenty-five he was. The Archbishop ordained him priest, his first mass was celebrated with great pomp; there were three days of feasting and his mother died contented and pleased, leaving him all her fortune.

But in that struggle Florentino received a wound from which he never recovered. Weeks before his first mass, the woman he had loved most married a nobody out of despair. That blow was the hardest he would ever feel; he lost his moral energy; life became heavy and unbearable. If not virtue and respect for his calling, that unfortunate love saved him from the abyss into which regular and secular *curas* in the Philippines were often plunged. He devoted himself to his parishioners out of duty, and to the natural sciences out of natural inclination.

When the events of 1872 took place,[9] Padre Florentino feared that his parish, because of the huge benefices it yielded, would draw attention to him, and a pacifist before anything else, he sought retirement, living since then as a private citizen on his family estate, situated on the shores of the Pacific. There he adopted a nephew, Isagani, who according to malicious gossip was his son by his old love when she was widowed; or a natural son of a cousin of his in Manila, according to the more sober and knowledgeable.

The skipper of the ship had seen the cleric and urged him to go into the lounge and up on deck. To prod him to make up his mind, he added:

"If you do not go up, the friars will believe that you do not wish to join them."

Padre Florentino had no alternative but to accept, and he had his nephew called to keep him abreast of the latest happenings and to warn him not to come near the lounge while the priest was there.

"If the skipper sees you he will invite you and we would be abusing his hospitality."

"One of my uncle's tricks," thought Isagani, "all so that I will not have a chance to talk to Doña Victorina."

- 3 -

Legends

Ich weiss nich was soll es bedeuten
Dass ich so traurig bin!

I want to cry,
I do not know why!

When Padre Florentino greeted the little group there were no longer traces of the ill humor of the past discussions. Perhaps they were influenced by the spirits, by the charming houses of the town of Pasig, the glasses of sherry they had taken to whet the appetite, or the prospects of a good meal; whatever the reason, they were laughing and jesting, even the gaunt Franciscan whose smiles were like the grimaces of the dying.

"Bad times! bad times," said Padre Sibyla laughing.

"Come on! don't say that, Vice-Rector!" replied the canon Irene, pushing the chair in which the other was seated. "In Hong Kong you are doing good business and putting up such buildings that...well there!"

"Look, look!" he answered. "You do not see our expenses, and the tenants on our estates are beginning to complain..."[1]

"Come on! enough griping, *puñales*, or else you will make me cry," gaily shouted Padre Camorra. "We do not complain, and we do not own estates or banks. And know that my *Indios* are starting to haggle over the fees and make available to me price schedules. Look here, they now cite to me rates, and no less than the rates fixed by the archbishop Don Basilio Sancho, *puñales*, as if since then, the prices of articles have not gone up.[2] Ha, ha, ha, why should a baptism cost less than a chicken? But I act dumb, charge what I can and do not complain at all. We are not greedy, it is true, Padre Salvi?"

At that moment Simoun's head appeared at the hatchway.

"But where have you been keeping yourself?" cried Don Custodio who had already completely forgotten his annoyance. "You have missed the best part of the trip!"

"Psh!" Simoun replied, going up. "I have already seen so many rivers and so many landscapes that I am interested only in those that bring legends to mind."

"Legends, well, the Pasig has some," replied the skipper, who did not welcome criticism of the river where he sailed and earned a living. "You have the legend of the *Malapad-na-bato*, a rock held sacred before the coming of the Spaniards, as the dwelling place of spirits. Afterwards, when the superstition was nullified and the rock profaned, it was converted into a hangout of *tulisanes* or bandits, from the summit of which they made easy prey of the helpless *bancas* which not only had to struggle against the current, but also against man. Much later in our times, despite the fact that man had touched it with his hand, the tale is told of a capsized boat and if I, upon making a turn, do not move with all my six senses, I would dash against its sides. There is another legend, that of the cave of Doña Jeronima, which Padre Florentino can relate to you..."[3]

"All the world knows it," remarked Padre Sibyla disdainfully.

But no one—not Simoun, or Ben Zayb, or Padre Irene, or Padre Camorra—knew the tale, and they asked to be told, some jokingly, others out of true curiosity. The cleric, adopting the same jesting tone of those who asked, like a nursemaid telling a tale to children, said:

"Once upon a time there was a student who gave his word to marry a maiden of his village who, it seems, he later failed to remember. She, faithful, waited for him for years and years, wasted her youth, became a spinster. One day she heard that her old love had become Archbishop of Manila. She disguised herself as a man, came by the Cape and presented herself to His Most Illustrious Person, demanding the fulfillment of his promise. What she asked for was impossible, and the archbishop had a cave built, which you must have seen, draped and decorated at the entrance with tangled vines. There she lived and died and there was buried, and tradition relates that Doña Jeronima was so fat that to enter she had to go sideways. Her fame as a charmer came from her custom of throwing into the river all the silver plates on which she served lavish banquets to which came many a gentleman. A net was stretched under water to catch the pieces which were thus washed. It is not more than twenty years since the river passed close by, almost kissing the mouth of the cave, but little by little it has receded from it, as its memory fades among the *Indios*."

"Beautiful legend!" said Ben Zayb, "I am going to

write an article. It is so sentimental."

Doña Victorina was thinking about living in another cave and was about to announce it, when Simoun took the words from her.

"But what do you think about it, Padre Salvi?" he asked the Franciscan who was absorbed in some meditation. "Does it not seem to you that His Most Illustrious Person, instead of giving her a cave, should have placed her in a cloister, in Santa Clara for example?"[4]

Padre Sibyla showed startled surprise, seeing Padre Salvi shudder and look askance at Simoun.

"Because it is not gallant," continued Simoun with great casualness, "to give a crag as a dwelling to someone whose hopes we have defrauded; neither is it charitable to expose her thus to temptations, in a cave, by the bank of a river. It smells somewhat of nymphs and druids. It would have been more gallant, more charitable, more romantic, more in conformity with the customs in this country to shut her up in Santa Clara like a new Heloise, and to visit and comfort her now and then. What do you say?"

"I cannot nor should I judge the conduct of the Archbishop," retorted the Franciscan grudgingly.

"But you, who are the ecclesiastical governor of the Archdiocese, he who stands in place of our archbishop, what would you have done if it had happened to you?"

Padre Salvi shrugged his shoulders and added calmly:

"It is not worth the pain of pondering what cannot happen...but since we are talking of legends, let us not forget the loveliest for being the truest, that of the miracle of San Nicolas, the ruins of whose church you must have seen. I am going to relate it to Señor Simoun, who cannot have known it. It seems that formerly, the river, like the lake, was infested with crocodiles, so huge and voracious that they attacked the bancas and overturned them with blows of their tails. Our chronicles narrate that one day an infidel Chinaman, who until then had refused to be converted, was passing by the church when all of a sudden the devil appeared to him as a crocodile, and overturned his banca to devour him and take him to hell. Inspired by God, the Chinese at that moment invoked San Nicolas, and instantly the crocodile turned into stone.[5] The ancients tell that in their time the monster was easily recognizable in the scattered pieces of rock which were left of it. I myself can assure you that I still was able to distinguish clearly the head, and judging by it, the monster must have been enormous."

"Marvelous, marvelous legend!" Ben Zayb exclaimed, "which lends itself to an article. The monster's description, the Chinaman's terror, the waters of the river, the cane brakes ... and it lends itself to a study of comparative religions. For look, a heathen Chinaman invoking in the midst of great peril precisely a saint whom he must have only heard of, and whom he did not believe in...Here the saying does not hold: *better the evil already known than the good still to be known.* Should I find myself in China and in a similar situation, the first thing I would do is to call upon the least known saint in the calendar rather than on Confucius or Buddha. Whether this proves the superiority of Catholicism, or an illogical inconsistency of the mental endowments of the yellow race, can be made clear only through a profound study of anthropology."

Ben Zayb adopted the tone of a professor, and with his index finger traced circles in the air, admiring his own imagination which knew how to draw from inconsequential things so many allusions and consequences. Seeing Simoun thoughtful, and believing him to be cogitating on what he had just said, he asked him what he was thinking.

"About two very important things," replied Simoun, "two questions you could include in your article. First, what could have become of the devil on seeing himself all of a sudden imprisoned in a stone? Did he escape? Did he remain there? Was he crushed? And secondly, could the petrified animals I have seen in various museums of Europe, have been victims of some antediluvian saint?"

The tone in which the jeweler spoke was very serious, and he leaned his brow on his index finger, indicating deep thought, such that Padre Camorra commented gravely:

"Who knows? who knows?"

"Well, since we speak of legends, we are entering the lake," replied Padre Sibyla, "the skipper must know many..."

At that moment the steamship was entering the bar and the panorama extending before their eyes was truly magnificent. Everyone was impressed. Before them lay the beautiful lake circled by green shores and blue mountains, like a colossal mirror with a border of emeralds and sapphires, in whose moon heaven could look at her image. To the right extended its lower shore, forming small bays with graceful curves, and there, far away, almost hazy, the hook of Sugay. Ahead, and in the background rose Mount Makiling, majestic, imposing, crowned with light clouds. To the left Talim island, the *Susong-dalaga* or Maiden's breast, with the deformed undulations which gave it its name.[6]

A cool breeze delicately curled over the great expanse.

"By the way, skipper," said Ben Zayb turning to the former, "do you know in which part of the lake was killed a certain Guevara, Navarra or Ibarra?"

Everyone looked at the skipper except Simoun, who turned his head elsewhere as if searching for something along the shores.

"Ah, yes!" said Doña Victorina, "where, skipper? Could he have left traces in the water?"

The good man winked several times, a sign that he was very much annoyed, but seeing the pleading in the eyes of everybody, advanced some paces to the prow and stared at the shore.

"Look there," he said in a scarcely audible voice, after making sure that there were no strangers listening. "According to the headman who organized the pursuit, Ibarra, upon seeing himself hemmed in, flung himself from the banca near the *Kinabutasan* or break[7] and, swimming and swimming between two waters, he negotiated all that distance of more than two miles, pelted by bullets every time he raised his head to breathe. Much farther ahead was where they lost trace of him and a little farther, near the shore, they discovered something like the color of blood...Today it is exactly thirteen years to the day that this happened."

"And so his body?..." asked Ben Zayb.

"Joined that of his father," answered Padre Sibyla.[8] "Was he not also another *filibustero*, a subversive, Padre Salvi?"

"Those are really cheap burials, eh, Padre Camorra," remarked Ben Zayb.

"I have always averred that it is the subversives who do not pay for pompous funerals," replied the former, laughing merrily.

"But what is the matter with you, Señor Simoun?" Ben Zayb asked upon seeing the jeweler motionless and deep in thought. "Are you seasick, you a voyager, and in a mere drop of water like this one?"

"Well, let me tell you," replied the skipper who had ended up loving all those places. "Don't you call this a drop of water. It is larger than any Swiss lake and all those of Spain put together.[9] I have seen old mariners become seasick here."

- 4 -

Cabesang Tales

T hose who have read the first part of this story will remember, perhaps, an old woodcutter who lived in the thick of the forest.

Tandang (Old) Selo still lives, and although his hair has all turned white, he nevertheless is still in good health. He no longer hunts or cuts down trees. Since his fortunes improved, he spends his time making brooms.

His son Tales (short for Telesforo) had first worked as a tenant in the lands of a capitalist, but later, owning two carabaos and a few hundred pesos, he wanted to work on his own helped by his father, his wife and his three children.

So they felled trees within the boundaries of the town, and cleared some thick forests which they believed

belonged to no one. During the breaking and draining of
the land the whole family, one after the other, fell sick
with fever, his wife and their oldest daughter, Lucia,
succumbing to consumption in the prime of their lives.
That was a natural consequence of the turning over of soil
plagued with various organisms, but they attributed it to
the vengeance of the spirits of the forest, were resigned
and continued with their labors confident that these had
been appeased. When they were about to reap the fruits
of their first harvest, a religious order which owned lands
in the neighboring town, claimed ownership of those fields,
alleging that they were within their property lines, and to
prove it attempted to sink at that moment their boundary
markers.[1] The administrator of the religious, however, for
humanity's sake, allowed them the use of the land as long
as they paid annually a small amount, a trifle, twenty or
thirty pesos.

Tales, a peaceful man as much as an enemy of
lawsuits like most, and submissive to the friars like some,
not to break his *palayok* or clay pot against a *kawali* or iron
pan, according to him, (for him the friars were containers
of iron and he, one of clay) had the weakness to yield to
such a claim, thinking that he did not know Spanish and
did not have the wherewithal to pay lawyers. And besides,
Tandang Selo told him:

"Patience! you would be spending more for litigation
in a year, than what you would pay in ten years that the
white Padres demand. Hmm! Maybe they will pay you
back in Masses. Make believe that you lost thirty pesos in
gambling, or that you dropped them in the water and a
crocodile swallowed them."

The harvest was good and sold well, and Tales
thought of building himself a house of wood in the barrio

of Sagpang of the town of Tiani, in the neighborhood of San Diego.[2]

Another year passed, another good harvest came, and because of this and that pretext, the friars raised the rental to fifty pesos, which Tales paid to avoid trouble and because he expected to sell his sugar well.

"Patience! Make believe the crocodile has grown," said old Selo, consoling him.

That year they were finally able to realize his dream: to live in a built-up area, in a wooden house in the barrio of Sagpang, and the father and the grandfather thought of giving some education to the two brethren, particularly to the girl, Juliana or Juli, as they called her, who gave promise of being gifted and pretty. A young male friend of the household, Basilio, was already studying in Manila and that young man was from the same humble cradle as theirs.

But this dream appeared destined not to be realized.

The first concern which the community had, upon seeing the family prosper gradually, was to name its most hard-working member *Cabeza de Barangay*.[3] Tano, the eldest son, was only fourteen years old. They therefore named Tales *Cabesa*. He had a jacket made, bought himself a felt hat, and prepared himself for further expenses. In order to avoid disputes with the parish priest and the local authorities he funded out of his own pocket the deficits in the tax census, paid for those who had left and those who had died, spent many hours in revenue collection and in trips to the capital.

"Patience; pretend that the relatives of the crocodile have turned up," said Tandang Selo, smiling placidly.

"Next year you will wear a long dress with a train, and will go to Manila to study like the young ladies in

town," Cabesang Tales said to Juli every time he heard
her talk of Basilio's progress.

But the year to come did not come, and in its place
there was another increase in rentals. Cabesang Tales
sobered up and scratched his head. The clay pot was giving
up its rice to the iron pan.

When the rental ascended to two hundred pesos,
Cabesang Tales was not content to scratch his head, or to
sigh; he protested and grumbled. The friar administrator
informed him then that if he was unable to pay this,
another one would take over to cultivate those lands. Many
who wanted it were offering to do so.

Cabesang Tales thought that the friar was not in
earnest; but the friar was serious, and assigned one of his
servants to take possession of the land. The poor man
blanched, his ears rang and a red cloud interposed itself
before his eyes, and in it he saw before him his wife and
daughter, pale and emaciated, agonizing, victims of
intermittent fever. And then he saw the thick forest,
converted into fields; he saw arroyos of sweat watering
the furrows; he saw there himself, poor Tales, plowing in
the heat of the sun, crushing his feet against the stones
and roots; while the lay brother went around in his
carriage, with the one who was to inherit the land following
behind like a slave to his master: Ah no! a thousand times
no! Rather let the fields sink first into the depths of the
earth and they all bury themselves underneath. Who was
that stranger to have rights over his lands? Had he brought,
coming over from his country, even a handful of its dust?
Was one of his fingers ever bent to pluck a single root
from the earth?

Exasperated by the threat from friars who attempted
to have their authority prevail at all costs before the other
tenants, Cabesang Tales rebelled, refused to pay a single

cuarto, and, always having before him the red cloud, said that he would surrender his fields only to the first man who would water them with blood from his own veins.

Old Selo, upon seeing his son's face, dared not mention his crocodile, but tried to soothe him, talking to him of clay pots and reminding him that in lawsuits he who wins is left without a shirt.

"To the dust we will return, father, and we were born without shirts on," he replied.

He resolutely refused to pay or to surrender even a palm's length of his lands, unless the friars proved the legitimacy of their claims with the presentation of whatever document. Since the friars had none, there was litigation, and Cabesang Tales accepted it in the belief that at least some people, if not all, loved justice and respected the laws.

"I serve and have been serving the king these many years with my money and my labors," he said to those who tried to discourage him. "I am asking him now to do me justice, and he must give it to me."

Dragged by some fatal compulsion, and as if he had staked on the litigation all his future and that of his children, he spent his savings to pay lawyers, notaries and solicitors without counting the officials and clerks who were exploiting his ignorance and his situation. He went back and forth to the capital, spent days without food and nights without sleep, and his conversation was all about pleadings, evidence, appeals, and the like. He saw himself involved in a struggle never before seen under the Philippine sky: that of a poor *Indio*, unlettered and friendless, confident of his rights and the worthiness of his cause, fighting against a most powerful Order before which justice had bent its neck, judges allowed the scales to drop and surrendered the sword. He fought tenaciously, like the ant which bites knowing that it will be crushed, like the fly seeing space through a glass. Ah! the earthen vessel defying the iron pan and breaking into a thousand pieces had something imposing about it: it had the sublimity of despair.

The days that left him free from making trips, or going to court, he spent patrolling his fields armed with a shotgun, saying that there were *tulisanes* hovering around and he had need to defend himself so as not to fall into their hands and lose his case. As if to practice his aim he shot even the butterflies with such accuracy that the lay brother administrator no longer dared to come to Sagpang without being escorted by *guardias civiles*; and the protegé who espied from afar the imposing height of Cabesang Tales inspecting his fields like a sentry over the walls, full of fear, gave up claiming the property.

But the justices of the peace and those from the capital dared not judge in his favor, fearful of losing their jobs and were justified, for one of them, who showed signs of being partial, was immediately dismissed. Those judges were not evil men, they were conscientious, moral, good citizens, excellent fathers of families, good sons...and knew how to consider poor Tales's situation better than Tales himself could. Many of them knew the scientific and historic foundations of the property; they knew that the friars by their own statutes were forbidden to own lands. But they also knew that coming from afar, across the seas, with an occupation earned at great pains, to pursue discharging it with the best of intentions, and to lose it because an *Indio* took it into his fancy to have justice meted out on earth as it is in heaven, come on, that, is another story...

They had their families, who surely had much greater

needs than did the family of that *Indio*. One had a mother
to support, and what task could be more sacred than to
take care of a mother? The other had sisters, all
marriageable, and there were many tiny children waiting
for bread like birds in the nest and who would surely die
the day he lost his position; and the least of them, the least
had far, far away a wife who, if she did not receive her
monthly pension, would find herself in hardship...And all
those judges, men of conscience the best of them, and of
the most sound morality, believed they had done the best
they could in advising on the settlement, that Cabesang
Tales should pay the required rent. But Tales, like all simple
clear consciences, once aware of what is just, would not
swerve from his path. He demanded proofs, documents,
papers, land titles, and the friars did not have any, but
argued solely on his past willingness.

Cabesang Tales countered:

"If every day I gave alms to a beggar to avoid his
molesting me, who would compel me afterwards to
continue giving him if he abused my bounty?"

And here nobody could sway him, and there were
no threats capable of intimidating him. *Gobernador* M—
made a trip expressly to talk to and make him afraid; to
all he responded:

"You can do what you will, Señor Gobernador. I am
an ignorant man and I lack resources. But I have cultivated
those fields, my wife and my daughter died helping me to
clear them, and I am not going to surrender them except
to another who could do with them better than I have
done. Let him first water these lands with his own blood
and inter in them his own wife and daughter!"

As a result of Tales's obstinacy the honorable judges
decided in favor of the friars and everybody laughed at

him, saying that one does not win lawsuits with right. He appealed. He carried his shotgun and calmly patrolled his boundaries. During this interval his life was a frenzy. His son Tano, a youngster as tall as his father, and good like his sister, was drafted; he let him go instead of buying the services of a substitute.

"I have to pay lawyers," he told his daughter, who was weeping. "If I win the case I will know how to make him come back, and if I lose I have no need for sons."

The son left and nothing more was known of him, except that his hair was shaved off; and that he slept under a cart.[4] Six months later it was said that he had been seen embarking for the Carolines; others believed they had seen him in the uniform of a *guardia civil*.

"*Guardia civil! Tano! Susmariosep!*"[5] exclaimed some, and others, wringing their hands, said, "Tano, so good and so honest! May he rest in peace!"

The grandfather spent many days without talking to the father; Juli fell ill, but Cabesang Tales shed not a single tear. For two days he did not go out of his house, as if fearing the reproachful eyes of the whole barrio. He was afraid that they would call him his son's executioner. On the third day, however, he stepped out with his shotgun.

They suspected him of murderous intentions, and some well-meaning ones murmured about having heard him threaten to bury the lay brother in the furrows of his field; the friar was frightened out of his wits. As a consequence of this, the Capitan General sent down a decree prohibiting all use of firearms, and ordering them confiscated.[6] Cabesang Tales had to give up his shotgun, but armed with a long bolo, he continued his rounds.

"What are you going to do with that bolo if the *tulisanes* have firearms?" old Selo asked him.

"I need to guard my sown fields," he replied. "Each sugar cane that grows there is a bone of my wife's." They took his bolo, finding it too long. He then got hold of his father's old axe, and with it over his shoulder continued his brooding walk.

Every time he left his house, Tandang Selo and Juli feared for his life. She would rise from her loom, go to the window, pray, make promises to the saints, recite novenas. The grandfather did not know at times how to finish the hoop of a broom and spoke of going back to the woods.

Life in that household became impossible.

Finally what they feared happened. As the fields were far from town, Cabesang Tales, notwithstanding his axe, fell into the hands of the *tulisanes* who had revolvers and shotguns. The *tulisanes* told him that since he had money to give the judges and to the lawyers, he should also give to the derelicts and the persecuted. So they demanded from him five hundred pesos for ransom through a peasant, assuring him that if something happened to the messenger the prisoner would pay with his life. They gave him two days of respite.

The news plunged the poor family into great dismay, more so when they learned that the *guardias civiles* were going in pursuit of the bandits. If there were to be an encounter the first casualty would be the prisoner, this everyone knew. The old man remained numb and the daughter, wan and terrified, tried to talk several times but could not. But a more terrible thought, a more cruel idea shook them out of their stupor. The peasant sent by the *tulisanes* said that the band would probably have to move faster, and that if they delayed in paying the ransom the two days would be over and Cabesang Tales would be beheaded.

This drove the two, both weak, both impotent, out of their wits. Tandang Selo would stand up, seat himself, go down and up the stairs; he did not know where to go, or whom to turn to. Juli turned to her images, counted and recounted her money, but her two hundred pesos did not increase, they did not multiply. Suddenly she got dressed, gathered all her jewels, asked her grandfather's advice, went to see the *gobernadorcillo*, the judge, the clerk, the *teniente* of the *guardia civil*. The old man said yes to everything and when she said no, also said no. Finally there arrived some neighbors among relatives and friends, some poorer than the others, matching each other in simplicity and excitability. The smartest of them all was Sister Balî, a great *panguinguera*[7] who had been in Manila to do spiritual exercises in the retreat house of the Society.[8]

Juli would sell all her jewels, except a locket of diamonds and emeralds with which Basilio had gifted her. This locket had its history: it was given by a nun, the daughter of Capitan Tiago, to a leper.[9] Basilio, having treated the leper in his illness, received it as a gift. She could not sell it without advising him beforehand.

They quickly disposed of the combs, earrings and the rosary beads of Juli to her richest neighbor, and that added fifty pesos. Two hundred fifty pesos were still not enough. Would she pawn the locket? But Juli shook her head. A neighbor proposed to sell the house, and Tandang Selo approved of the idea, happy to return to the woods, again to chop firewood as in the old times, but Sister Balî said that it could not be, the owner being absent.

"The judge's wife sold me once her *tapis*[10] for one peso and the husband said that the sale was not valid because it did not have his consent. *Abá*, she took back her *tapis* and she has not returned my peso until now, but I do not pay her in the *panguingi* when she wins, *abá!* This way I have been able to collect twelve *cuartos*, and for this only I play. I cannot stand it when they do not pay me back a debt, *abá!*"

A neighbor was on the point of asking Sister Balî why then had she not paid a tiny debt, but the smart *panguinguera* smelled it, and added immediately.

"You know, Juli, what can be done? Ask for a loan of two hundred fifty pesos on the house, payable when the case is won."

This seemed the best suggestion so far, and they decided to act on it that very same day. Sister Balî offered to accompany her, and both went the rounds of the homes of the rich of Tiani, but no one would accept the condition: they said the case was lost and to favor an enemy of the friars would expose oneself to their vengeance. Finally, a devout old woman took pity on her, and lent the amount on condition that Juli would stay with her to serve as long as the debt remained unpaid. Furthermore, Juli would not have much to do beyond sewing, praying, accompanying her to mass and fasting for her now and then. The young woman accepted with tears in her eyes, and received the money, promising to enter the following day, Christmas day, into her service.

When the grandfather learned of what amounted to a transaction, he wept like a child. What! The granddaughter whom he did not allow to walk under the sun so as not to burn her complexion, Juli of the slender fingers and rosy heels? What? That young woman, the most beautiful in the barrio, and perhaps in the town too, under whose window many had passed the night serenading and singing in vain? What? His only granddaughter, his only daughter, the only joy of his tired eyes, the one he had dreamt about dressed in a long gown with a train, speaking Spanish, fanning air with a painted fan like the daughters of the rich, she, to enter as a maidservant to be scolded and rebuked; to spoil her fingers, to sleep in any part of the house and to be awakened at any hour!

And the grandfather wept, spoke of hanging himself, or letting himself die of hunger...

"If you leave," he said, "I will return to the forest and I will never set foot in town."

Juli soothed him, saying that it was necessary that her father return; that they would win the case and soon they would be able to redeem her from servitude.

The night was sad: neither could taste a mouthful and the old man stubbornly refused to go to bed, spending the night huddled in a corner, silent, without saying a word, motionless. Juli, for her part, wanted to sleep, but for a long time could not close her eyes. Somewhat reassured of her father's fate, she now thought of herself, and she wept and wept, drowning her sobs so that the old man would not hear them. The following day she would become a maidservant, and that would be the precise day on which Basilio would arrive from Manila and bring her small gifts...From now on she would have to renounce that love; Basilio, who soon would be a doctor, should not marry one who is poor...And she saw him in her imagination going to church in the company of the richest and most beautiful maiden in town, well-dressed, happy and smiling both of them, while she, Juli, followed behind her mistress, carrying novenas, *buyos* and a spittoon. And here the maiden felt a knot in her throat, pressure on her heart, and asked the Virgin to let her die first.

"But at least," her conscience told her, "he will know

that I preferred to have myself pledged rather than pawn the locket he gave me."

This thought somewhat consoled her and she indulged herself in vain illusions. Who knows? A miracle might happen: she might find two hundred fifty pesos under the image of the Virgin. She had read of so many miracles of this sort. Or the sun might not rise and the morning might not come, and in the meantime the case might be won. Her father could return, and Basilio present himself; she might find a sack of gold in the orchard; the *tulisanes* could send her the sack. Padre Camorra, who always teased her, might come with the outlaws...her thoughts became more and more confused and disordered until finally, overcome by fatigue and by grief, she fell asleep dreaming of her childhood in the heart of the forest: she was bathing in the stream with her two siblings; there were tiny fish of many colors which allowed themselves to be caught like idiots, and she was getting impatient because she did not want to catch fish that were so stupid. Basilio was under the water, but she could not understand why Basilio had the face of her brother Tano. Her new mistress was observing her from the bank.

- 5 -

A Cochero's Christmas Eve

Basilio reached San Diego just as the Christmas Eve procession[1] was traversing the streets. He was delayed in his journey, losing many hours because the *cochero* or rig driver, who had forgotten his *cedula* or identification, was detained by the *guardia civil*, hit with some rifle butts and taken to the barracks to face the commandant.

Now the carriage had been detained anew to allow the procession to go through, and the pummelled cochero reverently uncovered himself and prayed one *padre nuestro* before the first image on wheels, which seemed to be that of a great saint. It represented an old man with a long, long beard, seated on the edge of a grave, under the shade of a tree with branches loaded with all kinds of stuffed birds. A *kalan* or earthen stove with a pot, a mortar and pestle and a *kalikut* to grind the betel nut, were his only furnishings, as if to show that the old man lived at the edge of the grave itself and cooked there. That was Methuselah in the Philippine list of religious icons. His colleague or perhaps contemporary is in Europe called Noel, the most cheerful and happiest of men.

"During the time of the saints," mused the *cochero*, "there surely were no *guardias civiles*, because with rifle butt strokes one cannot live long."

After the grand ancient, came the three Kings, the Magi riding on little horses which reared, particularly that of the black King Melchor which seemed about to knock down those of his companions.

"There must not have been any *guardias civiles*," concluded the *cochero*, envying those happy times; "otherwise that black who indulges in such antics beside those two Spaniards (Gaspar and Baltazar), would have gone to jail."

And, observing that the black was wearing a crown and was a king like the other two Spaniards, he naturally thought of the King of the *Indios* and sighed.

"Do you know, Señor," he asked Basilio respectfully, "if the right foot is free by now?"

Basilio repeated the question.

"The right foot? Whose?"

"The King's!" answered the *cochero* in a low voice with much mystery.

"Which King?"

"Our King, the King of the *Indios*...."

Basilio smiled and shrugged his shoulders.

The *cochero* sighed again. The *Indios* in the countryside treasure a legend that their king, imprisoned and chained in the cave of San Mateo, will one day come to deliver them from oppression.[2] Every hundred years he breaks one of his chains and he already has his hands and his left foot loose; only the right foot remains chained. This king causes earthquakes and tremors when he breaks his chains, or when he struggles or is agitated. He is so strong that one can shake his hand only by holding out a bone, which upon contact with him is reduced to powder. For no explainable reason, the natives call him King Bernardo, perhaps confusing him with Bernardo Carpio.

"When the right foot is set free," murmured the *cochero*, letting out a sigh, "I will give him my horses. I will place myself at his service and die for him...He will free us from the *civiles*."

And with a melancholy look he followed the Three Kings moving away.

The young boys came next in two files—sad and solemn, visibly coerced to join the procession. Some lighted the way with *huepes*[3] or torches, others with tapers and still others with paper lanterns on shafts of bamboo, praying aloud the rosary as if quarreling with someone. Then came St. Joseph, on a modest float, with a resigned and mournful attitude, his staff adorned with *azucena* flowers. He was between two *guardias civiles*, as if they had taken him captive. Now the *cochero* understood the expression on the saint's face. And whether it was the sight of the two guards that upset him, or he had little respect for a saint who was in their company, he did not pray even a *requiem aeternam*.

Behind St. Joseph came the girls bearing candles, their heads covered with kerchiefs knotted under their chins, also praying the rosary but with less ire than the boys. Among them some could be seen pulling little rabbits of Japanese paper lighted by little red candles with their cut-out little paper tails raised. The youngsters joined the procession with those toys to enliven the birth of the

Messiah. And the little animals, plump and round like eggs, seemed so contented that sometimes they would jump, lose their balance, fall and burn up. The owner would run to put out such ardor, puff, huff, extinguish the flames by beating them and, seeing it destroyed, would burst into tears. The *cochero* observed with a certain sadness that the breed of little paper animals decreased each year as if the plague had attacked them as it does live animals. He, Sinong the beaten one, remembered his two magnificent horses, to keep which from contagion he had had blessed as advised by the *cura*, spending ten pesos— neither the Government nor the priests had found a better remedy against the epidemic—and yet the animals had died. However, he felt consoled, for since those sprinklings of holy water, the Latin jargon of the priests and the ceremonies, the horses had become so conceited, affecting an air of importance, that they would not allow themselves to be hitched, and he, like the good Christian that he was, dared not punish them because a lay brother had told him they were *benditados*, thus blessed.

The Virgin closed the procession attired as the Divine Shepherdess, wearing a feathered hat, wide-brimmed and long-plumed, to indicate the journey to Jerusalem. With the purpose of explaining the Nativity, the curate had ordered that her waist be enlarged, and rags and cotton padded underneath the skirts, so that nobody could place in doubt the state in which she was found. It was a most beautiful image, equally sad of mien as are all the other images carved by the Filipinos, with an embarrassed air on account of the condition in which the curate, perhaps, had placed her. In front came some carolers; behind, some musicians and the corresponding *guardias civiles*. The priest, as was to be expected after what he had perpetrated, did not come: that year he was very much disgusted for having to use all his diplomacy and sly native wit to convince the parishioners that they should pay thirty pesos for each *misa aguinaldo* or early Christmas morning mass instead of the twenty that it used to cost.

"You are turning into subversives," he had told them.

The *cochero* must have been very preoccupied with the things he had seen in the procession because, when it had passed and Basilio ordered him to proceed on his way, he did not notice that the rig's light had gone out. Neither did Basilio, for his part busy looking at the houses, illumined within and without by little paper lanterns of fancy shapes and varied colors, stars encircled by hoops with long tails which, waved by the breeze, produced sweet murmurs; long-tailed fish with movable heads and oil lamps in their bellies, suspended from the window eaves with a delicious fiesta air, familiar and happy. Basilio also observed that the illumination was getting weaker, that the stars were on the eclipse and that year had less ornaments and pendants than the year before, just as last year's had less than the year before that... There was scarcely any music in the streets, cheerful kitchen noises could not be heard in all the homes, and the young man attributed this to bad times and sugar not selling well; the rice harvest had been lost; half of the work animals had died; rentals and taxes were rising and increasing without anyone knowing why and for what, while abuses of the *guardia civil* became more frequent, killing the merrymaking in the towns.

He was thinking precisely of these when a sharp order to halt resounded in the air. They were passing in front of headquarters, and one of the guards saw that the lights of the rig had been extinguished. A rain of insults fell upon the poor *cochero*, who was trying in vain to explain that the procession had lasted too long. Because it was bound to lead to an arrest for violation of edicts and publication afterwards in the newspapers, the peaceful and prudent Basilio got down from the rig and continued his way on foot, lugging his suitcase.

That was San Diego, his own town, where he had not a single relative.

The only house which seemed to him merry and busy was that of Capitan Basilio. Hens and chickens were crying songs of death to the accompaniment of sharp and frequent blows, as if someone were mincing meat on a chopping block, and the sputtering of lard boiling in the frying pan. In the house there was feasting, and the succulent aroma of stews and sweetmeats reached out to the streets.

In the mezzanine Basilio saw Sinang, as short as when our readers first met her, although somewhat plumper and rounder since she had married. And with great surprise he espied there, farther in, chatting with Capitan Basilio, the parish priest and the *alferez* of the *guardia civil*, none other than Simoun, the jeweler, always with his dark glasses and carefree air.

"It is understood, Señor Simoun," said Capitan Basilio, "we will go to Tiani to have a look at your jewels."

"I too would like to go," said the *alferez*, "I need a watch chain, but I have many things to attend to... If Capitan Basilio would like to undertake..."

Capitan Basilio took responsibility with the greatest of pleasure, and since he wanted to be in the good graces of the military so that he would not be molested in the persons of his laborers, he would not accept the amount that the *alferez* was forcibly digging out of his pocket.

"It will be my Christmas present!"

"I cannot allow that, Capitan...I cannot!"

"Well, well! We will settle accounts later," said Capitan Basilio with an elegant gesture.

The Curate, too, wanted a pair of lady's earrings, and likewise asked Capitan Basilio to get them for him.

"I want them to be *mabuti*, of the best quality. We can settle accounts later."

"Don't worry, Padre *Cura*," said the good man who also wanted to be at peace with the Church.

A piece of hostile information from the priest could be prejudicial to him and make him spend twice. Those earrings were compulsory gifts. Meanwhile Simoun was praising his jewelry.

"This man is unbearable!" thought the student. "He does business everywhere...If we are to believe *someone*, he buys back at half price from certain gentlemen the jewels he himself had sold to be given to them as presents ... Everybody makes business in this country except us!"

And he headed for his house, or rather that of Capitan Tiago, inhabited by a trusted man. The latter had great respect for him since the day he saw him perform surgical operations with the same calmness as if he were treating chickens. He had been waiting for him to give him some news. Two of the workers were in prison, one was going to be exiled...a number of carabaos had died.

"Always the same old stories," replied Basilio in bad humor. "You always meet me with the same complaints!"

The young man, who was often scolded by Capitan Tiago, liked in turn to scold those under him. The old man searched his mind for some fresh news.

"A tenant, the old man who takes care of the forest, has died and the parish priest will not give him burial as a poor man, alleging that his master is rich!"

"And what did he die of?"

"Of old age!"

"You don't say! To die of old age! If only he had died of some sickness!"

Basilio, in his zeal to conduct autopsies, wanted the sick.

"Don't you have anything to tell me? You take away my appetite by telling me the same things. Have you heard anything from Sagpang?"

Then the old employee told him about the kidnapping of *Cabesang* Tales. Basilio became thoughtful and did not say anything. His appetite had left him completely.

- 6 -

Basilio

When the bells were beginning to peal for the midnight mass and those who preferred a good sleep to feasts and ceremonies woke up grumbling against the sounds and the bustle, Basilio cautiously went downstairs and doubled back two or three times along various streets and, convinced that nobody was watching or following him, took the unfrequented paths towards the forest of the Ibarras, which had been acquired by Capitan Tiago when these properties were confiscated and sold.

Since in that year the Nativity coincided with a moon on the wane, there reigned absolute darkness. The ringing of the bells had ceased; only their echoes resounded in the midst of the silence of the night, through the murmur of the windswept branches and the rhythmic beat of the waves of the nearby lake, like the heavy breathing of nature sunk in deep slumber.

Inspired by the place and the moment, Basilio walked

head down as if trying to penetrate the darkness. Now and then, he would raise his head to seek the stars across the clearings left among the treetops, proceeding on his way, parting aside the bushes and tearing down the vines that impeded his progress. Sometimes he retraced his steps, his feet getting entangled in a shrub, or stumbling against a protruding root or a fallen tree trunk. After half an hour, he reached a small stream on the opposite bank on which stood a kind of hillock, a black shapeless mass which, in the obscurity, acquired the proportions of a mountain. Basilio crossed the stream, jumping over stones that stood out dark on the brilliant surface of the water, climbed the hillock, went towards a small enclosure surrounded by old crumbling walls and headed for a *baleté* tree which loomed in the center, enormous, mysterious, venerable, formed of roots that rose and fell with many other trunks confusedly intertwined.

He stopped before a pile of stones, uncovered himself and seemed to pray. Here was buried his mother, and his first visit every time he came to town was to that unknown and unmarked grave. Having to visit the family of Cabesang Tales the following day, he took advantage of the night to fulfill his duty.

He seated himself on a stone and seemed to be in deep thought. His past appeared before him like a long black ribbon, rosy at first, somber afterwards, with bloodstains, then black, very black, fading into gray and clear, much clearer every time. He could not see its end, hidden under a cloud suggestive of lights and dawns...

It was almost thirteen years, to the day, to the hour, since his mother had died in the midst of deepest misery during a splendid night when the moon shone brightly and Christians all over the world were rejoicing. Wounded and limping, he had reached the place, following her. She, mad and terror-stricken, was fleeing from her son like a shadow. Here she died. A stranger came and ordered him to build a funeral pyre. He obeyed mechanically, and when he returned, found himself facing another stranger near the dead body of the first stranger. What a morning and a night that had been! The unknown man helped Basilio build a fire, in which they burned the body of the dead man. He dug a pit in which they buried his mother. After giving him some coins the unknown man ordered him to leave the place. It was the first time he had seen that tall man with reddened eyes, bloodless lips, a sharp nose...

Completely orphaned, without brothers or parents, he left the town whose authorities filled him with terror. He went to Manila to serve in the household of some rich man and study at the same time, as many others did.[1] His journey was an odyssey of sleepless nights and sudden fears, in which hunger counted the very least. He fed on the fruits of the forest where he was wont to hide every time he saw a uniform of the *guardia civil*, a uniform which reminded him of the origin of all his misfortunes. One time in Manila, ragged and ill, he went from door to door offering his services: a youngster from the province who knew not a single word of Spanish and on top of that sickly! Discouraged, hungry and lonely, he traversed the streets calling attention to his miserable attire. How many times had he been tempted to throw himself beneath the hooves of the horses which passed like lightning flashes, pulling shiny carriages of silver and varnish, to end once and for all his miseries! By good fortune he saw Capitan Tiago pass by, accompanied by Tía Isabel. He had known them since San Diego, and in his happiness he saw them as townmates. He followed the carriage, then lost sight of it. He asked for their house and since it was precisely the day on which Maria Clara had entered the cloister, and Capitan Tiago was very depressed, he was admitted with the standing of a servant, without salary, of course, allowed to study instead, when he would so desire, in San Juan de Letran.[2]

Unkempt, poorly attired and shod only in a pair of wooden clogs, after the end of several months' stay in Manila, he enrolled in the first year of Latin. His classmates, seeing his attire, distanced themselves from him. His professor was a handsome Dominican who never asked him a single question and who frowned every time he saw him. The only words exchanged between the two of them in eight months were his name read in the roll call, to which the student daily answered *adsum*. With what great bitterness he came out of the classroom each time, and, guessing the motive of the manner in which he was treated, what tears would fill his eyes, and what griefs were stifled and died within his heart. How he had wept and sobbed over his mother's grave, telling her of his hidden pains, his humiliation and grievance when Christmas approached and Capitan Tiago took him along to San Diego.

Nevertheless, he learned his lessons by memory without missing a comma, although without understanding much of it. In the end he became resigned when he saw that among the three or four hundred students of his class only some forty deserved the honor of being asked questions, because they attracted the professor's attention through their looks, or buffoonery, or out of fellow-feeling, or for any reason whatsoever. Many of them congratulated themselves for being spared the ordeal. In that way they did not have to exert effort to think and understand.

One goes to college not to learn or study, but to complete the course; and if they could memorize the textbook nothing more could be expected from them and they would be sure to pass the year.

Basilio passed the examinations by answering the only question asked of him, like a machine, without pausing to breathe; and earned the passing mark to the great surprise of his examiners. His nine companions—they were examined in groups of ten to make things go faster—did not have the same luck and were condemned to repeat another year of brutalization.

In the second year, the fighting cock under his care having won a vast amount, he received a generous tip from Capitan Tiago, which he invested immediately in the purchase of a pair of shoes and a felt hat. With these and with the clothes given by his master which he fixed to fit him, his appearance became more decent, but he did not go beyond this. In a class of so many, much is needed to attract the professor's attention, and the pupil who since the first year had not been noticed through an outstanding quality, or had not captured the sympathy of the professors, would be very difficult to recognize for the rest of his student days. However, he continued well, perseverance being his main trait.

His luck took a turn for the better in his third year. He had the good fortune of having for his professor a jovial Dominican, fond of jesting, who made his pupils laugh, and was somewhat easygoing because almost always he made his favorites explain the lessons in his place. The truth was also that he was satisfied with almost anything. By this time Basilio could spend for boots and shirts almost always clean and well-pressed. As his professor observed him hardly laughing at the jokes, and saw in his eyes, sad and large, something like an eternal question, he considered him an imbecile. One day he wanted to prove this by asking him about the lesson. Basilio recited from head to tail without missing a single letter. The professor dubbed him a parrot; he narrated a tale that made all of the class laugh, and to increase the hilarity and justify the nickname, asked him some questions, winking at his favorites as if telling them:

"You will see how we will have some fun!"

Basilio by then knew Spanish, and was able to answer with the obvious intention of not making anyone laugh. That disappointed all; the fun they were expecting did not come. Nobody could laugh, and the good friar never forgave him for having defrauded the whole class of their expectations and belied his pronouncements. But who would expect that something sensible could come out of the unkempt head in which terminated an *Indio*, so poorly shod, classified, until lately, among the climbing animals? And just as in other centers of learning where the students are eager to learn and the professors rejoice over this fact, so, on the other hand, it is with schools run by men who are convinced for the most part that learning is a necessary evil, at least for the students. Basilio's case had bad repercussions and he was never called again the rest of the year. What for, since he could not make anyone laugh?

Although sufficiently discouraged and tempted to give up his studies, he passed the fourth year of Latin. Why learn, why not fall asleep like the others and leave it to chance?

One of the two professors was very popular, liked by all; he was considered a sage, a great poet and full of very progressive ideas. One day, when he was accompanying the students on a walk, the professor had a misunderstanding with some cadets, which resulted in a skirmish and then a challenge. The professor, who perhaps recalled his gallant youth, proclaimed a crusade and promised high grades to all who at the next Sunday's walk would take part in the melee. The week was full of excitement: there were partisan encounters in which canes and sabers crossed, and in one of these Basilio distinguished himself.[3]

He was carried in triumph by the students and presented to the professor, and since then was recognized and became his favorite. Partly for this and partly for his diligence, that year he finished with outstanding marks and with accompanying medals. In view of this, Capitan Tiago, who since his daughter had become a nun had shown an aversion towards the friars, in a moment of good humor, persuaded Basilio to transfer to the Ateneo Municipal, the fame of which was then at its summit.[4]

A new world opened before his eyes, a system of instruction in that college which he had never suspected could exist. Superfluities and puerilities aside, he was filled with admiration for the method followed there and with gratitude for the zeal of its professors. His eyes would sometimes fill with tears when he recalled the four previous years in which for lack of means he had not been able to study in that center. He had to exert the most extraordinary efforts to put himself on the same level as those who had begun well; it can be said that in that single year he finished five years of the Secondary Course. He took his bachelor's degree to the great satisfaction of his professors, who manifested their pride in him during the examinations before the Dominican judges sent there to test them.[5] One of these, as if to dampen a little such enthusiasm, asked him where he had learned his early years of Latin.

"At San Juan de Letran College, Padre," replied Basilio.

"Ah, in Latin he is not too bad," then observed the Dominican, half-smiling.

Out of a natural inclination and in keeping with his character, he chose to take up Medicine. Capitan Tiago preferred for him to study Law so that he could have a lawyer for free, but it is not enough to know and learn well the laws to have clientele in the Philippines; it is necessary to win lawsuits and for this one needs connections, influence in certain circles, and knowing one's way around. In the end Capitan Tiago gave in when he remembered that medical students were always playing around with corpses. For some time now Capitan Tiago had been looking for an effective poison to temper the gaffs of his cocks and the most deadly that he knew of was the blood of a Chinese who had died of a venereal disease.

With the same progress, if not greater, the young man pursued the years of medical studies and, from his third year, started to cure people successfully, which promised for him not only a brilliant future, but also gave him enough funds to dress with a certain elegance and even save money.

This year was the last of his studies and in two months he would be a physician. He would retire to his home town, and marry Juliana and live happily ever after. His graduation was not only assured, but also expected to be the crowning success of his student life. He had been chosen to deliver the valedictory address at the graduation ceremonies. Already he could see himself in the middle of the central hall before the assembly, the object of all eyes and public attention. All those intellects, eminences of

Manila science, half-shrouded in their capes of colors, all the women who would come in curiosity, and who, years before, had regarded him, if not with disdain then with indifference; all those gentlemen whose coaches would have run him over in the mud as a youngster as if he were a dog, now would listen to him attentively; and he would tell them something that was not trivial, something that had never before resounded in that audience. He would forget self and would speak for the needy students of the future. With that speech he would make his entry into the world.

- 7 -

Simoun

These things were in Basilio's thoughts when he visited his mother's grave. He was about to leave and return to town when he thought he saw a brightness filtering among the trees and heard a crackle of branches, the sound of footsteps, the rustle of leaves...The light dimmed, but the sound became more distinct, and soon he saw a shadow appear in the midst of the enclosure and march directly to where he stood.

Basilio was not by nature superstitious, and even less so after having dissected so many cadavers and assisted so many dying, but the ancient legends about that somber place, the hour, the darkness, and the melancholic moaning of the wind and certain tales heard in his childhood influenced his spirit and his heart beat violently.

The shadow stopped on the other side of the *baleté*, and the young man was able to see it through a cleft between its two roots which had acquired with time the proportions of two tree trunks. It took out from under its

attire a lamp with a powerful refraction lens, and set it on
the ground, where it lit a pair of riding boots, the rest
remaining hidden in the darkness. The shadow seemed to
search through its pockets. Afterwards it bent to adjust
the blade of a spade at the end of a thick cane. To his
surprise Basilio thought he saw something like the contours
of Simoun the jeweler. In fact it was he himself.

The jeweler was digging in the ground, and from
time to time the lantern illumined his face. He was without
the blue glasses that altered his features. Basilio shuddered.
This was the same unknown he had met thirteen years
ago, who had dug there the grave of his mother, except
that now he had aged, his hair had turned white, and he
sported a moustache and a goatee, but the look in his eyes
was the same, the same bitter expression, the same troubled
brow, the same muscular arms although a bit leaner now,
the same furious energy.

The past memories were revived in him. He thought
he felt the heat of the bonfire, the hunger, the
discouragement then, the smell of freshly turned earth...His
discovery filled him with terror. So the jeweler Simoun
who was posing as a British Indian, a Portuguese, an
American, a mulatto, the Brown Cardinal, his Black
Eminence, the evil spirit of the Capitan General, as he was
called by many, was no other than the mysterious stranger
whose appearance and disappearance coincided with the
death of the heir of those lands. But of the two unknowns
who had presented themselves to him, the dead and the
living, which was Ibarra?

This question which he asked of himself several times,
whenever the death of Ibarra was spoken of, came back to
his mind in the light of that enigmatic man he was looking
at now.

The dead one had two wounds which must have

been inflicted by firearms, according to what he had learned later, and could have been the result of the pursuit in the lake. The dead would be Ibarra then, come to die over his ancestor's grave and his desire to be cremated was very well explained by his stay in Europe where cremation was in vogue. So who was the other one then, the living one, this jeweler Simoun, miserable looking, now returned loaded with gold and a friend of the authorities? There must be some mystery here, and the student with his characteristic cold-bloodedness promised himself to clear this up, and watched for an opportunity.

Simoun was digging and digging in the meantime, but Basilio noted that his former vigor had diminished: Simoun was panting, breathing with difficulty and he had to rest every now and then.

Basilio, fearing he might be discovered, suddenly made a quick decision; he rose from his seat and in his most natural voice:

"Can I help you, Señor...?" he asked, coming out from hiding.

Simoun straightened and leaped up like a tiger attacked directly. He brought a hand to the pocket of his jacket, looked at the student, pale and dismayed.

"It has been thirteen years since you did me a great service, Señor," proceeded Basilio without batting an eyelash, "in this very place, burying the corpse of my mother, and I would be happy if I could be of service to you!"

Simoun, without taking his eyes off the young man, drew a revolver from his pocket. A click was heard, like that of a gun being cocked.

"Whom do you take me for?" he said, stepping back two paces.

"For someone I hold sacred," replied Basilio somewhat

moved, thinking his last hour had come, "for someone who all, except I, believed to be dead, and whose misfortunes I have always lamented."

Imposing silence followed these words, a silence that to the young man sounded like eternity. Simoun, however, after a long hesitation, approached him and, placing a hand on his shoulder, said to him in a voice that broke with emotion:

"Basilio, you possess a secret which can ruin me; and now you have surprised me in another which puts me entirely in your hands, and the disclosure of which can upset all my plans. For my security and for the good of the objective I pursue I should seal your lips forever, because what is the life of a man worth before the end that I pursue? The occasion is propitious to me; no one knows I have come. I am armed, you are defenseless; your death would be attributed to the *tulisanes* if not to a supernatural cause...but nevertheless I will let you live and I trust I will not regret it. You have labored, you have struggled with energetic perseverance ... and like me, you have accounts to settle with society. Your little brother was murdered, and your mother driven to madness, and society has not persecuted the murderer or the tormentor.[1] You and I both belong to those who thirst for justice, and instead of destroying each other, we should help one another."

Simoun stopped, drowned a sigh and afterwards continued slowly with a faraway look.

"Yes, I am that one who came thirteen years ago, ill and heartbroken, to render my homage to a great and noble soul, who wished to die for me. Victim of a vicious system, I have wandered throughout the world, working night and day to gather a fortune and bring my plan to fruition. Today I have returned to destroy this system, precipitate its corruption, push it to the abyss to which it runs insensate, even if I have to spill torrents of blood and tears...It has condemned itself and I do not wish to die without seeing it dashed to pieces at the bottom of the precipice!"

And Simoun extended both arms towards the earth as if with that movement he would maintain there the broken remnants. His voice had acquired a tone sinister, forlorn, which made the student shudder.

"Summoned by the vices of those who rule, I have returned to these islands and, beneath a businessman's cloak, I have traversed the towns. With my wealth I have opened the way, and wherever I have been, greed in the most execrable forms, now hypocritical, now shameless, now cruel, feeds on a dead organism like a vulture devouring a cadaver. And I have asked myself why the poison, the toxins, the venom of the graves, do not ferment in its guts, to kill the loathsome bird? The corpse is left destroyed; the vulture is satiated with flesh, and since it is not possible for me to give it life so that it would turn against its executioner, and since corruption sets in gradually, I have incited greed; I have favored it; the injustices and the abuses I have multiplied; I have fomented crime, the acts of cruelty to accustom the people to the prospect of death; I have encouraged anxiety so that flight from it would lead to any solution whatever. I have placed obstacles to commerce so that the country, made poor and reduced to misery, would fear nothing. I have instigated ambitions to impoverish the treasury; and this being insufficient to lead to a popular uprising, I have wounded the people in their most sensitive fibers; I have driven the vulture itself to degrade the same cadaver that gives it life and corrupts it...

"But, when I was about to achieve from this supreme

rottenness, from this supreme garbage, an accumulation of such loathsome refuse fermented from the venom, when exacerbated greed in its bewilderment hastened to grab all that it could lay hands on, like an old woman surprised by fire, then lo, you all showed up with your cry of pro-Hispanism, with calls for confidence in the Government, in what will never come! Here was flesh palpitating with warmth and life, pure, young, lush, vibrant with blood and enthusiasm, sprouting suddenly to be offered anew as fresh food...

"Ah Youth, always inexperienced, always dreaming, running after the butterflies and flowers! You bond together so that with your efforts you can bind your country to Spain with garlands of roses, when in reality you are forging her chains harder than the diamond! You ask for parity rights, the Hispanization of your way of life and you fail to see that what you are asking for is death, the destruction of your national identity, the annihilation of your Motherland, the consecration of tyranny.

"What will you be in the future? A people without character, a nation without liberty. Everything in you will be borrowed, even your very defects. You are asking to be Hispanized and you do not blanch with shame when it is denied you! Even if it is conceded, what would you want? What would you gain? At best, to become a country of pronouncements, a country of civil wars, a republic of the rapacious and the discontented, like some republics of South America. Why do you now come with your teaching of Spanish, a pretension that would be ridiculous were it not for its deplorable consequences? Do you wish to add another idiom to the more than forty already spoken in the islands, so that you may understand each other, each time, less...?"

"On the contrary," replied Basilio, "if the knowledge of Spanish can unite us with the Government, on the other hand it could unite as well all the islands."

"A crass error!" interrupted Simoun. "You allow yourselves to be misled by big words and you never get to the bottom of things to examine the effects in their ultimate manifestations. Spanish will never be the common language in the country; the people will never speak it because for the ideas of its mind and the sentiments of its heart there are no words in that idiom. Each country has its own, as it has its manner of feeling. What will you gain with Spanish, the few who speak it? To stamp out your originality, subordinate your thoughts to other minds and instead of making yourselves free, make yourselves truly slaves! Nine out of ten of those among you who presume to be enlightened, are renegades to your motherland. Those among you who speak that language are indifferent to their own tongue, so much so that they neither write nor understand it. How many have I seen who pretend not to know a single word of it!

"Luckily you have an imbecilic government. While Russia, in order to enslave Poland, compels her to speak Russian, while Germany prohibits French in the conquered provinces, your government endeavors to have you keep your own tongue, and you, in turn, an extraordinary people under an incredible government, you forcibly strip yourselves of your national identity. Both of you forget that as long as a people conserve their language they preserve the security of their liberty, as a man his independence while he keeps his way of thinking. Language is the people's thought. Happily your independence is secure: human passions stand watch over it."

Simoun paused and passed his hand over his brow.
The waning moon was rising and sending its fragile sheen
through the branches. With his white hair and severe
features, lighted from top to bottom by the light of the
lantern, the jeweler seemed to be the portentous spirit of
the woods, meditating on something sinister. Basilio, silent
before those stern reproaches, was listening with head bent.
Simoun continued:

"I saw the start of that pro-Spanish movement and
spent whole nights in anguish because I knew that among
the youth there were those of rare intelligence and
exceptional hearts sacrificing themselves for a cause they
believed was good, when in reality they were working
against their own country...How many times have I been
tempted to approach you, unmask myself and disillusion
you, but in view of the reputation that I exude, my words
would have been misinterpreted and perchance would
have had a counterproductive effect...How many times
did I want to address your Macaraig, your Isagani.
Sometimes, I thought of their death; I wanted to destroy
them...!"

Simoun paused.

"This is the reason I am allowing you to live, Basilio,
and although I run the risk that through any imprudence
whatsoever you might betray me some day...You know
who I am, you know how much I have suffered; you
believe in me. You are not of the common run that sees in
the jeweler Simoun the trader who impels the authorities
to commit abuses so that the victims may buy his wares...I
am the Judge come to punish a social system through its
own crimes; make war against it by flattering it...

"I need you to help me; that you may use your
influence on the youth to fight those senseless yearnings

of Hispanization, of assimilation, of equal rights...That way can only lead to at best a poor imitation, and our people should aim higher! It is madness to try to influence the thinking of those who rule; they already have their plans laid out; they are blindfolded and it is losing time uselessly to delude the people with vain hopes and help to bend their necks before the tyrant. What you should do is to take advantage of their prejudices and to use them for your own purposes.

"They refuse to integrate you into the Spanish nation? Well, congratulations! Stand out then, molding your own individuality; try to lay the foundations of the Filipino nation...They give you no hopes? Well and good! Hope only in yourselves and work. They deny you representation in their parliament? All the better! Even if you were able to send representatives elected by your own choice, what could you do there but drown among so many voices and, by your presence, sanction the abuses and wrongs which may afterwards be committed? The less rights they give you, the more rights you will have later to shake off their yoke and return evil for evil. If they refuse to teach you their language then develop your own, understand it and make it more widely known. Keep alive in the people their own way of thinking, and instead of aspiring to be a mere province, aspire to be a nation; instead of subjugated thoughts, think independently so that neither in rights, nor customs, nor language, the Spaniard may be considered here as being in his own home or thought of by the people as a fellow citizen, but always, as an invader, a foreigner and, sooner or later, you will be free. This is why I want you to live."

Basilio breathed as if a great burden had been lifted from him, and replied after a brief pause:

"Señor, the honor you do me by confiding your plans to me is so great that I must be frank with you and tell you that what you demand of me is beyond my strength. I do not play politics, and if I have signed the petition for the teaching of Spanish it was because I saw it as a help in my studies, and nothing more. My objective is something else; my aspiration is to reduce and alleviate the physical ills of my countrymen."

The jeweler smiled.

"What are physical ills compared to moral ills?" he asked. "What is the death of one man beside the death of a society? One day you may become a great physician if they would leave you to practice in peace; but greater still would be he who infuses new life into this anemic nation! You, what are you doing for the land that gave you being, which gives you life and which enables knowledge? Do you not know that a life that is not dedicated to a great idea is a useless life? It is a pebble lost in the fields instead of being part of an edifice."

"No, Señor, no," answered Basilio modestly. "I do not just cross my arms; I work as others work to raise from the ruins of the past a country whose citizens will be united, each one of them conscious in himself of the conscience and of the life of the totality. But no matter how enthusiastic our generation may be, we realize that in the great fabric of human society there must be a division of labor. I have chosen my task and devote myself to science."

"Science is not the end of man," observed Simoun.

"It is the goal of the most cultured nations."

"Yes, but only as a means to procure their happiness."

"Science is more eternal, more humane, more universal," replied the young man in a burst of enthusiasm.

"Within a few centuries, when humanity shall have been redeemed and enlightened; when there shall no longer be races; when all peoples shall have become free; when there are no longer tyrants nor slaves, colonies nor empires; when one justice reigns and man becomes a citizen of the world, only the cult of Science will remain; the word patriotism will sound as fanaticism, and whosoever will take pride in patriotic virtues will surely be locked up as a dangerous maniac, as a disturber of the social harmony."

Simoun smiled sadly.

"Yes, yes," he said shaking his head, "but to reach that condition it is necessary that there should be neither tyrants nor enslaved people; it is necessary that man should be where he goes free; he should know how to respect in the rights of others that of his own person, and to achieve this, much blood should first be shed; it demands the struggle as necessary...To vanquish the ancient fanaticism which oppressed consciences it is expedient that many perish on the stakes so that the conscience of society, horrified, would set free the conscience of the individual. It is also necessary that all answer the question which every day the nation asks them when she lifts up her shackled hands. Patriotism can only be a crime in the oppressor nations, because then it will be rapacity baptized with a beautiful name, but no matter how perfect humanity may become, patriotism will always be a virtue among the oppressed peoples because it will signify for all time love of justice, freedom and self-dignity. Let us not have then illusory dreams and idylls fit only for women! The greatness of man lies not in being ahead of his times, something impossible anyway, but in divining his wants, responding to his needs and guiding himself to march forward. The geniuses who the common man thinks are ahead of their times appear only so because those who judge them see them from afar, or take for an era the tailend in which the stragglers move."

Simoun held his peace. Seeing that he had failed to arouse a spark of enthusiasm in that cold soul, he resorted to another argument and asked, changing his tone:

"And what are you doing on behalf of your mother's and your brother's memories? Are you satisfied to come here each year and weep like a woman over a grave?"

And he laughed mockingly.

The shot hit the mark. Basilio was shaken and took a step forward. "What would you have me do?" he asked angrily: "without means, without social position, what justice could I obtain against their murderers? I would become another victim and I would be dashing myself like a piece of crystal thrown against a rock. You are wrong to remind me of them because it is useless to touch a wound."

"And if I offered you my support?"

Basilio shook his head and remained thoughtful.

"All the vindications of justice, all the vengeance of the earth, would not bring back a single lock of my mother's hair, or renew a smile on my brother's lips. Let them sleep in peace...What would I get out of revenge?"

"You would avoid having others suffer what you have suffered, such that in the future there may be no murdered sons and mothers driven to madness. Resignation is not always a virtue. It is a crime when it encourages tyrannies. There are no despots where there are no slaves. Ah! man is in himself so evil that he always commits abuses when he meets complacency.

"I once thought as you did, and you know what was my fortune. Those who caused your misfortune watch you day and night; they suspect that you are waiting for an opportune moment; they interpret your zeal for learning, your love for study, your very indifference as burning desires for vengeance...The day when they can get rid of you they will do so as they did to me, and they will not allow you to progress because they fear and hate you!"

"Hate me? Hate me after the evil they have done me?" asked the young man, surprised.

Simoun let out a laugh.

"It is natural in man to hate those he has injured, said Tacitus confirming the *quos laeserunt et oderunt* of Seneca. When you want to measure the grievances or the good that one country does to another, you have only to see whether one loves or hates the other. This explains why some here who have enriched themselves from the high positions they occupy, return to the Peninsula and lavish slander and insults on those who were their victims. *Proprium humani ingenii est odisse quem læseris*—it is natural for man to hate those he has injured!"

"But if the world is large, if one leaves them in peace to enjoy power...I am not asking more than to be allowed to work and live my own life..."

"And to raise peace-loving sons who will in their turn submit to the yoke," continued Simoun cruelly mimicking the tone of Basilio. "Brave future you prepare for them, and they will have you to thank for a life of humiliation and sufferings? Congratulations, young man! When a body is inert it is useless to galvanize it. Twenty years of uninterrupted slavery, of systematic humiliation, of constant prostration, can create a hump on a soul which cannot be straightened out by the work of one day. All consciousness, good or evil, is inherited and transmitted from parents to children.

"Long live therefore your idyllic ideas, long live the dreams of the slave who asks only for a little rag with which to wrap his chains so these would make less noise and not bruise the skin. You dream of a little home with some comfort, a woman and a handful of rice. Behold the ideal male in the Philippines! Good; if they give it to you, consider yourself fortunate!"

Basilio, accustomed to obey and suffer the whims and ill humor of Capitan Tiago, and dominated by Simoun, who appeared sinister and terrible, backed against a background tinted with blood and tears, tried to explain, saying that he did not consider himself to have the aptitude to involve himself in politics; that he did not have a single opinion because he had not studied the matter, but that he was always ready to render his services on the day when they would be needed, that for the time being he only saw one necessity: the enlightenment of the people, and so on and so forth. Simoun cut him short with a gesture, and since it would soon be dawn, said:

"Young man, I will not suggest that you guard my secret, because I know that discretion is one of your good qualities. And even if you would want to betray Simoun the jeweler, the friend of the authorities and of the Religious Orders will always carry more weight than the student Basilio, already suspected of subversion, by the very fact that being native, he stands out and distinguishes himself; and because in the profession he has chosen he will encounter powerful rivals. Although you have not met my expectations, the day that you change your mind, look for me in my house at the Escolta, and I will serve you with good will."

Basilio thanked him briefly and took his leave.

"Have I hit the wrong note?" murmured Simoun,

finding himself alone. "Does he doubt me or does he meditate in secret on his own plan of vengeance that he fears to entrust to the very solitude of the night? Or have the years of servitude stifled in his heart all human sentiment, leaving only the animal instinct to survive and reproduce? In this case the mold would be defective, and it will be necessary to recast it...the sacrifice certainly exacts it...Let the unfit perish and the strongest survive!"

And he added dismally, as if addressing someone:

"Have patience, all you who have left me the legacy of a name and a home, have patience! One by one I have lost them, country, future, well-being, your very own graves...but have patience! And you, noble spirit, great soul, magnanimous heart, who lived only for one ideal and sacrificed your life without counting the gratitude or admiration of anyone,[2] have patience, have patience! The means I am using are not yours, perhaps, but they are the shortest and the swiftest...The day nears and when it dawns I myself will go to announce it to all of you. Have patience!"

- 8 -

Merry Christmas

When Juli opened her grief-stricken eyes, the house was still in darkness. The cocks were crowing. The first thing that came to mind was that perhaps the Virgin had caused a miracle, and that the sun was not going to rise despite the cocks invoking it.

She arose, crossed herself, recited with much fervor her morning prayers and, trying to make as little noise as possible, she went out to the *batalan*.[1]

There was no miracle; the sun was going to come out; the morning promised to be magnificent; the breeze was deliciously cool; the stars in the eastern sky were fading and the cocks were crowing lustily. That was too much to ask. It was easier for the Virgin to send the two hundred fifty pesos. What would it cost her, the mother of God, to give it? But underneath the image she found only her father's letter asking for five hundred pesos for ransom...There was no other remedy but to leave. Seeing that her grandfather did not move, she thought him asleep; she made *salabat*, ginger tea,[2] for breakfast. How odd! She was calm, even desiring to laugh. What was there, therefore, to be so much upset about that night? She was not going far; she could come every two days to check on the house. Her grandfather could see her and, as for Basilio, he had known for some time the bad shape her father's affairs were taking, because he would tell her repeatedly:

"When I become a doctor and we are married, your father will not need his fields."

"It was foolish of me to weep so much," she thought, while she fixed her *tampipi* or clothes basket.

And because her hands came across the locket, she raised it to her lips and kissed it, but immediately wiped them, fearing contagion. That locket of diamonds and emeralds had come from a leper...Ah, then, if she contracted the same infirmity she would not be able to marry.

Since it was beginning to clear and she could see her grandfather seated in a corner, following with his eyes all her movements, she took her *tampipi* of clothes, approached him smiling, to kiss his hand. The old man blessed her without saying a word. She felt like jesting.

"When father returns you can tell him that I have finally gone to school. My mistress speaks Spanish. It is the cheapest college that you can find."

And seeing the old man's eyes fill with tears, she placed her *tampipi* on her head and went hurriedly down the stairs. Her slippers resounded merrily on the wooden steps.

But when she turned her face to look once more toward her house, the house wherein had vanished her last dreams of childhood, and where she had painted the first illusions of maidenhood; when she saw it sad, lonely, abandoned, with its half-closed windows, empty and dark like the sightless eyes of the dead; when she heard the faint noise of the reeds and saw them swaying at the push of the morning breeze as if bidding her farewell, her liveliness dissipated. She lingered, her eyes filled with tears and, allowing herself to sit down on a tree trunk which had fallen beside the road, she wept disconsolately.

It had been some hours since Juli had left, and the sun was high in the heavens. Tandang Selo, from the window, viewed the people who, in holiday attire, headed for the town to hear High Mass. Almost all held by the hand, or carried in their arms a little boy or a little girl dressed as for a feast.

Christmas day in the Philippines is, according to the elders, the feast for the children; perhaps children may not be of the same opinion, and it can be presumed that they have an instinctive fear of it. In effect: they are awakened early, they are washed, they are dressed and on them are put all that is new, expensive and precious that they own: clothes, silken boots, wide hats, costumes of wool, of silk or of velvet, including four or five small scapulars bearing the gospel of Saint John, and, thus burdened, the children are taken to High Mass which lasts almost an hour; they are obliged to suffer the heat and the stench of so many sweating people pressing against each other. If they are not made to pray the rosary they have to be quiet, bore themselves or sleep. For every movement or prank that may soil their garments, a pinch, a rebuke. So they do not laugh, nor are they happy, and in their round eyes can be read the nostalgia for the old *camisola*, the one-piece shirt of ordinary days, and they protest against so much embroidery.

Afterwards they are taken from house to house to visit relatives for the hand kissing. There they have to dance, to sing and to display all the graces they know, whether they feel like it or not, whether they are comfortable or not in their attire, always with pinches and scoldings when they try to have their own way. The relatives give them *cuartos* which the parents take away, and of which nothing is ever heard again. The only positive things the children get from these celebrations are the marks of the said pinches, the discomforts and, at best, an indigestion from the surfeit of candies and biscuits in the good relatives' homes. But such is the custom, and Filipino children enter the world through these trials which, after all, turn out to be the least sorrowful, the least difficult in their lives.

The grown-ups who live by themselves have a share of their own in the holiday. They visit their parents and uncles, bend a knee and wish them a merry Christmas: their presents consist of a sweet, a fruit, a glass of water or some insignificant gift.

Tandang Selo saw all his friends pass by and thought sadly: that year, he had no presents for anyone, and his granddaughter had left without hers, without wishing him a Merry Christmas. Was it *delicadeza* or tact in Juli or did she merely forget?

When Tandang Selo attempted to greet his relatives who came to visit him bringing their children, to his great surprise he found that he could not articulate a single word. In vain he tried; not a single sound could he utter. He brought his hands to his throat, shook his head. Useless! He tried to laugh, and his lips trembled convulsively: a dull sound like the puffing of a bellows was the most that he could produce. The women looked at one another in dismay.

"He is mute! he is mute!" they screamed, full of consternation, creating immediately a regular turmoil.

- 9 -
Pilates

The news of that misfortune soon spread within the town. Some were sorry; others shrugged their shoulders. No one was to blame, and no one carried it on his conscience.

The *teniente* of the *guardia civil* was not even moved. He had orders to seize all weapons, and he had done his duty. He pursued the *tulisanes* always, whenever he could, and when they kidnapped Cabesang Tales, he immediately organized a team and brought to town handcuffed, elbow to elbow, five or six peasants who seemed suspicious to him. If Cabesang Tales failed to appear, it was because he could not be found in the pockets, nor under the skins of the prisoners who had been actively searched.

The lay brother *hacendero* shrugged his shoulders. He had nothing to do with it: it was a matter of *tulisanes* and he had only complied with his duty. He was certain that if he had not complained, perhaps there would not have been a recovery of weapons, and poor Tales would not

have been sequestered. But he, Padre Clemente, had to
look after his own security, and that Tales had a way of
looking at him which seemed as if he were picking a target
in some part of his body.[1] Defense is natural. If there are
tulisanes, the fault is not his. It is not his duty to go after
them; that is the job of the *guardia civil*. If Cabesang Tales,
instead of wandering around his lands, had stayed at home,
he would not have fallen prisoner. In short that was a
punishment from heaven against those who resisted the
demands of his Order.

Sister Penchang, the old devotee in whose home Juli
was serving, heard about it, let go of two or three
susmariosep, crossed herself and added:

"Many times God sends us these things because we
are sinners or we have relatives who are sinners whom
we should have taught piety, and we have not done so."

Those sinning relatives meant Juliana; for the pious
old woman, Julí was a great sinner.

"Just imagine! a young woman of marriageable age
who does not yet know how to pray! Jesus, what a scandal!
Well, this unworthy does not recite the *Hail Mary* without
pausing after *is with you*, and the Holy Mary without
pausing after *sinners*, which all good Christians who fear
God should be doing! *Susmariosep!* She does not know the
oremus gratiam and says *mentíbus* for *méntibus!* Anyone
who heard her would think she was talking of *suman de
ibus* or sweet rice rolls. *Susmariosep!*"

And she made a scandalized sign of the cross, and
gave thanks to God for permitting the sequestration of the
father so that the daughter might be delivered from sin,
and learn the virtues that, according to the *curas*, should
adorn all Christian women. And that was why she was
retaining her in her service and did not allow her to return

to the barrio to take care of her grandfather. Julí had to learn how to pray, had to read the booklets distributed by the friars, and had to work until she paid the two hundred fifty pesos.

When she learned that Basilio had gone to Manila to withdraw his savings and redeem Julí from the house where she served, the good woman thought that the young woman was going to be lost forever, and that the devil would appear to her in the form of the student. Boring and all, that booklet which the parish priest had given her had reason. The young men who go to Manila to learn are lost, and they lead others to be lost, too. And thinking to save Julí, she made her read and reread the booklet of *Tandang Basio Macunat*,[2] urging Julí always to go and see the priest in the convent, as did the heroine its author, the priest, praised so fully.

In the meantime the friars were congratulating themselves: they had definitely won the lawsuit and they took advantage of the captivity of Cabesang Tales to deliver his lands to those who had applied for them, without the least scruple, without the slightest twinge of shame.[3]

When the former owner returned and learned what had taken place, when he saw his lands in the possession of another, those lands which had cost him the lives of his wife and daughter; when he discovered his father dumb, his daughter serving as a maid, and even more, an order from the Tribunal transmitted by the *teniente del barrio*[4] to evacuate the house and leave it within three days, Cabesang Tales said not a word. He seated himself beside his father and scarcely spoke the whole day.

- 10 -
Wealth and Misery

The following day, to the great surprise of the barrio, Simoun the jeweler sought lodging in the house of Cabesang Tales, followed by two servants each carrying canvas-covered suitcases. In the midst of his misery, Cabesang Tales did not forget the good old Filipino customs, and was very much upset at the thought that he had nothing with which to express hospitality to the stranger. But Simoun had brought everything with him: servants and provisions, and only wanted to spend a day and a night in that house for being the most comfortable in the barrio, and for finding it between San Diego and Tiani, towns from where he expected many buyers.

Simoun inquired about conditions on the highways, and asked Cabesang Tales whether his revolver would be sufficient to defend himself against the *tulisanes*.

"They have firearms that shoot far," Cabesang Tales observed, somewhat absent-mindedly.

"This revolver has no less reach," replied Simoun,

firing a shot at a *bonga* palm[1] some two hundred paces away.

Cabesang Tales saw some nuts fall, but he did not say anything, and remained in deep thought.

The various families of the neighboring towns were gradually arriving, attracted by the fame of the jeweler's gems. They greeted each other, wishing each other a Merry Christmas; they spoke of masses, saints, poor harvests, but all the same they were there to spend their savings on gems and trinkets which had come from Europe. They knew that the jeweler was a friend of the Capitan General's, and there was nothing better than to be on good terms with him for whatever may happen.

Capitan Basilio came with his wife, his daughter Sinang and his son-in-law, ready to spend at least three thousand pesos.

Sister Penchang was there to buy a diamond ring which she had promised to the Virgin of Antipolo. She had left Julí behind in the house to commit to memory the booklet which had been sold by the priest for two *cuartos*, with forty days of indulgences granted by the Archbishop to all those who read or listened to it.[2]

"Jesus!" said the good devotee to Capitana Tikâ, "that poor wench grew up here like a mushroom planted by the *tikbálang*[3]...I have made her read the booklet in a loud voice at least fifty times, and nothing remained in her memory. She has a head like a basket, full while it is in the water. All listening to her, even the dogs and the cats, must have gained at least twenty years of indulgences!"

Simoun arranged on the table the two suitcases that he had brought: one was somewhat larger than the other.

"You would not want to buy plated jewels or imitation gems...The lady," he said turning to Sinang, "would want diamonds..."

"That is right, Señor, diamonds, and antique diamonds, antique stones, you know?" she answered. "Papá will pay, and he likes antique things, antique gems."

Sinang liked to joke about how much Latin her father knew, and how little and how poorly he knew her husband.

"I have precisely jewels of great antiquity," answered Simoun, removing the canvas cover of the much smaller suitcase.

It was a chest of polished steel with many bronze decorations and solid, complicated locks.

"I have necklaces of Cleopatra, genuine and legitimate, found in the pyramids, rings of Roman senators and gentlemen found among the ruins of Carthage...."

"Probably those that Hannibal sent back after the Battle of Cannae!" added Capitan Basilio seriously and shivering with excitement.

The good Señor, although he had read much about the ancients, had never seen anything of those times because of the lack of museums in the Philippines.

"I have brought, besides, valuable earrings of Roman matrons, found in the villa of Annius Mucius Papilinus in Pompeii..."

Capitan Basilio nodded his head, giving to understand that he was aware of and was in a hurry to see such precious relics. The ladies were saying that they also wanted to have things from Rome, like rosaries blessed by the Pope, relics which forgive sins without need of confession, and so forth.

Simoun opened the casket and lifted the raw cotton which protected it, uncovering a compartment full of rings, lockets, crucifixes, pins and so forth. Diamonds combined with stones of different colors sparkled, stirred among golden flowers of different hues with veins of enamel, with fanciful designs and rare arabesques.

Simoun lifted the tray and displayed another full of fantastic jewels which could have overwhelmed the imagination of seven young women on the eve of seven balls in their honor. Such fantastic designs, combinations of precious stones and pearls, imitating insects with bluish backs and transparent wings; the sapphire, the emerald, the ruby, the turquoise, the diamond were arranged together, to create dragonflies, butterflies, wasps, bees, scarabs, serpents, lizards, fish, flowers, clusters, and others. There were combs in the shape of diadems, necklaces, chokers of pearls and diamonds so beautiful that a few *dalagas* or maidens could not contain a *nakú* of admiration, and Sinang clicked with her tongue so that her mother Capitana Tikâ pinched her, fearing that for this the jeweler would raise his price. Capitana Tikâ had continued pinching her daughter even after she had married.

"There you have your antique jewelry," replied the jeweler. "That ring belonged to the Princess of Lamballe, and those pendants to a lady-in-waiting of Marie Antoinette."

They were beautiful diamond solitaires, large as grains of maize, of somewhat bluish tinge and gleaming with a severe elegance as if they still remembered the horror of the days of terror.

"Those two earrings," said Sinang looking towards her father and protecting instinctively with her hand the arm close to her mother.

"Something older still, the Roman ones," answered Capitan Basilio, winking.

The pious Sister Penchang decided that with such a gift the Virgin of Antipolo would soften and would grant her most vehement desire; she had long been praying for a sensational miracle with which her name would be associated, and which would immortalize her on earth and in Heaven afterwards like the curates' Capitana Ines,[4] and she asked about the price. But Simoun demanded three thousand pesos. The good woman crossed herself. *"Susmariosep!"*

Simoun displayed the third compartment.

This was full of watches, purses, match-holders and reliquaries garnished with diamonds; the most exquisite was finely enameled with elegant miniatures.

The fourth contained loose stones, and a murmur of admiration resounded throughout the living room when it was displayed. Sinang again clicked her tongue; her mother returned to pinch her arm without herself letting go a *Sus Maria!* of admiration.

Nobody had ever seen such wealth before. In that box lined with dark blue velvet, divided into sections, could be realized the dreams of a *Thousand and One Nights*, the dreams of Oriental fantasies. Diamonds as large as chickpeas were scintillating, spewing sparks of fascinating hues as if they were melting or burning perfectly in the colors of the spectrum; emeralds from Peru of all shapes and cuts; rubies from India, red like drops of blood; sapphires from Ceylon, blue and white; turquoises from Persia; Oriental mother-of-pearl, some rosy, gray and black. Those who have seen in the night a giant rocket exploding against the dark blue sky into thousands of sparks of all colors, so brilliant that the eternal stars pale beside them, can imagine the aura that compartment radiated.

Simoun, as if to increase the admiration of all those present, stirred the precious stones with his long brown fingers, taking pleasure in their crystalline tinkle, in their slippery brilliance, like so many drops of water colored by the rainbow. The flash of so many facets, the thought of their extremely elevated prices fascinated the onlookers. Cabesang Tales, who had approached, curiosity aroused, closed his eyes and immediately moved away as if to drive away an evil thought. So much wealth was an insult to his poverty. That man had come to display his immense riches on the very eve of the day that he, for lack of money, for lack of *padrinos* or godfathers, would have to leave the house that he had built with his own hands.

"Here you have two black diamonds, among the largest there are," remarked the jeweler. "They are very difficult to cut, being the hardest...This somewhat rosy stone is also a diamond, like this green one which is often mistaken for an emerald. The Chinaman Quiroga has offered me six thousand pesos for it, to offer as a gift to a very powerful matron.[5] It is not the green ones that are most expensive, but these blue ones."

And he laid aside three stones, not very large, but thick and well cut, with a slight bluish tint.

"Although they are smaller than the green ones," he continued, "they cost twice as much. Note that this which is the smallest—it does not weigh more than two carats—has cost me twenty thousand pesos and I am not giving it for less than thirty. I had to make a trip expressly to buy it. This other one, found in the Golconda mines, weighs three carats and a half and is worth more than seventy thousand. The Viceroy of India, in a letter I received the day before yesterday, is offering me twelve thousand pounds sterling."

Before so much wealth gathered in the power of that man who expressed himself so naturally and casually, his audience felt a certain respect mixed with awe. Sinang clicked her tongue several times and her mother no longer pinched her, perhaps because she was sunk in deep thought, or because she was thinking that a jeweler like Simoun was not likely to gain five pesos more or less for an indiscreet exclamation. All were regarding the stones; no one evinced the least desire to touch them; they were afraid. Wonder got the better of their curiosity. Cabesang Tales was looking toward the fields and thinking that with one single diamond, perhaps with the smallest one, he could recover his daughter, keep his house, and till another field...God! that one of those stones should be worth more than a man's home, a young woman's freedom, the peace of an old man in his last days!

And, as if divining his thoughts, Simoun said, addressing the families surrounding him:

"See for yourselves! see! with one of these small blue stones which look so innocent and harmless, pure as stardust detached from the vaults of heaven; with one such as this, gifted opportunely, a man was able to exile his enemy, a family man, a disturber of the community... and with one other little stone equal to this, red as the blood of the heart, as the thirst for vengeance and brilliant as the tears of the orphans, he gave him his liberty. The man was restored to his family's bosom, the father to his children, the husband to his wife and he has saved, perhaps, the whole family from a dismal future."

And patting the box:

"Within this box I have, as does the doctor's bag," he added in a loud voice and in bad Tagalog, "life and death; poison and its antidote; and with this handful I can drown in tears all the inhabitants of the Philippines!"

Everyone stared at him with terror, and they knew he was right. In the voice of Simoun was noted a strange timbre, and sinister sparks seemed to fly through his blue glasses.

As if to break the spell cast by the sight of the jewels

over those simple folk, Simoun lifted the tray and revealed
the bottom where he kept the *sancta sanctorum* or holy of
holies, Russian leather cases, separated from each other
by layers of cotton wool, the bottom lined with gray velvet.
All expected marvels. Sinang's husband was confident he
would see carbuncles, stones throwing fire and brilliance
in the midst of the darkness. Capitan Basilio was before
the threshold of immortality. He was going to see
something, something real, the shape of which he had
dreamed much about.

"This is the necklace of Cleopatra," said Simoun lifting
up very carefully a plain box in the shape of a half-moon.
"It is a treasure which cannot be assessed, a museum piece,
only for rich governments."

It was the kind of necklace composed of different
medallions of gold representing tiny idols among green
and blue scarabs, and in the center the head of a vulture
made of a rare jasper stone, between two outstretched
wings, the symbol and ornament of the Egyptian queens.

Sinang, seeing it, wrinkled her nose and pouted with
childlike contempt, and Capitan Basilio, for all his love of
antiquity, could not suppress an *abá* of disappointment.

"It is a magnificent treasure, well-preserved, and
almost two thousand years old."

"Psh!" Sinang hastened to exclaim so that her father
would not fall into temptation.

"Fool!" he said to her, overcoming his initial
disillusionment. "For all you know this necklace is
responsible for the present state of all society! With this
Cleopatra may have captivated Caesar, Marc Antony"...he
had heard the ardent declarations of love of the two
greatest warriors of their times; these he heard in the purest
and most elegant Latin. "You would have been lucky to

have worn it!"

"Me? I would not give three pesos for it!"

"Twenty can be given, *gonga*, silly!" said Capitana Tikâ with the air of a connoisseur. "You could give twenty pesos for it. The gold is genuine and melted would serve for other jewelry."

"This is a ring that may have belonged to Sulla," continued Simoun.

It was a wide ring, of solid gold, with a seal.

"With this he may have signed the sentences of death during his dictatorship," said Capitan Basilio, pale with emotion.

And he tried to examine and decipher the seal, but not conversant with paleography, he could not make out anything.

"What a finger Sulla must have had," he finally remarked, "it fits two of ours; as I have said, we are deteriorating!"

"I still have other jewels..."

"If they are all of that kind, thank you!" answered Sinang, "I prefer the modern ones."

Each one chose a jewel, one a ring, another a watch, one a comb. Capitana Tikâ bought a reliquary which contained a chip of the stone on which Our Lord rested after his third fall; Sinang a pair of earrings, and Capitan Basilio the watch chain for the *alferez*, the lady's earrings for the priest, and other gifts besides. The other families from the town of Tiani, not to be outdone by those of San Diego, equally emptied their pockets.

Simoun was also buying old jewelry, making exchanges. The thrifty mothers had also brought those pieces that no longer served them.

"And you Sir, don't you have anything to sell?" asked

Simoun of Cabesang Tales, seeing him watch with covetous eyes all the selling that was being done.

Cabesang Tales said that the jewelry of his daughter had been sold and the pieces that were left were not worth much.

"And how about the locket of Maria Clara?" asked Sinang.

"That's right!" exclaimed the man, and for a moment his eyes flashed.

"It is a locket with diamonds and emeralds," Sinang told the jeweler. "My friend was wearing it before she entered the cloister."

Simoun did not answer; he was looking anxiously at Cabesang Tales.

After opening various drawers, Cabesang Tales came across the jewel. Simoun studied it carefully, opened and closed it several times. It was the same locket which Maria Clara had been wearing at the fiesta of San Diego, and which in a gesture of compassion she gave to a leper.

"I like the shape," said Simoun. "How much do you want for it?"

Cabesang Tales scratched his head, perplexed, then his ears, and looked at the women.

"I have a fancy for that locket," Simoun repeated. "Do you want a hundred...five hundred pesos for it? Do you want to barter it with another? Take your choice."

Cabesang Tales was silent, and looked at Simoun stupefied, as if he doubted what he had heard.

"Five hundred pesos?" he muttered.

"Five hundred," repeated the jeweler in an altered voice.

Cabesang Tales held the locket and turned it round and round. His temples were beating violently, his hands were shaking. What if he asked for more? That locket could save them. It was an excellent opportunity and there would not be another like it.

All the women winked at him so he would sell it, except Sister Penchang who, fearing this would redeem Julí, observed: "I would keep it as a relic...Those who saw Maria Clara at the convent found her so thin, so thin that they say she could scarcely speak and it is believed she will die a saint...Padre Salvi speaks very well of her, he being her confessor. It will be for this reason that Julí had not wanted to give it up, preferring instead to pledge herself."

The remark had its desired effect.

The memory of his daughter stopped Cabesang Tales.

"If you will allow me," he said, "I will go to town and consult with my daughter about it. I will be back before nightfall."

They agreed and Cabesang Tales left the house.

But when he found himself outside the barrio, he perceived from afar on a trail that led to the woods the friar-*hacendero* and another man whom he recognized as the one who had taken his lands. A husband who sees his wife entering with another man a secret room could not have felt greater anger and jealousy than Cabesang Tales, seeing those two heading for his fields, the fields he had tilled and which he had hoped to will to his children. He figured that those two were mocking his impotence. The memory of what he had said, 'I will not give them except to him who would water them with his blood and would bury in them his wife and daughter.'...

He stopped, laid a hand on his brow and closed his eyes. When he opened them he saw that the man was shaking with laughter and the lay brother was holding his stomach in as if to keep it from bursting with happiness, and then he saw they were pointing at his house and they were laughing again.

A sound seemed to ring in his ears; he felt around his temples the sting of a whip, the red cloud reappeared, and before his eyes he saw again the bodies of his wife and daughter, and beside them the man and the friar laughing and holding on to their waists.

He forgot everything; he made a half turn and followed the pathway taken by the two men: it was the path that led to his fields.

Simoun waited in vain on the evening Cabesang Tales was to return.

The following morning when he woke up, he noticed that the leather holster of his revolver was empty. He opened it and inside he found a piece of paper which held the gold locket with diamonds and emeralds and some lines written in Tagalog:

> *Forgive me, Sir, that while you are staying in my house, I have taken what is yours, but necessity obliges me and in exchange for your revolver I am leaving you the locket that you wanted so much. I need weapons and I leave to join the tulisanes.*
>
> *I advise you not to go on your way, because if you fall into our hands, since you are no longer my guest, we will demand a considerable ransom.*
>
> *Telesforo Juan de Dios*

"At last I have my man!" murmured Simoun, breathing in relief. He is somewhat scrupulous...but all the better; he will know how to keep his pledges!"

And he ordered his servant to proceed to Los Baños on the lake, taking with him the larger suitcase, and wait for him there. He was going by land, taking with him that which contained his famous stones.

The arrival of four *guardias civiles* definitely put him in good humor. They had come to arrest Cabesang Tales. Not finding him they took Tandang Selo with them.

Three assassinations had been committed during the night. The friar-*hacendero* and the new tenant of the lands of Tales were found dead on the boundaries of his land, their heads blown up and their mouths filled with soil. The tenant's wife had also been murdered, her mouth equally stuffed with soil, her throat slashed, and a piece of paper beside her on which the name *Tales* was written in blood as if traced by a finger...

Do not be alarmed, peaceful citizens of Calamba. Not one of you is called Tales, not one of you has committed the crime. You are called Luis Habaña, Matias Belarmino, Nicasio Eigasani, Cayetano de Jesus, Mateo Elejorde, Leandro Lopez, Antonino Lopez, Silvestre Ubaldo, Manuel Hidalgo, Paciano Mercado—you are called the whole town of Calamba![6] You have cleared your own fields, you have spent on them the labor of a lifetime, savings, sleepless nights, privations, and you have been deprived of them, expelled from your own homes and they have forbidden the rest to give you hospitality. They were not content with violating justice; they stepped on the sacred traditions of your country...You have served Spain and the King and when in their names you asked for justice and you were exiled without due process of law, you were snatched away from the arms of your spouses, from the kisses of your children...Any one of you has suffered more than Cabesang Tales and nevertheless no one, not one has had justice...There was neither pity nor humanity for you, and you have been persecuted beyond the grave like Mariano Herbosa.[7] Weep or laugh in the lonely islands where you roam useless and uncertain of the future! Spain, generous Spain, watches over you and sooner or later you shall obtain justice!

- *11* -

Los Baños

H is Excellency, the Capitan General and Governor of the Philippine Islands, had been out hunting in Bosoboso.[1] But because he had to go accompanied by a brass band—since such an exalted personage could be no less esteemed than the wooden images carried in processions—and since Saint Cecilia's divine art had not yet been popularized among the stags and wild boars of Bosoboso, His Excellency, with the music band and his cortege of friars, military men and bureaucrats, was not able to bag a single mouse or one solitary bird.

The first authorities of the province foresaw future layoffs and a change of destiny; the poor *gobernadorcillos* and *cabezas de barangay* were alarmed and could not sleep, fearing that it might occur to the exalted hunter to substitute with their persons the lack of submissiveness of the quadrupeds of the forest, as had been done years ago by an *alcalde* traveling, borne on the shoulders of bearers because there were no horses tame enough to answer for his person. Nor was there lacking a malicious rumor that His Excellency had decided to do something with the situation for he saw in it the first symptoms of a rebellion which was convenient to quelch in its cradle, and that a hunt without a catch would depreciate the Spanish name, and so forth. And an eye was being cast at a hapless one to dress as a stag, when His Excellency, in a gesture of clemency which Ben Zayb could not find adequate words to extol, dissipated the inquietude, declaring that it gave him pain to sacrifice for his pleasure the beasts of the forest.

Truth to tell, His Excellency was contented and pleased *inter se*, for what would have happened if he had missed a game animal, perhaps a stag not too familiar with political expediencies? Where would the sovereign prestige have gone? What? Imagine a Capitan General of the Philippines missing a quarry like an amateur hunter! What would they say, the *Indios* among whom there were regular hunters? It would endanger the motherland's integrity...

Thus it was that His Excellency, with a fatuous smile and exuding the air of a disappointed hunter, ordered an immediate return to Los Baños, not without relating during the journey, his hunting feats in this or that forest of the Peninsula, as one who did not care much, adopting a somewhat deprecating tone, rather conveniently, for hunting in the Philippines, pshaw! The baths at Dampalit (Daan pa liit),[2] the sunbathing on the shores of the lake, and the games of cards in the palace with this and that excursion to the neighboring falls or the lake of crocodiles,[3] offered more attraction and less risk to the integrity of the nation.

There, in the last days of December, His Excellency found himself in the sala playing *tresillo*⁴ while waiting for the lunch hour. He had come from the bath with the well-known glass of coconut water and its tender meat, and was in the best possible disposition to grant privileges and favors. His good humor was increased by his winning many rounds. Padre Irene and Padre Sibyla, who were playing with him, were each employing their wits to simulate losses, to the great irritation of Padre Camorra who, having arrived only that morning, was not aware of what was being hatched.

The friar-gunner who was playing in good faith and with the utmost attention, would flush and bite his lips every time Padre Sibyla was distracted or calculated badly, but dared not say a word because of the respect which the Dominican inspired in him. On the other hand, he got even with Padre Irene whom he looked at as contemptible and sleek, and whose crudeness he detested. Padre Sibyla did not even deign to look at him, allowing him to snort; Padre Irene, more humble, tried to make excuses, fondling the tip of his large nose. His Excellency was enjoying himself and took advantage, being the excellent tactician that he was, as suggested by the canon, of the mistakes of his opponents. Padre Camorra was unaware that on the table was at stake the intellectual development of the Filipinos, the teaching of Spanish, and had he known it, would have perhaps taken part in the subterfuge.

Throughout the length of the open balcony the breeze blew, fresh and pure, and one could see the lake whose waters murmured softly at the foot of the building as if paying homage. To the right, from afar, could be seen the island of Talim, of a pure blue; in the middle of the lake and almost in front, a green islet, the isle of Calamba,

desolate, shaped like a half-moon; to the left the lovely
shoreline embroidered with bamboo reeds, a hill
overhanging the lake; and beyond it vast fields, then red
roofs visible through the dark green branches of trees, the
town of Calamba, finally the coast losing itself in the
distance.[5] The sky closing on the horizon descending on
the waters, gave the lake the appearance of a sea, justifying
the name given it by the *Indios: dagat na tabang* or fresh-
water sea.

On the far end of the sala, seated before a small table
where could be seen some papers, was the secretary. His
Excellency was very hardworking and did not want to
waste time, so that he tended business with him while he
served as *alcalde* in the *tresillo* and while the cards were
being dealt.

In the meantime, the poor secretary yawned and was
frustrated. That morning he was working as on all
weekdays, on changes of assignment, suspension of
employees, deportations, concessions, etc., but had not yet
touched the great issue which aroused so much curiosity:
the petition of the students soliciting a permit to open an
academy for the teaching of Spanish.

Walking from one end to the other and conversing
animatedly although in a low voice were Don Custodio, a
high official,[6] and a friar who carried his head downcast
with a pensive mood or disappointment; he was called
Padre Fernandez.[7] From an adjoining chamber came the
sound of balls hitting against each other, laughter, guffaws,
in their midst the voice of Simoun, dry and cutting. The
jeweler was playing billiards with Ben Zayb.

All of a sudden Padre Camorra rose to his feet. "The
hell with this game, Christ, *puñales!*" he cursed, throwing
the two cards that were left at the head of Padre Irene;

"*puñales*, that bet was for sure, even if not the rest, and we lost by collusion! *Puñales!* The hell with this game, Christ!"

Furious, he explained to all those in the sala, particularly to the three strolling by, as if taking them for judges: "It was the General's play, he dealt against; Padre Irene already had his move; he pulled out his card and *puñales*, that idiot of a Padre Irene did not respond, he did not discard the bad one. The hell with this game, Christ! His mother's son did not come here to break his own head for nothing and to lose his money!"

"If this dolt believes," he added, turning very red, "that I earn this from nothing, without lifting a finger!...On top of this my *Indios* are now beginning to haggle..."

Grumbling and without paying attention to the excuses of Padre Irene, who was trying to explain, rubbing his nose to conceal a subtle smile, he marched off to the billiard room.

"Padre Fernandez, would you like to sit?" asked Padre Sibyla.

"I am a very bad *tresillista*," answered the friar, making a face.

"Then let Simoun come," said the General. "Eh, Simoun, hey, Mister, do you want to play a hand?"

"What is the decision on sporting firearms?" asked the secretary, taking advantage of the lull.

Simoun's head appeared.

"Do you want to take Padre Camorra's place, Señor Sinbad?" asked Padre Irene. "You will put your diamonds in place of tokens."

"I have no objection to that," replied Simoun, drawing near and shaking the billiard chalk dust off his hands. "And you, Sirs, what will you bet?"

"What will we place?" Padre Sibyla retorted. "The

General will bet what he likes, but we religious, priests..."

"Bah!" Simoun interrupted with irony, "You, Sir, and Padre Irene will pay with acts of charity, prayers, virtues, eh?"

"You should know, Sir, that the virtues one may possess," argued Padre Sibyla gravely, "are not like diamonds that can be passed from hand to hand, or sold and resold... They reside in one's being, are attributes inherent in the subject..."

"Then I will be satisfied with your paying me with mere words," replied Simoun cheerfully. "You Sir, Padre Sibyla, instead of giving me five tokens will tell me, for example: 'I renounce for five days poverty, humility and obedience...' you Sir, Padre Irene: 'I renounce chastity, generosity etc.,' You see that it is a small thing and I stake my diamonds!"

"What a singular character this Simoun is, what witty remarks," said Padre Irene, laughing.

"And *this one*," continued Simoun, touching His Excellency familiarly on the shoulder, *this one* will pay me five tokens, an IOU for five days of incarceration; another one, for five months; a codicil, a blank deportation order; an authorization, let us say, a summary execution expedited by the *guardia civil* while my man is being conducted from one town to another, etc."

The challenge was unique. The three strollers drew near.

"But Mr. Simoun," asked the high official, "what do you gain from mouthed virtues, and lives, and deportations and summary executions?"

"Quite a lot! I am tired of hearing talk about virtues and I would like to have them all, all there are in the world, enclosed in a sack to throw into the sea, even if I have to make use of all my diamonds for ballast..."

"What a whim!" exclaimed Padre Irene, laughing;
"And the deportations and summary executions?"

"Why, to clean up the country and destroy all the
evil seeds..."

"Come now, you are still furious at the *tulisanes* and
worried that they might well have exacted a bigger ransom
or kept all your jewels. Man! do not be so ungrateful!"

Simoun told them that he had been held up by a
band of *tulisanes* who, after entertaining him for one day,
allowed him to continue his journey, taking from him no
ransom other than his two magnificent Smith & Wesson
revolvers and two boxes of cartridges which he carried
with him. He added that the outlaws were sending their
best regards to His Excellency, the Capitan General.

And on account of this, and because Simoun
recounted that the *tulisanes* were very well equipped with
shotguns, rifles and revolvers; and that against such
individuals a man alone, no matter how well armed he
might be, could not possibly defend himself, His
Excellency, to prevent the *tulisanes* from acquiring any
more weapons in the future, was about to issue a new
decree regarding sporting firearms.

"On the contrary, on the contrary," Simoun protested,
"in my opinion the *tulisanes* are the most honest men in
the country; they are the only ones who earn their rice
properly...Do you think that If I had fallen into the
hands...well, into your hands, you would have allowed
me to escape without stripping me of half of my jewels, at
the very least?"

Don Custodio was about to protest: that Simoun was
undoubtedly a gross American mulatto who was abusing
his friendship with the Capitan General to insult Padre

Irene, although it was also true that Padre Irene would really not have allowed him to go for less.

"The evil is not," continued Simoun "in that there may be *tulisanes* in the mountains and in uninhabited places. The trouble lies in the *tulisanes* of the towns and the cities..."

"Like you," added the canon, laughing.

"Yes, like me, like us: let us be frank; here there is no *Indio* to overhear us," continued the jeweler. "The trouble is that we are not *tulisanes* in the open. When we become that and if we went to live in the forests, that day the country would be saved, that day would bring forth a new society which would, alone, put herself in order...and His Excellency would then be able to play *tresillo* tranquilly without need of being distracted by the secretary..."

The secretary was yawning at that moment, extending both arms over his head and stretching his crossed legs as far as possible under the table.

All burst into laughter, seeing him. His Excellency wanted to cut short the turn of the conversation. Dropping the cards he had been shuffling, he said between seriousness and smiles:

"Come, come, enough of jokes and games. To work, let us get down to some serious work; there is still half an hour before luncheon. Are there many matters to attend to?"

— All lent their attention. That day they would give dispute over the issue of teaching Spanish, for which Padre Sibyla and Padre Irene were there since three days. It was known that the former, as Vice-Rector, was opposed to the project and that the latter supported it and his efforts were, in turn, backed up by the Madame Countess.[8]

"What is there, what is there?" asked His Excellency impatiently.

"Aahh mazz-ah zh-zhov zzo-parr-tin fii-iar-mzzz,"

repeated the secretary suppressing a yawn.

"Let them be forbidden."

"I beg your pardon, my General," said the high official gravely. "Your Excellency will permit me to observe that the possession of sporting arms is allowed in all the countries of the world."

The General shrugged his shoulders.

"We do not imitate any country in the world," he said dryly.

Between His Excellency and the high official there always were divergences of opinion, and it was enough for the latter to make whatever observation for the former to maintain his own stand.

The high official tried another approach.

"Those sporting arms can only harm rats and chickens," he said, "they might say..."

"That we are chickens?" continued the General, shrugging his shoulders again; "What do I care? I have given proof that I am not."

"But there is another thing," observed the secretary. "It is now four months since the use of firearms was prohibited; the foreign importers were given the assurance that sporting arms would be allowed."

His Excellency frowned.

"But there is a way out," Simoun said.

"What?"

"Very simple. Almost all sporting arms have a caliber of six millimeters, at least those that are on the market. Let the sale be authorized only for those that may not have those six millimeters."

Simoun's suggestion was well-received by all except the high official, who whispered into the ears of Padre Fernandez that that was not proper, nor could it be called governing.

"The schoolmaster of Tiani," continued the secretary, leafing through some papers, "requests that he be given a better place for..."

"What better place, when he has a schoolhouse to himself?" interrupted Padre Camorra who had already returned, forgetting the *tresillo.*

"He said that it is roofless," replied the secretary, "and that having bought from his own pocket maps and paintings, he cannot expose these to the inclement..."

"But I have nothing to do with that," murmured His Excellency, "Let him direct it to the director of administration, to the governor of the province or the nuncio..."

"What I want to tell you, Sir," said Padre Camorra, "is that this insignificant schoolmaster is a discontented *filibusterillo* or petty subversive; figure it out yourselves: this heretic preaches that those who are buried with pomp putrefy just as much as those without it. Some day I will punch him in the face!"

And Padre Camorra clenched his fists.

"Truth to tell," observed Padre Sibyla, as if directing himself to no one but Padre Irene, "he who wants to teach teaches everywhere, in the open air: Socrates taught in the public plazas, Plato in the gardens of the academy, and Christ in the mountains and lakes."

"I have various complaints against this little schoolteacher," said His Excellency, exchanging a glance with Simoun. "I think the best solution would be to suspend him."

"Suspended!" repeated the secretary.

The fate of that hapless one who sought aid and encountered dismissal pained the high official, and he wanted to do something for him.

"What is certain," he insinuated with some timidity, "is that education is not at all well-tended to..."

"I have already decreed numerous sums for the purchase of materials," said His Excellency with arrogance, as if wanting to imply: "I have done more than I should!"

"But for lack of appropriate sites, the materials that have been bought are thrown to waste."[9]

"Not everything can be done at once," dryly interrupted His Excellency; "The schoolteachers here do wrong to ask for edifices when those of the Peninsula die of hunger. It is great presumption to want to be better than the mother country itself!"

"Subversion..."

"Before anything else, Country! Before anything else, we are Spaniards!" added Ben Zayb, eyes shining with patriotism, and who blushed somewhat when he found himself alone.

"In the future," concluded the General, "all those who complain will be suspended."

"If my project is accepted," ventured Don Custodio, as if speaking to himself.

"Regarding the school buildings?"

"It is simple, practical and economical like all my projects, born out of extensive experience and the knowledge of the country. The towns will have schools without costing the government a *cuarto*."

All burst into laughter.

"No sir, no sir," cried Don Custodio, piqued and turning red. "The buildings have been built and only wait to be used—they are hygienic, unsurpassable, spacious..."

The friars looked at each other with some uneasiness. "Would Don Custodio be proposing that the churches, the convents or parish house be converted into schoolhouses?"

"Let us see it," said the General frowning.

"Well, my General, it is very simple," replied Don Custodio straightening himself and drawing out the echoing voice of ceremony, "the schools are open only during the weekdays, and the cockpits during fiestas...Well, the cockpits could be converted into schools, at least during the week."

"Man, man, man!"

"Yes, yes, it is beautiful!"

"What things occur to you! Don Custodio!"

"I say, it is an attractive project!"

"This puts the others to shame!"

"But Señores," explained Don Custodio upon hearing so many exclamations, "let us be practical. What places are more appropriate than the cockpits? They are large, are well constructed and maligned for what they are used for during the week. From a moral point of view, my project is very acceptable: it would serve as some sort of weekly purification and expiation for the temple of gambling, if we may call it thus."

"But sometimes there are cockfights on weekdays," observed Padre Camorra, "and it is not fair that the cockpit concessionaires pay the government..."

"Come, for those days classes are cancelled!"

"Man, man!" said the Capitan General, scandalized. "Such a travesty will not happen while I govern! That the schools are closed because there are games! Man, man, man! I would rather resign first!"

And His Excellency was really scandalized.

"But my General, it is better to close for a few days than for months."

"That would be immoral," added Padre Camorra, even more indignant than His Excellency.

"Even more immoral is that the vices have good buildings and for letters, there are none...Let us be practical, gentlemen, and not allow ourselves to be carried away by sentimentalism. While out of respect for human dignity, we prohibit the cultivation of the opium plant in our colonies, we tolerate it because it can be smoked, and the result is that we do not combat the vice but we impoverish ourselves..."

"But note that this produces for the government, without effort of any kind, more than four hundred fifty thousand pesos," replied Padre Irene who was leaning more and more towards government.

"Enough, enough, *Señores*," said His Excellency, cutting the discussion: "I have my projects regarding this, and I dedicate my particular attention to the branch of public education. Anything else?"

The secretary looked at Padres Sibyla and Irene with a certain uneasiness. The fat was coming out. Both prepared themselves.

"The request of the students seeking authorization to open an academy for the teaching of Spanish," answered the secretary.[10]

A general movement was noted among those who were in the sala, and after looking at each other, they fixed their eyes on the *General* to read how he would dispose of it. The application had been lying there for six months awaiting a decree, and had been converted to some sort of *casus belli* in certain spheres. His Excellency had his eyes down, as if to impede what they might read in his thoughts.

The silence was becoming awkward, and the General knew why.

"What do you think?" he asked the high official.

"What should I think, my *General*," answered the one
asked, shrugging his shoulders and smiling bitterly; "What
should I think but that the petition is fair, very fair and it
appears strange that it would take six months to think
about it."

"It is because it had to be gone over due to other
considerations," replied Padre Sibyla coldly, half-closing
his eyes.

Once again, the high official shrugged his shoulders
as if he did not understand what considerations these
could have been.

"Apart from the untimeliness of the proposition,"
continued the Dominican, "apart from being an assault on
our prerogatives..."

Padre Sibyla did not dare to continue, and looked at
Simoun.

"The solicitation has a somewhat suspicious
character," concluded the latter, exchanging a look with
the Dominican.

This other one winked twice. Padre Irene, who saw
this, knew that his cause was now almost lost: Simoun
was against it.

"It is a peaceful rebellion, a revolution on stamped
paper," added Padre Sibyla.

"Revolution? rebellion?" the high official asked,
looking at one and the others as if he understood nothing.

"It is headed by some youths accused of extreme
reformism and radicalism, not to say more," added the
secretary, looking at the Dominican. "There is among them
a certain Isagani, head somewhat askew...a nephew of a
native priest..."

"He is a student of mine," replied Padre Fernandez,
"and I am pleased with him..."

"*Puñales*! he is also pleased with himself," explained Padre Camorra. "On the ship we nearly came to fisticuffs: because he is rather insolent, I gave him a push and he retaliated with another."

"There is also a certain Macaragui or Macaraig..."

"Macaraig," replied Padre Irene, in turn joining in; "a lad who is very amiable and charming."

And he murmured within the hearing of the General:

"Of this one, I have spoken to you about, he is very rich...the Madam Countess recommends him persuasively."

"Ah!"

"A student of medicine, a certain Basilio..."

"Of this Basilio I say nothing," replied Padre Irene raising his hands and opening them as if to say *Dominus vobiscum;* "this one is deep water for me. I have never been able to fathom what it is he wants or what he thinks. A pity that Padre Salvi is not here to give us some of his antecedents. I believe I heard that when he was a boy he had scrapes to settle with the *guardia civil*...his father was killed in, I do not remember in what mutiny..."

Simoun smiled slowly, soundlessly, showing his well-aligned white teeth.

"Aha! Aha!" said His Excellency, shaking his head, "What do we have here? Take note of that name!"

"But my General," said the high official, sensing that the thing was taking a turn for the worse, "up to now nothing positive is known against these young men; their petition is just, and we do not have any right to deny it grounded only on mere conjectures. My opinion is that the government, giving proof of its confidence in the people and the stability of its tenure, should grant what they ask of it; and be free afterwards to revoke permission when it sees that its kindness has been abused. There is no lack of motives or excuses, we can watch them...Why offend some youths who later can resent us when what they ask for is ordered by royal decrees?"

Padre Irene, Don Custodio, and Padre Fernandez nodded in assent.

"But the *Indios* should not understand Spanish, you know!" cried Padre Camorra. "They should not learn, because then they will dare to argue with us; and the *Indios* should not argue, but only obey and pay...they should not involve themselves in interpreting what the law says, nor the books; they are nitpickers and very frustrating. As soon as they know Spanish, they become enemies of God and of Spain...but read the *Tandang Basio Macunat;* that, yes, is what a book should be! It has truths like this!" And he raised his clenched fist.

Padre Sibyla passed his hand over his brow to show impatience.

"One word!" he said, adopting a most conciliatory tone in the midst of his irritation. "Here we are not only treating of the teaching of Spanish; here is a silent confrontation between the students and the University of Santo Tomas. If the students come out with their school, our prestige will be left in the dirt. They will say that they have defeated us and they will exult, and *adios* moral strength, farewell everything. The first dike destroyed, who will contain that youth? With our fall we can do nothing more but announce to you: 'After us, the government.'"

"*Puñales*, no to that!" cried Padre Camorra, "Let us see first who has more fists!"

Then spoke Padre Fernandez who, during the discussion, had been contented with smiling. Everybody became attentive because they knew that he had a thinking head.

"Do not wish me ill, Padre Sibyla, if I differ with your manner of looking at the matter, but mine is the singular fate of being almost always in contradiction with my brothers. I say therefore that we should not be such pessimists. The teaching of Spanish can be conceded, without danger whatsoever, and so it may not appear as a defeat for the University, we Dominicans should make efforts to be the first to celebrate it: this should be our policy. Why should we be in continuous tension with the people, when after all, we are the few and they are the many, when we need them and they do not need us— wait, Padre Camorra, wait!—Let it pass that the people are weak, and unlettered, I also believe that, but that will not be so tomorrow, nor after then. Tomorrow or after tomorrow, they will be stronger, they will know what suits them and we cannot prevent it as we cannot prevent children, reaching a certain age, to get to know many things...I say then, why should we not take advantage of this state of ignorance to completely overhaul our policy to anchor it on a solid undying foundation, justice, for example, instead of basic ignorance. For there is nothing better than to be just, this I have always said to my brethren and they do not want to believe me.

"The *Indio*, like all young people, idolizes justice, asks for punishment when he has wronged, as he is outraged when he has not deserved it. Is what they desire just? Then allow it, give them all the schools they would want until they tire of them. Youth is indolent and what impels their activity is our opposition. Our shackle of prestige, Padre Sibyla, is already very tired; let us forge another one, the chain of gratitude, for example. Let us not be fools, let us do as the cunning Jesuits..."

"Oh, oh, Padre Fernandez!"

No, no; anything can be tolerated by Padre Sibyla except to propose to him the Jesuits as a model. Trembling and pale, he burst into bitter recriminations.

"First, a Franciscan...whatever thing before a Jesuit!" he said, quite beside himself.

"Oh, oh!"

"Eh, eh Padre P...!!"

A discussion ensued in which everybody, ignoring the Capitan General, intervened; all talked at the same time, they shouted, they misunderstood each other, they contradicted each other; Ben Zayb argued with Padre Camorra and both thrust fists at each other; one talked of dimwits and the other of pencil-pushers; Padre Sibyla talked of readings from the Bible and Padre Fernandez of the *Summa* of St. Thomas until the *cura* of Los Baños entered to announce that lunch was being served.

His Excellency stood up and thus the discussion was cut short.

"Here, *Señores*, today we have labored like blacks and yet we are on vacation. Somebody has said that grave matters should be treated during dessert. I am absolutely of that opinion."

"We might have indigestion," observed the secretary, alluding to the heat of the discussion.

"Then let us leave it for tomorrow."

Everyone stood up.

"My General," murmured the high official, "the daughter of this Cabesang Tales has returned, asking for the release of her sick grandfather, a prisoner in place of the father..."

His Excellency looked at him disgustedly and passed a hand over his wide forehead.

"*Carambas*! can one not be allowed to have his breakfast in peace?"

"It is on the third day that she will come; she is a poor girl..."

"Ah, the devil!" exclaimed Padre Camorra, "I knew it, I have something to say to the General, for that I have come...to support the appeal of that girl!"

The General scratched behind the ears.

"Well, go!" he said, "have the secretary send a note to the *teniente* of the *guardia civil* to release him. Let them not say that we are neither forgiving nor compassionate."

And he looked at Ben Zayb. The journalist winked.

- 12 -
Plácido Penitente

U nwillingly and with almost tearful eyes, Plácido Penitente was going through the Escolta to get to the University of Santo Tomás.

It has hardly been a week since he arrived from his town, and he has already written his mother twice, reiterating his desire to leave his studies, return home and go to work. His mother had answered him, saying that he should be patient, that he should at least become a graduate with a Bachelor of Arts degree because it was a pity to abandon his books after four years of expenses and sacrifices on his part and hers.

Whence came Penitente's disenchantment with learning when he was one of the most dedicated in the famous college run by Padre Valerio in Tanauan?[1] Penitente graduated there for being one of the best Latinists and brilliant debaters who knew how to weave or untangle the simplest or most abstract questions. Those of his town considered him the smartest, and his parish priest, influenced by that reputation, dubbed him a subversive, indisputable proof that he was not a fool nor dim-witted. His friends were at a loss to explain his desire to go home and leave his studies. He did not have sweethearts, was not a gambler, hardly knew *hunkían* and seldom ventured at *revisino;*[2] he did listen to the advice of the friars, laughed at *Tandang Basio*, had money in excess, elegant clothes, and yet went to class reluctantly and looked at his books with revulsion.

On the Puente de España, the bridge which has only its name from Spain[3]—even its iron girders came from other shores—he met with a procession of young people directing their ways to Intramuros to their respective schools. Some were dressed in European attire, walking fast, carrying books and notebooks; preoccupied, they were thinking of their lessons and their compositions: these were the students of the Ateneo.[4] The Letranites[5] could be distinguished by their being mostly dressed *a la Filipina*, being more numerous and less loaded with books. Those from the University[6] dressed more neatly and smartly, walked slowly and, instead of books, often carried canes.

The student youth of the Philippines are not noisy nor rowdy; they walk as if preoccupied. Seeing them, one would say that before their eyes no hope whatsoever shines, no smiling future. Even though here and there the procession is made pleasant by the graceful charm and the richness in colors of the female students of the Escuela Municipal,[7] ribbons over their shoulders and books on their arms, followed by their maids, yet hardly a laugh breaks out, hardly a joke is heard, no songs, no light banter, at most a few serious jokes, tussles among the smaller ones. The older ones almost always move seriously and are as well-behaved as German students.

Plácido continued along the Paseo de Magallanes to enter by the breach— before the gate—of Sto. Domingo,[8] when suddenly he received a slap on his shoulders which made him turn around immediately in bad humor.

"Olé, Penitente, olé Penitente!"

It was his classmate Juanito Pelaez, the *barbero*[9] or favorite of the professors, crafty and ill-mannered as could be, with a roguish look and the smile of a clown. Son of a Spanish *mestizo*—a rich merchant in one of the suburbs, who pinned all his hopes and dreams on the youth's talent—he promised much with his naughtiness, and thanks to his habit of playing dirty tricks on everyone, crouching afterwards behind his companions, he grew a particular hump which was enhanced every time he did his thing and laughed.

"How did you enjoy yourself, Penitente?" giving him hard slaps on the shoulder.

"So, so," answered Plácido, somewhat irritated, "and you?"

"Well, divinely! Just imagine: the parish priest of Tiani invited me to spend the vacation in his town; I went...*Chico*, good fellow! You know him, Padre Camorra? Well, he is a liberal *cura*, very hearty, frank, very frank, in the style of Padre Paco...And because there were very pretty girls, we took to *harana* or serenading, he with his guitar and Andalucian songs and I with my violin...I tell you, *chico*, we enjoyed ourselves greatly; there was not a house to which we did not go."

He whispered some words into Plácido's ear, then broke out into laughter. And since Plácido showed some surprise, he added:

"I can swear to you! They have no other remedy, because with a government order you can undo the father, husband or brother, and there is no other way. However, we met up with a simpleton, the sweetheart, I believe, of Basilio, you know? Look, what a fool this Basilio is; he has a sweetheart who does not know a single word of Spanish, who has no money and has been a maid. As shy as can be, but beautiful. Padre Camorra tackled with cane blows two poor chaps who were serenading her, and I don't know why he didn't kill them. But with all that, she is still as unsociable as ever. But it will happen to her as to all women, like all of them."

Juanito Pelaez laughed with mouth full as if he thought this delightful. Plácido looked at him disgustedly.

"Listen, and what did the professor explain yesterday?" he asked, changing the conversation.

"There was no class yesterday."

"Oho! And the day before yesterday?"

"Man, that was Thursday!"

"That's right, stupid of me! You know, Plácido, that I am turning stupid? And Wednesday?"

"Wednesday? Wait...Wednesday, it was drizzling."

"Great! and Tuesday, *chico*?"

"Tuesday was the birthday of the professor and we went to greet him with a band, a bouquet of flowers and some gifts."

"Ah, *carambas!*" exclaimed Juanito, "I forgot about it. How stupid am I. Listen, did he ask for me?"

Penitente shrugged his shoulders.

"I don't know, but they gave him a list of his well-wishers."

"*Carambas!*...Listen, and Monday, what happened?"

"As it was the first day of class, he read the roll and indicated the lesson: about mirrors. Look, from here to there, by memory, word for word...skip this part and study this."

And he indicated with a finger in the *Physics* of Ramos

the points that had to be studied, when suddenly the book jumped into the air due to a slap given it by Juanito from below.

"Man, forget the lessons. Let us have a *día pichido!*"

Día pichido is what the students of Manila call a day found between two holidays, on which class is cancelled, as though squeezed by the students' will.

"Do you know that you really are stupid," replied Plácido, furiously picking up his book and his papers.

"Let's have a *día pichido!*" repeated Juanito.

Plácido refused; for only two they would not suspend a class of more that one hundred fifty. He remembered his mother's toil and scrimping, which sustained him in Manila, depriving her of everything.

At that moment they were entering the breach of Sto. Domingo.

"Now I remember," exclaimed Juanito upon seeing the small plaza in front of the ancient building of the *Aduana*,[10] "do you know that I am in charge of collecting the contribution?"

"What contribution?"

"That for the monument!"

"What monument?"

"Come on! that of Padre Baltazar, did you not know that?"

"And who is this Padre Baltazar?"[11]

"My word! but of course, a Dominican! That is why the Padres turn to the students. Come on, let go three or four pesos so they see how generous we are! Let it never be said that to put up a statue they had to turn to their own pockets. Come *Plácidete*, it is not money wasted!"

And he accompanied these words with a meaningful wink.

Plácido remembered the case of a student who passed courses by giving away canaries, and gave three pesos.

"Look, you know? I will write your name clearly so that the professor reads it, see? Plácido Penitente, three pesos. Ah! Listen! Within fifteen days comes the birthday of the professor of natural history[12]...Do you know that he is very free, that he never puts down absences nor asks about the lesson. *Chico*, you have to be grateful!"

"That's true!"

"Well, don't you think that we should fete him? The band should be no less than what you took to the professor of Physics."

"That is right!"

"What do you say we set the contribution at two pesos? Come, Pláciding, you give first, that way you will be at the top of the list."

Seeing that Plácido gave without hesitation the two pesos asked, he added: "Listen, put in four, two of which I will then return afterwards; it is to serve as bait."

"Well, if you are going to return them to me, why should I give them to you? It is enough to write down four."

"Ah! true, how stupid I am! Do you know, I am turning stupid? But, all the same, give them to me, so as to show them."

Plácido, so as not to deny the *cura* who had baptized him, gave what he asked for.

They arrived at the University.

At the entrance and along the sidewalks which extended from one to the other side, the students stayed, waiting for the professors to come down. Students of the preparatory year of law, of the fifth of the second course, of preparatory medicine, formed animated groups: the

latter were easy to distinguish by their attire and by a
certain air that was not apparent in others; the majority
came from the Ateneo Municipal, and among them we
see the poet Isagani explaining to a companion the theory
of the refraction of light. In one group were discussed,
disputed, cited the pronouncements of the professor,
textbooks, scholastic principles; in another they gesticulated
with books, waving them in the air; they demonstrated,
tracing with the cane figures on the ground. Farther off,
entertaining themselves by looking at devotees entering a
nearby church, the students made exuberant comments.

One old lady, leaning on a young girl, limps devoutly;
the young girl walks with eyes cast down, timid, and shy
to pass in front of so many observers; the old lady lifts her
skirts, the color of coffee, of the Sisterhood of Sta. Rita, to
show a pair of big feet and white stockings, smiles at her
companion, and hurls furious looks at the inquisitive ones.

"*Saragates!*"[13] she snarls, "Don't look at them; drop
your eyes."

Everything calls attention, everything occasions jokes
and comments.

Now, it is a magnificent Victoria that stops beside
the door to deposit a devout family; they go to visit the
Virgin of the Rosary on her favorite day; the prying eyes
sharpen to glimpse the shape and size of the feet of the
señoritas getting out of the carriage. Now it is a student
who comes out of the door with devotion still written on
his face: he had passed by the temple to plead with the
Virgin to make the lesson more understandable, to see if
his girlfriend was there, to exchange glances with her and
to go to class with the memory of her loving eyes.

Soon, among the groups a certain movement is
noticed, a certain expectation, and Isagani cuts himself

short and turns pale. A carriage stops beside the door; the pair of white horses is well-known. It is the carriage of Paulita Gomez and she has already alighted, weightless as a bird, without giving the rascals time to catch a glimpse of her foot. With a gracious movement of the body and a pass of the hand, she smooths the folds of her skirt, and with a quick glance, and rather carelessly, looks at Isagani, greets him and smiles. Doña Victorina descends in turn, looks through her spectacles, sees Juanito Pelaez, smiles and greets him affably.

Isagani, glowing with passion, replies with a timid wave of the hand; Juanito bows deeply, takes off his hat and performs the same gesture as that of the celebrated clown and opera buffoon Panza when he receives applause.

"*Mecachis*! what a lass!" exclaimed one, preparing to leave; "tell the professor I am seriously ill."

And Tadeo, as the sick one was called, entered the church to follow the young girl.

Tadeo went every day to the University to ask if there were classes, and each time he wondered more and more that there should be; he had this positive idea of a potential and eternal *cuacha*[14] or lark, and he waited for it to come one day or another. Every morning, after vainly proposing that they play truant, he would leave, pretending to have huge concerns, agreements, ailments, at exactly the moment that his companions entered the classroom. But, by some unknown art of the occult and by extraordinary means, Tadeo passed courses, was liked by the professors and had a bright future ahead of him.

In the meantime a movement started and the groups began to stir; the professor of Physics and Chemistry had gone down to class.

The students, mocked by their hopes, directed

themselves inside the building, letting out sighs of
discontent. Plácido Penitente followed the crowd.

"Penitente, Penitente!" someone called him with a trace
of mystery, "sign this!"

"And what is this?"

"It doesn't matter, sign it!"

Plácido felt as if his ears were being twisted. He still
remembered the history of a *cabeza de barangay* of his town
who, for having signed a document he had not read, was
imprisoned for months and months and almost deported.
An uncle of his, to engrave the lesson in his mind, had
given him a forceful tug at the ears. And every time he
heard talk of signatures it reproduced in the cartilage of
his ears the sensation experienced.

"*Chico*, forgive me, but I do not sign anything before
acquainting myself with it."

"What a fool you are; if two *carabineros celestiales*[15]
signed it, what have you got to fear?"

The name of *carabineros celestiales* infused confidence.
It was a holy company created to aid God in the war
against the spirit of evil, and to impede the introduction
of contraband heresy into the market of the New Zion.

Plácido was about to sign to end it all as he was in a
hurry: his companions were already praying the *O Thoma*,
but he seemed to feel his uncle again pulling him by the
ear, and he said:

"After class; I want to read it first."

"It is very long, you understand? It treats of addressing
a counter-petition, better said, a protest. You know?
Macaraig and others have petitioned that an Academy of
Spanish be opened, which is clear-cut foolishness."

"Sure, sure, *chico*, but later, they are already starting,"
said Plácido, trying to escape.

"But your professor does not call the roll!"

"Yes, yes, but he reads it at times. Later, later! Furthermore, I do not want to go against Macaraig."

"But it is not going against, it is only..."

Plácido did not hear any more; he was far and moving fast towards his class. He heard the different *adsum! adsum!* "*Carambas*, the roll was being read!"...He hastened his steps and arrived exactly at the door when they were at the letter Q.

"*Tinamáan ng*...!"[16] he murmured, biting his lips.

He vacillated on whether to enter or not: the *raya*[17] or line had already been placed and was not to be erased. To class, one goes not to learn, but not to get the *raya*; the class is reduced to reciting lessons from memory, to reading a book and, at most, to answering one or two trivial abstract, profound, cunning, enigmatic questions. True, there was no lack of the small sermon—always the same— about humility, submissiveness, and respect for the religious and he, Plácido, was humble, submissive and respectful. He was about to leave then, but he remembered that the examinations were nearing and his professor had not asked him a question yet, nor appeared to have noticed him. This was as good an occasion as any to call attention and be recognized. To be recognized is to have gained the year, since, if it would not cost anything to suspend one who is unknown, one has to have a hard heart not to be stirred by the sight of a youth whose presence is a daily reproach on a year's loss of his life.

Thus Plácido entered, not on tiptoe as was his wont, but making noise with his heels. And he achieved more than he had intended! The professor looked at him, knitted his brows and shook his head as though saying:

"Measly insolent, you will pay for this!"

- 13 -
A Class in Physics

The classroom was a broad rectangular space with large grilled windows which gave abundant access to air and light. Along the walls could be seen three wide seats of stone covered with wood, filled with students arranged in alphabetical order. At the end, opposite the entrance under a portrait of Saint Thomas of Aquinas, rose the chair of the professor, elevated, with a small stairway on each side. Except for a beautiful narra-framed blackboard hardly used, since on it still remained written the *viva* which appeared on the first day, nothing was to be seen there by way of furniture, useful or useless. The walls, painted white and protected in part by glazed tiles to prevent abrasions, were totally bare; not a sketch, not an engraving, not even a diagram of an instrument of Physics.

The students had no need for more; no one missed the practical instruction of a science eminently experimental. For years and years, it had been taught that way, and the Philippines was not disturbed; on the contrary it continued as always. Now and then, a little instrument would drop from heaven which would be shown to the class from afar, like the Holy Sacrament to the prostrated faithful: look at me and touch me not. From time to time, when some professor wanted to please, a day of the year was set aside to visit the mysterious laboratory and to admire from outside the enigmatic apparatuses placed inside the cabinets; no one could complain; on that day could be seen much brass, much glass, many tubes, discs, wheels, bells, etc.; and the bazaar did not go beyond that, nor was the Philippines disturbed. Besides, the students were convinced that those instruments had not been bought for them; the friars would be real fools. The laboratory had been set up to be shown to the guests and the high officials who came from the Peninsula, so that upon seeing it they could shake their heads with satisfaction while he who guided them smiled as if to say:

"You thought that you were going to encounter some backward monks, eh? Well, we are on the top of the century, we have a laboratory!"

And the guests and the high officials, gallantly entertained, would later on write in their travel memoirs that The Royal and Pontifical University of Santo Tomas de Manila, in the charge of the illustrious Dominican Order, possessed a magnificent Physics laboratory for the teaching of the youth. Some two hundred fifty students annually studied this course, and whether by apathy, indolence, limited capacity of the *Indio* or some other ethnological or inconceivable reason...up to now there has not flourished a Lavoisier, a Secchi nor a Tyndall, even in miniature, in the Malay-Filipino race!!!

However, to be accurate, we will say that in this

laboratory, the preparatory classes of thirty or forty students[1] are held and, indeed, under the direction of a professor who sufficiently complies with his duties, but the majority of these students coming from the Ateneo of the Jesuits, where the science is practically taught in the laboratory itself, its value does not come as great as it would have if taken advantage of by the two hundred and fifty who pay their matriculation, buy their books, study and spend a year only to know nothing afterwards. The result of this is that except for some rare *capista* [2] or servant who had the museum under his care for years and years, no one has ever known how to take advantage of the lessons learned by memory with much effort.

But let us return to our classroom.

The professor was a young Dominican who had discharged with much rigor and excellent prestige a number of professorships in the College of San Juan de Letran. He had the reputation of being an excellent dialectician as well as a profound philosopher, and was one of most promising in his field. The elders regarded him highly, and the younger ones envied him, since cabals also existed among themselves. It was the third year of his professorship, and although it was the first in which he taught Physics and Chemistry he already passed as an expert, not only among the complacent students but also among the other transient professors.

Padre Millon[3] was not of the common run, who every year changed their courses to gain some scientific knowledge, students among other students, without further difference except that they went through a single course, asked questions instead of being asked, understood Spanish better, and did not have to take examinations at the end of the course. Padre Millon deepened science; he knew the physics of Aristotle and that of Padre Amat; he read Ramos with care, and now and then took a look at Ganot.[4] Despite this, he would often shake his head with an air of doubt, smile and murmur, *"transeat."*

In the case of Chemistry, they attributed to him less common knowledge since, basing himself on a statement of Saint Thomas that water was a mixture, he proved clearly that the angelic doctor had more than anticipated Berzelius, Gay Lussac, Bunsen and other more or less presumptuous materialists. Moreover, despite his having been professor of Geography, he still maintained certain doubts about the roundness of the earth and would smile with malice when speaking of its rotary and revolutionary movements around the sun, reciting:

> *El mentir de las estrellas*
> *Es un cómodo mentir...*

> (The lying of the stars
> Is a comfortable lying...)

He would smile with malice before certain physical theories and took as a visionary, if not insane, the Jesuit Secchi,[5] imputing to him the drawing of triangulations on the host as a result of his astronomical manias, for which reason, he said, he was prohibited from saying Mass. Many also noticed in him a certain dislike for the science he explained, but such aberrations are trifles, prejudices of learning and religion and easily explained, not only because the physical sciences are eminently practical, of pure observation and deduction, while his strength lay in the philosophical, purely speculative, abstract and inductive, but also because, outside of being a good Dominican, protective of the prestige of his order, he could not feel fondness for a science in which none of his brethren had excelled—he was the first not to believe in the Chemistry of Saint Thomas—and in which so many glories have been conquered by contending Orders, let us say their rivals.

This was the professor who that morning called the roll, ordered many of the students to recite the lesson from memory, word for word. The recorders played, some good, some bad; others stammered, were marked. He who recited without mistake earned a *raya buena* or good mark, and he who committed more than three errors a *mala*.

A fat boy with a sleepy face and hair stiff and hard like the bristles of a brush, yawned almost to the point of dislocating his jaw, stretched himself, extending his arms as if he were in his bed. The professor saw him and wished to startle him.

"Oy! You, sleepy head, *abá*! what gives? Also lazy, maybe, you don't know your lesson, ha?"

Padre Millon not only tutored all the students like a good friar, but also spoke to them in the language of the streets, a practice which he had learned as professor of canon law. Whether the Reverend wanted to disparage the students or the sacred decrees of the councils is a question not settled yet, however much has been said about it.

The interpellation, instead of offending the class, amused it and many laughed: it was a daily routine. However, the sleepyhead did not laugh; he got up with a jump, rubbed his eyes and, like a steam engine gyrating a record player, started to recite:

"The name mirror is given to all polished surfaces destined to produce by reflection of light the images of objects situated before the said surface by the substances that these surfaces are formed they are divided into metal mirrors and mirrors of glass..."

"Stop, stop, stop!" interrupted the professor, "Jesus, what rattling...We are saying that mirrors are divided into those made of metal and of glass, ha! And if I present you with a piece of wood, *Camagong*,[6] for example, well polished and varnished, or a piece of black marble well burnished, a coating of jet, which reflect images of objects placed before them, how would you classify those mirrors?"

The one asked, whether because he did not know how to answer or did not understand the question, attempted to get out of the way by demonstrating that he knew the lesson, and continued like a torrent:

"The first are formed by brass or by an alloy of different metals and the second are formed by plates of glass whose two sides are well-polished and one of which has an amalgam of tin adhering to it."

"Tut, tut, tut! That is not it! I say to you *Dominus vobiscum* and you answer me *requiescat in pace!*"

And the good professor repeated the question in the language of the streets punctuating it with *cosas* and *abás* at each moment.

The poor young man did not know how to wiggle out of his straits: he doubted whether to include *Camagong* among the metals, the marble among the glasses and to leave the jet as neutral, until his neighbor Juanito Pelaez surreptitiously hinted to him:

"The mirror of *Camagong* is among the mirrors of wood!..." The unwary repeated it and half the class split their sides with laughter.

"A good *Camagong* you are," the professor said to him, laughing in spite of himself. "Let us see how you are going to name your mirror: from a surface *per se, in quantum est superficie*,[7] or from the substance which forms this surface, that is, the material on which this surface rests, the prime material, modified by the accidental surface, since it is clear, being the surface from which bodies cannot exist without substance. Let us see, what do you say?"

"I? Nothing!" the wretch was about to answer since he no longer knew what was being discussed, having been made giddy by the many surfaces and many accidents which cruelly hammered his ears, but a feeling of shame detained him and, filled with anguish and starting to sweat, he began to repeat between clenched teeth:

"The name mirror is given to all polished surfaces..."

"*Ergo, per te,* the mirror is the surface, fished out the professor. "Well, good, resolve for me this difficulty. If the surface is the mirror, it does not make any difference to the essence of the mirror what is in front of it, *id est,* of the surface, *quae super faciem est, quia vocatur superficies facies ea quae supra videtur*;[8] do you or do you not concede this?"

The hair of the poor youth became stiffer than ever as if animated by an upward force.

"Do you or do you not concede?"

"Whatever, what you wish, Padre," he was thinking, but he did not dare to say so for fear of being laughed at. This was a predicament and he had never seen a greater one. He had the vague idea that to the friars you cannot concede the most innocent thing without their extracting all imaginable consequences and advantages, or better said, their haciendas and parishes. Thus, his good angel suggested that he deny whatever thing with all the energy of his soul and the obstinacy of his hair, and he was about to let loose an arrogant *nego!* because he who denies everything commits to nothing, a court official had told him; but, the bad habit of not listening to the voice of one's own conscience, of having little faith in the people of the legal profession and of seeking assistance from others when one alone would suffice, made him lose himself. His companions were making signs to him to concede, above all Juanito Pelaez, and allowing himself to be carried by his evil destiny, he emitted a "concedo Padre" in a voice so faint as if to say: "*In manus tuas commendo spiritum meum*; Into thy hands I commend my spirit."

"*Concedo antecedentem*," repeated the professor, smiling maliciously; "*ergo*, I can scrape the quicksilver off a mirror of glass, substitute it with a piece of *bibingka*⁹ and we would still have a mirror, ha? What would we have?"

The youth glanced at his inspirators and seeing them amazed and not knowing what to say, he etched on his face a most bitter reproach. "*Deus meus, Deus meus, quare dereliquiste me*—My God, my God, why hast thou forsaken me," said his worried eyes while his lips murmured: "*linintikan!*"¹⁰ In vain did he cough, tug at his shirt front, lean on one foot then on the other; he did not see any solution.

"Come, what have we?" repeated the professor relishing the effects of his argument.

"The *bibingka*!" huffed Juanito Pelaez, "The *bibingka*!"

"Quiet, stupid!" finally shouted the youth, desperate, wishing to get out of the bind by transforming it into a complaint.

"Let us see, Juanito, if you can resolve the question for me!" the professor asked Pelaez instead.

Pelaez, who was one of his favorites, slowly stood up, not without first nudging with his elbow Plácido Penitente, who followed him in the order of the roll call. The nudge meant:

"Take note and prompt me!"

"*Nego consecuentiam*, Padre," he answered unwaveringly.

"Hola, then *probo consecuentiam*! *Per te*, the polished surface constitutes the essence of the mirror..."

"*Nego suppositum*!" interrupted Juanito upon feeling that Plácido was pulling at his coat.

"How? *Per te*..."

"*Nego*!"

"*Ergo*, you opine that that which is behind has an influence over what is in front?"

"*Nego*!" he shouted with much more ardor then before, feeling another tug at his coat.

Juanito, or rather Plácido, who was the one prompting him, was unwittingly employing Chinese tactics: not to admit the most harmless foreigner so as not to be invaded.

"Where are we then?" asked the professor, somewhat disconcerted and looking with uneasiness at the intransigent student; "Does the substance behind have any influence on the surface or not?"

To this precise, categorical question, a sort of ultimatum, Juanito did not know how to respond, and nobody was tugging at his coat. Vainly did he make signs with his hand at Plácido: Plácido was undecided. Juanito took advantage of a moment when the professor was looking at a student who was secretly removing his half-boots which were very tight, and stepped hard on Plácido, saying:

"Prompt me, hurry, prompt me!"

"I distinguish...Ouch! what an idiot you are!" shouted Plácido without wishing to, looking at him with irritated eyes while he brought his hand to his patent leather boots.

The professor heard the shout, saw them and divined what was happening.

"Oy, you! *Espiritu-sastre*, busybody," he summoned him, "I am not asking you, but since you value saving others, let us see, save yourself, *salva te ipsum*, and resolve for me the difficulty."

Juanito sat down happily, and as proof of his gratitude, put his tongue out at his prompter who, in the meantime, red with shame, stood up and murmured unintelligible excuses.

Padre Millon considered him for a moment like one who was savoring with his eyes a luscious dish. How nice it would be to humiliate and put to ridicule that smart aleck, always well-dressed, head erect and looking serene. It was a work of charity, and so the charitable professor set himself to it with all his consciousness repeating the question slowly:

"The book says that metallic mirrors are made of brass or of an alloy of different metals, is this true or is it not true?"

"So the book says, Padre..."

"*Liber dixit ergo ita est*;[11] do not pretend to know more than the book...It follows then that mirrors of glass are formed by a sheet of glass whose two surfaces are well polished, having an amalgam of tin adhering to one of them, *nota bene*! an amalgam of tin. Is this true?"

"If the book says so, Padre..."

"Tin is a metal?"

"Yes, it seems, Padre; so the book says..."

"It is, it is, and the word amalgam means it is united with mercury which is another metal. *Ergo*, a mirror of glass is a mirror of metal; *ergo*, the terms of the difference are confusing, *ergo* the classification is defective, *ergo*...How do you explain that, you busybody?"

And he stressed the *ergos* and the *yous* with unutterable relish and winked an eye as if to say: "You are fried!"

"It is that...it means that..." stuttered Plácido.

"It means that you have not studied the lesson, miserable soul, that you do not understand it and yet you prompt your neighbor."

The class was not slighted; on the contrary, many found the tone entertaining and laughed. Plácido bit his lips.

"You, what are you called?" the professor asked him.

Plácido answered dryly.

"Aha! Plácido Penitente, although you are more like Plácido *Soplon*, Tattle-tale, or *Soplado*, Swellhead. But I am going to impose penance on you for your *sopladurias*, tattle-telling."[12]

Delighted with his word play, he ordered him to recite the lesson. The young man, in the state of mind he was in, committed more than three errors. The professor then, moving his head up and down, slowly opened the list and deliberately went through it as he repeated the names in a low voice...

"Palencia...Palomo...Panganiban...Pedraza...Pelado... Pelaez...Penitente, aha! Plácido Penitente, fifteen voluntary absences from actual presence..."

Plácido bolted up:

"Fifteen absences, Padre?

"Fifteen voluntary absences from actual presence," continued the professor; "with which one more absence means failure."

"Fifteen absences, fifteen absences?" repeated Plácido stunned; "I have not been absent more than four times and with today, perhaps five!"

"*Júsito, júsito, señolía*, dasrite, dasrite, señol!"[13] mimicked the professor, peering at the youth from over his gold-rimmed spectacles. "You confess that you have been absent five times and God knows how many more times! *Atqui*, as I rarely call the roll, each time I catch any one I place five *rayitas*, *ergo*, how many are five times five? Have you forgotten the multiplication table! Five times five?"

"Twenty-five..."

"*Júsito, júsito*! Thus you still swallowed ten, since I have not caught you more than three times...*Uy*! if I had caught you in all...And how much are three times five?"

"Fifteen..."

"Fifteen, *parejo camaron con cangrejo*, shrimp exactly like to crab!" finished the professor closing the list. "You make a mistake once more, *sulung*, out! *apuera de la fuerta*, outta da door![14] Ah! and now a little failure on the day's lesson."

And he opened the list anew, found the name and placed the *rayita*.

"Come! a small *raya*!" he said; "since you never had any before!"

"But, Padre," argued Plácido, holding himself back, "if Your Reverence marks me for failing the lesson, Your Reverence should erase that for absence, which he has placed against me for this day!"

The Reverend did not answer; he first slowly indicated the fault, contemplated it, tilting his head—the *rayita* should be artistic—closed the list and then with great malice, asked:

"Abá! and why, ..*ñol*?"[15]

"Because I cannot conceive, Padre, how one may be absent from class and at the same time recite the lesson in it...Your Reverence says that to be is not to be..."

"*Nacú! metapisico pa*, also a metaphysician, premature, no less! With what can you not conceive, ha? *Sed patet experientiâ y contra experentiam negantem, fusilibus est argüendum*, you understand? And you cannot conceive, philosopher, that you may be absent from class and not know the lesson at the same time. Is it that not being actually present necessarily implies knowledge? What do you have to say to me, philosophaster?"[16]

This last sentence was the last drop of water which made the vessel run over. Plácido, who among his friends was known as a philosopher, lost his patience, threw down his book, stood up and confronted the professor.

"Enough, Padre, enough! Your Excellency can mark me with all the absences he wishes, but he has no right to insult me. Your Reverence may stay with the class; I cannot stand it any longer."

And without further farewells, he left.

The class was shocked; such an act of dignity had never been seen before: who would think that Plácido Penitente...? The professor, surprised, bit his lips, moving his head somewhat menacingly and looked at him leaving. With a trembling voice, he began a sermon on the same theme as always, albeit with much more forcefulness and more eloquent delivery. It dwelt on the increasing arrogance, the innate ingratitude, the vanity, the excessive pride which the demon of darkness had infused into the youth, the little education, the lack of courtesy, etc., etc. From there he passed on to throwing obscenities and sarcasms at the pretensions which some *sopladillos*, petty swellheads, have, to teach their teachers by setting up an academy for the teaching of Spanish.

"Ha, Ha!" he said, "those who before yesterday hardly knew how to say yes Padre, no, Padre, now want to know more than those who turned grey-haired from teaching? He who wants to learn, learns with academies or without them. Surely that, that one who has just left, is one of those of the project. Spanish does well with such partisans. Where will you find the time to attend the academy when you hardly have enough of it to comply with the obligations of the classroom? We would like all of you to know Spanish, and to pronounce it well, so that you do not ruin your eardrums with your twists and your 'Ps', but first duty, and then, satisfaction; fulfill your studies first and then learn Spanish and turn to pen-pushers if you so desire..."

And thus he continued talking and talking until the bell rang and class ended, and the two hundred and thirty-four students, after praying, trooped out as ignorant as when they entered, but sighing as if a tremendous weight over them had been lifted. Each youth had lost one hour more of his life, and with it, a part of his dignity and self-respect, and in exchange discouragement had gained ground, along with a distaste for study, and a resentment in their hearts. After all this, ask them for knowledge, dignity, gratitude!

De nobis post hœc, tristes sententia fertur; after all this, you still speak ill of us!

And like the two hundred and thirty-four, the thousands and thousands of students who preceded them had passed their class hours, and if matters are not repaired, so will still pass those who are to come; they will be brutalized, their dignity wounded, the enthusiasm of youth vitiated and transformed into hatred and indolence, like the waves which, turning muddy in certain parts of the beach, follow one after the other, leaving behind each time more sediment of muck. However, He who sees from eternity the consequences of an act unravels them like a thread in the course of the centuries. He who

weighs the value of a second and has imposed progress
and perfection for all his creatures as the prime law; He, if
He is just, will demand strict accounting from those who
should render it, of the millions of darkened and blind
intelligences, of the human dignity diminished in millions
of creatures and the unaccountable amount of time lost
and labor wasted. And if the doctrines of the Gospel have
a heart of truth, they also have to answer to the millions
and millions who knew not how to keep the light of their
intelligences and the dignity of their spirits, as the *Señor*
seeks accounting from the cowardly servant who allowed
his own talents to be stolen!

- 14 -

A Students' Lodging House

It was worth visiting the house where Macaraig lived.[1] Large and spacious, with two mezzanine floors provided with elegant gratings, it looked like a school during the first hours of the morning, and like pandemonium from ten o'clock onward. During the boarders' recreation hours, from the spacious entrance hall up to the main floor, there bustled laughter, tumult and movement. Youths in scanty house clothes played *sipa*,[2] did gymnastic exercises making use of improvised trapezes, while the staircase supported a fencing match among eight or nine armed with canes, pikes, crooks and lassoes, but neither the attackers nor the attacked generally did any great damage to each other, their blows stopping on rebound upon the shoulders of the Chinese peddler on the stairway, who was selling a mess of victuals and indigestible pastries. Crowds of boys surrounded him, pulled on his pigtail, already undone and in disarray; they snatched a pie, haggled over the prices, and committed a thousand deviltries on him. The Chinaman yelled, swore and cursed in all the languages he jabbered, including his own; he whined, laughed, pleaded, put on a smiling face when an ugly one would not serve or vice versa.

"Ah, dassa no good, you bad consien, velly bad Clistian, you devil, balbalian, lascal, etc., etc.!"

Piff, paff! it did not matter! He would turn a smiling face if the cane blows fell only on his shoulders; he dauntlessly continued with his trade, contenting himself with crying: "*No jugalo, eh? no jugalo*! don't play, eh? Enough of jokes!" But if the blows fell on the *bilaó*[3] that contained his pastries, then he swore never to return, and spewed forth all imprecations and maledictions imaginable. The boys redoubled their efforts to enrage him all the more, and when they finally saw his phraseology exhausted and were satisfied with too much *hopia* and salted melon seeds, they then paid him religiously and the Chinaman marched off contented, chuckling, winking and receiving as caresses the light cane blows that the students tipped him with in a manner of farewell.

"*Huaya, homia*! Go hopia!"[4]

Concerts of piano and violin, of guitar and accordion, alternated with the repeated impact of canes from the fencing lessons. Gathered around a long wide table the Ateneo students write, make their compositions, solve their problems beside others who write to their sweethearts on rose-colored embossed paper. One composes a melodrama alongside another who is learning the flute, and the harmonies bring forth disapproving whistles from the onset. Further in, the older ones, students of the arts and sciences, sporting silk socks and embroidered slippers, amuse themselves, teasing the younger ones by pulling their ears, which are already red from receiving so many

flicks. Two or three hold down a little fellow who yells
and cries, defending with kicks the cords of his drawers:
the project was to return him to the state in which he was
born...kicking and screaming. In one room, around a small
night table, four are playing *revisino* amid laughter and
jests to the great annoyance of another who feigns to study
his lesson but who in reality waits for his turn to play.
Another comes in with overwhelmed emotions, deeply
scandalized; he approaches the table.

"How corrupt you are!" he says, "So early in the
morning and already at cards! Let us see, let us see: You
ass! take it with the three of spades!"

And he closes his book, and joins in the game.

Shouts are heard; blows resound. Two are fighting
in the adjoining room: a lame student, very touchy, and
an unhappy newcomer from the province. He has hardly
begun to study, dealing with a treatise on philosophy and
reads innocently in a loud voice, improperly accentuating
the Cartesian principle:

"*Cogito, ergo sum*! I think, therefore I am!"

The lame one feels alluded to, and the others
intervene to restore peace, but in reality to sow discord,
and they end up knocking each other.

In the dining room, a young man with a can of
sardines, a bottle of wine and the provisions which he has
brought from his hometown, makes heroic effort to have
his friends join him in his snack; his friends, in turn, offer
heroic resistance. Others are bathing in the azotea and,
with water from the well, make like firemen in combat
with pails of water, to the great delight of the onlookers.

But the noise and the uproar slowly cease with the
arrival of distinguished students convoked by Macaraig
for an account of the progress on the Academy for the

teaching of Spanish. Isagani is cordially greeted, as is the Peninsular Sandoval who had come to Manila as an employee and was finishing his studies, completely identified with the aspirations of the Filipino students. The barriers that politics creates between races disappears in the schoolrooms as though melted by the fire of science and youth.

For lack of athenæums and scientific centers, literary or political, Sandoval took advantage of all gatherings to display his great oratorical gifts, delivering speeches, arguing on any subject and drawing applause from his listeners and friends. In those moments the theme of conversation was the teaching of Spanish.

Since Macaraig had not yet arrived conjectures were the order of the day.

"What could have happened?—What has the *General* decided?"

"Has he denied the permit?—Has Padre Irene won?— Has Padre Sibyla won?"

These were the questions they asked each other, and which only Macaraig could answer.

Among the young men gathered were optimistic ones like Isagani and Sandoval, who saw the thing done, and were talking of congratulations and praises from the Government for the patriotism of the students, optimism that made Juanito claim for himself a large part of the glory of the creation of the society. To all this the pessimistic Pecson—a flabby person with the ample smile of a madcap—responded by speaking of other influences, of whether Bishop A., Padre B., or Provincial C. were or were not consulted, and had or had not advised that all those in the movement be thrown into jail, a warning which made Juanito uneasy and stammer: "*Carambas*, do not get me mixed up in..."

Sandoval, like the Peninsular and the liberal that he was, lost his temper.

"But, *puñeta!*" he said, "that is to have a low opinion of His Excellency! I know that he is very friar-bent, but in matters such as these he would not allow himself to be influenced by the friars. Will you tell me, Pecson, on what you base your belief that the *General* does not have his own judgment?"

"I did not say that, Sandoval," answered Pecson, grinning until he showed his wisdom teeth. "I believe the *General* has his own judgment; that is, the judgment of all those within his reach... That is clear enough!"

"Do not confuse things! But cite me one example; cite me just one case!" yelled Sandoval. "Let us stay away from hollow talk, from empty phrases, and let us go into the area of facts," he added, gesticulating with a flourish. "Facts, *Señores*, facts! The rest is bias which I do not wish to call subversion."

"There you go! subversion, indeed! But can there be no discussion without resorting to accusations?"

Sandoval protested and, in a small speech, asked for facts.

"Well, not too long ago there was a court suit here between some persons and certain friars, and the Acting *General* judged it, deciding that the Provincial of the litigating order should determine it,"[5] answered Pecson.

And he broke out anew into a grin, as though speaking of an innocent matter. He cited names, dates, and promised to bring documents which would prove the manner in which justice was administered.

"But on what can it be based, tell me, on what can they base a decision not to allow that which appears immediately to the eye as highly useful and necessary?" asked Sandoval.

Pecson shrugged his shoulders.

"It is because it threatens the integrity of the nation..." he replied, in the tone of a court clerk reading a summary.

"That sounds beautiful. What does the integrity of the nation have to do with the rules of syntax?"

"Doctors, the Holy Mother Church has...What do I know; perhaps it is feared that we might understand the laws and obey them...What would happen to the Philippines on the day when we can understand one another?"

Sandoval did not like the dialectical turn and the leg-pulling trend of the conversation. Through that avenue he could not launch any speech that would be worth the trouble.

"Don't take these things as a joke," he exclaimed, "these are serious matters."

"God deliver me from jesting when there are friars involved!"

"But on what could it be based...?"

"On the fact that class hours have to be at night," continued Pecson in the same tone, as if he were dealing with familiar and well-known formulae, "and so immorality can be invoked as an impediment, as with the school of Malolos..."[6]

"Again! But are not the classes of the Academy of Design, as well as novenas and processions, also sheltered by the dark mantle of night...?"

"It attacks the dignity of the University," continued the fat one without minding what had been said.

"What attack! the University has to dedicate itself to the needs of the students. And if this be true, what then is a University? Is it an institution where one may not learn? Have a few men, perhaps, conspired together in the name of knowledge and education to impede the learning of others?"

"It is that initiatives that come from below are called discontent..."

"And those that come from above, projects," insinuated another one, "there's the School of Arts and Trades!"[7]

"Take it easy, *Señores*," said Sandoval. "I am not friar-bent; my liberal ideas are well-known, but render unto Caesar what is Caesar's! Of that School of Arts and Trades, of which I am a most enthusiastic defender and whose realization I will hail as the first break of dawn for these fortunate Islands, of that School of Arts and Trades of which the friars have taken charge..."

"Or the gardener's dog, which is the same thing," added Pecson.

"Oh come on, *puñeta!*" cursed Sandoval, furious at the interruption and losing the thread of his sentence. "While we know nothing negative, let us not be pessimists, let us not be unjust, suspicious of the liberty and independence of the government..."

And he launched in elegant phrases a defense of government and its good objectives, a subject which Pecson dared not interrupt.

"The Spanish Government," he said among other things, "has given you everything, has not denied you anything. We had absolutism in Spain, and you also have absolutism; the friars covered our soil with convents, and convents occupy a third part of Manila; in Spain, the garrote reigns, and the garrote here is the ultimate penalty; we are Catholics and we made you Catholics; we were scholastics and scholasticism shines in your school halls. In brief, *Señores*, we weep when you weep, we suffer when you suffer, we have the same temples, the same tribunal,

the same punishments, and it would be just to give you as
well our own rights and our own happiness."

And because nobody interrupted him he became
more and more enthusiastic and went on to speak of the
destiny of the Philippines.

"As I said, *Señores*, the dawn is not far away; Spain
opens the Orient for her beloved Philippines, and the times
are changing and, it is evident to me, more than we think.
This Government, according to you, vacillates and has no
will; it is good that we fortify her with our confidence,
that we make her see that we hope in her. Let us remind
her by our conduct (when she forgets that which I do not
believe will happen) that we have faith in her good intent
and that she should not rule by any other norm except
that of justice and the well-being of all those governed.

"No, *Señores*," he continued, shifting more and more
to a rhetorical pitch, "we should not, in this matter, even
consider the possibility of a consultation with other entities,
more or less adverse; the thought alone would imply a
tolerance of the deed. Your conduct has till now been frank,
loyal, without vacillations, without misgivings; you guided
it simply and directly; the considerations you have
expounded cannot be more worthy of attention; your
objective is to lighten the task of the teachers in the first
years and to facilitate study for hundreds of students who
crowd the classrooms, and those whom one teacher alone
cannot take care of. If till now the expedient measure has
not been resolved, it has been because, it is clear to me,
there has been so much material accumulated. I foresee,
however, that the campaign has been won, and the
rendezvous with Macaraig is to announce to us the victory,
and tomorrow we will see our efforts rewarded with the
applause and gratitude of the country. And who knows,

Señores, if the Government might not propose for you some honorable decoration for meritorious service to the nation!"

Enthusiastic applause resounded; all already believed in the victory, and many in the commendation.

"Let it be recorded, *Señores*," said Juanito, "that I was one of the principal instigators!"

The pessimist Pecson was not so enthusiastic.

"Let us not have that decoration on the ankles!"[8] he said.

Fortunately for Pelaez, his observation was not heard in the midst of the applause. When it died down somewhat, Pecson replied:

"Good, good, very good, but a conjecture...and if in spite of everything, the *General* consults, consults and consults and afterward denies us the authorization?"

The conjecture fell like cold water.

Everybody stared at Sandoval, who found himself unable to speak.

"Then...," he murmured, stammering.

"And then?"

"Then," exclaimed Sandoval, still intoxicated with the applause and in the grip of enthusiasm, "seeing that in writing and in print it flaunts the intent to enlighten you, and impedes and denies it when reality calls upon it, then, *Señores*, your efforts shall not have been in vain; you would have accomplished that which nobody else has, that of pulling off the mask and having the gauntlet thrown at you!"

"Bravo, bravo!" some roared enthusiastically.

"Good for Sandoval! Bravo for the gauntlet!" added others.

"Let them throw down the gauntlet!" repeated Pecson contemptuously, "and afterwards?"

Sandoval stopped frozen in the midst of his triumph, but with the vivacity fitting to his race and his calling as an orator, he replied immediately.

"Afterwards?" he asked, "then if none of the Filipinos dare to respond to the challenge, then I, Sandoval, in the name of Spain, will pick up the gauntlet because such a policy would belie the good objectives which she has always preserved for the benefit of her provinces, and because he who prostitutes in such a manner the trust given to him, and abuses his absolute powers, deserves neither the protection of the motherland nor the favor of any Spanish citizen."

The tumult of his listeners bordered on delirium. Isagani embraced Sandoval; the others followed suit. They talked of native land, of unity, of fraternity, of fidelity; the Filipinos said that if there were nothing but Sandovals in Spain, all would be Sandovals in the Philippines. Sandoval's eyes gleamed, and one could well believe that if at that moment anybody had flung whatever gauntlet at him, he would have mounted whatever horse to die for the Philippines. Only the 'cold water' replied:

"Good, that is very good, Sandoval. I could also say the same if I were a Peninsular, but not being one, if I said only half of what you have, you yourself, would take me for a subversive."

Sandoval began a speech filled with protests, but was interrupted.

"Hurrah! friends, hurrah! Victory!" shouted at that moment a youth entering and embracing everybody.

"Hurrah, friends! Long live the Spanish language!"

A salvo of applause received the newcomer; everybody embraced each other; all eyes sparkled with tears. Pecson was the only one who maintained his ever skeptical smile.

He who came bearing such good tidings was Macaraig, the youth who headed the movement.

This student occupied in that house, for himself alone, two rooms luxuriously furnished, had a servant and a *cochero* to take care of his *araña*[9] and his horses. He was of graceful countenance, had fine manners, was elegant and very rich. Although he studied law only to have an academic degree, he nevertheless enjoyed the reputation of being industrious, and as a dialectitian in the scholastic tradition he had nothing to envy in the most frantic sophists of the university staff. He did not, however, fall behind with respect to ideas and modern trends; his fortune supplied him with all the books and magazines that prior censorship had been able to restrain.[10] With these qualities, with his reputation for valor, his fortunate encounters in his younger years and his refined and delicate gallantry, it was not strange that he would exercise such influence over his companions, and was chosen to endow with finality such a difficult endeavor as the teaching of Spanish.

Gone were the first manifestations of enthusiasm that the youth always take in the most exaggerated form, in the same manner that all they see is beautiful. Now they desired to know how the matter had proceeded.

"This morning I saw Padre Irene," said Macaraig with an air of mystery.

"Long live Padre Irene!" shouted an enthusiastic student.

"Padre Irene," continued Macaraig, "recounted to me all that had happened in Los Baños. It seems that they discussed for at least a week, he sustaining and defending our cause against everybody, against Padre Sybila, Padre Hernandez, Padre Salvi, the General, the second top official, the jeweler Simoun..."

"The jeweler Simoun!" interrupted one, "but what does this Jew have to do with matters of our country. And we who enrich him by buying..."

"Keep quiet!" said another, impatient and anxious to know how Padre Irene had been able to defeat such powerful enemies.

"There were even high officials who were against our project, the administrative director, the civil governor, the Chinaman Quiroga..."

"Quiroga! The procurer of the..."[11]

"Quiet, man!"

"In the end," continued Macaraig, "they were going to shelve the file and leave it dormant for months and months, when Padre Irene remembered the Superior Commission of Primary Instruction and proposed that, since this has to do with the teaching of the Spanish language, the document should pass through that body, that it may issue an opinion on it..."[12]

"But that Commission has not been functioning for a long time," observed Pecson.

"That is precisely what they answered Padre Irene," continued Macaraig, "and he replied that it was an opportune occasion to revive it, and taking advantage of the presence of Don Custodio, one of its members, he proposed right away that a committee be formed. The energy of Don Custodio being known and acknowledged, he was named chairman, and now the petition is in his hands. Don Custodio promised to act on it within the month."

"Long live Don Custodio!"

"And if Don Custodio rules against...?" asked the pessimist Pecson.

They had not counted on this, intoxicated as they

were with the thought that the matter would not be
shelved. Everyone looked at Macaraig to learn how it could
be resolved.

"I made the same objection to Padre Irene, but with
his mischievous smile, he told me: 'We have gained a lot;
we have made the matter move toward a solution; the
opponent sees itself obliged to accept the challenge...If we
can influence the mind of Don Custodio so that, following
his liberal bent, he expresses his opinion favorably, all is
won; the *General* shows himself absolutely neutral.'"

Macaraig paused.

"And how to influence him?" asked an impatient one.

"Padre Irene indicated two ways to me..."

"The Chinese Quiroga!" said another.

"Come now! too much ado about Quiroga..."

"A fitting gift!"

"But he prides himself in being incorruptible."

"Ah yes, I know that!" exclaimed Pecson laughing.
"Pepay the *bailarina*."

"Ah, yes! Pepay the dancing girl," several agreed.

This Pepay was a tawdry girl who passed for a close
friend of Don Custodio: to her ran the contractors, the
employees and the intriguers when they wanted to secure
something from the influential councilor. Juanito Pelaez,
who was likewise Pepay's friend, offered to arrange
things himself, but Isagani shook his head and said that
it was enough to have had the services of Padre Irene,
and it would be too much to make use of Pepay in the
same matter.

"Let us look at the other means!"

"The other way is to resort to his lawyer-adviser, Señor
Pasta, the oracle before whom Don Custodio bows."

"I prefer that," said Isagani; "Señor Pasta is a Filipino

and was a classmate of my uncle's. But how to get him interested?"

"There's the *quid*," replied Macaraig looking thoughtfully at Isagani; Señor Pasta has a *bailarina*, I mean...a *bordadora*, an embroiderer..."

Isagani again shook his head.

"Don't be such a puritan," Juanito Pelaez told him; "the end justifies the means! I know the embroiderer, Matea, who has a shop where many girls work..."

"No, *Señores*," interrupted Isagani. "Let us resort first to honest means...I will go and present myself at the residence of Señor Pasta, and if I achieve nothing, then you can do what you wish with the *bailarinas* and the *bordadoras*."

They had to accede to the proposition, and agreed that Isagani should talk to Señor Pasta that very day and in the afternoon give an account of the result of the meeting to his companions at the University.

- 15 -

Señor Pasta

Isagani presented himself at the residence of the lawyer, one of the most gifted minds of Manila, whom the friars consulted in their gravest concerns.[1] The young man had to wait for some time because of the many clients, but finally his turn came, and he entered the study or *bufete*, as it is usually called in the Philippines.

The lawyer received him with a slight clearing of the throat, looking furtively at his feet; he did not stand up nor bid him take a seat, but continued writing. Isagani had occasion to observe and study him well. The lawyer had aged much, was white-haired, and his baldness extended almost throughout the upper part of his head. He had dour and gloomy features.

In the study everything was quiet; one could hear only the whispering of the clerks or assistants who were at work in the adjoining room: their pens screeched as though scuffling with the paper.

At last the lawyer finished what he was writing, laid

the pen down, raised his head and upon recognizing the youth, his face brightened and he affectionately held out his hand.

"Hello, young man! but do sit down, forgive me...I did not know it was you.[2] And your uncle?"

Isagani took heart and believed that his case would go well. He briefly recounted what had happened, studying well the effect his words had. Señor Pasta listened impassively at the beginning and, although he had been informed of the students' actions, feigned ignorance as if to show that he had nothing to do with such childish acts. But when he suspected what was wanted of him, and heard that it had to do with the Vice-Rector, the friars, the Capitan General, the project, etc., his face gradually darkened and he ended up exclaiming:

"This is a country of projects! But continue, continue."

Isagani was not disheartened; he spoke of the solution he was offering and ended by expressing the confidence of the youth that he, Señor Pasta, would intercede in their favor in case Don Custodio should consult him, as was expected. Isagani did not dare to say *would counsel* Don Custodio, in view of the face the lawyer made.

But Señor Pasta had already made his decision, which was not to be involved in the case either as consultant or the consulted. He was aware of what had happened at Los Baños; he knew that two camps existed, and that Padre Irene was not the only champion on the students' side, nor was he the one who had proposed the submission of the papers to the Superior Commission of Primary Instruction, but quite the contrary. Padre Irene, Padre Fernandez, *the countess*, a trader who foresaw the sale of materials for the new Academy, and the high official who was citing royal decrees after royal decrees, were going to triumph, when Padre Sybila, wanting to gain time, remembered the Superior Commission. All these things the great lawyer had in his mind, so that when Isagani finished speaking, he resolved to bewilder him with evasions, to embroil the matter, to carry the conversation to another realm.

"Yes!" he said, pursing his lips and scratching his pate, "no one exceeds me in love of country and in progressive aspirations, but...I cannot compromise myself...I do not know if you are aware of my position, a very delicate position...I have many interests... I have to work within the limits of a strict prudence...it is a compromise..."

The lawyer wanted to befuddle the youth with a wealth of words, and began to speak of laws, of decrees, and spoke so much that instead of confounding the youth, he almost enmeshed himself in a labyrinth of quotations.

"Not in any way do we wish to put you in a difficult position," replied Isagani very calmly. "God deliver us from molesting in the least way those persons whose lives are so useful to the rest of the Filipinos! But little versed as I am in the laws, royal decrees, writs and measures that are in force in our country, I do not believe that there can be any ill in seconding the lofty vision of government by seeking its beneficial interpretation; we pursue the same end, and only differ in the means."

The lawyer smiled: the youth had allowed himself to be led to another sphere, and there he was going to ensnare him; he was already caught.

"Precisely, there is the *quid* as is vulgarly said. It is clearly laudable to help the government when one helps it with submissiveness, following its measures, the true spirit of the laws in consonance with the just beliefs of those who govern, and not standing in contradiction to the primary and general mode of thinking of those persons who have in their hands the common well-being of the individuals which make up a society. And that is why it is criminal, it is punishable, because it is offensive against the lofty principle of authority, to attempt an action contrary to its initiative, even assuming that it would be better than that of government, because such behavior could damage the prestige which is the primary foundation on which rest all the colonial structures."

And the old lawyer, sure that that tirade had, at the very least, muddled Isagani, reclined himself on his chair, looking very serious but laughing within himself.

Isagani, however, replied:

"I believe that governments seek more solid foundations when they are more threatened ...For colonial governments the foundation of prestige is the weakest, because it does not depend on them, but on the free will of the governed while they wish to recognize it...The foundation of justice or reason appears to me more durable."

The lawyer raised his head; how did that young man dare to reply to him and argue with him, he, Señor Pasta? Had he not yet been confused by his glorious words?

"Young man, you have to set those considerations aside because they are dangerous," interrupted the lawyer, making a gesture. "What I am telling you is to leave the government to do its job."

"Governments were set up for the welfare of the people, and to comply properly with their end they must follow the manifestations of the citizens, who best know their needs."

"Those who form the government are also citizens, and among the most distinguished."

"But, as men, they are fallible and they should not ignore the opinions of others."

"You have to trust them; they have to take care of everything."

"There is a Spanish saying which says that he who does not cry does not get milk. He who does not ask is not given."

"On the contrary!" answered the lawyer, smiling sarcastically, "with the government exactly the opposite happens..."

But he suddenly restrained himself, as if he had said too much, and wanted to make up for the imprudence:

"The government gives us things that we have not asked for, that we could not ask for...because to ask...to ask assumes that government is deficient in some way, and therefore does not live up to its obligations...to suggest to it a means, to attempt to guide it when not even battling it, is to consider it capable of making mistakes, and as I have already told you, such assumptions are threats to the existence of colonial governments...The common people ignore this, and the youth who work thoughtlessly, do not know, do not understand, do not want to understand how counter-productive it is to ask...what subversiveness there is in that idea."

"Sir, forgive me," interrupted Isagani, offended by the arguments which the jurist was using on him, "when through legal means a people asks a government for something, it is because it assumes that it is beneficent and disposed to concede a good, and this action, instead of irritating it, should be seen as praise; one asks from a mother, never from a stepmother. The government, in my modest opinion, is not an omniscient being that can see and foresee everything, and even if it were, it should not be offended, for you see that even the church does nothing but ask and ask from God, who sees and knows everything; and you yourself ask and demand many things in the courts of this same government, and neither God nor the courts have till now taken offense.

"It is held in the consciences of all that the government, as the human institution that it is, needs the help of the rest of us; it needs to be made to see and feel the reality of things. You yourself are not convinced of the truth of your objection; you yourself know that it is a tyrannical and despotic government that, to display its power and independence, denies everything out of fear and suspicion, and you know that only tyrannized and enslaved peoples have the duty never to ask. A people who detest their government should not demand more of it than that it abdicate its power."

The old lawyer made faces, shaking his head from side to side as a sign of displeasure and, passing a hand over his baldness, said in the tone of a compassionate protector:

"Hm! those are wrong doctrines, wrong theories, hm! It is evident that you are young and have no experience of life. See what is happening to the inexperienced boys who in Madrid ask for so many reforms: they have all been accused of subversion; many dare not return.[3] And yet what were they asking for? Things pious, old and clearly known as harmless...But there are matters that I cannot explain to you because they are very delicate...come...I confess to you that reasons exist other than those which impel a sensible government to systematically deny the wishes of a people...no...it may happen that we find ourselves with leaders so fatuous and ridiculous...but always, there are other reasons...even though what is being asked appears to be most just...distinct conditions inform different governments..."

And the old man faltered, gazed fixedly at Isagani, and taking resolve, made a gesture with a hand as if moving away from a thought.

"I can guess what you want to say," continued Isagani smiling sadly, "you want to say that a colonial government for the reason that it is imperfectly formed and because it is founded on premises..."

"No, no, that is not so, no!" sharply interrupted the old man, searching for something among his papers. "No, I wanted to say...but where are my glasses?"

"There you have them," said Isagani.

Señor Pasta put on his glasses, pretended to read some papers, and seeing that the youth was waiting, stammered:

"I wanted to say one thing...I wanted to say, but it has now escaped me...you with your zest have interrupted me...it was a matter of small import...If you only knew how my head goes, I have many things to do!"

Isagani understood that he was being told to leave.

"This means," he said, getting up, "that we..."

"Ah!...you will all do well to leave the matter in the hands of government; it will settle it as it wills...You say that the Vice-Rector is against the teaching of Spanish. Perhaps he may be, not in the substance but in the form. They say that the Rector who is coming brings a project to reform education...you wait awhile, bide your time, study, seeing that the examinations are nearing and what, *carambas*! you who now speak Spanish very well and express yourself with facility, why do you get yourself into fights? What interest do you have in its being specially taught? I am sure that Padre Florentino thinks as I do!

Give him my fondest regards."

"My uncle," answered Isagani, "has always advised me to think of the rest as much as I think of myself...I did not come here for myself, I have come in the name of those who are in worse conditions..."

"What the devil! Let them do what you have done; let them burn their eyebrows studying and become as bald as I from learning entire paragraphs by memory...I believe that if you speak Spanish it is because you learned it; you are not from Manila, nor are you the son of Spanish parents! So let them learn it as you did and as I have done...I have been servant to all the friars,[4] I prepared their chocolate, and while I whipped it with my right hand, with my left I held a grammar book, I learned, and, thank God, I had no need of more teachers nor more academies, nor permits from the government...Believe me, he who desires to learn, learns and comes to know."

"But how many among those who wish to learn become what you are? One among ten thousand and more!"

"Psch! and what for?" replied the old man, shrugging his shoulders. "Of lawyers, there are more than enough; many become clerks. Doctors insult, slander and kill one another arguing about a patient...Muscles, *Señor*, muscles are what we need for agriculture!"

Isagani knew that he was wasting time, but wanted to reply.

"Undoubtedly," he answered, "there are many doctors and lawyers, but I will not say we have a surplus, since we have towns that sorely lack them, but if they abound in quantity; perhaps we lack them in quality. And seeing that the young cannot be impeded from study and no other careers are open to us, why let them waste their time and efforts? If the defects in education cannot stop the many who become lawyers or doctors, if we have to have them in the end, why not have them good? And with all this, even if what is desired is only to make this an agricultural country, a country of workers, giving them at least an education will allow them to perfect themselves and perfect their work, putting them in a state of knowing many things which at the present they do not know."

"Bah, bah, bah!" exclaimed the lawyer, tracing with his hand circles in the air as if to banish the thoughts evoked. "To be a good farmer, there is no need for much rhetoric. Dreams, illusions, ideology! Eeea! do you want to follow some advice?"

He stood up and, affectionately placing a hand on Isagani's shoulder, continued:

"I am going to give you one piece of advice, and a good one, because I see that you are smart and the counsel would not be wasted. You are going to study medicine? Well, limit yourself to learning how to place plasters and how leeches are applied, and never seek to improve or worsen the fate of your equals. When you receive your licentiate, marry a rich and devoted girl, make cures and charge well; distance yourself from all things that relate to the general condition of the country; hear mass, go to confession and communion when the others do, and you will see afterwards how you will thank me, and I will see it if I still live. Always remember that charity well understood begins at home; man should not look in this world for more than the greatest sum of happiness for himself, as Bentham says; if you involve yourself in quixoticisms, you will neither have a career, nor marry, nor amount to anything. All will abandon you, and your own countrymen will be the first to laugh at your innocence. Believe me, you will remember me and will know I am correct when you have white hair like mine, white hair like this."

And the old lawyer touched his sparse white hair, smiling sadly and shaking his head.

"When I have white hair like that, Señor," answered Isagani with equal sadness, "and my vision goes back to my past and I see that I have worked only for myself, without doing the good that I could or should for the country that has given me everything, for the citizens who have helped me live, then, Señor, each white hair would be a thorn and instead of glorying in them, I would feel shame."

That said, he bowed deeply and left.

The lawyer remained motionless in his place, with an astounded look. He heard the footfalls fading, and sat down murmuring:

"Poor young man! Similar thoughts also crossed my mind once! What more would they all want than to be able to say: I have done this for my country, I have consecrated my life for the good of the others...? A crown of laurels drenched in aloes, dried leaves which hide thorns and worms. That is not life, that does not bring home food, nor does it win honors; the laurels hardly serve as sauce...nor give one tranquility...nor win lawsuits—on the contrary! Each nation has its own ethics as it has its own climate and diseases, different from the climate and diseases of other nations!"

And then he added:

"Poor young man!...If all thought and worked as he does, I don't say that no...Poor young man! Poor Florentino!"

- 16 -
The Tribulations
of a Chinaman

In the evening of that same Saturday, Quiroga, the Chinaman who aspired to set up a consulate for his nation, was hosting dinner at the top floor of his large bazaar on Escolta Street. His feast was very well attended: friars, bureaucrats, officers, merchants, all his customers, partners or sponsors, were in attendance. His store provided the parishes and convents with all their needs; he accepted the *vales* or IOUs of all employees, had loyal attendants, active and eager to please. The friars themselves did not disdain to stay in his store for hours, sometimes in full view of the public, and at other times in the inner chambers in pleasant company...

That night, therefore, the sala presented a curious ambience. Friars and bureaucrats filled it, seated on Vienna chairs and on stools from Canton of dark wood with seats of marble, in front of small square tables, playing *tresillo* or conversing among themselves by the brilliant light of gilt lamps or the dim flicker of Chinese lanterns ornately decorated with long silken tassels. On the walls were a mix-up: a lamentable assortment of placid blue landscapes, painted in Canton and Hong Kong; brazen chromoliths of odalisques and half-naked women; lithographs of effeminate Christs; the deaths of the Just Man and of the Sinner made by Jewish houses of Germany to be sold in the Catholic countries. Nor was there a lack of Chinese prints on red paper representing a man seated, of venerable aspect with a calm and smiling face, behind whom stood his servant, ugly, horrible, diabolical, threatening, armed with a lance with a wide cutting blade. Some *Indios* call him Mohammed, others, Santiago or St. James, we do not know why; the Chinese do not give a clear explanation of this prevalent duality. The popping of champagne corks, the clink of glasses, laughter, cigar smoke and a certain odor peculiar to Chinese homes, a mixture of aromatic burning incense, opium and preserved fruits, completed the gathering.

Dressed as a mandarin with a blue-tasseled cap, the Chinaman Quiroga moved from room to room, stiff and straight, but casting watchful glances here and there as if to make sure that nobody shanghaied anything. And despite this instinctive distrust he exchanged firm handshakes, greeted some with a courteous and humble smile, others with a guarded air, still others with a certain contempt that seemed to say:

"I know! you do not come for me but for my dinner."

And the Chinaman was right! That fat gentleman who now praises him and speaks of the convenience of establishing a Chinese consulate in Manila, giving to understand that for this task there could be no other than Quiroga, is the same Señor Gonzales who signs himself *Pitili* when he attacks Chinese immigration in the columns of the newspapers. That other one, more advanced in years, who examines objects closely, the lamps, the picture frames and the like, and makes grimaces and exclamations of disdain, is Don Timoteo Pelaez, Juanito's father, a merchant who clamors against the Chinese competition that ruins his business. Still another, the one farther off, that dark slender man with sharp eyes and a pallid smile, is the celebrated author of the Mexican peso affair[1] which gave such grief to one of Quiroga's protegés, a bureaucrat notorious in Manila for his cunning! A fourth, the one with the swarthy look and unkempt mustache, is a government official who passes for the most worthy because he has had the courage to speak ill of the business in lottery tickets[2] carried on between Quiroga and a high society matron. In fact, if not half, two-thirds of the tickets go to China and the few that are left in Manila are sold at a premium of half a real. The worthy gentleman is of the conviction that he would one day win the first prize, and it infuriates him to find himself before such mischief.

Meanwhile the dinner is nearly over. From the dining room to the sala ranged snatches of toasts, pleasantries, interruptions, laughter. The name of Quiroga is heard repeated many times, mixed with such words as consul, equality, rights...

The host, who does not eat European dishes, contents himself with drinking a glass of wine now and then with his guests, promising to dine with those who are not seated at the head table.

Simoun had arrived already through with supper, and was talking in the sala with some merchants who were complaining about the state of business: everything was going wrong, commerce was paralyzed, the exchanges with Europe were at an exorbitant cost; they asked the jeweler for enlightenment or insinuated to him some ideas hoping that these would be passed on to the Capitan General. For each remedy they proposed, Simoun responded with a sarcastic and brutal smile: "Come now! Nonsense!" until one, exasperated, asked him for his opinion.

"My opinion?" he asked; "study, all of you, why other nations prosper, and do the same as they."

"And why do they prosper, Señor Simoun?"

Simoun shrugged his shoulders and did not answer.

"The port works which weigh so much on trade and the port are not yet finished!"[3] sighed Don Timoteo Pelaez, "a cloth of Guadalupe, as my son says, which weaves and unweaves itself...the duties..."[4]

"And you complain!" exclaimed another. "Now that the General has just decreed the demolition of houses of light material! You who have a shipment of galvanized iron!"

"Yes," responded Don Timoteo; "But how much did that decree cost me! And then, the demolition will not be done for a month, till Lent comes; other shipments may arrive...I would have wanted them demolished immediately, but... Besides, what are the owners of those houses going to buy from me since each is as poor as the others?"

"You would always be able to buy the houses for a pittance..."

"And make sure afterwards that the decree is withdrawn, then resell them at double the price...That is business!"

Simoun smiled his cold smile and, seeing the Chinaman Quiroga advancing, left the plaintive merchants to greet the future consul who, as soon as he saw him, lost his satisfied expression, took on a face similar to those of the merchants, and became slightly bent.

The Chinese Quiroga has great respect for the jeweler, not only because he knew him to be rich, but also for the rumored understanding with the Capitan General which was attributed to him. It was said that Simoun favored the ambitions of the Chinaman, was partisan to the consulate, and a certain Chinophobic newspaper alluded to him with the use of many circumlocutions and ellipses, in the famous literary controversy with another newspaper partial to people with pigtails.[5] Prudent persons added with winks and mumbled words that the Black Eminence was counseling the General to favor the Chinese in order to humble the stubborn pride of the natives.

"To have a people submissive," he had said, "there is nothing better than to humiliate and degrade them in their own eyes."

Soon enough an occasion had presented itself.

The fraternities of *mestizos* or half-breeds and those of the natives were always watching one another and devoting their energy and quarrelsome spirits to jealousy and distrust. One day, at mass, it occurred to the *gobernadorcillo* of the natives, who was seated in the pew on the right and who was extremely thin, to cross one leg over the other, adopting a nonchalant posture to display more thigh and show off his handsome boots. That of the *mestizos*, who was seated on the opposite pew, because he had bunions and could not cross his legs for being too fat and big-bellied, adopted the posture of spreading his legs wide to bring forth his paunch sheathed in a crimpless waistcoat adorned with a beautiful chain of gold and diamonds. The two factions understood these maneuvers and the fray began.

At the next mass all the *mestizos*, even the thinnest, developed paunches and spread their legs wide apart as if they were on horseback. All the natives crossed one leg over the other, even the fattest, and there was a Cabeza de Barangay who tumbled down. The Chinese who saw them adopted their own posture. They sat as in their shops, one leg tucked and raised and the other dangling and swinging. There were protests, letters, proceedings etc., the municipal police armed themselves, ready to ignite a civil war; the priests were delighted, the Spaniards were amused and made money at everyone's expense until the General resolved the conflict, decreeing that all should sit as the Chinese did for these were the ones who paid the most although they were not the most Catholic. And this was the bane of the *mestizos* and the natives, because having narrow trousers, they could not imitate the Chinese. And so that the intention of humiliating them would be more manifest, the measure was enforced with all pomp and circumstance, surrounding the church with a cavalry squad while inside all were sweating.

The affair reached the *Córtes* or parliament, but there it was reiterated that the Chinese, because they paid, could impose their law even in religious ceremonies,[6] even when afterwards they should forsake and make a mockery of Christianity. The natives and *mestizos* accepted the situation and learned not to fritter away their time on similar trifles.

Quiroga, with his smooth tongue and most humble smile, entertained Simoun. His voice was caressing and his bows repetitive, but the jeweler cut short his words, asking him brusquely:

"Did they like the bracelets?"

At this question all Quiroga's animation vanished like a dream; the caressing voice transformed into one of lamentation, he bent even more and, joining both hands and raising them to the level of his face in a Chinese salutation, moaned:

"Ah, Siño Simoun, me loss, me luined!"

"What? Chinaman Quiroga, lost and ruined? With so many bottles of champagne and so many guests?"

Quiroga closed his eyes and made a grimace. The events of the afternoon, the affair of the bracelets, had ruined him. Simoun smiled: When a Chinese merchant complains, it is because everything goes well for him; when he pretends that all goes like a thousand miracles, he foresees bankruptcy or is about to flee to his country.

"You not know, my losses!, me luined, Ah, Siño Simoun me *hapay!*"[7]

And the Chinaman, to make his situation more comprehensible, illustrated the word *hapay* by assuming the manner of one collapsing.

Simoun felt like laughing, but he contained himself and said that he knew nothing, nothing, absolutely nothing.

Quiroga took him to another room, locked the door carefully and explained to him the cause of his misery.

The three diamond bracelets which he had ordered from Simoun to show to his *Señora*, were not intended for her, poor *India* locked in a room like a Chinese woman; they were for a beautiful and enchanting lady,[8] the friend of a big *señor*, and whose influence was necessary for him in a certain business in which he could cleanly gain some six thousand pesos. And because the Chinaman did not understand feminine tastes and wanted to be gallant, he had ordered the three best bracelets which the jeweler had, which cost three or four thousand pesos apiece. The Chinaman, affecting candor and with his most caressing smile, asked the lady to choose the one she liked best, but the lady, even more ingenuous and caressing, declared that she liked all three and kept them all.

Simoun roared with laughter.

"Ah *siñolia*, me lost, me luined!" cried the Chinaman slapping himself lightly with his slender hands.

The jeweler continued to laugh.

"Huu! bad people, mebbe no tlue *siñola*!" continued the Chinese shaking his head disconsolately. "What? She 'as no shame, even dat me Chino, me also people. Ah, mebbe no tlue *siñola*, cigalela, cigarette girl, 'ab more shame!"

"You have been taken, you have been taken," exclaimed Simoun, poking him in the belly.

"An all the woll bollow money and no pay it, what's sa matta?" And he counted with his fingers armed with long nails: "employee, opisial, lotenan, soliel. Ah, Siño Simoun, me loss, me *hapay*!"

"Come on! Let us have less complaints," said Simoun. "I have saved you from many officials who were borrowing money from you...I have lent them some so that they would not bother you, and I knew they could not pay me..."

"But Siño Simoun, you len only opisial, I len del women, wibes, sailols, all de woll..."

"Well, later you will be able to collect."

"Me collec?" Ah, mebbe you not know! When loss in gambling, nebel come back. Goot, you 'ab consul, yu kan fols. Me no 'ab..."

Simoun was thinking.

"Listen, Chinaman Quiroga," he said somewhat distracted, "I will take charge of collecting what is owed you by these officials and sailors. Give me their notes."

Quiroga started again to whine: "They never gave me any notes."

"When they come to borrow money, always send them over to me; I want to save you."

Quiroga thanked him gratefully, but soon returned to his lamentations; he spoke of the bracelets and repeated:

"Even cegalela, 'as more shame!"

"*Carambas*," Simoun said, looking askance at the Chinaman as if to study him, "just now I needed money and thought you could pay me. But everything can be worked out and I do not want you to go bankrupt for such a small thing. Come now, a favor and I will reduce to seven the nine thousand you owe me. You can bring through customs anything you wish, crates of lamps, ironware, chinaware, copper, Mexican pesos; you supply the convents with arms, do you not?"

The Chinese affirmed this with his head, but he had to bribe many.

"Me gib it all to the *Pales*."

"Well, look here," added Simoun in a low voice. "I need you to bring in some crates of guns which arrived this evening...I want you to keep them in your warehouses; they cannot all fit in my house."

Quiroga grew alarmed.

"Do not be alarmed, you do not run any risk: those rifles are to be concealed, a few at a time, in certain homes, and afterwards a search will be made and many will be sent to prison...you and I can earn much, procuring liberty for those detained. Do you understand me?"

Quiroga hesitated; he was afraid of firearms. In his desk he had an unloaded revolver which he never touched without turning his head and closing his eyes.

"If you cannot do it I shall go to someone else, but then I shall be needing my nine thousand pesos to grease palms and keep eyes shut."

"Al-light, al-light," Quiroga finally said, "but you put mucha peepel in plison, you mek sealches soon, eh?"

When Quiroga and Simoun returned to the sala they found those who had come from dinner discussing animatedly. The champagne had loosened tongues and excited the cerebral mass. They were speaking with a certain freedom.

In a group where there were many who held offices, some *señoras* and Don Custodio were talking of a commission sent to India to make certain studies on the footwear of soldiers.

"And who compose it?" asked a prominent lady.

"A Colonel, two officers and His Excellency's nephew."

"Four?" asked an employee, "What a commission! And if opinions are divided? Are they at least competent?"

"That is what I was asking," added another: "It is said that one civilian ought to go, one who has no military biases...a shoemaker, for instance."

"That is right!" added an importer of shoes, "but since it would not do to send an *Indio* or a *Macanista* (Chinese), and the only Peninsular shoemaker demanded such large fees..."

"But why must there be a study of footwear?" asked an elderly *Señora*. "It is not for the Peninsular artillery men. The *Indios* can go barefoot, as in their towns."

"Exactly, and the treasury would save more," added another *Señora*, a widow who was not satisfied with her pension.

"But you must note," replied one of those present, a friend of the members of the Commission, "it is true that many *Indios* go barefoot in their towns, but not all of them, and marching as volunteer is not the same as being in the service: one cannot choose the hour, nor the road, nor rest when one wishes. Consider, *Señora*, that the sun at noon heats the ground such that you could bake bread on it. And you have to march over sandy stretches, where there are stones, sun above and heat below, bullets in front..."

"It is a matter of getting used to it."

"Like the donkey which accustomed itself not to eat! In the present campaign, the greater number of our casualties was due to wounds on the soles of the feet...I say it of the donkey, *Señora*, of the donkey."

"But son," countered the *Señora*, "consider so much money lost on sole leather. There has to be a pension for many orphans and widows to maintain our prestige. And do not smile, I am not talking about myself because I have my pension even though small, insignificant, for the services rendered by my husband, but I am talking of others who are dragging out a miserable existence. It is not just that after so much pressure to come, and after crossing the sea, they end up here dying of hunger...What you say about the soldiers may be true, but it is a fact that I have been in the country more than three years, and I have not seen anyone limping."

"In that I opine as the *Señora* does," said her neighbor, "why give them shoes when they were born without them?"

"And what for give them shirts?"

"And what for give them trousers?"

"Figure out how much we could save with an army in raw skin!" concluded the one who had defended the soldiers.

In another group the discussion was more heated. Ben Zayb was speaking and orating, interrupted as usual at every step by Padre Camorra. The journalist-friar, for all his respect for the cowled folk, was always at odds with Padre Camorra, whom he considered a very simple semi-friar; thus he gave himself an air of detachment, and

demolished the accusations of those who dubbed him
Padre Ybañez. Padre Camorra liked his adversary: he was
the only one who took seriously what he called his logic.

They discussed magnetism, spiritism, magic and the
like, and words flew through the air like the knives and
balls of jugglers: they were throwing them and they were
catching them.

That year in the Quiapo Fair, a great deal of attention
was aroused by a mummified human head, inaccurately
called sphinx, exhibited at the fair by Mr. Leeds, an
American. Huge posters, mysterious and somber, covered
the walls of houses and excited curiosity. Neither Ben Zayb
nor Padre Camorra, nor Padre Irene, nor Padre Salvi had
seen it yet; only Juanito Pelaez had gone to see it one
night and was telling the group of his admiration.

Ben Zayb, in the manner of a journalist, wanted to
seek a natural explanation; Padre Camorra spoke of the
devil; Padre Irene smiled; Padre Salvi was serious.

"But Padre, even if the Devil no longer comes, we are
more than enough to damn ourselves..."

"In another manner, it cannot be explained..."

"If science..."

"The devil with science! *puñales!*"

"But listen, I am going to demonstrate it to you. All is
a matter of optics. I have not yet seen the head nor do I
know how they present it. The *Señor,*" pointing to Juanito
Pelaez, "tells us that it is not at all like the talking head
ordinarily exhibited—let it be! But the principle is the same;
all is a question of optics. Wait, you place a mirror thus,
another one behind, the image is reflected...I say, it is purely
a problem of Physics."

And he took down various mirrors from the walls,
combined them, tilted them, and because the effect he

wanted did not emerge, concluded:

"As I said, nothing more or less than a matter of optics."

"But what mirrors do you want, if Juanito tells us that the head is inside a box which is placed on a table...I see spiritism in this, because the spiritists always avail themselves of tables; and I believe Padre Salvi, as the ecclesiastical governor that he is, should forbid the spectacle."

Padre Salvi was silent. He neither said yes nor no.

"To know whether there are devils or mirrors inside," replied Simoun, "the best thing is for you to go and see the famous Sphinx."

The suggestion seemed sound and was accepted, but Padre Salvi and Don Custodio showed a certain reluctance. They, at a fair, elbow to elbow with the public, to see sphinxes and talking heads! What would the *Indios* say? They might be mistaken for ordinary men, endowed with the same passions and flaws as the others. Ben Zayb, with his newsman's creativity, promised to ask Mr. Leeds not to allow the public entry while they were inside. They were doing him enough honor by seeing his show for him not to agree; and surely, he should not even charge them admission. And to whitewash this pretense, Ben Zayb was saying:

"Because, figure it out, if I discovered the fraud of the mirrors before a crowd of *Indios*! We would deprive the poor American of his daily bread!"

Ben Zayb was a very scrupulous man.

About twelve went down, among them our acquaintances Don Custodio, Padre Salvi, Padre Camorra, Padre Irene, Ben Zayb and Juanito Pelaez. Their carriages left them at the entrance of the Quiapo square.

- 17 -

The Quiapo Fair

The night was lovely, and the plaza offered a most lively aspect. Taking advantage of the freshness of the breeze and the splendid January moon, the people crowded into the Fair to see, to be seen and to amuse themselves. The music from the cosmoramas and the lights from the lanterns communicated animation and merriment to everyone.

Long rows of booths glittering with tinsel and colored decorations, displayed clusters of balls, masks strung through the eyes, tin toys, trains, little carts, tiny mechanical horses, carriages, steamships with their diminutive boilers, porcelain tableware of Lilliputian size, small Nativity cribs of pine wood, foreign and native dolls, the former blonde and smiling, the latter, serious and pensive, like little *señoras* beside gigantic girls. The beat of tiny drums, the toot of tin horns, the wheezy music of the accordions and chamber organs combined in a carnival concert. And in the midst of all this the crowds came and went, shoving and tripping over each other, their faces turned to the booths, so that the collisions were frequent and uproarious. The coaches had to hold back the sprint of the horses, the *tabi! tabi!*[1] of the *cocheros* resounding at every moment; office clerks, military men, friars, students, Chinese, young girls with their mothers or aunts, crossed each other, greeting one another, winking at each other, calling to each other, in more or less merriment.

Padre Camorra was in seventh heaven, seeing so many pretty maidens. He stopped, turned his head, nudged Ben Zayb, clicked his tongue, swore and said: "And that one, and that, ink-slinger? And that other one, what do you say?" In his exuberance he addressed his friend and adversary familiarly. Padre Salvi looked at him now and then, but little did he care for Padre Salvi. On the contrary he would stumble towards the girls to brush against them; he winked at them and made roguish eyes.

"*Puñales!* When shall I ever become parish priest of Quiapo?" he asked himself.

All of a sudden, Ben Zayb let go of an oath, started, and brought a hand to his arm. Padre Camorra, at the height of his enthusiasm, had pinched him. A dazzlingly beautiful señorita had arrived, attracting the admiration of the whole plaza. Padre Camorra, unable to restrain his glee, took the arm of Ben Zayb for that of the maiden.

It was Paulita Gomez, loveliest of the lovely, who was accompanied by Isagani; behind followed Doña Victorina. The young woman was resplendent with beauty: everybody stopped, necks turned, conversations were suspended, eyes followed her, and Doña Victorina received respectful greetings.

Paulita Gomez displayed an exquisite *camisa* and *pañuelo*[2] of embroidered *piña*, different from those she had

worn that morning to go to Sto. Domingo. The ethereal
cloth of the pineapple turned her lovely head into an ideal,
and the *Indios* who saw her compared her to the moon
surrounded by white and airy clouds. The rose-colored
silk *saya*, gathered in rich and graceful folds by a
diminutive hand lent majesty to her erect body whose
movements, graced by an undulating neck, revealed all
the triumphs of vanity and coquetry. Isagani appeared
upset: so many glances disturbed him, so many curious
who focused on the beauty of his beloved. The stares
seemed to him robberies, the maiden's smiles near
infidelities.

    Juanito, upon espying her, accentuated his hunch and
greeted her; Paulita responded casually. Doña Victorina
called him; Juanito was her favorite, and she preferred
him to Isagani.

    "What a girl! what a girl!" murmured Padre Camorra,
captivated.

    "Come on, Padre, pinch your own belly and leave us
in peace!" said Ben Zayb peevishly.

    "What a girl, what a good-looking girl!" he repeated.
"And she has for a fiancé my student, he of the shovings."

    "She is fortunate that she is not of my parish!" he
added afterwards, turning his head several times to follow
her with his eyes. He was tempted to leave his companions
and to follow the young lady. Ben Zayb was hardly able
to dissuade him.

    Paulita continued walking, showing off a lovely
profile, a torso proudly erect and her dainty head, tastefully
combed, moving with innate coquetry.

    Our promenaders continued their way, not without
sighs on the part of the friar-artillery man, and reached a
booth surrounded by the curious, who readily made way
for them.

It was a shop filled with diminutive wooden figurines carved in the country, which represented in all shapes and sizes, the types, races and professions of the Archipelago—*Indios*, Spaniards, Chinese, *mestizos*, friars, clerics, bureaucrats, *gobernadorcillos*, students, military and so forth. It could be that the artists had more fondness for the padres, the folds of whose habits could have been more convenient for their fine esthetics or that the friars, playing a greater role in Philippine society, preoccupied the mind of the sculptor more. For whatever reason, the fact is that their little figures abounded, well-done, elaborately finished and representing them in the most sublime moments of life, the opposite of what is done in Europe where they are depicted sleeping over casks of wine, playing cards, emptying cups, reviving themselves or passing a hand over the fresh cheeks of some buxom lass. No, the friars of the Philippines were different: elegant, comely, well-attired, their tonsures smartly trimmed, their features regular and serene, their looks contemplative, saintly of expression, somewhat rosy in the cheeks, a staff of *palasan* in hand and patent-leather shoes on their feet— making one wish to adore them and display them under glass globes. Instead of the symbols of gluttony and incontinence of their European brothers, those of Manila held a book, a crucifix, the palm of martyrdom; instead of kissing rustic maidens, those of Manila gravely offered a hand to be kissed by children and elderly men, bent and almost kneeling; instead of the replete pantry and dining room, the scenarios in Europe, in Manila they had the oratorio, the study table; instead of the mendicant friar going from door to door with his donkey and his sack begging for alms, the friar of the Philippines poured from his full hands, gold among the impoverished *Indios*...

"Look, here is Padre Camorra!" said Ben Zayb, still

touched by the effects of champagne.

And he pointed to the figure of a thin friar with a contemplative air, seated at a desk, his head resting on the palm of one hand, apparently writing a sermon. A lamp was there to illuminate him.

The contrast with the likeness made many laugh.

Padre Camorra, who had already forgotten Paulita, understood the intent and in his turn, asked: "And whom does this other figure resemble, Ben Zayb?" And he burst into laughter with his clownish laugh.

It was a one-eyed old woman, dishevelled, squatting on the floor like the *Indio* idols, ironing clothes. The appliance was well reproduced. It was of copper, the coals were made of tinsel and the whirls of smoke were small strong bundles of dirty twisted cotton.

"Eh, Ben Zayb, he who thought of this was no fool, was he?" asked Padre Camorra, sneering.

"Well, I do not see the point!" said the journalist.

"But, *puñales!* do you not see the label: *The Philippine Press*? That gadget with which the old woman irons here is called the press."

Everyone burst into laughter and even Ben Zayb laughed good-humoredly.

Two soldiers of the *guardia civil*, with the name tags *civiles* on them, were shown behind a man manacled with strong cords, his face covered with a hat. It was titled *The Land of Abaca* and it seemed that they were going to shoot him.

Many of our visitors did not relish the exhibit. They spoke of rules of art; they sought proportions; one said that such and such a figure did not have seven heads; that a face lacked a nose, it did not have more than three— making Padre Camorra somewhat thoughtful; he could not understand how one figure, in order to appear right, should have four noses and seven heads; another said that they were too muscle-bound and the *Indios* could not be so; or was that sculpture or merely carpentry? and so forth, each one putting in his spoonful of criticism. Padre Camorra, not to be outdone, ventured to suggest no less than thirty legs for each figure. Why? If some suggested noses, why should he not ask for thighs? And right there they discussed whether the *Indio* did or did not have a talent for sculpture; if it was convenient to encourage such art, and a general dispute ensued which Don Custodio cut short by saying that the *Indios* certainly had the disposition but that they should dedicate themselves exclusively to carving saints.

"Anyone would say," replied Ben Zayb who was full of bright ideas that night, "that the Chinese is Quiroga, but on close observation it looks like Padre Irene."

"And what do you say about that British Indian? He looks like Simoun!"

Fresh peals of laughter resounded. Padre Irene stroked his nose.

"It is true...it is true...it is himself!"

"But where is Simoun? Let Simoun buy it!"

Simoun had disappeared. No one had seen him.

"Puñales!" said Padre Camorra. "How stingy that American is! He is afraid that we will make him pay for the admission of all into the booth of Mr. Leeds."

"No!" retorted Ben Zayb. "What he is afraid of is that he might be compromised. He must be foreseeing the joke that awaits his friend Mr. Leeds and that, he is shirking."

And without purchasing a single item, they proceeded on their way to see the famous sphinx.

Ben Zayb offered to manage the whole affair, for the

American would not refuse a journalist who could retaliate with an unfavorable article.

"You will all see how it is all a question of mirrors," he said, "because you see..."

He embarked again into a long explanation, and since he did not have before him that which could compromise his theory, he introduced all the possible absurdities, and ended up not knowing himself what he was saying.

"Finally," he said, "you will see that it is all a matter of optics."

- 18 -

Deceptions

D r. Leeds, a genuine Yankee, dressed completely in black, received them with great deference. He spoke Spanish well, having stayed for many years in South America. He raised no opposition to our visitors' ruse; he said they could examine all, everything, before and after the show, requesting them only to maintain silence while it was going on. Ben Zayb smiled, and savored the discomfiture which he had in store for the American.

The sala was draped entirely in black, illumined by ancient lamps nourished with the spirit of wine. A rail draped in black velvet divided the place in two parts almost equally: one was filled with seats for the spectators; and the other was occupied by a floor with a checkered carpet. On a raised platform in the middle of the floor was a table covered by black cloth and adorned with skulls and cabalistic figures. The *mise en scéne* resulted in gloom and affected the mirthful visitors. Jests ceased and talk was in hushed tones, and even though some wanted to appear unconcerned, no smile formed on their lips. All felt as if they had entered a house where there was death. A smell of incense and wax augmented this illusion. Don Custodio and Padre Salvi discussed in whispers whether if would be proper or not to prohibit similar spectacles.

Ben Zayb, to shock the naive and to put Mr. Leeds in a quandary, said in a familiar tone:

"Eh, Mister, seeing there are none but ourselves here and we are not *Indios* who can be fooled, can we see the trick? We know, of course, that it is a matter of pure optics, but since Padre Camorra does not want to be convinced..."

Here he made as if to jump over the rail instead of passing through the proper entrance, while Padre Camorra broke out into protests, afraid that Ben Zayb might be right.

"And why not, Señor?" answered the American, "but do not break anything. Agreed?"

The journalist was already on the floor.

"With your permission," he said.

And, without waiting for permission, fearing that Mr. Leeds would not give it, he raised the cloth and searched for the mirrors he expected should have been between the legs. Ben Zayb let out half an oath, drew back, then inserted anew both hands under the table and moved them about: he encountered nothing. The table had three thin legs of iron sunk into the floor.

The journalist looked around as if searching for something.

"Where are the mirrors?" asked Padre Camorra

Ben Zayb looked and looked, felt the table, raised the cloth and raised a hand to his forehead time and again, as if trying to remember something.

"Have you lost something?" asked Mr. Leeds.

"The mirrors, Mister, where are the mirrors?"

"Your mirrors, I do not know where they might be; I keep mine at my hotel...Do you want to look at yourself? You look somewhat upset and pale."

Many, in spite of their prejudice, and noting the American's nonchalant banter, laughed, and Ben Zayb, much abashed, returned to his seat, muttering:

"It cannot be. You will see: he cannot do it without mirrors. He will have to change the table afterwards..."

Mr. Leeds put the cloth back on the table and, addressing the illustrious inquisitors, asked them:

"Are you satisfied? Can we begin?"

"*Anda*! what gall he has!" said the widowed *señora*.

"Well, *Señoras* and *Señores*, take your seats and have your questions ready."

Mr. Leeds disappeared through a door and in a few moments returned with a box of worm-eaten black wood bearing inscriptions of birds, mammals, flowers, human heads and the like.

"*Señoras* and *Señores!*" said Mr. Leeds with a certain gravity: "Visiting once the great pyramid of Khufu, a Pharaoh of the Fourth Dynasty, I came upon a sarcophagus of red granite in a forgotten chamber. My joy was great; I believed I had found a mummy of the royal family, but even greater was my disappointment when, opening the coffin after immense labors, I found nothing but this box, which you may examine."

And he handed the box to those seated in the first row. Padre Camorra drew back his body as if disgusted; Padre Salvi looked closely at it as if things sepulchral attracted him. Padre Irene smiled with the smile of the knowing; Don Custodio assumed an air of gravity and disdain; and Ben Zayb searched for his mirror; it had to be there, because it was all done by mirrors.

"How it smells of death!" remarked one of the *señoras*; "Puff!" And she fanned herself furiously.

"It smells of forty centuries!" commented one with emphasis.

Ben Zayb forgot all about the mirrors in order to find out who had made that remark. It was a military man who had read Napoleon's history. Ben Zayb envied him; and to make another remark which would annoy Padre Camorra a bit, he said:

"It smells of a church!"

"This box, *Señoras* and *Señores*," continued the American, "contained a handful of ashes and a fragment of papyrus on which some words were written. See for yourselves, but I beg you not to breathe on it heavily because if any part of the ashes is lost my sphinx will appear mutilated."

The farce, declared with such seriousness and conviction, sank in deeply, so much so that when the box was passed no one dared to breathe. Padre Camorra, who many times had described in the pulpit at Tiani the tortures and the sufferings in hell while he was laughing to himself at the terrified looks of the women sinners, covered his nose; and Padre Salvi, the very same Padre Salvi who on All Souls Day had done a phantasmagoria of the souls of Purgatory with fires and figures illumined to transparency with lanterns of alcohol and bits of tinsel on the main altar of a church in a suburb to secure masses and alms, the lean and silent Padre Salvi now held his breath, and stared with foreboding at that handful of ashes.

"*Memento, homo, quia pulvis es!* Remember, man, that thou art dust!" murmured Padre Irene smiling.

"P—!" swore Ben Zayb.

He had prepared the same thought and the Canon had taken it from his mouth.

"Not knowing what to do," Mr. Leeds went on, carefully closing the box. "I examined the papyrus, and saw two words of a meaning unknown to me. I deciphered them and tried to pronounce them in a loud voice and had hardly articulated the first when I felt the box slipping through my hands as if dragged down by an enormous weight, and it rotated on the floor from where I attempted to retrieve it in vain. My surprise turned to horror when I opened it and found inside a human head which stared at me with extraordinary intensity. Terrorized and not knowing what to do before such a monster, I remained dazed for a moment, trembling as if agitated...I recovered...Believing that it was sheer illusion, I tried to divert myself by proceeding to read the second word. Hardly had I pronounced it than the box closed, the head disappeared and in its place I found again the handful of ashes. Without suspecting it I had discovered the two most powerful words in nature: the words of creation and extinction, that of life and that of death!"

He paused for a few moments to see the effect of his account. Then with grave and measured pace, he approached the table and placed the mysterious box on it.

"The cloth, Mister!" said the incorrigible Ben Zayb.

"Why not?" replied Mr. Leeds very complacently.

Lifting the box with his right hand, he caught up the cloth with his left, completely exposing the table sustained on its three legs. Again he placed the box in the center and with much seriousness approached the audience.

"Now I would like to see it," said Ben Zayb to the one next to him, "you will see how he comes out with an excuse."

The greatest attention was discernible on the faces of

all; silence reigned. The noise and sounds of the street could be heard distinctly, but all were so intensely caught up that the scraps of dialogue which reached them had not the least effect.

"Why *ba* can't we enter?" asked a woman.[1]

"*Aba, ñora*, because there meni *prailes* and meni *imployii*" answered a man; "is jas alone for dem de hed of sphinx."

"Curios also de meni *prailes*," said the voice of the woman fading away. "Dey no want yet us know when dey comes out ignoran. Why, *querida* ba de *praile* de hed?"

In the midst of a profound silence, and with an emotional voice, the American continued:

"*Señoras* and *Señores*, with one word I shall now bring to life the handful of ashes and you will be talking with someone who knows all the past, present and much of the future!"

And the magician slowly launched a cry, first mournful and then lively, a medley of sharp sounds like imprecations and hoarse notes like threats, which made Ben Zayb's hair stand on end.

"*Deremof!*" cried the American.

The curtains around the salon rustled, the lamps threatened to go out, the table creaked. A feeble groan responded from the interior of the box. All stared at one another, pale and uneasy; a *señora*, full of terror and feeling a hot excretion under her skirt, hung on to Padre Salvi.

The box then opened of its own accord and presented to the eyes of the audience a head of cadaverous aspect, surrounded by long and abundant black hair. The head slowly opened its eyes and looked around the whole audience. Those eyes were of a vivid radiance deepened perhaps by their dark circles, and as *abyssus abyssum invocat*, abyss calls to abyss, those eyes fixed themselves on the deep and cavernous eyes of Padre Salvi, who had them now wide open as if beholding a specter. Padre Salvi was trembling.

"Sphinx!" said Mr. Leeds, "tell the audience who you are!"

A profound silence reigned. A chill wind blew through the room and made the bluish flames of the sepulchral lamps flicker. The most skeptical shuddered.

"I am Imuthis," replied the head in a sepulchral and menacing voice. "I was born in the time of Amasis, and was killed during the domination of the Persians, while Cambysses was returning from his disastrous expedition into the interior of Libya. I had come to finish my studies after long journeys throughout Greece, Assyria and Persia, and I was returning to my country to live there until Thot would summon me before his dreaded tribunal. But to my misfortune, as I was passing through Babylon I discovered a terrible secret, the secret of the false Smerdis who had usurped power, the rash magician Gautama who governed through a ruse. Fearing he would be discovered by Cambysses, he decided on my perdition, availing himself of the Egyptian priests. In my country these ruled then, owners of two-thirds of the lands, monopolizers of science. They plunged the people into ignorance, and in tyranny brutalized them and made them ready to pass without repugnance from one domination to another. The invaders made use of them, and knowing their usefulness, protected and enriched them, and several not only depended on their goodwill but were also reduced to being their mere instruments. The Egyptian priests lent themselves to execute the orders of Gautama with greater willingness since they too feared me, and so that I would not reveal their impostures to the people. They availed themselves for their ends of the passions of a young priest of Abydos who passed for a saint!..."

Anguished silence followed these words. The head spoke of intrigues and priestly deceptions, and although he referred to another epoch, other times and other creeds, it annoyed all the friars present, perhaps because they saw at base some analogy to the actual situation. Padre Salvi, a prey to convulsive trembling, worked his lips and with bulging eyes followed the head's gaze as if fascinated. Beads of sweat began to break out on his gaunt brow, but no one noticed it: so deeply absorbed and emotionally upset were they.

"What was the plot concocted against you by the priests of your country?" asked Mr. Leeds.

The head flung out a painful groan that seemed to come from the depths of the heart, and the spectators saw his eyes, those fiery eyes, darkening and brimming with tears. Many shuddered and felt their hair stand on end. No, this was not fiction, nor deception, nor quackery; the head was a victim and what it was telling was its own story.

"Ay," it cried shaking with grief, "I loved a damsel,[2] daughter of a priest, pure as light, like the lotus when it just opens! The young priest of Abydos also coveted her and raised a mutiny using my name, thanks to some papyrus of mine which he had obtained from my beloved. The mutiny broke out at the very moment that Cambysses was returning in a fury from the disasters of his unfortunate campaign. I was accused of rebellion, jailed, and, having escaped, in the pursuit I was killed in the lake of Moeris...From eternity I saw the triumph of imposture, saw the priest of Abydos hound day and night the virgin

sheltered for refuge in a temple of Isis in the island of
Philoe...I saw him persecute and hound her even in the
vaults of the earth, turn her mad with terror and suffering,
like a gigantic bat tormenting a white dove...Ah! priest,
priest of Abydos! I return to life to reveal your infamies,
and after so many years of silence I call you murderer,
sacrilegious, slanderer!"

A hollow dry laugh followed these words while a
choked voice responded:

"No! mercy!..."

It was Padre Salvi who, overcome with terror, was
stretching both hands and falling down.

"What is the matter with Your Reverence, Padre Salvi?
Are you ill?" asked Padre Irene.

"It is the heat of the sala..."

"It is the smell of death that one breathes here!"

"Assassin, calumniator, sacrilegious!" repeated the
head. "I accuse you, murderer, murderer, murderer!"

And again resounded the dry, cavernous and
menacing laughter as if the head, absorbed in the
contemplation of its grievances, did not see the tumult
which reigned in the sala. Padre Salvi had completely
passed out.

"Mercy! He still lives..." repeated Padre Salvi and lost
consciousness. He was pale like a corpse. The other *señoras*
thought they should faint too and faint they did.

"Delirious...Padre Salvi!"

"I told him that he shouldn't take the birds' nest soup,"
said Padre Irene, "that was what upset him."

"But he has not taken anything," replied Don Custodio
trembling, "as the head had been staring fixedly at him, it
hypnotized..."

There was confusion; the sala looked like a hospital,

a battlefield. Padre Salvi appeared dead, and the *señoras*, seeing that no one had come to their rescue, took it upon themselves to recover.

Meanwhile, the head had been reduced to ashes and Mr. Leeds replaced the black cloth on the table and bowed to his audience.

"The spectacle must be forbidden," said Don Custodio on leaving, "it is highly impious and immoral."

"Above all, because it does not use mirrors!" added Ben Zayb.

But before leaving the sala he wanted to assure himself for the last time. He jumped the rail, approached the table and raised the cloth—nothing, always nothing.*

The following day he wrote an article in which he spoke of the science of the occult, of spiritism and the like. An order came immediately from the Ecclesiastic Governor suspending the show, but Mr. Leeds had already disappeared, carrying his secret with him to Hong Kong.

---

*Ben Zayb, however, was not very much mistaken. The three legs of the table had grooves in them on which slid the mirrors, hidden below the floor and concealed by the squares of the carpet. Placing the box on the table pressed a spring, and the mirrors rose gently. The cloth was then removed, taking care to lift it instead of leaving it to slide, and revealing the ordinary table of the talking heads. The table was connected to the bottom of the box. The exhibition finished, the prestidigitator again covered the table, pressed another spring, and the mirrors descended. —*Author's note*

- 19 -
The Fuse

Plácido Penitente left class, his heart spilling bitterness, somber tears in his gaze. He was most worthy of his name when he was not shaken up, but once irritated, he was a veritable torrent, a wild beast stopped only by dying or killing. So many affronts, so many pinpricks which, day by day, had made his heart tremble, hoarded within himself to sleep the sleep of benumbed vipers, were now awakened and agitated, roaring with fury. The hisses resounded in his ears, along with the sneering words of the professor, phrases in the language of the marketplace, and he seemed to hear whiplashes and laughter. A thousand plans for revenge surged in his brain, crowding one another, only to vanish immediately like images in a dream. His self-respect, with the tenacity of a desperado, cried out to him what should be done.

"Plácido Penitente," said the voice, "show all those youths that you have dignity, that you are the son of a brave and gallant province where an insult is washed off by blood. You are a *Batangueño*, Plácido Penitente! Avenge yourself, Plácido Penitente!"

And the young man growled and gnashed his teeth, stumbling against everyone in the street, on the Puente de España, as though looking for trouble. At this juncture he saw a carriage carrying the Vice-Rector Padre Sibyla, accompanied by Don Custodio, and this gave him a great impulse to take hold of the religious and hurl him into the water.

He went along the Escolta and was tempted to come to blows with two Augustinians who were seated at the entrance of Quiroga's bazaar, laughing and jesting with other friars who must have been inside the shop, preoccupied with some social event; their merry voices and loud laughter could be heard. A little farther on, two cadets blocked the pavement, chatting with a shop clerk in shirt-sleeves. Plácido Penitente headed towards them to force his way through. The cadets were in good humor and, seeing the young man's serious mien, prudently gave way. Plácido was, in those moments, under the influence of *hamok*,[1] as the Malay experts say.

Plácido, on nearing his home—the house of a silversmith where he lived as a boarder—endeavored to gather his thoughts together and hatch a plan. He would go home to his town and avenge himself by showing the friars that they could not insult a youth with impunity, nor laugh at him. He thought of immediately writing a letter to his mother, Cabesang Andang, to let her know what had happened, and to inform her that for him the schoolroom had closed forever. Although there existed the Ateneo of the Jesuits in which he could finish his studies for that year, it was most probable that the Dominicans would not concede the transfer; and even if he obtained it, for the next course he would have to return to the University.

"They say that we do not know how to get even," he muttered. "Let the lightning strike and we shall see!"

But Plácido did not reckon with what awaited him in the house of the silversmith.

Cabesang Andang had just arrived from Batangas, having come to do her shopping, visit her son and bring him some money, dried venison, and silk handkerchiefs.

The first greetings over, the poor woman who, from the start, had noted her son's gloomy face, could no longer contain herself and began to question him. The first excuses Cabesang Andang took for a ruse; she smiled and calmed her son down, reminding him of the sacrifices and the privations and the like... and she spoke of the son of Capitana Simona who, having entered the Seminary, now appropriated unto himself the affectations of a bishop. Capitana Simona now considered herself the Mother of God; clearly, her son was to be another Jesus Christ!

"If the son becomes a priest," said Cabesang Andang, "the mother will no longer pay us what she owes us...who will collect from her then?"

But upon seeing that Plácido was talking in earnest, and reading in his eyes the tempest brewing inside him, she understood that, unfortunately, what he was recounting was the sheer truth. For some moments she remained speechless, then broke out into lamentations.

"Ay!" she said, "and I, who promised your father to take care of you, to educate you and make a lawyer of you! I have deprived myself of all so that you could study! Instead of going to *panguingui* where they play at half a peso, I went only to that of half a *real*, suffering the foul stench and the dirty cards! Look at my mended *camisas*. Instead of buying new ones, I spend the money on masses and offerings to San Sebastian, although I do not believe much in his virtue because the *cura* mentions them so fast and effortlessly, and the saint is entirely new, and still does not know how to perform miracles, and he is not made of *batikulin* but of *laniti*[2]... Ay! What will your father say to me when I die and see him?"

The poor woman mourned and sobbed; Plácido became even more gloomy and from his breast escaped stifled sighs.

"What will I gain by being a lawyer?"

"What will become of you?" asked his mother, clasping her hands. "They will call you a *pilibistiero* and you will be hanged. I told you that you should have patience, you should be humble! I am not telling you to kiss the hand of the *curas*; I know that you have a sensitive sense of smell, like your father who could not eat the cheese of Europe...but we have to suffer, to silence ourselves, to say yes to everything...What are we going to do? The friars have all. If they do not wish it, no one becomes a lawyer or a doctor... Have patience, my son, have patience!"

"But I have had enough, mother; for months and months I have suffered!"

Cabesang Andang continued with her lamentations. She was not asking him to declare himself a supporter of the friars; neither was she one. But she knew that for every good friar there are ten bad ones who take money from the poor and send the rich into exile. One must be silent, suffer, and endure; there was no other recourse. And she cited this and that *señor*, who by showing himself to be patient and humble, even though in the bottom of his heart he hated his masters; from the servant of friars that he was, he attained the position of district counsel. And so-and-so, who is rich now and could commit atrocities, being assured of patrons who would shield him against the law; he was no more than a poor *sacristan*, humble and obedient, who married a pretty girl and for whose child the parish priest was the godfather.

Cabesang Andang continued with her litany of Filipinos who, according to her, were humble and patient; and was about to cite others who, for not being so, found themselves exiled and hounded, when Plácido, on an insignificant pretext, left the house to wander among the streets.

He traversed Sibakong, Tondo, San Nicolas, Santo Cristo, distracted and in ill humor, not minding the sun nor the hour, and it was only when he felt hunger that he realized that he had no money, having given it all to *fiestas* and contributions, and went back home. He did not expect to find his mother there, since her custom whenever she was in Manila, was to go at this hour to the house of a neighbor where *panguingui* was played. But Cabesang Andang was waiting for him in order to make known her plan. She would make use of the Procurator of the Augustinians to make her son enter into the grace of the Dominicans. Plácido cut her words short with a gesture.

"I would throw myself into the sea first," he said, "I would become a *tulisan* or outlaw first, rather than return to the University."

And because his mother started with her sermon on patience and humility, Plácido, without having eaten anything, went out again and headed toward the docks where the ships cast anchor.

The sight of a steamer raising anchor for Hong Kong gave him an idea: to go to Hong Kong, run away, get rich there and then wage war against the friars. The idea of Hong Kong awoke in his mind a recollection, a story about rich altar panels, *ciriales*[4] and candelabra of pure silver, which the charity of the faithful had gifted to a certain church. The friars, recounted his landlord the silversmith, had ordered from Hong Kong other altar fronts, *ciriales* and candelabra of Ruolz silver which they substituted for the real ones which they ordered minted and converted into Mexican pesos. This was the story he had heard, and even if it did not go beyond a tale or rumor, his resentment colored it with the character of truth, and he remembered other tricks of the same style. The desire to live free, and certain half-outlined plans, made him decide on the idea of going to Hong Kong. If the Orders took all their money there, business must be going well, and he could get rich there. "I want to be free, to live free!"

Night caught him still wandering around in San Fernando[5] and, not having run into any sailor friend, he decided to return home. Since the night was beautiful and the moon gleamed in the heavens, transforming the miserable city into a fantastic kingdom of fairies, he went to the fair. There he went to and fro, wandering through the shops without noticing the goods, thinking of Hong Kong, of living free, of enriching himself...

He was about to leave the fair when he thought he recognized the jeweler Simoun bidding farewell to a foreigner, both of them speaking in English. For Plácido, any language spoken in the Philippines by Europeans that was not Spanish had to be English. Besides, the young man caught the word Hong Kong.

If only the jeweler Simoun could recommend him to that stranger who must be leaving for Hong Kong!

Plácido stopped. He knew the jeweler, who had once

been in his hometown, selling jewels. He had accompanied
him on one of his trips during which Simoun had shown
himself very amiable, telling him of the life he lived in
Universities, the life in the free countries—what a difference
there was!

Placido followed the jeweler.

"Señor Simoun, Señor Simoun!" he said.

The jeweler at that moment was about to board a
carriage. When he recognized Plácido he stopped.

"I would like to ask of you a favor....to exchange with
you a few words!" he said.

Simoun made a gesture of impatience which Plácido,
in his confusion, did not notice. In a few words the young
man narrated to Simoun what had happened to him,
manifesting his desire to go to Hong Kong.

"What for?" asked Simoun looking at Plácido intensely
through his blue eyeglasses.

Placido did not answer. Then Simoun raised his head,
smiled his silent and cold smile and said to Plácido:

"All right! Come with me! To Iris Street,"[6] he said to
the cochero.

Simoun remained wordless during the whole transit
as if absorbed in very important thoughts. Plácido, waiting
for the man to speak to him, did not say a single word,
and distracted himself by looking at the many promenaders
taking advantage of the brightness of the moon: young
people, pairs of lovers, enamored ones followed by vigilant
mothers or aunts;[7] groups of students in white apparel
which the moon made even whiter; half-drunken soldiers
in a carriage, six together, on their way to visit a *nipa*
temple dedicated to Cytherea; children playing *tubigan*;[8]
Chinese peddlers of sugarcane and so forth, were filling
the streets, and were acquiring from the resplendent light

of the moon fantastic shapes and imaginary contours. In a house an orchestra was playing waltzes and some couples could be seen dancing under the light of _quinques_ and kerosene lamps...what a paltry spectacle they presented compared with what was offered in the streets! And thinking of Hong Kong he asked himself whether the moonlit evenings in that city were as poetic, as sweetly melancholic as those in the Philippines, and a deep sadness settled in his heart.

Simoun bade the carriage stop and both went down. At that moment Isagani and Paulita Gomez, murmuring endearments, passed by them. Behind came Doña Victorina with Juanito Pelaez, who was talking in a loud voice, gesticulating much and even more humped than ever. Pelaez, distracted, did not see his ex-schoolmate. "That one is indeed happy!" murmured Plácido, sighing and looking toward the group which had melted into shadowy silhouettes—with only Juanito's arms, going up and down like the arms of a windmill, distinguishable.

"He only serves for that!" muttered Simoun in turn. "It is nice to be young!"

To whom were Placido and Simoun alluding?

The latter made a sign to the young man; they left the avenue and entered a maze of footpaths and alleys which formed various areas among themselves. At times they leaped over stones to avoid little pools of water; other times they descended to pass a curve, badly designed and even more badly cared for. Placido was puzzled to see the rich jeweler move among such places as if familiar with them. Finally they reached a kind of large yard where a lone miserable hut stood surrounded by banana plants and _bonga_ palms. Some frames and lengths of tubes, both of bamboo, made Plácido suspect that they were at the house of some *castillero*⁹ or pyrotechnist. Simoun rapped at the window. A man showed himself.

"Ah, Señor..."

And immediately he came down.

"Is the gunpowder here?" Simoun asked.

"In sacks; I am waiting for the cartridge shells."

"And the bombs?"

"All ready."

"All right then, *maestro*...This very night you leave, and speak with the lieutenant and the corporal...and immediately proceed on your way; in Lamayan¹⁰ you will meet a man in a *banka*; you will say *Cabesa* and he will answer *Tales*. It is necessary that he be here tomorrow. There is no time to lose!"

And he gave him some gold coins.

"How is this, Señor?" asked the man, who spoke very good Spanish; "Is there anything new?"

"Yes, it will be done within the coming week."

"The week to come!" repeated the stranger, stepping back. "The suburbs are not ready; they hope that the General will withdraw the decree...I thought it was being left for the beginning of Lent."

Simoun shook his head.

"We will not have need of the suburbs," he said, "with the men of Cabesang Tales, the ex-carbineers, and a regiment, we have enough. Later, Maria Clara may be dead. You leave at once!"

The man disappeared.

Plácido was present at this brief interchange, and heard everything; when he thought he understood his hair rose on end and he stared at Simoun with terrified eyes. Simoun smiled.

"Does it surprise you," he said with his cold smile,

"that this *Indio*, so poorly dressed, should speak Spanish well? He was a schoolmaster who endeavored to teach Spanish to children and did not stop until he lost his position and was exiled for disturbing the peace and for having been the friend of the unfortunate Ibarra.[11] I took him from exile where he had been trimming coconut palms, and made him a pyrotechnist."

They returned to the main street and on foot headed towards Trozo.[12] Before a house of wood of pleasant and clean aspect, a Spaniard leaned on a crutch, relishing the light of the moon. Simoun approached him; the Spaniard, on seeing him, tried to stand up, stifling a groan.

"Be prepared!" Simoun told him.

"I always am!"

"The coming week?"

"Already?"

"At the first volley!"

And he moved away, followed by Plácido, who was beginning to ask himself if he was not dreaming.

"Does it startle you," Simoun asked him," to see a Spaniard so young and so wasted by disease? Two years ago he was just as vigorous as you are, but his enemies were able to send him to Balábak to work in a penal colony, and there he contracted rheumatism and malaria which will carry him to the grave. The hapless one had married a very beautiful woman..."

An empty carriage passed, Simoun halted it and, Plácido still with him, directed it to his house on Escolta Street. At that moment the church clocks rang half-past ten.

Two hours later, Placido left the jeweler's house and, grave and thoughtful, continued on the Escolta, by then almost deserted, in spite of the cafés which were still sufficiently animated. A few carriages were passing rapidly, producing an infernal noise on the worn pavement.

Simoun, from a room in his house which looked out on the Pasig river, turned his gaze toward the Walled City, which could be glimpsed through the open windows, with its galvanized iron roofs gleaming under the moon, its towers etched—sad, heavy and melancholic—in the serene atmosphere of the night. Simoun had removed his blue glasses; his white hair was like a silver frame for his bronzed features, dimly lighted by a lamp whose flame threatened to die for lack of oil. Simoun, apparently preoccupied by a thought, did not perceive that little by little the lamp was agonizing and darkness was at hand.

"Within a few days," he murmured, "when from her four sides flames burn that wicked city, den of presumptuous nothingness and the impious exploitation of the ignorant and the unfortunate; when tumult breaks out in the suburbs and there rush into the terrorized streets my avenging hordes, engendered by rapacity and wrongdoing, then I will shatter the walls of your prison; I will snatch you from the clutches of fanaticism; white dove, you will be the phoenix that will be reborn from the glowing ashes...! A revolution plotted by men in obscurity tore me from your side. Another revolution will bring me to your arms, will revive me and that moon, before reaching the apogee of its splendor, will light the Philippines, cleansed of her repugnant refuse!"

Simoun stopped suddenly as if interrupted. A voice was asking in the depths of his conscience if he, Simoun, were not also part of the refuse of the wicked city, perhaps its most malignant ferment. And like the dead who are to rise at the sound of the oracular trumpet, a thousand bloody ghosts, desperate shadows of murdered men, of women violated, fathers torn from their families, vices stimulated and fomented, virtues outraged, now rose in echo to the mysterious question. For the first time in his criminal career since in Havana, by the use of vice and bribery, he sought to forge an instrument to execute his plans, a faithless man, without patriotism and without conscience; for the first time in that life, something rose up within and protested against his actions. Simoun closed his eyes and remained motionless for some time.

He passed a hand over his forehead; he refused to look into his own conscience, and felt fear. No, he did not want to analyze himself; he lacked the courage to cast a glance at his past...To be wanting in courage precisely when the moment to act neared; to lack conviction, faith in himself! And as the ghosts of the wretches in whose destiny he had an influence continued hovering before his eyes, as if issuing from the brilliant surface of the river, and invading his room, crying out to him and stretching out their hands; as the reproaches and laments seemed to fill the air, audible with threats and accents of vengeance, he turned his gaze from the window and for the first time perhaps, started to tremble.

"No, I must be ill; I must not be feeling well," he murmured. "There are many who hate me, those who ascribe their misfortunes to me, but..."

And feeling his forehead burning, he stood up and approached the window to breathe in the fresh breeze of the night. At his feet the Pasig dragged along its silver current, on whose surface lazily glittered the foam, rolling, advancing and receding, following the course of the little eddies. The city rose on the opposite bank, its black walls looking fateful, mysterious, losing its penury in the moonlight that idealizes and embellishes everything.

Simoun shivered again; he seemed to see before him his father's severe countenance, dying in prison, but dying for having done good; and the face of another man, more severe still, a man who had given his life for him because he believed that he was going to bring about the rebirth of his country.

"No, I cannot turn back," he exclaimed, wiping the sweat from his forehead. "The work has gone far and its success will justify me... If I had conducted myself like you, I would have succumbed...away with idealism! Away with fallacious theories! Fire and steel to the cancer, chastisement to vice, and afterwards destroy the instrument, if it be bad! No! I have planned well, but now I feel feverish...my reason wavers...it is but natural...if I have done evil it was with the objective of doing good, and the end justifies the means...what I will do is not to expose myself..."

And with his brain swirling he went to bed and tried to go to sleep.

Plácido, the following morning, listened submissively and with a smile on his lips to his mother's preaching. When she spoke of her plans to interest the Procurator of the Agustinians, he did not protest or oppose her; on the contrary, he offered to speak himself to spare his mother further troubles; he begged her to return to the province as early as possible, if she could, that very same day. Cabesang Andang asked him why.

"Because...because if the Procurator learns of your presence in the city, he will not do it before you send him a gift and several masses."

- 20 -

The Ponente

That Padre Irene had said was true: the question of the Academy of Spanish, pending for so long, was on its way to a solution. Don Custodio, the active Don Custodio, the most energetic of all the *ponentes* or arbitrators of the world, according to Ben Zayb, was occupied with it, and was spending days reading the *expediente* or documents and falling asleep without having decided anything, then awakening on the following day, doing the same, going back to sleep again, and so on for successive days on end.

How the poor man labored, the most active of all the *ponentes* of the world! He wished to get out of the predicament by pleasing everybody, the friars, the high official, the Countess, Padre Irene and his liberal principles. He had consulted with Señor Pasta, and Señor Pasta had left him stupefied and confused after advising him of a million contradictory and impossible things. He had consulted Pepay the *bailarina*, who had no idea what it was all about, executed a pirouette and asked him for twenty-five pesos to bury an aunt of hers who had just died for the fifth time; or for the fifth aunt who had died, according to more elaborate explanations, not without asking if he could appoint a cousin of hers who knew how to read, write and play the violin, as assistant in the ministry of public works, all things that were very far from inspiring Don Custodio with any saving idea.

Two days after the events at the Quiapo Fair, Don Custodio is working as always, studying the *expediente* without finding the happy solution. But, while he yawns, coughs, smokes and thinks about the pirouettes and the legs of Pepay, we will say something about this exalted personage, in order to understand why Padre Sibyla had proposed him to finish such a thorny matter and why those of the other party accepted him.

Don Custodio de Salazar y Sanchez de Monteredondo, (a) *Buena Tinta* or Good Authority, pertained to that class of Manila society which cannot take a step without having the newspapers hang, before and after them, a thousand appellations, calling them *indefatigable, distinguished, zealous, active, profound, intelligent, knowledgeable, influential,* and so on, as if it were feared that they might be confused with others of the same name who were indolent and stupid. Besides, no harm resulted from this, and the previous censorship was not upset. *Buena Tinta* came to him from his friendship with Ben Zayb, when the latter, in two pieces of noisy polemics which he sustained for weeks and months in the columns of the newspapers—whether bowler hat, top hat or *salakot* should be worn; and whether the plural of *carácter* or character should be *carácteres* and not *caractéres.* To reinforce his arguments, he always came out with: "We have this on *buena tinta* or good authority, we know it from *buena tinta*, etc.," letting it be known later, for in Manila everything is known, that this *buena tinta* was no other than Don Custodio de Salazar y Sanchez de Monteredondo.

He had come to Manila very young, with a good job which allowed him to marry a beautiful *mestiza* who belonged to one of the wealthiest families of the city. As he had natural talent, daring, and much tact, he knew well how to make use of the society in which he found himself, and with his wife's money he dedicated himself to business, to contracts with the government and the Ayuntamiento or municipal administration for which he was made councilor, then mayor; director of the Sociedad Económica de Amigos del Pais;[1] counselor to the Administration; president of the administrative board of the *Obras Pías*;[2] director of the board of *Misericordia*;[3] adviser of the Banco Español Filipino[4] etc., etc., etc.

These etceteras should not be taken to be like those which are ordinarily placed after a long enumeration of titles. Don Custodio, without having ever seen a treatise on hygiene, even came to be vice-president of the Board of Health of Manila,[5] although it is true that of the eight that compose it only one had to be a physician and this one could not be he. Likewise, he was also a member of the Central Vaccination Board,[6] composed of three physicians and seven laymen, among them the archbishop and three provincials. He was a brother of confraternities and archconfraternities and, as we have seen, *ponente*, member-arbitrator of the Superior Commission of Primary Instruction which usually did not function; more than enough reasons for the newspapers to surround him with adjectives when he travelled as when he sneezed.

Despite the many burdens of office, Don Custodio

was not one of those who went to sleep during the sessions, contenting himself, like those timid and lazy members of parliament, to vote with the majority. Unlike the many kings of Europe who carry the title of King of Jerusalem, Don Custodio made his dignity prevail and derived from it all the gain he could, knitted his brow much, deepened his voice, coughed out words and many times spent a whole session relating a tale, sponsoring a project or debating with a colleague who had placed him in disfavor. In spite of not having passed forty, he already spoke of behaving with prudence, of allowing the figs to ripen by themselves, adding under his breath, "idiots"; of thinking profoundly and moving with feet of lead, of the need to know the country, because of the conditions of the *Indio*, because of the prestige of the Spanish name, because above all they were Spaniards, because religion etc., etc.

A speech of Don Custodio's is still remembered in Manila when for the first time kerosene lighting was proposed to replace the old coconut oil.[7] In such an innovation, far from seeing the end of the coconut oil industry, he merely noticed the interests of a certain councilor—because Don Custodio was far-seeing—and he opposed it with all the eloquence he was capable of, finding the project premature, and predicting great social upheavals. No less famous was his opposition to a sentimental serenade which some wanted to give a certain governor on the eve of his departure. Don Custodio, who was somewhat resentful over something, some slight, which we cannot now remember, was able to insinuate that the coming governor was a mortal enemy of the one departing, such that in fear, those who were for the serenade, desisted.

One day he was advised to return to Spain to cure

himself of a liver ailment, and the newspapers spoke of
him as an Antaeus who needed to set foot in the Mother
Country to recover new strengths.[8] However, the Manila
Antaeus found himself in the midst of the *Corte* or Spanish
Court, feeling small and insignificant. There he was a
nobody and his favorite adjectives meant little. He could
not relate to the great fortunes; his lack of education did
not give him much importance in scientific circles and
academies, and because of his backwardness and
monastery politics he came away from court circles
bewildered, disgusted, disappointed, seeing nothing clearly
except that there they habitually borrowed and gambled
excessively. He had looked down on the submissive
servants of Manila who had suffered all his impertinences,
but they now seemed preferable to him.

As the winter kept him between a fireplace and
pneumonia, he sighed for the winter of Manila where a
simple scarf was enough for him; in the summer he missed
his lounging chair and the *batá* or boy to fan him. In short,
in Madrid he was only one of the many, and in spite of his
diamonds, he was once taken for a bumpkin who did not
know how to conduct himself and, in another instance,
for an Indian—they mocked his scruples and some
borrowers whom he rebuffed made fun of him impudently.
Disgusted with the Conservatives who did not make a
great thing of his advice, as well as with the parasites who
were sucking his pockets, he declared himself as belonging
to the Liberal Party, and returned to the Philippines within
a year, if not with a cured liver, then completely perplexed
in thought.

The eleven months of life in the *Corte*, spent among
cafe politicians, almost all retired; the various speeches
caught here and there; such-and-such an article of
opposition; and all the political life which he absorbed in

the atmosphere, from the barbershops where between scissor cuts the Figaro expounded his program, up to the banquets where they discussed during harmonious periods and in impressive phrases the different shades of political creeds, the divergences, disagreements, discontents, etc.,— while he distanced himself from Europe, all this aroused the lifeblood within him, much like a seed sown whose growth was impeded by thick foliage, so much so that when he dropped anchor in Manila he believed that he was going to regenerate it, and in effect, had the most virtuous aims and the purest ideals.

In the first months after his arrival everything was talk about the *Corte*, of his good friends Minister so-and-so, ex-minister such-and-such, delegate C, writer B; there was not a single political event or court scandal that he was not acquainted with in its smallest detail; no public figure whose private life he did not know the secrets of; nor could anything happen that he had not foreseen; nor a reform commanded on which he had not been previously consulted before its appearance—all this seasoned with attacks against the Conservatives with ardent indignation, with apologies of the Liberal Party, with a little anecdote here, a phrase there from some great man, intercalated by one who did not wish offices and employments, which he refused so as not to owe anything to the Conservatives. Such was his zeal in those first days that several of his cronies who gathered at the grocer's shop which he was wont to visit now and then, affiliated themselves with the Liberal Party and called themselves liberals, among them Don Eulogio Badana, a retired sergeant of the carabineers, the reputable Armendía, sailing master and rabid Carlist, Don Eusebio Picote, customs surveyor, and Don Bonifacio Tacon, shoe and belt-maker.

But the enthusiasm gradually petered out for lack of

incentives and opposition. He did not read the newspapers
which came from Spain because they arrived in bundles,
and looking at them made him yawn. The ideas that he
had acquired, all used up, needed reinforcement, and their
verbalizers were not there: although in the casinos of
Manila there was as much gambling and money borrowed
as in the circles of the *Corte*, but then any speech that
would nourish political ideas was not permitted there.

Don Custodio was not lazy, he did more than wish,
he worked, and foreseeing that he would leave his bones
in the Philippines, and judging the country to be his own
world, he devoted his care to it and thought of liberalizing
it, imagining a series of reforms and projects, which were
strange to say the least. It was he who, having heard in
Madrid mention of the pavement of wood for the streets
of Paris, not yet adopted in Spain, proposed its application
in Manila by extending on the streets planks nailed in the
manner seen in the houses. It was he who, lamenting the
accidents of two-wheeled vehicles, in order to prevent them
argued that they should be provided with at least three. It
was he also who, while Acting Vice-President of the Board
of Health, took to fumigating everything, even the
telegrams which came from infected points. He it was too
who, pitying on the one hand the convicts who were
laboring under the sun, and wishing on the other to save
the government from spending on their clothing, proposed
to dress them in simple loin-cloths and put them to work
at night instead of in the daytime. He was puzzled, he
was enraged when his plans encountered objectors, but
he consoled himself with the thought that a worthy man
has enemies, and got even by attacking and rejecting
several projects, good or bad, presented by the others.

Since he boasted of being a liberal, when asked what

he thought of the *Indios,* he was wont to answer, like someone doing a great favor, that they were fit for mechanical work and the "imitative arts" (he wanted to say music, painting and sculpture), and added his usual rejoinder that to know them, one must have spent many, many years in the country. However, if he heard that one of them had excelled in something that was not mechanical work or imitative art, in chemistry, medicine or philosophy for example, he would say: "Psh, he shows promise...he is not dumb!" And he was sure that much Spanish blood must be running in the veins of that *Indio,* and if it could not be found despite his good will, he would then seek a Japanese origin. He began, at that time, the fashion of attributing to Japanese and to Arabs whatever good the Filipinos manifested. For Don Custodio the *kundiman,* the *balitaw,* the *kumintang*[9] were Arabian music like the alphabet of the ancient Filipino, and of this he was sure, although he knew no Arabic, nor had he ever seen that alphabet.

"Arabic and of the most pure Arabic!" he would say to Ben Zayb in a tone that could not be gainsaid. "At best, Chinese."

And he added with a significant wink:

"Nothing can be, nothing could be original with the *Indios,* you understand? I like them a lot, but they must not be praised for anything, because they would become intoxicated and disgrace themselves."

At other times he would say:

"I love the *Indios* passionately. I have made myself their father and defender, but it is necessary for things to be in their place. Some are born to command, others, to serve. It is obvious that this truism cannot be said in a loud voice, but it is practised without many words. And look here, the game consists of small things: when you wish to subjugate a people convince them that they are subjugated—the first day they will laugh; the second, they will protest; the third, they will doubt; and on the fourth they will be convinced. To keep the Filipino docile, it must be repeated to him day after day what he is, to convince him that he is incompetent. What good would it do, besides, to have him believe in something else that would make him wretched? Believe me, it is an act of charity to keep everyone in the place that he is in, then there is order, harmony. In this consists the science of governing."

Don Custodio, in referring to his policy, was not contented with the word *art*. And when he mentioned *government* he would extend his hand downwards to the height of a man on his knees, bent.[10]

With regard to religious ideas, he prided himself in being Catholic, very Catholic, ah, Catholic Spain, land of the *Maria Santissima*, Most Holy Mary...a liberal can and should be Catholic where the reactionaries call themselves gods and saints at least, just as a mulatto passes for a white man in Kaffir. But with all that, he ate meat during Lent except on Good Friday, and never went to confession; he did not believe in miracles nor in the infallibility of the Pope and when he heard mass it was at ten o'clock or at the shortest one, the mass for the troops.

Although in Madrid he had spoken ill of the religious orders so as not to be out of harmony with the ambience in which he was living, considering them anachronisms, hurling curses at the Inquisition, while relating this or that dirty or droll story where the cassocks were dancing, or rather friars without cassocks; however, in speaking of the Philippines which should be ruled by special laws, he would cough, look wise and again extend his hand downwards to that mysterious height.

"The friars are necessary, they are a necessary evil," he would say.

And he would rage when some *Indio* dared doubt miracles or did not believe in the Pope. All the torments of the Inquisition were not sufficient to punish such audacity.

When it was pointed out to him that to rule or to live at the expense of ignorance had another name, somewhat ugly-sounding and which the laws punished when the culpable acted by himself, he came right back, citing other colonies.

"We," he would say in his ceremonial voice, "we can speak out loud! We are not like the English and the Dutch who, to maintain peoples in submission, make use of the lash....We use other means, much milder and surer. The salutary influence of the friars is superior to the English whip..."[11]

This phrase of his made his fortune, and for a long time Ben Zayb had been paraphrasing it and with him all of Manila; thinking Manila applauded it. The phrase reached up to the *Corte*; was cited in parliament as from a liberal of long residence etc., etc., etc., and the friars, flattered by the comparison, and seeing their prestige reinforced, sent him *arrobas*[12] of chocolate, gifts which were returned by the incorruptible Don Custodio, whose virtue Ben Zayb immediately compared with that of Epaminondas.[13] Yet the modern Epaminondas availed of the whip in his moments of anger and counseled it!

In those days, the *conventos*, afraid that he would issue an opinion favorable to the petition of the students, renewed their gifts, and on the afternoon on which we see him, he was more harassed than ever, for his reputation as a man of action was at stake. For more than fifteen days he had had in his possession the *expediente*, and that morning the high official, after praising his zeal, had asked him for his recommendation. Don Custodio had replied with a mysterious seriousness, giving to understand that he had it already finished. The high official smiled, and that smile now bothered and hounded him.

As we said, he was yawning and yawning. In one of those acts, in the moment when he opened his eyes and closed his mouth, he fixed his eyes on a long row of red folders arrayed in order on a magnificent shelf of *camagong* or ebony; on the back of each one could be read in large letters: PROJECTS.

For a moment he forgot his tiredness and the pirouettes of Pepay to consider that everything that was contained in those tiers had come out of his fertile brain in moments of inspiration! So many original ideas, so many sublime thoughts, so many remedial measures for the miseries of the Philippines! Immortality and the gratitude of the country he would have for sure!

Like an old rascal who had stumbled upon a musty bundle of old love letters, Don Custodio stood up and approached the shelf. The first folder, thick, fat, overflowing, carried as its title "PROJECTS in projection."

"No!" he murmured, "this has excellent things but it would take a year to reread them."

The second, quite voluminous too, was titled "PROJECTS under study." "No, neither!"

Then came "PROJECTS in maturity...PROJECTS presented... PROJECTS rejected...PROJECTS approved... PROJECTS suspended...." These last folders contained very little, but the last still less, that of the "PROJECTS in execution."

Don Custodio wrinkled his nose. What could be in there? He had forgotten what could possibly be within.

A sheet of yellowish paper protruded between the two covers as if the folder were sticking out its tongue.

He took it out of the bookcase and opened it: it was the famous project of the School of Arts and Trades.

"What the devil!" he exclaimed; "but if the Augustinians have been in charge of this..."

All of a sudden he slapped his forehead, arched his eyebrows, an expression of triumph painted on his face.

"Yes I have the solution, *c*—!" he blurted, hurling out an offensive word which was not *eureka*, but which begins where this ends. "My decision is made."

And repeating five or six times his peculiar *eureka*, which assailed the air like happy reproofs, radiant with joy, he sat down at his table and began to scribble on sheets of paper.

- 21 -
Manila Characters

That night there was a grand performance at the Teatro de Variedades.[1]

The French operetta company of Mr. Jouy was giving its first performance, *Les Cloches de Corneville*, and he was going to exhibit to the eyes of the public his elite troupe whose fame the newspapers had been proclaiming for days. It was said that among the actresses was one with a very beautiful voice, a figure even more beautiful and, if rumors were to be believed, whose amiability surpassed even her voice and figure.

By seven-thirty in the evening there were no more tickets, not even for Padre Salvi himself, who was dying for one, and those entering general admission formed long queues. In the ticket office, there were brawls and quarrels, talk of subversion and of race, but this did not turn out more tickets. By a quarter of eight fabulous prices were being offered for gallery seats. The sight of the building profusely illuminated, with plants and flowers at all the entrances, enraged the latecomers, who broke out in exclamations and gestures. A great crowd swarmed around the surroundings, staring enviously at those entering, at those who came early fearful of losing their seats: laughter, murmurs, expectations, greeted the recent arrivals who disconsolately joined the curious crowd and, now that they could not enter, contented themselves with watching those who could.

There was one, however, who appeared aloof to so much eagerness, to so much curiosity. He was a tall thin man who walked slowly, dragging a stiff leg. He was dressed in a miserable brown coat and dirty checkered trousers that clung close to his thin and bony limbs. A bowler hat, artistic in spite of its being ragged, covered his enormous head, letting out a few strands of hair of a dirty gray that was almost blonde, long and curling at the ends like a poet's locks. What was most striking in the man was not his attire, nor his European face without a beard nor moustache, but its fiery red color, a color which earned him the nickname *Camaroncocido* or stewed shrimp, by which he was known.[2] He was an uncommon type: belonging to a distinguished family, he lived like a vagabond, a beggar; of the Spanish race, he made fun of the prestige which he flouted indifferently with his rags. He passed for some sort of news reporter, and in fact his gray bulging eyes, so cold and calculating, always showed up where there was something worth publishing. His way of living was a mystery to many; nobody knew where he ate or where he slept: perhaps he had a barrel some place.

Camaroncocido did not have at that moment his usual hard and indifferent expression. Something like amused sympathy was reflected in his looks. A little man, a diminutive oldster greeted him merrily:

"Frienddd," he said in a raucous voice as hoarse as a frog's, showing some Mexican pesos.

Camaroncocido saw the pesos and shrugged his shoulders. To him, what did these matter?

The little old man was his worthy contrast. Small, very small, his head covered with a top hat transformed into a huge hairy worm, he seemed lost in a wide frock coat much too wide and too long, which finally joined trousers too short, which did not pass his calves. His body seemed to be the grandfather, and his legs the grandchildren, while his shoes had the look of sailing on dry land—they were huge sailor's shoes, which protested against the hairy worm of his head with the energy of a *convento* beside a World Exposition. If Camaroncocido was red, he was brown; the person of the Spanish race did not waste a single hair on his face, the *Indio* had a goatee and white mustache, long and sparse. His look was alive. He was called Tio Quico, and like his friend, lived equally on publicity: he announced the shows on the streets and pasted up theater posters. He was, perhaps, the only Filipino who could walk around with impunity in a top hat and frock coat, just as his friend was the first Spaniard to laugh at the prestige of his race.

"The Frenchman has rewarded me very well," he said smiling and showing off his picturesque gums which looked like a street after a fire. "I had good luck in pasting up the posters!"

Camaroncocido again shrugged his shoulders.

"Quico," he replied in a cavernous voice, "if they give you six pesos for your labor, how much will they give the friars?"

Tio Quico, with instinctive alertness, raised his head.

"To the friars?"

"Because you must know," continued Camaroncocido, that all the admission tickets were bought by the *conventos!*"

In fact, the friars, at their head Padre Salvi and some laymen led by Don Custodio, had protested against such performances. Padre Camorra, who could not attend, had a gleam in his eyes and water in his mouth, but he argued with Ben Zayb, who weakly defended the other side, thinking of the free tickets the management would send him. Don Custodio spoke to him of morality, of religion, good conduct and the like.

"But," the writer stammered, "if our vaudeville with its play of words and phrases with double meanings..."

"But at least they are in Spanish," the virtuous councilor interrupted him shouting and aflame with holy indignation. "Obscenities in French, good God, man, Ben Zayb, in French!!! That, never!"

And he said "Never" with the energy of three Guzmans they might have threatened with death by a flea if he would not give up twenty *tarifas*.[3] Padre Irene naturally opined as did Don Custodio, and execrated the French operetta. Pfui! He had been in Paris, and had never even stepped on the pavement of a theater, God deliver him!

But the French operetta also counted with numerous supporters. The officers of the Army and the Armada, among them the aides of the General, government employees and many prominent *señores* who were anxious to savor the nuances of the French language from the mouths of genuine Parisiennes. They were joined by those who had traveled by the M.M.[4] and spoke badly a little French during the trip; by those who had visited Paris and by all those who wanted to pass themselves off as *ilustrados*. Manila society was thus divided into two camps:

into pro-operettas and anti-operettas who were backed by the elderly ladies, wives jealous of and concerned with the affection of their husbands; and by those who had beaus, while the free and the attractive declared themselves rabidly pro-operetta. Pamphlets and more pamphlets crossed each other; there were defections and comebacks, disputes about little things, meetings, lobbying, discussions, even talk of an uprising by the *Indios*, of indolence, of inferior and superior races, of prestige and other cock-and-bull stories; and much gossip and many rumors.

The permit was conceded, and Padre Salvi issued a pastoral letter which no one read except the printer's proofreader. There were conjectures about the *General* having quarreled with the Countess; about her spending her time in the halls of pleasure; about whether His Excellency was bored; whether the French consul...whether there had been gifts and so forth. Many names were bandied about: that of the Chinaman Quiroga, that of Simoun, even those of many actresses.

Thanks to this scandalous beginning, the peoples' excitement had been aroused and since the evening before, when the stars arrived, there was talk of nothing but attendance at the first performance. Since the red posters appeared announcing the *Les Cloches de Corneville*, the winners hastened to celebrate victory. In some offices, instead of spending time reading newspapers and conversing, they devoured the story plot, read French novelettes, and many went to the water closets and feigned dysentery to secretly consult their pocket dictionaries. Not for this reason were documents dispatched: on the contrary everyone was made to come back the next day, but the public could not take offense: they found numerous courteous employees, very affable officials, who greeted and sent them off with grand salutations in the French style. The clerks practised by brushing the dust off their French, calling out to one another *oui monsieur s'il vous plait* and *pardon* at every step, such that it was a pleasure to watch and hear them.

It was in the editorial offices of the newspapers, however, that the excitement and anxiety reached their climax. Ben Zayb, appointed as critic and translator of the story plot, trembled like some poor woman accused of witchcraft. He saw his enemies searching out his blunders and throwing to his face his poor knowledge of French. With the Italian Opera Company, he had nearly fought a duel, having translated erroneously the name of a tenor; an envious one immediately published an article referring to him as an ignoramus, he the leading intellectual in the Philippines! What it cost him to defend himself! He had to write at least seventeen articles and consult fifteen dictionaries. With this refreshed memory, the poor Ben Zayb moved with heavy hands, to say nothing of feet, in order not to imitate Padre Camorra, who once had the gall to reproach him on what he had written about them.

"You see, Quico," said Camaroncocido, "half of the public came because the friars said they should not—it is a kind of demonstration—and the other half because they said to themselves, 'Do the friars prohibit it? Then it must be instructive.' Believe me, Quico, your public notices were good, but the pastoral letter was even better, even considering the fact that no one read it."

"Frienddd," asked Tio Quico alarmed, "do youuu believe that the competence of Padre Salvi may in the futuuure abolish my operationnns?"

"Maybe so, Quico, maybe so," replied the other, gazing at the sky. Money is beginning to get scarce..."

Tio Quico muttered some words and incoherent phrases; if the friars engaged themselves in advertising the theater, he would become a friar. After taking leave of his friend, he moved away coughing and rattling his pesos.

Camaroncocido, with his usual indifference, continued to wander here and there, his leg in pain and his look drowsy. His attention was called by the arrival of unfamiliar faces, coming as they did from different points, and who made signals with a wink, a cough. It was the first time that he had seen at such an occasion such individuals, he who knew all the features in the city and all its faces. Men with dark faces, hunched shoulders, uneasy and uncertain and poorly disguised, as though they had put on coats for the first time. Instead of placing themselves in the front rows where they could see a wider range, they hid themselves among shadows as if to avoid being seen.

"Secret police or thieves?" Camaroncocido asked himself and immediately shrugged his shoulders, "And to me, what does it matter to me?"

The lamp of an approaching carriage lighted up upon passing, a group of four or five of these individuals talking with one who looked like a soldier.

"Secret police! It must be a new corps!" he muttered.

And he made his gesture of indifference. Soon, however, he noticed that the soldier, after communicating with two or three more groups, approached the carriage and seemed to be talking animatedly with some person inside. Camaroncocido took a few steps forward and, without surprise, thought he recognized the jeweler Simoun, while his sharp ears caught this brief dialogue:

"The signal is a shot!"

"Yes, Sir."

"Do not worry—it is the *General* who is ordering it, but be careful about saying so. If you follow my instructions you will be promoted!"

"Yes, Señor."

"So then....be ready!"

The voice quieted, and seconds later the carriage began to move. Camaroncocido, despite all his indifference, could not but murmur:

"Something is being hatched... look out for the pockets!"

And feeling his own empty, he again shrugged his shoulders. What was it to him if the heavens fell?

And he continued making his rounds. Upon passing near two persons who were talking, he caught what one of them, who wore scapulars and rosaries on his neck, was saying in Tagalog:

"The friars have more power than the *General;* do not be a fool! This one will go away but they will stay. So, if we do well, we will get rich. The signal is a shot!"

"Good gracious, good gracious!" muttered Camaroncocido, shaking his fingers. "The *General* there, and here, Padre Salvi...poor country....!But—and what is it to me?"

Shrugging his shoulders and spitting at the same time, two gestures which in him were the signs of the utmost indifference, he proceeded with his concerns...

Meanwhile the carriages were arriving at dizzying speed. They stopped, unswerving, close to the door and deposited the denizens of high society. The *señoras,* although it was scarcely cool, displayed magnificent waistcoats, shawls of silk, and even spring and autumn coats. The gentlemen, those who were in frock coats and white ties, wore overcoats, while others carried them on their arms to show off the rich silk linings.

In the group of the curious, Tadeo, he who fell ill the moment the professor appeared, accompanied his townmate, the newcomer whom we saw suffering the consequences of a badly read principle of Descartes. The newcomer was very curious and inquisitive, and Tadeo took advantage of his candor and inexperience by relating to him the most brazen lies. Each Spaniard who greeted him, whether he be a minor clerk or shop attendant, he presented to his companion as a department head, a marquis, a count and the like; on the other hand, if he passed without stopping, psh! he was a *bago*[5] or come-lately, a fifth-rank bureaucrat, a nobody. And when there was a lack of passersby to maintain the novice's admiration, he utilized the resplendent carriages passing by; Tadeo saluted graciously, made a friendly sign with his hand, and uttered a familiar "Adios!"

"Who is he?"

"Bah," he answered casually: "The Civil Governor...the Vice-Chief, Magistrate So-and-So...the *Señora* of....friends of mine!"

The novice admired him, listened agape and took good care to keep himself to the left. Tadeo, friend of magistrates and governors!

And Tadeo named all the persons who arrived and, when he did not know them, invented family names, histories and gave curious details.

"Do you see that tall señor with dark sideburns, somewhat cross-eyed, dressed all in black? That is Magistrate A, an intimate friend of the *señora* of Colonel B. One day, if not for me, the two almost came to blows...adios! Look! here comes the precise Colonel in question. Will they come to blows?"

The novice held his breath, but the colonel and the magistrate cordially shook hands; the military man, an old bachelor, asked after the health of the family and so forth.

"Ah, thank God!" sighed Tadeo. "It is I who made them friends."

"Could you ask them to let us enter," the newcomer queried somewhat timidly.

"No, indeed, man! I never ask for favors!" Tadeo said majestically. "I endow them, but disinterestedly."

The newcomer bit his lips, shrunk even more and placed a respectful distance between himself and his townmate.

Tadeo continued:

"That is musician H...that, Attorney J, who gave as his own a speech published in all the books, and the listeners congratulated and admired him!...Doctor K, the one getting off that hansom cab, a specialist in children's diseases, for that he is called Herod[6]...That one is banker L who only knows how to talk of piles and piles of money... the poet M, who speaks only of stars and the hereafter...There goes the beautiful *señora* of N whom Padre Q is wont to visit when her husband is away...the Jewish merchant P who came with a thousand pesos and is now a millionaire...That one with the long beard is Doctor R who has made it rich by creating patients, which is better than healing them."

"Creating patients?"

"Yes, man, in the examination of the draftees[7]... attention! that respectable gentleman who is so elegantly attired is not a physician but a homeopathist on his own, *sui generis*: he believes totally in the *similia similibus*, the attraction of likes. That young Cavalry captain with him is his favorite disciple...That one in a light-colored suit with tilted hat, is official S, whose maxim is never to be polite,

and who is carried away by the devils when he sees a hat
kept on the head of another; they say he does it to ruin the
German hat-makers. That one coming with his family is
the very wealthy merchant D, who has more than a
hundred thousand in income...but what would you say if
I told you that he still owes me four pesos, five reals and
twelve cuartos? But, who will collect from a *nouveau riche*
like that?"

"That señor owes you money?"

"Of course! one day I got him out of tight fix; it was a
Friday at seven-thirty in the morning, I still remember; I
had not had any breakfast yet...That *señora* followed by an
old woman is the celebrated Pepay, the *bailarina*...now she
no longer dances, since a very Catholic *señor* and a good
friend of mine...has forbidden it...There is that rake Z,
surely he is after Pepay to make her dance again. He is a
good chap, a great friend of mine, he has no defects save
one: he is a Chinese *mestizo* and yet calls himself a
Peninsular Spaniard. Sst! look at Ben Zayb, that man with
the face of a friar, who carries a pencil and a roll of papers
in his hand. That is the great writer Ben Zayb, a very good
friend of mine; he has talent!"

"Tell me—and that little man with white sideburns...?"

"He is the one who made his daughters, those three
little girls, assistants in the Public Works... so they can
collect from the payroll...He is a very smart *señor*, very
smart indeed! He makes a mistake and he blames it on the
others... he buys himself shirts and the Treasury pays for
them...he is smart, very smart, very smart indeed!"

Tadeo stopped himself.

"And that señor who has a fierce look and casts a
contemptuous eye at the whole world?" inquired the
newcomer, pointing to a man who nodded with
haughtiness.

But Tadeo did not answer. He was stretching his neck to see Paulita Gomez, who arrived in the company of a friend, Doña Victorina and Juanito Pelaez. The latter had gifted them with a box in the theatre, and was more stooped than ever.

More and more coaches drove up, the actresses arrived, entered by another door, followed by friends and admirers.

Paulita had already entered, and Tadeo continued:

"Those are the nieces of the rich Capitan D, those coming up in a landau, see how pretty and healthy they are? Well, in a few years they will be dead or crazy...Capitan D is opposed to their marrying; and the madness of the uncle manifests itself in the nieces...That one is señorita E, the wealthy heiress courted by the world and by the conventos...Hold on! This one I know! Padre Irene, disguised, with a false moustache! I know him by his nose! And he who so much opposed it!"...

The newcomer stared aghast and saw a well-cut frock coat behind a group of *señoras*.

"The Three Fates!" continued Tadeo, seeing three withered *señoritas* arrive, sunken, wide of mouth and very shabbily dressed...They are called..."

"Atropos?..." ventured the newcomer, who wished to show he also knew something, mythology at least.

"No, man, they are the *señoritas de Balcon*, fault-finders, old maids, indigent...They affect hatred for everybody, men, women and children...But look how on the side of evil God places the remedy, only that at times it arrives late. Behind the three Fates, terror of the city, come those three, pride of their friends, among whom I count myself. That slender young man with bulging eyes, somewhat stooped, who gesticulates with liveliness because he could not get a ticket, is the chemist S, author of many scientific studies and works, some prize winners and all of them worthy of note;[8] the Spaniards say of him that he is promising, promising...The one who is trying to calm him down with that Voltairean laughter is the poet T, a talented youth, a great friend of mine, and for the very reason of being talented, has thrown away his pen. The one who is suggesting that they enter with the actors through the other door, is the young physician U who has made many remarkable cures; it is also said of him that he is promising...he is not so stooped as Pelaez but is smarter and more clever still. I believe that death itself he can bluff and make dizzy."

"And that dark man with a moustache like bristles?"

"Ah! that is businessman F, who forges everything, even his birth certificate. He wants to be a Spanish *mestizo* at any cost, and makes heroic efforts to forget his language."

"But, his daughters are very white-skinned..."

"Yes, that is the reason rice has gone up in price, and yet they eat nothing but bread."

The newcomer did not understand the connection between the price of rice and the whiteness of those girls.

"There goes the lover, the young, slender man, dark, with slow gait, following them and who greets, with a protective air, the three friends laughing at him...He is a martyr of his beliefs, of his own importance."

The newcomer felt overwhelmed with admiration and respect for the young man.

"He looks like a fool, but he is," continued Tadeo, "he was born in San Pedro Makati. He deprives himself of many things; he almost never bathes; nor tasted pork, because according to him, the Spaniards don't eat it, and for the same reason does not eat rice, nor *patis* or fish sauce, nor *bagoong* or shrimp paste, although he may be dying of hunger or watering in the mouth...Anything that comes from Europe, rotten or preserved, tastes heavenly to him, and a month ago Basilio saved him from severe gastritis. He had eaten a jar of mustard to prove that he was European!"

At that moment the orchestra began to play a waltz.

"See that señor? That sickly looking one who is turning his head, fishing for greetings? That is the famous governor of Pangasinan,⁹ a good man who loses his appetite whenever an *Indio* fails to salute him...He would have died if he had not decreed the edict on salutes to which he owes his celebrity status. Poor *señor*, it is only three days since he arrived from the province and how much he has thinned! Oh! here is the great man himself, the acclaimed, open your eyes!"

"Who? that man with the knitted brows?"

"Yes, that is Don Custodio, the liberal Don Custodio. He has his brows knitted because he is thinking of some important project... if the ideas which he has in his head could only be put into practice, they would be something serious! Ah! here comes Macaraig, your housemate!"

As a matter of fact, Macaraig was arriving with Pecson, Sandoval and Isagani. Tadeo, upon seeing them, moved forward and greeted them.

"Are you not coming?" Macaraig asked him.

"We could not get any tickets."

"As it happens, we have a box," replied Macaraig. "Basilio cannot come....Come along with us."

Tadeo did not wait for the invitation to be repeated. The newcomer, fearing to be in the way, with the timidity natural to all provincial *Indios*, excused himself, and there was no way to persuade him to enter.

- 22 -

The Performance

The theater presented a most lively aspect; it was full to the brim: in the general admission section and in the aisles many people were standing, struggling to draw aside a head or place an eye between a neck and an ear. The open boxes, occupied mostly by ladies, looked like baskets of flowers whose petals were shaken by a light breeze (I speak of the fans), and in which hummed a thousand insects. Yet, as there are flowers of delicate and strong fragrance, flowers that kill and flowers that console, in these baskets of our theater similar scents are breathed in; dialogues are heard, conversation, phrases that sting and bite. About three or four boxes remained vacant despite the lateness of the hour. The performance had been announced for half past eight; it was already a quarter of nine and the curtain had not been raised because His Excellency had not yet arrived. Those in the gallery, impatient and uncomfortable in their seats, mounted an uproar, clapping and pounding the floor with their canes.

"Boom-boom-boom! Raise the curtain! Boom-boom-boom!"

The artillery men[1] were not the least among the uproarious. These emulators of Mars, as Ben Zayb called them, were not satisfied with this sound. Perhaps they thought themselves in a bullring. They saluted the ladies who passed before them with words which are euphemistically called flowers in Madrid, although at times, they seem more like smoking garbage.[2] Without heeding the furious looks of the husbands, they proclaimed loudly the sentiments and longings which in them were awakened by so many beauties...

In the orchestra seats—where the ladies seemed afraid to venture, since not one was visible there—reigned a murmur of voices, suppressed laughter amid clouds of smoke...They discussed the merits of the performers; talked of scandals, wondering whether His Excellency had quarrelled with the friars; whether the presence of the *General* at such a show was a provocation or simply a curiosity. Others were not interested in these matters but in capturing the attention of the ladies, adopting postures more or less interesting, more or less statuesque, displaying their diamond rings, particularly when they believed themselves observed by persistent opera glasses. Others directed respectful salutes to that *señora* or *señorita*, bowing the head with much earnestness while whispering to a neighbor:

"How ridiculous she is! What an aggravation!"

The lady would respond with the most gracious of her smiles and an enchanting movement of the head, and murmur to a friend sitting near, between two indifferent fan strokes:

"How conceited! *Chica*, he's madly in love!"

Meanwhile the uproar heightened: boom-boom-
boom! Toc-toc-toc! Now there was nothing left but two
vacant boxes and that of His Excellency, which could be
distinguished by its red velvet hangings. The orchestra
played another waltz. The public protested: fortunately
there showed up a charitable hero who distracted attention
and saved the impresario. It was a gentleman who had
occupied an orchestra seat and refused to relinquish it to
its owner, the philosopher Don Primitivo. Seeing that his
arguments could not convince him, Don Primitivo sought
the aid of the usher. "I do not care to," answered the hero,
calmly smoking his cigarette. The usher appealed to the
manager. "I do not care to," he repeated and settled back
into the seat. The manager left while the artillerymen in
the gallery started to sing a chorus:

"Yes he won't! Yes he will, No he won't! Yes he will!"

Our actor, who had already attracted everyone's
attention, thought that to yield would be to degrade
himself, so he held on to his seat while repeating his answer
to the pair of the veterans called in by the manager. The
guards, considering the rebel's rank, went in search of the
corporal, while the whole house broke out in applause,
celebrating the firmness of the *señor* who remained seated
like a Roman senator.

Whistles were heard, and the *señor*, who had an
inflexible character, turned his head angrily, thinking they
were whistling at him.[3] The sound of galloping horses
was heard; a stir was noticed. One might have said that a
revolution had broken out, or at least a riot; no, the
orchestra had stopped playing the waltz and struck up
the royal march; it was His Excellency, the Capitan General
and Governor of the Islands who had arrived: all eyes
sought him, followed him, lost him, and he finally

appeared in his box, and after looking all around him and making some happy with his vigorous salute, sat down in the armchair awaiting him. The artillery men had become silent, and from the orchestra surged the overture.

Our students occupied a box directly facing that of Pepay, the *bailarina*. This box was a present from Macaraig, who had already colluded with her to solicit Don Custodio's help. Pepay had written a letter that same afternoon to the famous *ponente*, making a rendezvous with him in the theater, and awaiting a reply. For this reason Don Custodio, notwithstanding the tough opposition which he had displayed against the French operetta, had gone to the theater, which earned for him subtle cutting remarks from Don Manuel, his inveterate opponent in the sessions of the Ayuntamiento.

"I come to judge the operetta!" he had replied in the tone of a Cato satisfied with his conscience.

So Macaraig was exchanging knowing glances with Pepay, who made him understand that she had something to say to him; and since the dancer had a happy look, all augured that success was assured. Sandoval, who had just arrived from visits made to other boxes, assured them that the judgment had been favorable and that that very same afternoon the Superior Commission had examined and had approved it. All thus was jubilation; even Pecson himself forgot his pessimism, seeing a smiling Pepay display a letter. Sandoval and Macaraig congratulated one another; only Isagani remained somewhat cold and hardly smiled.

What had happened to the young man?

Isagani, upon entering the theater, had seen Paulita in a box and Juanito Pelaez conversing with her. He blanched and thought he was just mistaken. But no, it was

Paulita herself, she who greeted him with a gracious smile while her lovely eyes seemed to be seeking his forgiveness and promising him explanations. As a matter of fact, they had both agreed that Isagani would go first to the theater to see that there was nothing in the show objectionable for a young woman, and now he found her there and in no less than the company of his rival.

What was going on within Isagani's soul was indescribable: wrath, jealousy, humiliation, resentment, raged inside him. There was a moment when he wished the theater would collapse; he had violent desires to laugh uproariously; to insult his beloved; to provoke his rival; to create a scandal; but he contented himself with sitting quietly and not looking at her at all. He heard Macaraig and Sandoval discussing their beautiful plans, and they sounded like distant echoes; the notes of the waltz seemed to him sad and mournful, all of that audience inane and idiotic, and many times he had to make an effort to contain his tears. The gentleman who refused to relinquish the box; the arrival of the Capitan General, he hardly perceived; he stared at the show curtain, which depicted a kind of gallery amid sumptuous red hangings with the view of a garden, in the midst of which rose a fountain. How sad the gallery looked to him and how melancholic the scenery! A thousand vague reminiscences surged in his memory like the distant echoes of music heard during the night; like the lullabyes of infancy; the murmur of lonely forests; dark rivulets; moonlit nights by the shores of a sea stretching endlessly before his eyes...And the enamoured youth who considered himself very wretched stared at the ceiling so that his tears would not drop from his eyes.

A burst of applause drew him from his meditation.

The curtain had just risen, and the gay chorus of the peasants of Corneville appeared before his eyes, attired in their cotton caps, and with heavy wooden clogs on their feet. The girls, some six or seven lasses, heavily painted with rouge on their lips and cheeks, with big round black circles around their eyes to enhance their sparkle; showed off white arms; fingers loaded with diamonds, and rounded, well-shaped legs. And while they sang the Norman refrain: *Allez, marchez! Allez, marchez!* they smiled at their respective admirers in the orchestra seats with such brazenness that Don Custodio, after glancing at Pepay's box as though to make sure that she was not doing the same thing to another admirer, jotted down in his notebook this indecency, and to be more sure, lowered his head a little to see if the actresses were not showing even their knees.

"Oh, these Frenchwomen!" he muttered while his imagination was lost in thoughts of a level more lofty, as he made comparisons and plans.

"*Quoi v' la tour les cancans d'la s'maine?* What is all the gossip of the week?..." sang Gertrude, a proud wench who looked obliquely and very roguishly at the Capitan General.

"We will have the cancan!" exlaimed Tadeo, the first prize winner of French in his class, who had been able to fish out the word. "Macaraig, they will dance the cancan!"

And he gleefully rubbed his hands.

Tadeo, ever since the curtain had been raised, paid no heed to the music; he was looking only for the scandalous, the indecent, the immoral, in the gesture and in the dresses and with his meager French, sharpened his ears to catch the obscenities which the censors of his country had severely warned against.

Sandoval, who pretended to know French, made himself into a sort of interpreter for his friends. He knew as much French as Tadeo did, but he aided himself with the published synopsis, and the rest his fancy supplied.

"Yes," he said, "they are going to dance the cancan and she is going to lead it."

Macaraig and Pecson became attentive and smiled to themselves in anticipation. Isagani looked elsewhere, embarrassed that Paulita should be present at such a show, and thinking that he should challenge Juanito Pelaez to a duel the following day.

But our young men waited in vain. Serpolette came, a delicious lass with her cotton cap, equally provocative and quarrelsome.

"*Hein! qui parle de Serpolette?*" she asked the gossipers, her arms akimbo and with a challenging air. A gentleman applauded, and after him so did all those in the orchestra seats. Serpolette, without a change in her demeanor of a virtuous girl, looked at the first who had applauded her, and rewarded him with a smile showing tiny teeth that looked like a string of pearls in a case of red velvet. Tadeo followed her gaze and saw a gentleman with a false moustache and an extraordinarily long nose.

"Good Lord! Little Irene himself!"

"Yes" answered Sandoval, "I have seen him inside talking with the actresses."

In effect Padre Irene, who was a melomaniac of the first degree and knew French very well, had been sent to the theater by Padre Salvi as a sort of secret religious police, or so at least he told the persons who recognized him. And, as a good critic who is not satisfied with viewing the piece from afar, he wanted to examine the actresses at close range, mixing himself into the group of admirers and gallants; he had introduced himself into the dressing room where, by necessity, French was whispered and spoken, a French of the *market*, an idiom highly comprehensible for the vendor when the buyer seemed disposed to pay well.

Serpollete was surrounded by two gallant officers, a sailor, and a lawyer, when she glimpsed him moving about, sticking the end of his long nose into all nooks and crannies as if he were sensing with it the mysteries of the stage.

Serpollete cut short her chatter, knitted her brows, raised them, opened her lips and with the vivacity of a Parisienne left her admirers and launched herself like a torpedo against our critic:

"*Tiens, tiens, Toutou! mon lapin!*" she broke out, catching Padre Irene by the arm and, shaking him merrily, made the air ring with silvery notes.

"Chut, chut!" said Padre Irene, trying to conceal himself.

"*Mais, comment! toi ici, grosse bête! Et moi quit' croyais...*"

"*Fais pas d'tapage, Lily! il faut m' respecter! 'suis ici l'Pape!*"

With great difficulty Padre Irene brought her back to reason. The joyful Lily was *enchantée* to meet in Manila an old friend who reminded her of the *coulisses* of the Grand Opera House. And thus it was that Padre Irene, complying at the same time with his duties of friend and of critic, had initiated the applause to inspire her. Serpolette deserved it.

In the meantime, our young men were waiting for the cancan. Pecson became all eyes; everything except cancan was there. There was a part in which, if people of the law had not arrived, the women would have come to blows and pulled one another's hair, egged on by the naughty peasants who expected, like our students, to see more than just a cancan.

> *Scit, scit, scit, scit, scit, scit,*
> Disputez-vous, battez-vous,
> Scit, scit, scit, scit, scit, scit,
> *Nous allons compter les coups.*

But the music stopped, the men left, the women returned, a few at a time and started between them a dialogue which our friends could not comprehend at all. They were speaking badly of someone absent.

"They look like the *Macanistas* of the *panciteria*!" observed Pecson in a low voice.

"And the cancan?" Macaraig asked.

"They are talking about the most suitable place to dance it." Sandoval gravely replied.

"They look like the Chinese of the *panciteria*," repeated Pecson, disgusted.

A *señora*, accompanied by her husband, entered at that moment and occupied one of the vacant boxes. She had the airs of a queen, and glanced with disdain at the hall as if to say:

"I have come later than all of you, you bunch of vulgarity and provincials! I have come later than you!"

Indeed, there are people who go to the theater like asses in a race: he who comes last wins, sensible men we know of who would rather climb the gallows first, than arrive at the theater before the first act. But the satisfaction of the lady was of short duration; she had seen the other box which remained vacant; she knitted her eyebrows, and started to scold her better half, causing such a disturbance that irritated many.

"Sst! Sst!"

"The stupid ones! As if they understood French!" said the lady, looking around with overbearing contempt and fixing her gaze on the box of Juanito where she thought she had heard the impudent *sst* issue.

Juanito was, in fact, guilty; from the start he had been pretending to understand everything and assumed airs, smiling, laughing and applauding at times as though nothing that was said escaped him. And he was not guided in this by the actors' miming, because he scarcely looked towards the stage. The rogue had intentionally told Paulita that there being so many more beautiful women, he did not wish to tire himself looking far away. Paulita had blushed and covered her face with a fan and would glance stealthily at Isagani who, without laughing nor applauding, was witnessing the show distractedly.

Paulita felt resentment and jealousy. Was Isagani enamored with those provocative actresses? This thought put her in a bad humor, and she scarcely heard the praises Doña Victorina was heaping upon her favorite.

Juanito was playing his part well: at times he would move his head in sign of disgust and then there would be heard coughs, murmurs in some parts; at times he would smile, approve and seconds later applause would resound. Doña Victorina was delighted, and even conceived vague desires to marry the young man herself the day Don Tiburcio died. Juanito knew French and de Espadaña did not. And she started to lavish on him flattery! But Juanito did not perceive the change of tactics, absorbed as he was in watching a Catalan merchant who sat next to the Swiss Consul. Juanito, who had seen them talking in French and was inspired by their expressions, was mimicking them magnificently.

Scene after scene came, characters after characters, comical and ridiculous like the bailiff and Grenicheux, noble and congenial like the marquis and Germaine. The audience laughed much at the blow by Gaspard intended for the coward Grenicheux and taken by the grave bailiff, at the wig of the latter which flew in the air, at the disorder and the confusion as the curtain dropped.

"And the cancan?" asked Tadeo.

But the curtain rose again immediately, and the scene represented the servant market, with three posts covered with streamers and bearing notices of *servantes, cochers* and *domestiques*. Juanito took advantage of the occasion and, in a sufficiently loud voice so that Paulita could hear him and be convinced of his knowledge, addressed Doña Victorina.

"*Servantes* means servants, *domestiques* domestics."...

"And how are they different, the *servantes* from the *domestiques*?" asked Paulita.

Juanito was not left short.

"*Domestiques*, those that are domesticated: have you not observed how some have the look of savages? Those are the *servantes*."

"It is true!" Doña Victorina added. "Some have bad manners...and I who thought that in Europe everybody was refined and...but, as it happens in France...well, I see!"

"Sst! Sst!"

But Juanito was in a predicament when the time for the market came and the barrier opened; the servants for hire placed themselves beside their respective signs, which indicated their kind! The man-servants, some ten or twelve rough types attired in livery and carrying little branches in their hands, situated themselves under the sign *domestiques*.

"Those are the domestics!" Juanito said.

"Truly, they have the appearance of having been recently domesticated," remarked Doña Victorina. "Let us have a look at the half-savages!"

Afterwards, the dozen girls, at their head the gay and lively Serpollete, dressed in their finest clothes, each carrying a large bouquet of flowers at the waist, laughing, smiling, fresh, attractive, placed themselves to the great dismay of Juanito beside the post of the *servantes*.

"How is that?" Paulita asked candidly. "Are those the savages that you mentioned?"

"No," replied Juanito unperturbed. "They have made a mistake...they have changed...Those who follow behind."

"Those who come with a whip?"

Juanito made signs that it was so, with his head, very uneasy and disturbed.

"So those lasses are the *cochers*?"

Juanito was attacked by a fit of coughing so violent that it provoked uneasiness in some spectators.

"Out with him! Out with the consumptive!" cried a voice.

Consumptive? To dub him consumptive before Paulita! Juanito wanted to see the loquacious one and make him swallow the consumption. Seeing that the women were intervening, he was further emboldened, and his spirits were raised. Fortunately it was Don Custodio who had made the diagnosis and, fearing to attract attention, looked disinterested, pretending to write down the critique of the piece.

"If it were not because I am with you..." said Juanito making his eyes roll like some puppets that move the pendulum of a clock. And to approximate it, he stuck his tongue out from time to time.

That night he earned himself before the eyes of Doña Victorina the reputation of being brave and punctilious, and she decided in her heart to marry him as soon as Don Tiburcio passed away.

Paulita felt much sadder every time, thinking how some girls called *cochers* could occupy the attention of Isagani. *Cochers* reminded her of certain terms which convent school girls use among themselves to explain a sort of passion.

Finally the first act came to an end with the Marquis taking Serpollete and Germaine with him as his servants, representing the timid beauty of the troupe; and for *cocher* the stupid Grenicheux. An outburst of applause made them appear on the stage holding hands, where five seconds before they had been chasing one another and were about to come to blows, bowing here and there to the gallant Manila audience and exchanging knowing looks with some spectators.

While the intermission tumult reigned, caused by those who stumbled against one another to go to the dressing room, and to acclaim the actresses, by those who were going to greet the ladies in the boxes, some declared their judgments of the operetta and the performers.

"Undoubtedly, Serpollete is the best," said one showing airs of genius.

"I prefer Germaine; she is an ideal blonde."

"But she does not have a voice,"

"And what do I care about the voice?"

"Well, as for shape, the tall one."

"Psh!" said Ben Zayb, "not one of them is worth a rush, not one is an artist."

Ben Zayb is the critic for *El Grito de la Integridad* and his air of disdain gave him much importance before the eyes of those who were contented with so little.

"Neither does Serpollete have a voice, nor does Germaine have grace, neither is that music, nor art nor anything!" he concluded with marked derision.

In order to appear as a great critic there is nothing like being contemptuous of everything. The management had not sent more than two tickets to the editorial office.

In the boxes they were asking who could be the owner of the empty box. That one would surpass everyone in chic since he would be the last to arrive.

Without knowing where the piece of news came from, it was said that it was Simoun's. The rumor was confirmed. No one had seen the jeweler in the orchestra seats or in the dressing room, or anywhere.

"However, I have seen him this afternoon with Mr. Jouy!" someone said.

"And he has gifted one of the actresses with a necklace..."

"Which one?" asked some of the inquisitive ladies.

"The best of all, the one who followed his Excellency with her eyes!"

Significant looks, winks, exclamations of doubts, of affirmation, and half-uttered comments.

"He is playing the role of the Count of Monte Cristo!" observed one who prided herself on being literary.

"Or purveyor of the Royal House,"[4] added her admirer, now jealous of Simoun.

In the box of our students, Pecson, Sandoval and Isagani had remained. Tadeo had gone to entertain Don Custodio, making conversation and talking about his pet projects, while Macaraig was interviewing Pepay.

"By no means, as I told to you before, friend Isagani," harangued Sandoval, making grand gestures and drawing out a melodious voice so that the neighbors of the box, the daughters of the rich man who owed Tadeo, might hear him. "By no means, the French language does not have the rich harmony, nor the varied and elegant cadences of the Castilian idiom. I cannot conceive, I cannot imagine, I cannot form any idea of the French orators and I doubt that they have ever had any or can have any orators, in the real sense of the word, in the strict sense of the idea. Because we must not confuse the word orators with the word talkers or charlatans. Talkers or charlatans can be found in any country, in all the regions of the inhabited world, among the cold and wry Englishmen as well as among the lively and impressionable Frenchmen..."

And he continued with a magnificent review of the nations with his poetical characterizations and most resounding epithets. Isagani nodded his head in assent while thinking of Paulita, whom he had surprised looking at him, with a glance that was expressive and wanted to say many things. Isagani wanted to decipher what those eyes were expressing, those eyes that certainly were eloquent and not loquacious!

"And you who are a poet, slave to rhyme and meter, son of the Muses!" continued Sandoval, making a very elegant gesture with his hand as if he were saluting on the horizon the Nine Sisters, "do you comprehend, can you figure out how a language so harsh and of such meager rhythm as is French, can give birth to poets of the gigantic measure of our Garcilasos, our Herreras, our Esproncedas and Calderones?"

"Nevertheless," observed Pecson, "Victor Hugo..."

"Victor Hugo, friend Pecson, if Victor Hugo is a poet it is because he owes it to Spain...because it is an established fact, it is a fact beyond all doubt, a fact admitted even by the Frenchmen themselves who are so envious of Spain, that if Victor Hugo was a genius, if he is a poet it is because his childhood had been spent in Madrid, there he imbibed the first impressions, there he molded his brain, there he colored his imagination, he fashioned his heart and there were born the most beautiful concepts of his mind. And, after all, who is Victor Hugo? Can he compare at all with our moderns?"

But the arrival of Macaraig in a despondent mood and with a bitter smile on his lips cut the perorations of the orator. Macaraig had in his hand a paper which he turned over to Sandoval without saying a word.

Sandoval read:

'My dove: Your letter has reached me late; I had already handed in my decision and it has been approved. However, as if I had divined your thoughts, I have resolved the matter according to the wishes of your protegés.

I will be at the theater and will wait for your departure.

Your tender little dove,
Custodining.'

"What a dear man he is!" exclaimed Tadeo, touched.

"And well," said Sandoval, "I see nothing wrong, on the contrary!"

"Yes," replied Macaraig with his rueful smile; "resolved favorably! I have just met with Padre Irene!"

"And what does Padre Irene say?" asked Pecson.

"The same as Don Custodio, and the rascal still had the gall to congratulate me. The Commission which made its own the decision of the *ponente*, approves the idea and congratulates the students for their patriotism and their zeal to learn..."

"Well, then?"

"Only that, considering our concerns, in the end it says that in order that the idea may not go to waste, it is understood that one of the religious corporations should take charge of the direction and execution of the plan, in case the Dominicans would not wish to incorporate the Academy into the University!"

Exclamations of disappointment greeted those words. Isagani rose to his feet but said nothing.

"And so that it is seen that we participate in the direction of the Academy," Macaraig continued, "we are entrusted with the collection of the contributions and dues with the obligation of turning them over afterwards to the treasurer whom the corporation in charge may designate, which treasurer will issue us receipts..."

"Cabezas de Barangay, barrio chieftains, then!⁵" Tadeo commented.

"Sandoval," said Pecson, "there is the gauntlet, pick it up!"

"Puf! that is no gauntlet, but by the smell, more like a sock."

"And the most ridiculous," Macaraig went on, "is that Padre Irene advises us to celebrate the event with a banquet or a serenade with torches, a demonstration by the students en masse to render thanks to all the persons who have intervened in this matter."

"Yes, after the blow we sing and give thanks. *Super flumina Babylonis sedimus*! By the river of Babylon we sat and wept!"

"Yes, a banquet like that of the convicts," said Tadeo.

"A banquet in which we are all in mourning and we

deliver funeral speeches," added Sandoval.

"A serenade with the Marsellaise and funeral marches," proposed Isagani.

"No, gentlemen," said Pecson with his rakish laugh, "in order to celebrate this affair there is nothing like a banquet in a *panciteria*[6] served by Chinamen in *camisa*, but without their *camisa*!"

The idea was accepted for its sarcasm and grotesqueness. Sandoval was the first to applaud it: for some time now he had wanted to see the interior of such establishments which during the night appeared so gay and animated.

Precisely at the moment when the orchestra played to begin the second act, our young men rose to their feet abandoning the theater, to the consternation of the whole house.

- 23 -

A Corpse

S imoun, in fact, did not go to the theater.

Since seven in the evening he had gone from his house, troubled and gloomy. His servants saw him return twice accompanied by different individuals. At eight o'clock Macaraig met him roving along the street of the Hospital,[1] near the cloister of Santa Clara, at the time when the bells of the church were tolling. At nine o'clock Camaroncocido saw him again in the surroundings of the theater talking to one who looked like a student, opening the door and again leaving, disappearing among the shadows of the trees.

"And what is that to me?" again said Camaroncocido. "What do I get out of warning the populace?"

Basilio, as Macaraig said, did not attend the performance either. The poor student, ever since his return from San Diego to ransom Juli his betrothed from her servitude, had returned to his books, spending his time in the hospital studying or nursing Capitan Tiago, whose ailments he was trying to combat.

The patient had turned into an intolerable character. In his worst moments, when he felt depressed for lack of a dose of opium which Basilio tried to moderate, he would accuse, maltreat, insult him; Basilio suffered, resigned in his conscience that he was doing the best for one to whom he owed so much, and only in final extremes would he yield. The passion satisfied, the monster of the vice, Capitan Tiago, would fall into good humor, turn sentimental, call him his son, would cry, remembering the young man's services, how well he administered his properties, and talked of making him his heir. Basilio would smile bitterly, thinking how in this life the gratification of vice is better rewarded than the fulfillment of duty. Not a few times did the young man feel tempted to give free rein to the disease and lead his benefactor to the grave along a path of flowers and pleasant illusions rather than lengthen his life on a road of privation.

"What a fool I am!" he often said to himself. "The masses are stupid and therefore pay for it..."

But he would shake his head thinking of Juli, of the untold future he had before him. He wanted to live without soiling his conscience. He would follow the prescribed treatment and keep watch.

Despite all this, the patient was, with slight respites, getting worse every day. Basilio, determined to gradually reduce the dosage, or at least not to allow him to abuse smoking more than he usually did, would find him, upon returning from the hospital or from some rounds, sleeping the heavy slumber of opium, slobbering and pale as a corpse. The young man could not explain where the drug could come from; the only ones who frequented the house were Simoun and Padre Irene. The former came very

rarely; and the latter never tired of urging him to be severe
and unyielding in his regimen and not to take notice of
the patient's outbursts since the objective was to save him.

"Do your duty, young man!" he would tell him, "Do
your duty!"

And he would give him a homily on this theme with
such conviction and enthusiasm that Basilio came to feel
sympathy for the preacher. Padre Irene had, besides,
promised to get him an appointment, a good province,
and even hinted to him of the possibility of having him
named professor. Basilio, without allowing himself to be
carried away by illusions, pretended to believe this, and
went on obeying what his conscience said.

That night, while *Les Cloches de Corneville* was being
presented, Basilio was studying in front of an old table by
the light of an oil lamp whose opaque glass shade
immersed his melancholy countenance in half brightness.
An ancient skull, some human bones and several volumes,
were neatly stacked on the table, where there were, besides,
a basin of water and a sponge. A smell of opium which
escaped from the adjoining room weighed heavily on the
atmosphere and made him drowsy, but the young man
resisted, moistening temples and eyes from time to time,
determined not to fall asleep until he had finished the
volume.

It was the *Medicina Legal y Toxicologia* of Dr. Mata, a
work he had borrowed and must return to the owner as
soon as possible. The professor did not want to lecture
except from that author,[2] and Basilio did not have enough
money to buy the work, since, with the pretext that it was
prohibited by the Manila censor[3] and they had to bribe
many officials to bring it in, the booksellers charged high
prices. The young man was so absorbed in his studies that

he had not even bothered himself with some pamphlets sent to him from abroad, no one knew from where, pamphlets dealing with the Philippines, among some that had aroused great interest at that time because of the harsh and insulting way they dealt with the sons of the country. Basilio had not had sufficient time to open them; perhaps he was also deterred by the thought that it is not pleasant to receive an insult or a provocation and not have the means to defend oneself or to reply. The censors, in effect, allowed insults against the Filipinos but prohibited them to reply.[4]

In the midst of the silence that reigned in the house, disturbed now and then by weak snores which came from the adjoining room, Basilio heard light footsteps on the stairs, steps that then crossed the *caida* directing themselves to where he was. He raised his head, saw the door open, and to his great surprise, there loomed the somber figure of the jeweler Simoun.

Since the incident of San Diego, Simoun had not seen the young man again nor Capitan Tiago.

"How is the patient?" he asked, throwing a quick look about the room and casting an eye on the pamphlets we mentioned, their pages still unopened.

"The beats of the heart, imperceptible...pulse very weak...appetite, completely gone," replied Basilio with a sad smile and in a low voice; "he sweats profusely towards the dawn..."

Seeing that Simoun, by the direction of his face, had noticed the pamphlets, and fearing he would renew the matter which they had talked about in the woods, he continued:

"The organism is saturated with poison; he may die any day as if struck by lightning...the least cause, an inconsequential thing, an excitement, can kill him..."

"Like the Philippines!" observed Simoun grimly.

Basilio could not suppress a gesture and, determined not to renew the matter, continued as if he had heard nothing:

"What weakens him most are his nightmares, his terrors..!"

"Like the Government," again observed Simoun.

"Some nights ago he awoke in the darkness and thought he had gone blind; he created a disturbance, bewailing his condition and insulting me, saying I had plucked out his eyes... When I entered with a lamp he mistook me for Padre Irene and called me his savior..."

"Like the Government precisely!"

"Last night," proceeded Basilio, turning a deaf ear, "he got up and asked for his fighting cock, dead since three years ago; I had to present him with a hen, and he showered blessings on me and promised me many thousands..."

At that moment a clock struck ten-thirty.

Simoun shuddered and interrupted the young man with a gesture.

"Basilio," he said in a low voice, "listen to me carefully for the moments are precious. I see that you have not opened the pamphlets which I have sent you. You do not care about your country?"

The young man wanted to protest.

"It is useless!" Simoun said dryly. "Within an hour the revolution will start at my signal and tomorrow there will be no more studying, there will be no University, there will be nothing but combat and killings. I have everything ready and my success is assured. When we win, all those who could have served us but did not will be treated as enemies. Basilio, I have come to propose your death or your future!"

"My death or my future!" he repeated as if he did not understand anything.

"With the Government or with us," Simoun replied. "With your oppressors or with your country. You decide now, for time demands it. I have come to save you because of the memories that bind us!"

"With the oppressors or with my country!" he repeated in a low voice.

The young man was stupefied. He stared at the jeweler with eyes etched with terror; he felt his limbs go numb, and a thousand confused ideas surged in his brain. He saw the streets flowing with blood; heard the gunfire; found himself among the dead and wounded; and in the singular impulse of his calling, he saw himself in his surgeon's smock amputating legs and extracting bullets.

"I have in my hands the will of Government," Simoun went on, "I have pledged and wasted its meager strength and resources in foolish expeditions, dazzling it with booty that it might seize; its leaders are now in the theater, tranquil, distracted, thinking of a night of pleasures, but none of them will again rest on a cushion...I have regiments and men at my disposal, some of them I have led to believe that the revolution is ordered by the *General*; others that it is being done by the friars. Some I have bought with promises, with employment, with money; many others, very many, work for vengeance, because they are oppressed and because they see themselves in a case of killing or being killed. Cabesang Tales is downstairs, and he has accompanied me here. I ask you again: Are you with us or do you prefer to expose yourself to the resentments of those who follow me? In grave moments

to declare oneself neutral is to expose oneself to the fury
of both contending parties."

Basilio drew his hand across his brow many times as
if wanting to rouse himself from a nightmare. He felt that
his temples were cold.

"Make up your mind!" repeated Simoun.

"And what...would I have to do?" he asked with stifled
voice, broken, weak.

"A very simple thing," replied Simoun whose features
lighted up with a ray of hope. "Since I have to direct the
movement, I cannot distract myself in any action. I need
to have you, while all the attention of the city is at different
points, head a detachment to force the gates of the cloister
of Santa Clara and take away from there a person whom
you alone, outside of myself and Capitan Tiago,
recognize...You do not run any risk."

"María Clara!" exclaimed the young man.

"Yes, María Clara!" repeated Simoun and for the first
time his voice took on sad and gentle tones; "I want to
save her; to save her, I want to live, I have returned...I
began the revolution because only a revolution will open
to me the gates of the cloister!"

"Ay!" said Basilio, wringing his hands, "You arrive
late, too late!"

"And why?" asked Simoun knitting his brows.

"María Clara has passed away!"

Simoun stood up with a bound and rushed towards
the youth.

"Has died?" he asked in a terrible voice.

"This afternoon, at six o'clock; now she should be..."

"It is not true!" roared Simoun, pallid and looking
very ill, "that is not true! María Clara lives, María Clara
has to live! It is a cowardly excuse...she has not died, and

this night I have to free her or tomorrow you die!"

Basilio shrugged his shoulders.

"Some days ago she was taken ill, and I went to the cloister to gather news. Look, here is the letter of Padre Salvi which Padre Irene brought. Capitan Tiago was crying all night, kissing and asking forgiveness from the portrait of his daughter until he ended up smoking an enormous quantity of opium...This afternoon they tolled her death knell."

"Ah!" cried Simoun and, grasping his head with both hands, remained frozen.

He remembered having, in fact, heard the death knell while moving about in the surroundings of the cloister.

"Dead!" he murmured in a voice so low it was as if a ghost were speaking, "dead! dead without having seen her, dead without knowing that I was living for her, dead suffering..."

And feeling that a horrible storm, a tempest of whirlwinds and thunder without a drop of rain, sobs without tears, cries without words, roared in his breast and was going to overflow like incandescent lava long ago suppressed, he hurriedly fled the room. Basilio heard him rush down the stairs with erratic steps, tumbling; he heard a silent cry, a cry that seemed to herald the coming of death, deep, unbridled, mournful, so much so that the young man stood up from his chair, pale and trembling, heard the footsteps that were soon lost and the gate at the street which was shut with a loud noise.

"Poor *señor!*" he murmured, and his eyes filled with tears.

And forgetting his studies, with his look wandering in space, he thought of the fate of those two beings: he, young, rich, lettered, free, master of his destiny, with a brilliant future ahead of him, and she, beautiful like a dream, pure, full of faith and innocence, cradled among loves and smiles, destined for a happy life, to be adored in the family and respected in the world, and yet, nevertheless, those two beings, full of love, of dreams and hopes; by a fatal destiny, he wandered around the world, dragged without respite by a whirlpool of blood and tears, sowing bad instead of doing good, dismantling virtue and fomenting vice, while she was dying in the mysterious shadows of the cloister where she had sought peace and may perhaps have encountered sufferings, where she had entered pure and without stain and expired like a crushed flower!

Sleep in peace, unhappy child of my unfortunate motherland! Bury in your grave the enchantments of your childhood, withered in their vitality! When a people cannot offer its virgins a peaceful home, the shelter of sacred liberty; when a man can only bequeath dubious words to his widow, tears to his mother and slavery to his children, you do well to condemn yourselves to perpetual chastity, choking within your breasts the seed of a cursed future generation!

Ah, you have done well, not to have to tremble in your grave hearing the cries of those who agonize in the shadows, of those who feel themselves with wings and yet are fettered, of those who choke themselves for lack of liberty! Go, go with the dreams of the poet to the region of the infinite, vestige of woman glimpsed in a beam of moonlight, whispered by the supple stalks of the cane-brakes...Happy she who dies wept for, she who leaves in the heart of those who love her, a pure vision, a sacred memory, not stained by common passions which ferment with the years!

Go, we will remember you! In the pristine air of our motherland, under her blue sky, over the waves of the lake which imprison mountains of sapphire and shores of emerald, in her crystalline streams which the bamboo-canes overshadow, the flowers border, and dragonflies and butterflies enliven with their uncertain and capricious flight as if playing with the wind, in the silence of our forests, in the singing of our creeks, in the diamond cascades of our waterfalls, in the resplendent light of our moon, in the sighs of our evening breeze, and all that in the end evoke the image of the beloved, we will see you eternally as we have dreamed about you: lovely, beautiful, smiling like hope, pure like the light and, nevertheless, sad and melancholy comtemplating our miseries!

- 24 -
Dreams

Amor, que astro eres?

Love, what heavenly body are you?

The following day, a Thursday, a few hours before sunset, Isagani was on his way along the beautiful Paseo de María Cristina headed for the Malecon[1] to keep an assignation which that morning Paulita had granted him. The young man did not doubt that they were going to talk about that which had occurred the night before, and because he was resolved to ask her for explanations, and knowing how proud and overbearing she was, he foresaw a breakup. Anticipating this eventuality, he had brought with him the only two notes he had from Paulita, two scraps of paper with a few lines scribbled in a hurry, with several blots and an even handwriting, things that did not prevent the lovestruck young man from preserving them with as much love as if they had been autographs of Sappho herself or of the muse Polyhymnia.[2]

This decision to sacrifice love at the altar of dignity, the conscience to suffer complying with a duty, did not prevent a deep melancholy from overwhelming Isagani, making him think of the lovely days and even lovelier nights, during which they whispered sweet nothings across the flower-decked grill of the ground floor, nothings which for the young man had such seriousness and importance of character that they seemed the only things worthy of the attention of the most lofty human intellect. Isagani was thinking of the promenades in the moonlit nights at the fair, on December mornings after the *misa de gallo*, of the holy water that he was wont to offer her, and which she would acknowledge with a look pregnant as a poem of love, both of them trembling when their fingers touched. Sonorous sighs, like little rockets, burst from his breast and he called to mind all the verses, all the sayings of poets and writers about the inconstancy of woman.

He cursed within him the creation of theaters, the French Operetta, swore to himself to take vengeance on Pelaez at the first opportunity. Everything that surrounded him appeared to be under the saddest and blackest colors: the bay, deserted and lonely, seemed to him more solitary than ever with the few steamers there anchored; the sun was about to sink behind Mariveles devoid of poetry and enchantment, without the clouds fanciful and rich in the colors of happier twilights; the Anda monument, in bad taste, mean and squat, without style, without grandeur, looked like a dish of ice cream, or at best, a pie.[3]

The gentlemen strolling along the Malecon, in spite of their having an air of satisfaction and contentment, appeared to him diffident, arrogant and vain; naughty and ill-bred, the youngsters who were playing on the beach, making flat stones skim over the waves; or searching in the sand for mollusks and crabs which they caught and killed without benefit to themselves. Even so the never-ending works of the port to which he had dedicated more than three odes, now looked to him absurd, ridiculous, child's play.

The port, ah! the port of Manila, a bastard that, since it was conceived, has caused all to weep tears of shame and humiliation! If only after so many tears, the fetus of an obscene abortion would not come forth!

Absentmindedly he greeted two Jesuits, his old professors; he barely noticed a tandem driven by an American, which excited the envy of some gallants who drove their rigs. Near the Anda monument he heard what Ben Zayb was saying to another of Simoun, that the night before, he had all of a sudden fallen ill. Simoun refused to receive anybody, even the aides of the *General*.

"Ya!" exclaimed Isagani with a bitter smile, "for him all the attention, because he is rich...the soldiers return from expeditions, sick and wounded, and no one visits them!"

Thinking of these expeditions, of the plight of the hapless soldiers and the resistance put up by the *insulares* against the foreign yoke, he thought that, death for death, if that of the soldiers was sublime because they had fulfilled their duty, the death of the *insulares* was glorious because they were defending their homes.

"Strange destiny, that of some nations," he thought. Because a traveler comes to their shores, they lose their freedom and become the subjects and slaves, not only of the traveler, not only of his heirs, but even of all his compatriots, and not for one generation, but for always!

Strange concept of justice! Such a situation gives ample right to exterminate every foreigner as the most ferocious monster that the sea can cast out!

And he was thinking that those *insulares* against whom his motherland was at war, after all had no crime other than their weakness. The travelers also arrived on the shores of the other nations but, finding these strong, did not undertake their singular pretension. Weak and all, to him the spectacle they represented seemed beautiful, and the names of the enemies, whom the newspapers were not careless in calling cowards and traitors, appeared to him glorious as they succumbed with glory at the feet of the ruins of their imperfect fortifications, with more glory yet than the ancient Trojan heroes; those *insulares* had abducted no Filipino Helen. And with his poet's enthusiasm, he thought of the young men of those islands who could cover themselves with glory before the eyes of their women, and because in love with despair, he envied them because they could find glorious suicide. And he exclaimed:

"Ah! I would like to die, be reduced to nothingness, leave my motherland a glorious name, die for her cause, defending her from foreign invasion, and that the sun afterwards illumine my corpse as an immobile sentinel on the rocks of the sea!"

The conflict with the Germans came to his mind, and he almost regretted its having been resolved: he would gladly have died for the Spanish-Filipino standard before submitting himself to the foreigner.

"Because, after all," he thought, "with Spain we are united with firm bonds, the past, history, religion, the language..."

"Language, yes, the language!" A sarcastic smile

etched itself on his lips. That night they would have a banquet at the *panciteria* to celebrate the death of the Spanish Academy.

"Ay," he sighed, "if the liberals in Spain were like the ones we have here, in a little while the mother country would be able to count the number of her faithful!"

Night descended gradually, and with it the melancholy was exacerbated in the heart of the young man, who was losing almost all hope of ever seeing Paulita. The strollers were gradually leaving the Malecon to go to the Luneta,[4] the music from which was heard in snatches of melodies wafted there by the fresh evening breeze. The sailors of a warship anchored on the bay were executing their before-evening maneuvers, climbing along the slender ropes like spiders; the boats, one by one, lighted their lamps thus giving signs of life, and the beach,

> *Do el viento riza las calladas olas*
> *Que con blando murmullo en la ribera*
> *Se deslizan veloces por si solas...*

> (Where the wind with gentle moan
> Sends the billows swiftly on
> In the silence and alone...)

which Alaejos says, exhaled in the distance thin vapors which the light of the moon, now in all its fullness, gradually converted into transparent and mysterious gauzes...

A distant sound was perceived, a noise that gradually came nearer. Isagani turned his head and his heart started to beat violently: a carriage came drawn by white horses, the white horses that he could distinguish among a hundred thousand. In the carriage came Paulita, Doña Victorina and Paulita's friend of the night before.

Before the young man could take a step, Paulita had alighted on the ground with the nimbleness of a sylph and smiled at Isagani with a smile pregnant with conciliation. Isagani smiled in turn, and it seemed to him that all the clouds, all the dark thoughts which before had besieged him, dissipated like smoke, the sky filled with light, the air with song, and flowers covered the grass by the road. Unfortunately Doña Victorina was there, Doña Victorina who took the young man to herself to ask him for news of Don Tiburcio. Isagani had pledged to find the latter's hiding place by inquiring among the students he knew.

"No one has been able to give me an account until now," he replied, and he was telling the truth, because Don Tiburcio was in hiding at the house of the same young man's uncle, Padre Florentino.

"Let him know," Doña Victorina said, furious, "and I will call on the *guardia civil*. Alive or dead, I want to know where he is...Because to have to wait ten years before being able to marry!..."

Isagani looked at her astonished. Doña Victorina herself thinking of marrying! Who could the hapless one be?

"What do you think of Juanito Pelaez?" she asked suddenly.

"Juanito?..."

Isagani did not know what to reply; it made him want to tell all the worst that he knew about Pelaez, but *delicadeza* triumphed in his heart and he spoke well of his rival for that reason. Doña Victorina, all contentment and enthusiasm, consumed herself in exaggerating the merits

of Pelaez, and was about to make of Isagani a confidant of
her new love, when Paulita's friend came running to say
that her fan had dropped among the rocks on the beach
beside the Malecon. Stratagem or accident, the fact was
that this mishap gave an excuse for the friend to remain
with the old woman and Isagani to be with Paulita. Besides,
Doña Victorina was overjoyed, and to stay with Juanito,
she favored Isagani's suit.

Paulita had her own strategy; upon thanking him
she took on the pose of the offended, the resentful, and
gently made him understand that she was surprised to
find him there, when all the world was at the Luneta,
even the French actresses...

"You have given me an appointment, how could I
do less..."

"Nevertheless, last night you were not even aware
that I was in the theater; all the time, I was observing you,
and you could not draw your eyes away from those
cochers..."

The roles were reversed; Isagani who had come to
demand explanations had to give them, and considered
himself very happy when Paulita said that she forgave
him. As for her presence in the theater, it was gratifying
for him to know that she had been forced by the aunt, and
had only decided to go in the hope of seeing him during
the performance. She scoffed at Juanito Pelaez!

"My aunt is the one who is in love," she said, laughing
merrily.

Both laughed; the marriage of Pelaez with Doña
Victorina made them crazy with joy and they saw it as a
fait accompli, but Isagani remembered that Don Tiburcio
still lived, and confided the secret to his beloved, after
making her promise that she would tell no one. Paulita

promised, but with the mental reservation of revealing it to her girlfriend.

This led the conversation to Isagani's town, surrounded by forests and situated on the shore of the sea which roared at the foot of the high rocks.

Isagani's eyes lit up when speaking of that obscure remote place, the fire of pride flamed in his cheeks, his voice trembled, his imagination was stirred like that of a poet and words came to him burning, filled with enthusiasm as if he were speaking to the love of his love, and he could not but explain:

"Oh, in the solitude of my mountains I feel free, free as the air, like the light rushing uncontrolled through space! A thousand cities, a thousand palaces I would give up for a remote place of the Philippines, where far from mankind I feel free with true liberty! There, with nature face to face, in the presence of the mysterious and the infinite, the forest and the sea, I think, speak and act like a man who knows no tyrants!"

Paulita, before such enthusiasm for his native town, an enthusiasm she could not understand, she who was so accustomed to hear her country spoken of badly and herself join in the chorus now and then, displayed some jealousy and, as always, resentment.

But Isagani immediately put her at ease.

"Yes," he said, "I loved it above all things before I knew you! It was for me a delight to wander through the thickets, sleep under the shade of trees, to seat myself upon the summit of a cliff, to contain with my gaze the Pacific rolling below me, its blue waves bringing back to me the echoes of songs learned on the shores of free America...Before knowing you, that sea was for me my world, my enchantment, my love, my illusions. When it slept calmly and the sun shone in the heavens, I delighted in scanning the abyss, fifty meters from my feet, searching for monsters in the forests of mother of pearl and corals which revealed themselves through the limpid blue, the enormous serpents which, according to the peasants, left the forests to dwell in the sea and acquired frightful forms...In the evenings which is when, they say, the sirens appear, I looked for them in one wave or another, with such eagerness that one time I believed I saw them amid the foam busy with their divine frolics; I distinctly heard their songs, songs of freedom, and I perceived the sound of their silvery harps.

"I used to spend hours and hours watching the clouds transform themselves, contemplating a solitary tree on the plains, a rock, without being able to give myself a reason, without being able to define the vague feeling aroused in me. My uncle would often preach to me long sermons and, fearing that I would turn into a hypochondriac, spoke of taking me to the house of a physician.

"But I saw you, I loved you, and in these vacations, it seemed that there was something missing there; the forest was gloomy, sad the river that flowed among the thickets, dreary the sea, deserted the horizon...Ah, if you could go there once, if your footsteps could tread those paths, if you could stir the waters of the rivulet with your fingertips, if you could gaze upon the sea, sit on the cliff, or make the air resound with your melodious songs, my forest would be transformed into Eden, the ripples of the brook would sing, light would burst from the dark leaves, the dewdrops would turn to diamonds and the sea-foam into pearls!"

But Paulita had heard it said that to reach Isagani's home it was necessary to cross mountains where little leeches abounded, and with this thought alone, the coward shuddered convulsively. Comfort-loving and spoiled, she said that she would travel only in a carriage or a railway train.

Isagani, who had forgotten all his pessimism and saw everywhere only roses without thorns, replied:

"In a little while all the islands are going to be crossed by a net of iron: 'Where rapid and winged engines will rush in flight,' as someone has said; then, the most beautiful places of the archipelago will be open to all."

"Then, but when? When I have become an old woman...?"

"Bah! you do not know what we can do within a few years," replied Isagani. "You do not realize the energy and enthusiasm that are awakening in the country after a lethargy of centuries...Spain pays attention to us; our young men in Madrid work day and night, dedicating to the Motherland all their intelligence, all their time, all their strength; generous voices there are joined to ours, statesmen who comprehend that there is no better bond than the community of interest and sentiments. Justice is being done to us and everything augurs for all a brilliant future[5]...It is true that we have just suffered a slight disaster, we the students, but victory triumphs all along the way...it is in everyone's consciousness. The treacherous defeat that we suffered witnesses the last gasps, the last convulsions of the dying! Tomorrow we will be citizens of the Philippines, whose destiny will be beautiful because it will be in loving hands.

"Oh, yes, the future is ours! I see it rosy, I see the movement stirring life in these regions so long dead, lethargic. I see towns arise along the railroads, and whatever factories, edifices like that of Mandaluyong[6]...I hear the boats whistle, the jolt of the trains, the clatter of engines...I see the smoke rising, its powerful breathing and I smell the odor of oil, the sweat of monsters occupied in incessant toil...This port, of difficult beginnings, that river where commerce seems to agonize, we shall see covered with masts and it will give us an idea of winter in the forests of Europe...This air so pure and these stones so clean will be covered with coal, with boxes and barrels, products of human industry, but it matters not, for we shall move on rapidly in comfortable coaches, to search in the interior for other winds, other panoramas in other shores, fresher temperatures in the folds of the mountain...the iron frigates of our navy will guard our coasts.

"The Spaniard and the Filipino will rival each other in zeal to repel all foreign invasion, to defend all your homes and leave you free to laugh and enjoy in peace, loved and respected. Freed from the system of exploitation, without spite or distrust, the people will work because then work will cease to be despicable, will no longer be servile, an imposition on the slave. Then the Spaniard will no longer sour his character with ridiculous despotic pretensions, buy with a frank look, a stout heart will give us a hand, and commerce, industry, agriculture, the sciences will develop under the umbrella of liberty and of wise and equitable laws as in prosperous England..."

Paulita smiled with an air of doubt, and shook her head.

"Dreams, dreams," she sighed. "I have heard it said that you all have many enemies. *Tía* Torina says this country will always be enslaved."

"Because your aunt is a fool, because she cannot live without slaves, and when she does not have them, she dreams of them in the future; and if they are not possible, she forges them in her imagination. It is true we have enemies, that there will be a struggle, but we shall overcome. The old system may convert the ruins of its castles into shapeless barricades, but we will take them with songs of liberty, in the light of all your eyes, to the applause of all your beloved hands! For the rest, be at ease, the struggle will be peaceful. It is enough that you all spur us to study, that you awaken in us noble, elevated thoughts and encourage us to constancy, to heroism with the reward of all your tenderness!"

Paulita maintained her enigmatic smile and seemed thoughtful; she gazed upon the river, giving herself on the cheeks light taps with the fan.

"And if you accomplish nothing?" she asked, distracted.

The question hurt Isagani's sensibilities. He fixed his eyes on those of his beloved, took her lightly by the hand and replied:

"Listen, if we accomplish nothing..."

And he paused, vacillating.

"Listen, Paulita," he continued, "you know how much I love you and how much I adore you; you know that I feel myself another person when your gaze enfolds me, when I catch in it a spark of love...but yet, if we accomplish nothing, I would dream of another look of yours, and I would die happy because a flash of pride could shine in your eyes and you would one day say to the world pointing at my corpse: 'My love died fighting for the rights of my Motherland!'"

"To the house, child! Let us go home, you are going to catch cold," Doña Victorina shrieked at that moment.

The voice brought them back to reality. It was time to return, and out of amiability they invited Isagani to come into the carriage, an invitation which the young man did not make them repeat. Since the carriage was Paulita's, naturally Doña Victorina and the friend occupied the front part and the two lovers the small bench.

To go in the same carriage, to have her beside him, to inhale her perfume, to rub against the silk of her dress, to see her pensive with arms crossed, bathed in the beams of the Philippine moon that lends to the meanest things idealism and enchantment, was a dream that Isagani had never hoped for! How wretched were those who returned on foot, alone and who had to give way to the passage of the swift vehicle. In the whole course of that drive along the beach, by the Paseo de la Sabana,[7] the Puente de España, Isagani saw nothing but a soft profile gracefully ending in an arched neck which lost itself in the gauze of *piña*. A diamond winked at him from the lobe of a diminutive ear, like a star amid silvery clouds. Isagani had heard faint echoes asking him for Don Tiburcio de Espadaña, the name of Juanito Pelaez, but they sounded to him like bells heard from afar, confused voices perceived during a dream.

It was necessary to advise him that they had arrived at the Plaza Santa Cruz.

- 25 -

Laughter and Tears

The dining hall of the Panciteria Macanista de Buen Gusto that night offered an extraordinary sight.

Fourteen young men from the principal islands of the Archipelago, from the pure *Indio* (if there be those that are pure) to the Spanish peninsular, were gathered together to celebrate the banquet that Padre Irene had proposed in view of the decision given on the matter of the teaching of Spanish. They had reserved for the occasion all the tables, ordering added lights and placing on the wall beside the Chinese landscapes and picture scrolls this curious verse:

"GLORY TO CUSTODIO FOR HIS CLEVERNESS, AND PANSIT ON EARTH TO YOUTHS OF GOOD WILL!"

In a country where all that is grotesque is disguised by a mantle of sobriety, where many rise by dint of smoke and hot air; in a country where what is profoundly serious and sincere, coming from the heart, may do damage and cause disturbances, that was probably the best way to celebrate the bright idea of the notable Don Custodio. The cheated answered the mockery with a guffaw, to the governmental pastry they responded with a plate of *pansit!*

They laughed, they jested, but it was obvious that in the merriment there was strain; the laughter rang with a certain nervous tremble; from eyes quick sparks were emitted, but in more than one a tear could be seen to shine. Yet those youths were cruel, they were unjust! That was not the first time that the most beautiful thoughts had been resolved thus, that hopes were defrauded by big words and small actions: before Don Custodio, there had been others, very many others!

At the center of the sala and beneath the red lanterns were four round tables, systematically arranged to form a square; equally round little wooden stools served as seats. In the middle of each table, according to the custom of the establishment, were laid out four small colored plates with four pastries on each one, and four tea cups with their corresponding lids, all of red porcelain. In front of each stool could be seen a bottle and two wineglasses of gleaming crystal.

Sandoval, in the manner of the curious, looked, scrutinized everything, tasted the pastries, examined the pictures, read the list of prices. The rest were discussing the topic of the day, the actresses of the French operetta and the mysterious ailment of Simoun who, according to some, had been found wounded in the streets; according to others, had attempted suicide, as was natural; they lost themselves in conjectures. Tadeo gave his own particular version, according to him, from trustworthy sources: Simoun had been assaulted by an unknown in the old plaza of Vivac;[1] the motive was revenge, and in proof of it

Simoun himself refused to give the least information. From there they passed on to talk of mysterious vengeances and naturally to monkish deeds, each one relating the prowess of the respective curates of their towns.

A quatrain in large black letters crowned the frieze of the sala and said:

> *De esta fonda el cabecilla*
> *Al público advierte*
> *Que nada dejen absolutamente*
> *Sobre alguna mesa ó silla.*

> (The manager of this eatery
> Warns the public
> That absolutely nothing may be left
> On any table or chair.)

"What a notice!" exclaimed Sandoval; "Is there trust among thieves, eh?" And what verses! Don Tiburcio converted into a stanza, two feet, one much longer than the other, between two crutches! If Isagani saw them he would give them to his future aunt as a gift!"

"Here is Isagani," replied a voice from the stairway.

And the happy young man appeared radiant with joy, followed by two *descamisados*, shirtless Chinese who carried in huge trays platters which diffused an appetizing odor. Merry exclamations greeted them.

Juanito Pelaez was missing, but since the time for dining had come, they seated themselves gaily at the table. Juanito was always unreliable.

"If we had invited Basilio in his place," said Tadeo, "we would have enjoyed ourselves more. We could have made him drunk and extracted some secrets."

"What! does the prudent Basilio keep secrets?"

"Come!" replied Tadeo, "and of the utmost importance! There are some enigmas to which he alone knows the key...the boy that disappeared, the nun..."[2]

"*Señores*, the *pansit lang-lang* is the soup par excellence!" cried Macaraig. "As you will note, Sandoval, it is made of mushrooms, lobsters or shrimps, egg noodles, *sotanjun*, chicken bits and I don't know what else.[3] As first-fruits, let us offer Don Custodio the bones, and see what projects he makes of them!"

A merry guffaw greeted this harangue.

"If he comes to learn of this..."

"He would come running!" added Sandoval. "The soup is excellent—what is it called?"

"*Pansit lang-lang*, that is, Chinese *pancit* to differentiate it from the other one peculiar to this country."

"Bah! that is a name difficult to remember. In honor of Don Custodio I christen it *proyecto de sopa* or project soup!"

The new name was accepted.

"*Señores*," said Macaraig, who was the one who had prepared the menu, "there are still three dishes more! Chinese *lumpia*, spring rolls made of pork ..."

"Which should be dedicated to Padre Irene!"

"Gracious! Padre Irene does not eat pork unless he moves his nose away," a young man from Iloilo observed in a low voice to his neighbor.

"Let him remove his nose!"

"Down with Padre Irene's nose!" cried everyone in chorus.

"Respect, gentlemen, more respect!" complained Pecson with droll gravity.

"The third dish is a *torta* or crab omelet..."

"Then it should be dedicated to the friars," added the Visayan.

"For being such crabs," Sandoval added.

"Just so, and it shall be called *torta* of friars!"

All repeated in a chorus: "*torta* of friars!"

"I protest in the name of one," said Isagani.

"And I, in the name of the crabs!" added Tadeo.

"Respect gentlemen, more respect!" Pecson again cried out with his mouth full.

"The fourth plate is *pansit guisado* or sautéed noodles, which should be dedicated...to the Government and to the country!"

All turned towards Macaraig.

"Until recently, *señores*," he continued, "*pansit* was believed to be Chinese or Japanese, but since in fact it is not known in China or in Japan, it seems to be Filipino, yet those who cook it and benefit from it are the Chinese, the same, the same which happens to the Government and to the Philippines: they seem to be Chinese, but whether they are or are not, the Holy Mother has her doctors...All eat and enjoy it, and yet have affectations and loathing, the same happens to the country, the same to the Government. All live at its expense, all share in the feast and afterwards there is no country worse than the Philippines, no Government more disorganized. Let us then dedicate the *pansit* to the country and to the Government!"

"It is so dedicated," they said in chorus.

"I protest!" exclaimed Isagani.

"Respect for the minority, respect for the victims," cried Pecson in a hollow voice, raising in the air a chicken bone.

"Let us dedicate the *pansit* to the Chinaman Quiroga,

one of the four powers of the Filipino world!" proposed
Isagani.

"No, to his Black Eminence!"

"Silence!" exclaimed one with a mysterious air. "In
the plaza there are groups watching us, and the walls
hear."

In fact, curious groups were standing in front of the
windows, while the uproar and merriment in the adjoining
establishments had ceased completely, as if attention were
being directed to what was taking place at the banquet.
The silence was somewhat unusual.

"Tadeo, make your speech!" Macaraig said to him in
a low voice.

It had been agreed that Sandoval, having the best
qualities as orator, would resume the toast.

Tadeo, lazy as usual, had nothing prepared, and
found himself in a predicament. While he sucked in a
long strand of *sotanjun*, he thought how he could extricate
himself, until he remembered a speech learnt in class, and
decided to plagiarize and adulterate it.

"Beloved brethren in project!" he started, gesticulating
with the two chopsticks Chinese use for eating.

"Beast, let go of those chopsticks! you have mussed
my hair!" said his neighbor.

"Elected by your choice to fill a vacancy that has been
left in..."

"Plagiarist," Sandoval interrupted him; "that speech
was delivered by the president of our academy!"

"Elected by your choice,"—continued Tadeo
unperturbed— "to fill the vacancy that has been left in
my....mind (and he pointed to his stomach) by a man
illustrious for his Christian principles and for his
inspirations and projects worthy of having a little more

than memory, what could I tell you who, like me, are hungry, not having had breakfast?"

"Have a neck, *chicooó*, mannn!" his neighbor countered, offering him a chicken neck.

"There is one dish, gentlemen, the treasure of a people which is today a fable and the scorn of the world, into which have chosen to thrust their hungry spoons, the greatest gluttons of the western regions of the globe..." pointing with his chopsticks at Sandoval struggling with an unruly chicken wing.

"And oriental!" replied the one alluded to, tracing a circle in the air with a spoon to include all the table companions.

"No interruptions, please!"

"I demand a word!"

"I demand *patis*, fish sauce!"[4] added Isagani.

"Bring in the *lumpia!*"

All asked for the *lumpia*, and Tadeo seated himself very much content at having gotten out of the predicament.

The dish dedicated to Padre Irene did not seem that good, and Sandoval manifested this cruelly:

"Shining with grease outside and tough pork inside! Bring in the third dish, the *torta* of friars!"

The *torta* had not yet been made; the sizzling of lard in the frying pan could be heard. They took advantage of the intermission to drink, and asked that Pecson speak.

Pecson crossed himself gravely, rose to his feet, restraining with difficulty his clownish laughter, mimicking a certain Augustinian preacher then famous. He started to murmur as though reciting the text of a sermon: *"Si tripa plena laudat Deum, tripa famelica laudabit fratres* (If a full belly glorifies God, a hungry belly glorifies the friars)— words that Don Custodio said through the mouth of Ben

Zayb, in the newspaper *El Grito de la Integridad*, article second, nonsense one hundred and fifty seventh!"

"Beloved brethren in Christ!

"Evil blows its foul breath over the verdant shores of Friarlandia, commonly known as the Philippine Archipelago! No day shines without an attack that resounds, without a sarcasm that is heard, against the reverend, venerable and preaching Orders, defenseless and devoid of all support. Allow me, brethren, for a moment to make myself knight errant, to sally forth in defense of the helpless, of the Holy Orders that educated us, confirming one more time the complementary concept of the adage 'a full belly glorifies God', which is, 'an empty belly will glorify the friars.'"

"Bravo, bravo!"

"Listen!" said Isagani seriously. "I am informing you that concerning friars, I respect one."

Sandoval, who was now cheerful, started to sing:

> *Un fraile, dos frailes, tres frailes en el coooro*
> *Hacen el mismo effecto que un solo tooooro!*

> (One friar, two friars, three friars in the choir-loooft
> Has the same effect as one solo horny buuull!)

"Hearken, my brethren; turn your gaze towards the beautiful days of your infancy; try to scrutinize the present and inquire into the future. What do you have? Friars, friars and friars! A friar baptizes you, confirms you; visits the school with loving zeal; a friar listens to your first secrets; he is the first to make you eat a God; to start you on the path of life. Friars are your first and last teachers; the friar is the one who opens the hearts of your sweethearts, disposing them to your sighs; a friar marries you; makes you travel to different islands adjusting you to changes in climate and distractions; he attends to you on your deathbeds; and even if you mount the scaffold, there is the friar too to accompany you with his prayers and tears and you can be tranquil that he will not abandon you, until he sees you completely dead.

"Moreover, his charity does not stop there either; dead he will try to bury you with all the pomp; he will fight to have your cadaver pass by the Church; he receives the suffrages and will rest content only when he can turn you over to the hands of the Creator purified here on earth, thanks to the temporal punishments, tortures and humiliations. Knowing the doctrine of Christ which closes heavens to the rich, they, the new redeemers, true ministers of the savior, invent all the astuteness to lighten your sins, commonly *cuapí*,[5] money, and transport it far, far away, to where the damned Chinese and protestants live, and leave this atmosphere limpid, pure, cleansed in such a way that even if afterwards we wished so, it would be impossible for us to find a single real for our damnation!"

"Since, therefore, his existence is essential to our happiness, since, wherever we may stick our noses, we will have to encounter the delicate hand, hungry for kisses, which flattens every day even more the maltreated probosces which on our faces we display, why not pamper and fatten them and why demand their anti-political expulsion?[6] Consider for a moment the immense void that their absence would leave in our society! Tireless workers, they improve and propagate the races. Divided as we are, thanks to jealousies and susceptibilities, the friars unite us in a common destiny, in a tight truss, so tight that many cannot move their elbows!

"Remove the friar, gentlemen, and you will see how the Philippine edifice will tumble, for lack of vigorous shoulders and hairy limbs; Philippine life will become monotonous without the happy note of the playful and gracious friar, without the booklets and sermons that make us break bones in laughter. Without the amusing contrast of great pretensions and small minds; without the live, daily images of the tales of Boccacio and La Fontaine! Without the girdles and scapulars, what would you have our women do in the future but save that money and become, perhaps, miserly and covetous? Without the masses, novenas and processions, where would you find *panguinguis* to entertain their leisure? They would have to reduce themselves to household chores, and instead of reading amusing stories of miracles, we may have to provide them works that do not exist. Take away the friar, and heroism will vanish, the political virtues will be under the control of the vulgar; take him away and the *Indio* would no longer exist.[7]

"The friar is the father, the *Indio* is the Word; the former the sculptor, the latter the statue, because all that we are, all that we think, all that we do, we owe to the friar, to his patience, to his efforts, to his perseverance of three centuries to modify the form that Nature gave us! And the Philippines without friar and without *Indio*, what would happen to the poor government in the hands of the Chinese?"

"It will be a *torta* of crabs," answered Isagani, who was bored with Pecson's speech.

"And that is what we ought to do. Enough of speeches!"

Since the Chinese waiter who should have served the plate did not appear, one of the students stood up and went to the back toward the balcony overlooking the river, but returned at once, making mysterious signs.

"We are being watched; I have seen the favorite of Padre Sibyla!"

"Yes?" exclaimed Isagani raising himself.

"It is useless; upon seeing me he left."

And approaching the window he looked toward the plaza. Then he made a sign to his companions to draw near. They saw coming out through the door of the *pansiteria* a youth who gazed about him, and entered with a stranger a carriage waiting at the curb. It was the carriage of Simoun.

"Ah!" exclaimed Macaraig: "the slave of the Vice-Rector served by the Master of the *General!*"

- 26 -
Pasquinades

B asilio rose very early in the morning to go to the hospital. He had his plans traced out: he would visit his patients, then go to the University to make inquiries about his degree, and finally see Macaraig about the expenses that this would entail. He had used up a great part of his savings to ransom Juli and get her a house where she could stay with her grandfather, and he dared not ask Capitan Tiago's help, fearing that he might interpret the request as an advance on the inheritance he was always promising him.

Distracted with these thoughts, he failed to notice the groups of students that so early in the morning returned from the city as if the schools had been closed; even less did he notice the worried attitude of some, the conversations in low voices, the mysterious signals exchanged among them. Thus when he reached the San Juan de Dios hospital, and his friends asked him about a conspiracy, Basilio was startled, remembering what Simoun had been plotting, which was aborted by the jeweler's mysterious accident. Full of apprehension and in an altered voice, he asked, feigning ignorance:

"Ah! What conspiracy?"

"It has been discovered!" replied another, "and it seems there are many implicated."

Basilio tried to control himself.

"Many implicated?" he repeated, trying to read something in the looks of the others, "and who are they...?"

"Students, many students!"

Basilio thought it imprudent to ask further, afraid to betray himself, and, pleading the need to visit his patients, left the group. A professor of clinical medicine went out of his way to approach him and, placing his hand on Basilio's shoulder with an air of mystery—the professor was his friend[1]—asked him in hushed tones:

"Were you at the dinner last night?"

Basilio, in the frame of mind in which he found himself, thought he heard "the *night before*." The night before had been his meeting with Simoun. He tried to explain.

"I will tell you," he stammered, "as Capitan Tiago was critical and besides I had to finish the Mata..."

"You did well not to go," said the professor, "but are you a member of the Association of Students?"

"I pay my dues..."

"Well, then, a piece of advice: resign at once and destroy whatever papers you have that might compromise you."

Basilio shrugged his shoulders. Papers, he had none; he had clinical notes, nothing more.

"Is Señor Simoun...?

"Simoun has nothing to do with this matter, thank

God!" the doctor added. "He was opportunely wounded by mysterious hands and is in bed. No, here, other hands moved, but they were no less terrible."

Basilio breathed. Simoun was the only one who could compromise him. However, he thought of Cabesang Tales.

"Are there *tulisanes* or bandits...?"

"No, man, nothing but students."

Basilio recovered his composure.

"What happened then?" he dared to ask.

"Subversive posters have been found; did you not know?"[2]

"Where?"

"F—! In the University."

" Nothing more than that?"

"Damn it! What else do you want?" asked the professor, almost furious; "The posters are attributed to the organized students, but, silence!"

The Professor of Pathology was coming, a man who looked more like a *sacristan* than a doctor. Appointed at the powerful pleasure of the Vice-Rector without requiring of him any merit or further qualifications than his unconditional adherence to the Order, he passed for a spy and a tattle-tale in the eyes of the other professors in the Faculty.

The first Professor coldly returned the other's greeting and, winking at Basilio, said in a loud voice:

"I know now that Capitan Tiago already smells like a cadaver; the crows and vultures hover over him."

And he entered the sala of the Professors.

Somewhat more tranquil, Basilio ventured to find out more information. All that he learned was that on the doors of the University posters were found which the Vice-Rector ordered removed to send to the Civil Government.

They said they were full of threats of attack and invasion and other bravado.

On this event the students were making their own comments. The news came from the caretaker; this he got from a servant of the University, who in turn, heard them from a *capista*. They predicted future suspensions, imprisonments and the like, and tagged those who were to be the victims, naturally members of the Association.

Basilio remembered the words of Simoun: "The day on which they can get rid of you...You will not finish your career..."

"Could he have known anything?" he asked himself. "We will see who may be the most powerful."

Recovering his equanimity, to find out where he stood and at the same time to inquire about his degree, Basilio walked towards the University. He took the street of Legaspi, followed Beaterio, and upon arriving at the angle this formed with Solana, he observed that effectively something important, indeed, must have occurred.

Instead of the merry and mischievous groups of before, on the sidewalks were seen pairs of the *guardia veterana* or veteran guards making the students move. The latter were coming out of the University, some silent, others taciturn, irritated, standing off at a distance or returning to their homes. The first one he encountered was Sandoval. In vain did Basilio call him; it seemed he had turned deaf.

"Effects of fear on the gastrointestinal juices!" thought Basilio.

Then he met Tadeo, who had on a Christmas face...At last the eternal holiday seemed to be coming true.

"What is happening, Tadeo?"

"We will not have classes for at least a week, *chico*! sublime! magnificent!"

And he rubbed his hands with glee.

"But what has happened?"

"They are going to throw us into jail, all those of the Association!"

"And you are happy?"

"There are no classes, no classes!" and he moved on, almost beside himself with joy.

He saw Juanito Pelaez approaching, pale and suspicious. This time his hump had reached the maximum; he was in such a hurry to get away. He had been one of the most active promoters of the Association when things were going well.

"Eh, Pelaez, what has happened?"

"Nothing, I know nothing. I have nothing to do with it," he replied nervously. "I have been telling them that these things are quixotic...It is true! you know that I said that."

Basilio did not remember whether he had said so or not, but to humor him he replied:

"Yes, man, yes, but what happened?"

"It is true, is it not? Look! you are a witness: I have always been opposed...You are a witness! Look! Do not forget!"

"Yes, man, yes, but what is going on?"

"Listen! You are my witness! I have never been involved with those of the Association except to advise them!...Do not deny it afterwards. Be careful, see?"

"I will not deny it; but, what has happened man, for God's sake!"

But Juanito was already far away. He had seen a guard approaching and feared he would be apprehended.

Basilio continued on his way to the University to see

if, perhaps, the secretariat was open, and to get news. The secretariat was closed, and in the building there was exceptional activity. Friars, officers, private individuals, seasoned lawyers and physicians went upstairs and downstairs, perhaps to offer their services to the cause which was in danger.

He espied from a distance his friend Isagani, pale and deeply concerned, radiant with youthful appeal, haranguing some fellow students, raising his voice, it did not matter in the least to him to be heard by all the world.

"It seems incredible, gentlemen, it seems preposterous, that an incident so insignificant should disperse us and that we should flee like sparrows because a scarecrow shakes itself! Is it perhaps the first time that the youth will enter prison for the cause of liberty? Where are the martyrs, those who have been shot? Why abandon our cause now?"

"But who could be the fool who wrote such posters?" asked an indignant one.

"What does that matter to us?" retorted Isagani. "It is not for us to find out; let them find out! Before we know how they were drawn up, we do not need to make a show of cohesion in moments like these. There, where danger is, that is where we should be, for that is where honor is! If what the posters declare is in harmony with our dignity and our feelings, whoever wrote them has done well: we should give him our thanks and hasten to add our signatures to his. If they are unworthy of us, then our conduct and our consciences would protest for themselves and defend us from every accusation!"

Basilio, hearing such language and although he greatly liked Isagani, turned around and left. He had to go to Macaraig's house to talk to him about a loan.

Near the house of the wealthy student, he noted

murmurs and mysterious signals among the neighbors. The young man, unaware of what was going on, calmly continued on his way and entered the doorway. Two *guardias de la Veterana* advanced to ask him what he wanted. Basilio realized that he had made a wrong move, but he could no longer withdraw.

"I came to see my friend Macaraig," he calmly replied.

The guards looked at each other.

"Wait here," one said to him. "Wait till the corporal comes down."

Basilio bit his lips, and the words of Simoun resounded anew in his ears... Have they come to arrest Macaraig? he thought, but dared not ask.

He did not wait long; in that moment Macaraig was coming down conversing amiably with the corporal, both preceded by a guard.

"What? You too, Basilio?" he asked.

"I came to see you..."

"Noble conduct!" said Macaraig laughing. In times of calm you avoid us..."

The corporal asked Basilio his name, and leafed through a list.

"Student of medicine, Anloague Street?" asked the corporal.

Basilio bit his lip.

"You have saved us a trip," added the Corporal, placing a hand on his shoulder. "You are under arrest!"

"What? I, too?"

Macaraig burst into laughter.

"Do not be alarmed, friend. Let us get into the carriage, and I will tell you about the dinner last night."

With a gracious gesture, as though he were in his own house, he invited the assisting officer and the corporal to board the carriage which awaited them at the door.

"To the Civil Government!" he ordered the driver.

Basilio, who had by then recovered, told Macaraig the object of his visit. The wealthy student did not wait for him to finish, and stretched out his hand. "Count on me and, to the festivities of our graduation, we will invite these gentlemen," he said indicating the corporal and the assisting officer.

- 27 -
The Friar
and the Filipino

Vox populi, vox Dei.

Voice of the people; voice of God.

We left Isagani haranguing his friends. In the midst of his enthusiasm, a *capista* approached to tell him that Padre Fernandez, one of the eminent professors, wanted to speak to him.

Isagani's face changed. Padre Fernandez was for him a highly respectable person; he was the one he always excepted when an attack on the friars was made.

"And what does Padre Fernandez want?" he asked.

The *capista* shrugged his shoulders; Isagani reluctantly followed him.

Padre Fernandez, the friar we saw in Los Baños, waited in his cell, grave and sad, with knitted brows, as though meditating. He stood up on seeing Isagani enter, greeted him and shook his hand, and closed the door. He started to pace back and forth in his room. Isagani, on his feet, waited for him to speak.

"Señor Isagani," he finally said, in a somewhat emotional voice, "from the window I heard you perorate; although I am a consumptive, I have good hearing; and I wanted to talk to you. I have always liked young men who express themselves clearly and who think and act for themselves; it does not matter to me that their ideas may differ from mine. You all, according to what I heard, had, last night, a dinner—do not make excuses..."

"But I do not make excuses!" interrupted Isagani.

"Better and better; that proves that you accept the consequences of your actions. Besides you would do ill in retracting. I do not censure you. I take no notice of what might have been said there last night. I do not accuse you, for after all, you are free to say of the Dominicans what you like; you are not a student of ours. It is only this year that we have had the pleasure of having you, and we probably will not have you anymore. Do not think that I shall invoke questions of gratitude, no; I am not going to waste my time on foolish trivialities. I had you called because I believe that you are one of the few students who act from conviction; and since I like men of conviction, I told myself, to Señor Isagani I am going to explain myself."

Padre Fernandez paused and continued pacing, his head lowered, looking at the floor.

"You may take a seat if you like," he continued; "I have the habit of talking while walking because that way the thoughts come to me better."

Isagani remained standing, head high, waiting for the professor to thresh out the issue.

"For more than eight years I have been a professor," continued Padre Fernandez, pacing, "and I have known and dealt with more than two thousand five hundred young men. I have taught them; tried to educate them; I have inculcated in them principles of justice, of dignity; and yet, in these times when so much is murmured against us, I have not seen anyone who could have the boldness to back his accusations, face to face with a friar...not even in a loud voice before a certain audience....There are young men who slander us behind our backs, and when face to face, kiss our hands and with vile smiles beg for a glance! Puf! What would you have us do with such creatures"?

"The fault is not all theirs, Padre," retorted Isagani. "The fault is in those who taught them to be hypocrites; in those who tyrannize freedom of thought, freedom of speech. Here, all independent thought, all words which are not an echo of the will of the powerful, are judged as subversion, and you know very well what that means. A fool is he who allows himself to say in a loud voice what he thinks, and risks suffering persecution!"

"What persecution did you have to suffer?" asked Padre Fernandez, raising his head. "Have I not allowed you to express yourself freely in my class? However, you are an exception, but if what you say is true, I should have corrected you to make the rule applicable to all, to avoid propagating a bad example."

Isagani smiled.

"I give you my thanks, and shall not argue whether or not I am an exception. I will accept your description so that you will accept mine. You too, are an exception, but since we are not talking of exceptions here, or speaking for our persons, at least as far as I am concerned, I beg my professor for another approach to this matter."

Padre Fernandez, despite his liberal principles, raised his head and stared with surprise at Isagani. That young man was even more independent than he thought. Even though he called the friar *professor*, in reality the young man was dealing with him as an equal to an equal, inasmuch as he allowed himself insinuations. As a good diplomat, Padre Fernandez not only accepted the fact but he himself stood on it.

"Congratulations!" he said, "but do not look at me as your professor; I am a friar and you a Filipino student, nothing more, nothing less! And now I am asking you, what would the Filipino students have us do?"

The question came as a surprise; Isagani was not prepared. It was a lunge which slithered in suddenly while they set up the defense, as they say in fencing. Thus surprised, Isagani responded with a violent parry, like a novice defending himself.

"That you all do your duty!" he said.

Padre Fernandez drew himself up. The answer sounded like a cannon shot.

"That we do our duty!" he repeated, holding himself erect. "Well, have we not then done our duty? What duties do you assign us?"

"The same which you most freely imposed upon yourselves on entering your order, and those which, once in it, you have wanted to impose! But, as a Filipino student, I do not feel myself called upon to examine your conduct in relation with your statutes, with Catholicism, with the government, the Filipino people and humanity in general, questions that you will have to resolve with your founders, with the Pope, the government, the people as a whole, or with God.

"As a Filipino student I will limit myself to your duties with respect to us. The friars, in general, being the local inspectors of education in these provinces, and the

Dominicans, in particular, in monopolizing within their hands all the studies of Filipino youth, have contracted the obligation, before eight million inhabitants, before Spain and before humanity, of which we form part, to improve each time the tender seed, morally and physically; to guide it to its welfare; to create a people honest, prosperous, intelligent, virtuous, noble and loyal. And now I ask you in my turn: Have the friars complied with their obligation?"[1]

"We are complying..."

"Ah, Padre Fernandez," interrupted Isagani, "you with your hand upon *your* heart can say that you *are* complying, but with a hand upon the heart of the Order, over the heart of all the Orders, you cannot say it without deceiving yourself!

"Ah, Padre Fernandez, when I find myself before a person whom I esteem and respect, I prefer to be the accused rather than the accuser; I prefer to defend myself than to offend; but since we have entered into explanations, let us go on to the end. How do they comply with their duty, those in the towns, who supervise education? By hindering it. And those who have monopolized the studies, those who wish to mold the mind of the youth, with the exclusion of whomever else, how are they complying with their mission? Curtailing, as much as possible, knowledge; extinguishing all ardor and enthusiasm; diminishing all dignity, the soul's only resort, and inculcating in us ancient ideas, rancid notions, false principles incompatible with a life of progress!

"Ah yes, when it has to do with feeding convicts and providing for the support of criminals, the government calls for bids to find the bidder who offers the best conditions of nourishment, or is the least likely to leave

them to perish of hunger. When it comes to nourishing
morally a whole people, to nourishing the youth, the part
most wholesome, that which afterwards makes the nation
and the whole of it, the government not only does not call
for any bid, but instead perpetuates in power that
organization which precisely takes pride in not wanting
instruction, not wanting any advancement.

"What would we say if the provider of prisons, after
having himself empowered by contractual intrigues,
then left the prisoners to languish in anemia, giving
them only what is stale and rancid, excusing himself by
saying it is not convenient to have the prisoners in good
health, for good health brings happy thoughts; because
happiness improves the man, and man should not improve
because it suits the purveyor that there should be more
criminals? What would we say if government and supplier
conspired between themselves, because of the ten or twelve
cuartos which one received for each criminal, the other
received five?"

Padre Fernandez bit his lips.

"Those are very harsh accusations," he said, "and you
trespass the limits of our understanding."

"No, Padre, I am still treating of the student question.
The friars, and I do not say all of you, because I do not
include you in the common crowd, the friars of all the
Orders have become our intellectual purveyors, and they
say and proclaim without any inhibition that it is not
convenient that we enlighten ourselves because we are
some day going to declare ourselves independent! That is
not wishing that the convict be nourished, so that he does
not improve himself and leave prison. Liberty is to man
what education is to the mind, and the friars not wanting
us to have it is the source of our discontent."

"Education is not given except to those who deserve it," replied Padre Fernandez curtly; "to give it to men without character and without morality is to prostitute it."

"And why are there men without character and without morality?"

The Dominican shrugged his shoulders.

"Flaws that they themselves suck from their mothers' milk, that they breathe in within the bosoms of their families...how would I know?"

"Ah no, Padre Fernandez!" exclaimed the young man impetuously. "You have no wish to be involved in the issue; you do not wish to look into the abyss for fear of finding there the shadow of your brethren. What we are, you have made us. A people which is tyrannized is obliged to be hypocritical; those to whom the truth is denied give you falsehood; he who makes himself a tyrant begets slaves. There is no morality, you say, so be it, even though statistics can prove you wrong, because here crimes are not committed as in many other countries, by people blinded by the presumption of moralizers. But, and without wishing now to analyze what constitutes character and how much the education received counts in morality, I agree with you that we are flawed. Who is at fault? Is it you, who for three centuries and a half have had our education in your hands, or we who have submitted to everything? If after three centuries and a half the sculptor has been able to produce nothing more than a caricature, indeed, he must be truly stupid."

"Or the material that he works on must be very bad."

"Still more stupid is he then, because, knowing that it is bad, he does not reject the material and continues wasting time...and he is not only stupid, he cheats and steals, because knowing the uselessness of his work he continues it in order to receive compensation...and he is not only stupid and a thief, but also a villain because he prevents another sculptor from exercising his skill to see if he might produce something worthwhile! The lamentable jealousy of incompetence!"

The reply smarted, and Padre Fernandez felt trapped. He stared at Isagani, who appeared to him towering, invincible, imposing, and for the first time in his life he felt vanquished by a Filipino student. He regretted having provoked the polemics, but it was too late. In his quandary, and finding himself in the presence of so formidable an adversary, he sought a strong shield and laid hold of the government.

"You all impute to us all the faults, because you do not see beyond us who are near," he said in a tone less arrogant, "it is natural and it does not surprise me. The people hate the soldier or the guard who makes the arrest, and not the judge who decreed the imprisonment. You and we both dance to the beat of the same music. If you lift your feet at the same time as we do, do not blame us for that. It is the music that directs our movements. Do you believe that the friars have no conscience and do not desire good? Do you believe that we do not think of you, that we do not think of our duty and that we eat only to live and live only to rule? I wish it were so. But, like yourselves, we follow the beat. We find ourselves between the sword and the wall. Either you throw us out or the government does. The government commands and whoever commands, rules, and loads the cannon!"

"With that it can be inferred," observed Isagani with a bitter smile, "that the government desires our demoralization."

"Oh, no, I did not mean to say that! What I wanted to

say was that there are beliefs, there are theories and laws which, dictated with the best of intentions, produce the most deplorable consequences. I will explain better, citing to you an example. To avert a minor evil numerous laws are decreed, which cause even greater evils. *Corruptissima in republica plurimae leges,* (the state is more corrupt when there are too many laws,) said Tacitus. To avoid one case of fraud, a million and a half measures, preventive and insulting, are dictated, which produce the immediate effect of awakening in the public the desire to evade and to mock such preventions. To make criminals of a people you have only to doubt their honesty. Let a law be promulgated, not necessarily here but in Spain, and you will see how the means to cheat it are studied, and it is because legislators have forgotten the fact that the more an object is hidden the greater the desire to see it.

"Why are knavery and cunning considered such great qualities among the Spanish people when there is no other like them, so noble, so proud, so chivalrous? Because our legislators, with the best intentions, have doubted their nobility, wounded their pride and challenged their chivalry. Do you want to open in Spain a road in the midst of rocks? Then put up there an arrogant sign prohibiting passage, and the people, protesting against such an imposition, would leave the highway to climb the boulders. The day that in Spain a legislator prohibits virtue and imposes vice, the next day every one would be virtuous."

The Dominican paused and, after a while, continued:

"But you will say that we are straying from the issue. I return to it...What I can say to convince you is that the imperfections that you suffer you should not blame on us nor on the government. They are due to the imperfect organization of our society, *qui multum probai, nihil probat,* which proving much proves nothing, which ruins itself with excessive prudence, short in what is necessary and long on the superfluous."

"If you confess those defects in *your* society," replied Isagani, "why then involve yourselves in straightening out alien societies instead of occupying yourselves first with your own?"

"We are departing from our issue, young man. The theory of consummated deeds must be accepted..."

"So be it! I accept it because it is a fact and I continue to ask: why, if your social organization is defective, why not change it or at least listen to the voices of those who come out prejudiced?"

"We are still far from the point; we were talking of what the students want from the friars..."

"From the moment friars hide themselves behind the government, the students must address themselves to the latter."

The observation was fair: from there, there was no escape.

"I am not the government, and I cannot be responsible for its actions. What do the students want us to do for them within the limits in which we are confined?"

"Not to oppose the emancipation of education but to favor it."

The Dominican shook his head.

"Without expressing my personal opinion, that is to ask of us suicide," he said.

"On the contrary, it is to ask you for passage, so as not to trample over and flatten those who seek it."

"Hm!" said Padre Fernandez, pausing and becoming thoughtful. "Begin by asking us something that does not cost much, something that each one of us might concede without reducing his dignity and privileges, because if we can understand one another and live in peace, why the hatred, why the mistrust?"

"Let us go down then to details."

"Yes, because if we touch the foundations we shall bring down the edifice!"

"Let us go down to details then; let us leave the sphere of principles," replied Isagani smiling, *"and without declaring my own opinion either,"*— and here the young man accentuated the phrase— "the students would cease in their attitude; and soften certain acrimonies, if the professors knew how to treat them better than they have done so far...This is in your hands."

"What!" asked the Dominican. "Have the students any complaint about my conduct?"

"Padre, we have agreed from the beginning not to talk of yourself or of myself. We are speaking in general. The students, besides not gaining any great benefit from the years spent in classes, often leave there shreds of their dignity, if not all of it."

Padre Fernandez bit his lips.

"No one compels them to study; the fields lie fallow," he observed curtly.

"Yes, but there is something that compels them to study," replied Isagani in the same tone, looking at the Dominican face to face. "Aside from each one's responsibility to seek his own perfection, there is the innate desire in man to cultivate his intelligence, a desire that here grows more powerful the more it is repressed. He who gives his gold and his life to the State, has the right to require of it that it give him the light to better earn his gold and better conserve his life. Yes, Padre, there is something that compels them, and that something is the same government; it is you yourselves who deride without compassion the uncouth *Indio* and deny him his rights on

the grounds that he is ignorant. You yourselves strip him
and then sneer at his shame!"

Padre Fernandez did not reply. He continued pacing,
but feverishly as though very much excited.

"You say that the fields lie fallow!" continued Isagani
in another tone, after a brief pause. "Let us not start now
to analyze why, for we shall stray far. But, you, Padre
Fernandez, you, a professor, you a man of science, you
wish a people of peons and peasants. Is the peasant in
your opinion, the perfect state at which man may arrive in
his evolution? Or is it that you wish knowledge for yourself
and labor for the rest?"

"No, I want knowledge for him who merits it, for him
who will know how to preserve it," the priest replied.
"When the students give proof of loving it, when one sees
young men of conviction, young men who will know how
to defend its dignity and win respect for it, then there will
be knowledge, then there will be considerate professors! If
there are now professors who abuse, it is because there
are pupils who acquiesce."

"When there are professors, there will be students."

"Begin by transforming yourselves, who are the ones
who have need of change, and we will follow."

"Yes," said Isagani with a bitter laugh, "ask us to begin
because on our side lies the difficulty! You know well
enough what is expected of a pupil who places himself
before a professor; you yourself, Padre Fernandez, with
all your love of justice, with all your kind sentiments,
have restrained yourself at great effort while I told you
bitter truths! You yourself, Padre Fernandez! What good
has been achieved by him among us who wanted to
germinate other ideas? And what evils have rained
down on you because you wanted to be fair and to fulfill
your duty?"

"Señor Isagani," said the Dominican extending his hand, "although it may seem that from this conversation nothing practical resulted, something has been gained. I will speak to my brethren about what you have told me, and I hope that something can be done. I only fear that they will not believe in your existence...."

"I fear the same," retorted Isagani, shaking hands with the Dominican. "I fear that my friends will not believe in your existence, as you have revealed yourself to me today."

And the young man, considering the interview ended, took his leave.

Padre Fernandez opened the door for him, followed him with his eyes and saw him disappear at the turn of the corridor. He listened for some time to the sound of his footsteps, then entered his cell and waited for him to appear on the street. He saw him, actually heard him say to a friend who asked him where he was going:

"To the Civil Government. I am going to see the posters and join the others."

The friend, startled, stared at him as one would look at someone about to commit suicide, then left running.

"Poor young man!" murmured Padre Fernandez, feeling his eyes moisten. "I envy the Jesuits who educated you."

Padre Fernandez was somewhat mistaken; the Jesuits disowned Isagani,[2] and when that afternoon they learned that he had been arrested, they said that he was compromising them.

"That young man has lost himself and is going to do us harm! It must be known that he did not imbibe those ideas from us."

The Jesuits did not lie, no: those ideas God only gives through native genius.

- 28 -
Panic

B en Zayb had a prophet's inspiration when he
maintained, days earlier in his newspaper, that
education was insidious, highly insidious, for the
Philippine Islands. Now, in the light of the events of that
Friday concerning the posters, the writer was crowing and
singing his triumph, leaving crushed and confused his
adversary *Horatius*, who had dared ridicule him in a section
of *Pirotecnia* in the following manner:

From our colleague *El Grito*:
•Education is disastrous, absolutely disastrous for the
Philippines.•
Understood.
For some time now *El Grito* has believed itself to be
representing the Filipino people; *ergo*...as Fray Ibañez
would say if he knew Latin.
But Fray Ibañez turns Muslim when he writes, and
we know how the Muslims treat education. *Witness*, as a
royal preacher said, the library of Alexandria.

Now he was right, he, Ben Zayb! He was the only
one in the Philippines who thought, the only one who
foresaw events!

Indeed, the news of the finding of subversive posters
on the University doors, not only took away the appetite
of many and spoiled the digestion of others, but also made
uneasy the phlegmatic Chinese, such that they dared not
sit themselves in their shops with a leg tucked under, as
was customary, for fear they would lack time to stretch it
to start running. At eleven in the morning, even though
the sun continued in its course and His Excellency, the
Capitan General, did not appear at the head of his
victorious cohorts, the restlessness had nevertheless
increased. The friars who often frequented Quiroga's
bazaar had not appeared, and this sign presaged terrible
disasters. If the sun had risen square and the Christs
dressed in pantaloons, Quiroga would not have been so
alarmed. He would have taken the sun for a *liampó* and
the sacred images for gamblers of *chapdiquí*[1] who had been
left without a *camisa*, but for the friars not to come when,
precisely, the latest goods had just arrived!

By command of a provincial friend of his, Quiroga
prohibited admission into his houses of *liampó* and *chapdiquí*
to every *Indio* not of previous acquaintance; the future
Chinese consul feared that they themselves would take
possession of the amounts the wretches lost there. After
laying out his bazaar in such a way that it could be closed
rapidly in a moment of danger, he had himself escorted
by a veteran guard along the short road which separated
his house from that of Simoun. Quiroga found that occasion
the most propitious for using the rifles and shells which
he had in his warehouse in the manner that the jeweler
had indicated: it was to expect that in the following days

searches would be undertaken, and thus how many
terrified people would not give all their savings! That was
a diversion of the old *carabineros* or excise collectors: to
slip underneath houses unlicensed tobacco and contraband
leaves, simulate a search afterwards, then oblige the hapless
owner to pay a bribe or fines. Except that the art was
being perfected and, tobacco now being open to trade,[2]
the game would now recur with contraband arms.

But Simoun did not want to see anyone, and had the
Chinese Quiroga told to leave things as they were. With
this he went to see Don Custodio to ask him whether he
should arm his bazaar or not, but Don Custodio did not
receive him either. Studying a defense strategy in case he
found himself under siege, he thought of Ben Zayb, to ask
him for news. Upon finding him armed to the teeth and
using two loaded revolvers as paperweights, Quiroga took
leave as fast as he could, locked himself up in his house
and went to bed on the pretext that he felt ill.

At four o'clock in the afternoon there was no longer
talk of simple posters. Rumors were whispered of an
understanding between the students and the fugitives of
San Mateo. It was ascertained that in a *panciteria* they had
pledged under oath to surprise the city; there was talk of
German boats outside the bay to support the movement;
of a group of young men who, under the guise of protest
and Hispanism, were going to Malacañang to place
themselves at the orders of the *General*, and who were
arrested upon the discovery that they were armed.

Providence had saved His Excellency, preventing him
from receiving those precocious criminals, for he was at
that time meeting with the Provincials, the Vice-Rector
and Padre Irene, who had been delegated by Padre Salvi.
There was much truth to these rumors, if we are to believe

Padre Irene, who in the afternoon went to visit Capitan Tiago. According to him, certain personages had counselled His Excellency to take advantage of the occasion to inspire terror and to give once and for all a good lesson to the petty subversives.[3]

"A number of them shot," one said, "some two dozens of reformists sent into exile immediately and in the silence of the night; that would extinguish forever the steam of the discontented!"

"No," replied another who had a kind heart, "it is enough for the troops to run through the streets, the battalion of cavalry for example, with sabers unsheathed; sufficient to drag along some cannons, that is enough! The people are very timid and all will enter their houses."

"No, no," insinuated another; "this is the occasion to do away with the enemy. It is not enough that they enter their houses, they should be made to come out like evil humors by means of poultices. If they do not decide to arm mutinies, they should be incited by means of agents provocateurs...I am of the opinion that the troops should be armed, and yet appear careless and indifferent, so that they may be emboldened and in any disturbance, we shall be on top, and—action!"

"The end justifies the means," said another. "Our end is our holy religion and the integrity of the Mother Country. Proclaim a state of siege, and at the least disturbance arrest all the rich and *ilustrados*...to clean up the country."

"If I had not arrived on time to counsel moderation," added Padre Irene, addressing himself to Capitan Tiago, "blood would surely now be running through the streets. I was thinking of you, Capitan...The violent faction could not get much from the *General* and were missing Simoun...Ah! if Simoun had not become ill..."

With the arrest of Basilio and the search made afterwards among his books and papers, Capitan Tiago had taken a turn for the worse. Now came Padre Irene to augment his terror with hair-raising tales. The hapless one was seized by an indescribable terror which he manifested, first by a slight shudder which rapidly became acute until it prevented him from speaking. Eyes staring and brow sweating, he clutched at Padre Irene's arm, tried to raise himself but could not, and launching two groans, fell heavily on his pillow. Capitan Tiago's eyes stared, and he frothed at the mouth: he was dead. Terrified, Padre Irene fled, and because the corpse had clutched at him, in his flight he dragged it out of the bed, leaving it in the middle of the room.

By nightfall the panic reached its maximum. Several incidents had taken place, leading the timid to believe in agents provocateurs.

On the occasion of a christening some *cuartos* were thrown to the children and naturally there was some tumult at the church door. By chance a daring officer happened to pass by and, somewhat preoccupied, mistook the commotion for subversion, and set out to attack the urchins. Sword in hand, he entered the temple, and if he had not entangled himself in the curtain hanging from the choir loft, he would not have left inside the church anything with a head. The cowardly saw this and took flight, thinking that the revolution had begun; it was just a matter of seconds. The few stores that were still open were hurriedly closed; some Chinese left bolts of cloth outside, and not a few women lost their slippers as they fled across the streets. Fortunately there was not more than one wounded and a few bruised, among whom was the soldier himself, who had stumbled while battling with the curtain, which to him smelt of the mantle of subversion. Such prowess gave him renown, and a renown so pure that would to God all fame were gained in analogous ways! Mothers would mourn less and the earth would be better populated!

In one suburb, the neighbors surprised two individuals who were burying weapons under a wooden house. The barrio was agitated; the inhabitants wanted to pursue the strangers to kill them and deliver them to the authorities, but a neighbor pacified them, saying that it was enough to deliver to the tribunal the corpus delicti. They were for the most part old shotguns, which would surely have hurt the first to wish to use them.

"Well then," said a vainglorious one, "if they want us to rebel, forward!"

But the bold one was assaulted with blows and cuffs, pinched by the women as if he were the owner of the shotguns.

In Ermita the events were even more serious, though not as clamorous, in spite of some shots heard. A certain employee, armed to the teeth, saw at nightfall a dark mass near his house, which he heedlessly took for a student and fired at it twice. The mass turned out afterward to be a veteran guard and they buried him and, *pax Christi! Mutis!* peace of Christ! Silence!

In Dulumbayan various shots also resounded, one of which felled a poor deaf old man who had not heard the *quien vive* (who goes there?) of the sentinel, and a pig which heard it, and did not answer *España*. The old man was not easily buried for he had nothing with which to pay for the funeral rites; the pig was eaten.

In Manila, in a confection shop which was near the University and well-frequented by students, people commented on the arrests in this manner:

"Have they catched *ba* Tadeo?" asked the proprietress.

"*Aba, ñora,*" answered a student who lived in the Parían, "*pusilau ya*! shot already!"

"*Pusilau! Naku! no pa ta* paid to me his debt."

"Ay, no talk voice *puelte,* strong *ñora, baká pa di quedá,* you may be yet taken as accomplice. Already I burn the book that they gave *prestau,* lent to me. *Baká pa di* search and it found, *anda,* be ready, *ñora!*"

"*Ta quedá dice,* you say, prisoner Isagani?"

"*Loco-loco,* fool-fool, also that Isagani," said the student, indignant. "*No sana di cogí con ele,* they not catch him, *ta andá pa presentá,* but he go present himself. *O, bueno ga,* serves him right, *que topá rayo con ele,* let lightning strike with him! *Siguro pusilau,* shot for sure!"

The woman shrugged her shoulders.

"With me *no ta debí nada*! no owe nothing! *Y cosa di jasé Paulita?* And what's the matter to Paulita?"

"*No di faltá novio,* no lack lover, *ñora. Siguro di llorá,* maybe she cry a little, *luego di casá,* after marry Spaniard!"

The night was one of the saddest ever. In the homes, the rosary was said and pious women offered strong *padrenuestros* (Our Fathers) and requiems to the souls of relatives and friends. By eight o'clock passersby could scarcely be seen. From time to time only the galloping of a horse could be heard, whose flanks were slapped scandalously by a saber, then whistles of *guardias,* coaches passing at full speed as if chased by subversive hordes.

Yet, not everywhere did terror reign.

At the silversmithy where Plácido Penitente lodged, they were also talking of the events and discussing among themselves with a certain freedom.

"I do not believe in those posters!" said a worker

grown thin and withered from working a blowpipe. "For me it is the doing of Padre Salvi."

"Ehem, ehem!" coughed the master silversmith, a very prudent man, who feared to seem a coward, and did not dare stop the conversation. The good man contented himself with coughing, winking at his aide and gazing toward the street as if to tell him: "They may be spying on us!"

"Because of the operetta!" continued the worker.

"Oho!" exclaimed one who had the face of an idiot, "I told you so! That is why..."

"Ehem," replied a clerk in a tone of compassion. "That of the posters is true, Chichoy, but I will give you its explanation."

And he added in a mysterious voice:

"It is a trick of the Chinaman Quiroga!"

"Ehem, ehem!" again coughed the *maestro*, shifting the *sapá* of *buyo* from one cheek to the other.

"Believe me, Chichoy, the Chinaman Quiroga! I heard it at the office!"

"*Naku*, seguro pues! perhaps!" exclaimed the simpleton, believing it beforehand.

"Quiroga," continued the clerk, "has a hundred thousand pesos in Mexican silver at the bay. How to get them in? Well, very simple; he invents the posters, taking advantage of the question of the students, and while the whole world is in uproar, pum! grease the officials' palms and the chests come in."

"*Justo, justo*! Da's right, da's right!" exclaimed the credulous one, striking a fist on the table. "*Justo! Por eso palá*, Da's right! Da's why so! the Chinaman Quiroga...*por eso, da*'s why!"

And he had to silence himself, not knowing what to say about the Chinaman Quiroga.

"And we will pay for the broken plates..?" asked Chichoy indignant.

"Ehem, ehem, ehhhem!" coughed the silversmith, hearing footsteps approaching from the street.

In fact, the footsteps were at hand, and everyone kept quiet in the smithy.

"San Pascual Bailon is a great saint," said the silversmith hypocritically in a loud voice, winking at the others; "San Pascual Bailon..."

At that moment Plácido Penitente appeared, accompanied by the pyrotechnist whom we had earlier seen receiving orders from Simoun. Everybody surrounded the recent arrivals, asking about the latest news. "I have not been able to talk to the prisoners," replied Plácido, "There are about thirty!"

"Be careful!" added the pyrotechnist, exchanging a knowing look with Plácido. "They say that tonight there is going to be a slaughter."

"Ha! Thunderation!" exclaimed Chichoy; he searched with his eyes for a weapon, saw none, and took up his blowpipe.

The *maestro* sat down; his legs were shaking. The credulous one saw himself already beheaded, and sobbed beforehand for the fate of his family.

"Oh no!" said the clerk. "There is not going to be a slaughter! The counselor of"—he made an enigmatic motion— "fortunately is ill."

"Simoun!"

"Ehem, ehem, ehhhem!"

Plácido and the pyrotechnist exchanged another look.

"If he had not gotten sick..."

"A revolution feigned," remarked the pyrotechnist casually, lighting a cigarette above the chimney of the *quinqué*, "and what shall we do then?"

"Well, make it real then, now that they are going to slaughter us..."

"The violent cough that seized the silversmith prevented the rest of the statement from being heard. Chichoy must have said terrible things because he made murderous gestures with his blowpipe and assumed the face of a Japanese tragedian.

"You should say that he feigns sick because he is afraid to go out! As may be seen..."

The *maestro* was attacked by another very violent cough and ended by asking all to retire.

"Nevertheless, prepare yourselves, prepare yourselves," said the pyrotechnist. "If they want to force us to kill or be killed..."

Another cough returned to attack the hapless patron, and the workmen or tradesmen retired to their homes carrying with them hammers and saws and other implements more or less cutting, more or less bruising, disposed to sell lives dearly. Plácido and the pyrotechnist went out again.

"Prudence, prudence!" counselled the *maestro* in a tearful voice.

You will now have to take care of my widow and orphans," begged the credulous one in an even more tearful voice.

The wretch already saw himself riddled with bullets and buried.

That night the sentries at the city gates were replaced by peninsular artillerymen and the following day, at the first rays of daylight, Ben Zayb, who ventured to take a morning walk to look over the state of the walls, found on a slope near the walls of the Luneta the corpse of a young *india*, half-naked and abandoned. Ben Zayb was horrified and, after prodding it with his cane and looking towards the direction of the gates, continued on his way, thinking of writing a sentimental little tale about it. In the days that followed, however, no reference appeared in the newspapers, which occupied themselves with accidents and falls caused by banana peels and, because of lack of news Ben Zayb himself had to make a lengthy comment on a certain cyclone in America which had destroyed towns and caused the death of more than two thousand people. Among other splendid things he said:

"*The sentiment of charity* more latent in Catholic countries than in others, and the memory of Him, who with the same motive sacrificed himself for *humanity, moves* us (sic) to compassion over the tragedies of our kind and to give thanks that *in this country,* so tormented by cyclones, there are no scenes so desolating as those which must have been witnessed by the inhabitants of the United States!"

Horatius did not allow the occasion to pass, and, likewise without mentioning the dead, nor the poor murdered *india,* nor the abuses, answered him in his *Pirotecnia:*

"After so much charity and such humanity, Fray Ibañez, I mean Ben Zayb, reduces himself to pleading for the Philippines.

But it is understandable.

Because he is not Catholic and the sentiment of charity is most latent, etc., etc., etc."

- 29 -
Last Words about Capitan Tiago

Talis vita finis ita.

His end befitted his life.

Capitan Tiago had a good end, that is, a funeral equalled by few. It is true that the parish priest remarked to Padre Irene that Capitan Tiago had died without confession, but the worthy cleric, laughing mockingly, rubbed the tip of his nose and replied:

"Come on, don't give me that! If we are to deny funeral rites to those who die without confession, we should forget the *De Profundis*. Those rigidities, as you well know, are observed when the impenitent is also insolvent, but with Capitan Tiago!...Off with you! you have buried Chinese infidels, and with a requiem mass!"

Capitan Tiago had named Padre Irene administrator and testamentary executor and bequeathed his estate partly to Santa Clara, partly to the Pope, to the Archbishop, to the Religious Orders, leaving twenty pesos for the tuition of needy students. This last clause was dictated at the suggestion of Padre Irene as protector of studious youths. Capitan Tiago had annulled a legacy of twenty-five pesos which he was leaving Basilio, in view of the young man's ungrateful conduct in the last days, but Padre Irene revived it and announced that he would take it from his own pocket and his conscience.

In the house of the deceased where old acquaintances and friends gathered the following day, there was much talk of a miracle. It was said that at the particular moment when he was dying, the soul of Capitan Tiago had appeared to the nuns surrounded by radiant light. God had saved him, thanks to the numerous Masses that he had ordered said, and to the pious legacies. The rumor was commented on, was embroidered, acquired details, and no one placed it in doubt. Capitan Tiago's attire, a swallow-tailed coat, of course, was described, his cheek lumped with the *sapá* of *buyo*[1], without forgetting the pipe for smoking opium or the fighting cock. The *sacristan mayor*, who was among the group, affirmed this gravely with his head, and visualized that he in death would turn up with his cup of *tajú blanco* or curdled soybean milk, for without that refreshing breakfast he could not conceive happiness in heaven nor on earth.

On this theme, and not being able to speak of the events of the preceding day, and since there were gamblers around, there sallied forth very rambling opinions. Conjectures were made about whether or not Capitan Tiago would invite St. Peter to a *soltada*,[2] whether they would exchange bets; whether the game cocks would be immortal, or invulnerable, and in this case, who would be the referee, who would win and so on, discussions to the taste of those who establish sciences, theories, systems based on a text which they deem infallible, revealed or dogmatic. Furthermore, they quoted passages from novenas, books of miracles, sayings of priests, descriptions of the heavens and other odds and ends. Don Primitivo, the philosopher, was in his glory citing opinions of theologians.

"Because nobody can lose," he said with much authority. "To lose would occasion displeasure, and in heaven there can be no quarrel."

"But someone has to win," the gambler Aristorenas protested; "in winning is the bounty!"

"Well, very simple, both win!"

This was incomprehensible to Martin Aristorenas, who had spent his life in the cockpit and had always seen one cock lose and the other win; at most there would be a tie, and in vain did Don Primitivo try to explain in Latin. Martin Aristorenas shook his head, and yet the Latin of Don Primitivo was easy to understand. He talked of *an gallus talisainus, acuto tari armatus, an gallus beati Petri bulikus sasabungus sit*, etc., until he decided to use the argument of which many avail themselves, to silence and convince.

"You are going to be damned, *amigo* Martin; you are falling into heresy. *Cave ne cadas!* (Be careful you do not fall!) Now I am not going to play *monte* with you and we will not be joint bettors. You deny the omnipotence of God, *peccatum mortale!* (mortal sin!) You deny the evidence of the Holy Trinity: three are one and one is three! Be warned! You indirectly deny that two natures, two understandings, and two wills can have only one memory! Take care! *Quicumque non crederit Anathema sit!* (He who does not believe let him be anathema!)"

Martin Aristorenas grew ashen and he trembled. The Chinaman Quiroga, who had been listening attentively to the argument, with much deference offered the philosopher a magnificent cigar and asked him in an assuaging voice: "*Sigulo, puele contalata aliendo galela con kilisto, ja?* (Sulely can contlact lent cackpit with a Klist, ha?)[3] *Cuando mia muele, mia contalatista, ja?* (When meselp die meselp contlactol, ha?)"

In other groups, they were talking more of the deceased; at least they discussed the attire they were to put on him. Capitan Tinong proposed the habit of a Franciscan; precisely, he had one, old, threadbare and patched, a precious piece which, according to the friar who gave it to him as alms in exchange for thirty-six pesos, would save the corpse from the flames of hell, citing in support various pious anecdotes taken from the books distributed by the curates. Although he held this relic in great esteem, Capitan Tinong was disposed to part with it for the sake of his intimate friend whom he was not able to visit during his illness. But a tailor objected with good reason, saying that, since the nuns saw Capitan Tiago ascending to heaven in a full dress suit, then in a frock coat he had to be dressed here on earth, and there was no need of embalming or water-proofing; he would go in a dress suit as if going to a ball, to a fiesta and nothing else would be expected in the skies...and look! incidentally he had one ready which he could cede for thirty-two pesos, four less than the Franciscan habit, because with Capitan Tiago he did not want to make any profit. He was his customer in life, and now would be his patron in heaven! But Padre Irene, administrator and testamentary executor, rejected one and the other proposals and ordered the corpse to be attired in any of his old suits, saying with holy unction that God does not take note of attire.

The funeral rites were therefore of the very first class.

There were responses in the house, on the street; three friars officiated as though one were not enough for such a great soul. They performed all the rites and ceremonies possible, and it is well known that others were improvised, having *extras* as in theater presentations. That was a delight: much incense was burned, much singing in Latin, much holy water expended—Padre Irene, in tribute to his friend, sang the *Dies Irae*, in falsetto from the choir—and the neighbors suffered real headaches from so much tolling for the dead.

Doña Patrocinio,[4] Capitan Tiago's ancient rival in religiosity, truly wanted to die the next day, so as to order even more pompous funeral rites. The pious old woman could not suffer the fact that he, whom she had always vanquished in life, would, upon dying, be resurrected with so much pomp. Yes, she wished to die and it seemed that she could hear the exclamations of the people who would present their responses:

"This indeed is a funeral! This indeed is knowing how to die, Doña Patrocinio!"

- 30 -
Juli

The death of Capitan Tiago and Basilio's imprisonment were soon known in the province, and to the credit of the simple inhabitants of San Diego, we will say that they felt more for the latter and spoke almost only of it. As was to be expected, the news took on various forms, was given sad, even dreadful details, that which was not understood was explained, the gaps were filled with conjectures. These passed for deeds done, and the phantasms thus created terrorized their very creators.

In the town of Tiani, it was said that, at the very least, the young man was to be exiled and very probably murdered during the trip. The timorous and pessimistic were not satisfied with this and spoke of gallows and councils of war. January was a fatal month; in January *those in Cavite* who, despite their being priests, had been hanged,[1] so a poor Basilio with neither protection nor friendships...

"I told him so!" sighed the Justice of the Peace, as if he had at some time given Basilio advice. "I told him so..."

"It was to be expected!" added Sister Penchang: "He would enter the Church and when he saw the holy water somewhat dirty, would not cross himself. He talked of germs and diseases, *aba*, chastisement of God! He deserved it! As if holy water could transmit diseases! Quite the contrary, *aba!*"

And she recounted how she had been cured of indigestion by moistening her navel with holy water at the same time that she was reciting the *Sanctus Deus*; and recommended the remedy to those present in case they should suffer from dysentery or flatulence or when an epidemic raged, except that then they should pray in Spanish:

> *Santo Dios*
> *Santo fuerte*
> *Santo inmortal*
> *Libranos Señor de la peste*
> *Y de todo mal.*

> God Most Holy
> God most powerful
> God immortal
> Deliver us Lord from pestilence
> And from all evil.

"The remedy is infallible, but the holy water must be brought to the part that is sore or diseased," she said.

But many men did not believe in these things nor did they attribute the imprisonment of Basilio to God's chastisement. Neither did they believe in insurrections nor in the posters, knowing the very peaceful and prudent character of the student, and preferred to attribute it to the vengeance of the friars, for his having rescued from servitude Juli, daughter of a *tulisan*, mortal enemy of a certain powerful Order. And since they had quite a negative idea of the morality of that same Order and could recall petty revenges, the conjecture was believed the most probable and justifiable.

"I did well in throwing her out of my house!" said Sister Penchang. "I do not want to earn the displeasure of the friars, so I urged her to look for money."

The truth was that she resented Juli's liberty. Juli prayed and fasted for her, and if she had stayed a little longer she would have done penance as well. Why, if the *curas* prayed for us and Christ died for our sins, should not Juli do the same for Sister Penchang?

When news reached the hut where poor Juli and her grandfather lived, the young woman needed to have it told to her twice. She stared at Sister Balî who was the one who said it, as if uncomprehending, unable to coordinate her ideas; her ears hummed; she felt a heaviness in her heart and a vague presentiment that the event would have a disastrous effect on her future. Nevertheless she wanted to clutch at a ray of hope; she smiled, she thought that Sister Balî was telling her a joke, a rather grave one, and she would forgive her if she would say it was one. But Sister Balî made a cross with her thumb and index finger, and kissed her as proof that she was telling the truth. Then the smile vanished from the lips of the young woman; she turned pale, horribly pale, felt her strength abandon her and for the first time in her life she lost consciousness, and fainted.

When by means of slaps, pinches, splashes of water,

crucifixes and applications of blessed fronds the young woman returned to herself and realized her situation, tears fell silently from her eyes, drop by drop, without sobs, without lament, without complaint! She thought of Basilio who had no protector other than Capitan Tiago, and who, with him dead, was now left completely without protection, and without freedom. In the Philippines it is a known fact that patrons are needed in everything, from the time one is baptized until one dies, to obtain justice, secure a passport or exploit whatever industry.[2] And since it was said that his imprisonment was due to vengeance on her account and that of her father, the maiden's sorrow bordered on desperation. Now it was her turn to free him as he had rescued her from servitude; an inner voice suggested the idea and presented to her imagination a horrible remedy.

"Padre Camorra, the *cura*," said the voice.

Juli bit her lips and was left immersed in gloomy thought.

In the wake of her father's crimes, her grandfather had been imprisoned, the authorities hoping by that means to make his son appear. The only one who had been able to secure his release was Padre Camorra, and Padre Camorra had shown himself unhappy with words of gratitude and, with his usual bluntness, had asked for sacrifices...Since then Juli had tried to avoid meeting him, but the priest made her kiss his hand, caught her by the nose, by the cheeks, jested with her with winks and laughing, laughing, pinched her. Juli was the cause of the beating which the good *cura* administered to some young men who had been going around the barrio serenading the girls. The malicious ones, seeing her pass sad and dejected, said so that she would hear:

"If she wished, Cabesang Tales would be pardoned."

The young woman reached her home gloomy, her eyes wandering.

Juli had changed greatly. She had lost her gaiety; no one now saw her smile. She scarcely spoke, and seemed afraid to even look at her own face. One day she was seen in the town with a big spot of soot on her forehead, she, who was wont to go ever trim and composed. Once she asked Sister Balî whether those who committed suicide went to hell.

"For sure!" replied the woman, and she described the place as though she had been in it.

With the imprisonment of Basilio, the simple and grateful relatives proposed to make all sorts of sacrifices to save the young man, but since among all of them they could scarcely raise thirty pesos, Sister Balî, as usual, had the best idea.

"What we should do is to ask the counsel of the clerk," she said.

To these simple folk, the municipal clerk was what the oracle of Delphi was to the ancient Greeks.

"Give him a *real* and a cigar," she added, "and he tells you enough law to bloat the heads of those listening to him. If you have a peso he will save you even if you were at the foot of the scaffold. When they threw my neighbor Simon into jail and beat him up for not being able to say anything on a robbery which was committed near his house, *aba*! for two *reales* and a string of garlic, the clerk saved him. And I saw Simon could scarcely walk and had to stay in bed for at least a month. Ay! his rear rotted *aba*! and he died as a result."

The advice of Sister Balî was accepted and she herself undertook to talk with the clerk; Juli gave her four reales and added pieces of dried meat of the deer her grandfather had hunted. Tandang Selo had taken to hunting once more.

But the clerk could do nothing. The prisoner was in Manila and his influence did not reach that far.

"If he were in the capital at least, notwithstanding...." he said, making a show of his influence.

The clerk knew very well that his clout did not pass beyond the boundaries of Tiani, but it suited him to keep his prestige and be left with the venison.

"But I can give you some sound advice, and that is for you to go with Juli to the Juez de Paz or Justice of Peace. It is necessary that Juli goes."

The Juez de Paz was a very brusque man, but seeing Juli, perhaps, he would be less rude: herein lay the wisdom of the advice.

With much gravity the *Señor Juez* listened to Sister Balî, who did the talking, not without taking a look now and then at the maiden whose eyes were downcast and who was very much embarrassed. People would say of her that she was much interested in Basilio; the people did not remember her debt of gratitude and that he had been imprisoned, it was said, because of her. After belching three or four times, because the *Señor Juez* had this ugly habit, he said that the only person who could save Basilio was Padre Camorra, *in case he would want to*—and he looked at the young woman with much meaning. He advised her to speak to the *cura* in person.

"You already know the influence he has. He got your grandfather out of jail...A report of his would be enough to exile a newborn babe or save from death one condemned to hang."

Juli said nothing, but Sister Balî regarded the advice as if she had read it in a novena. She was ready to accompany her to the parish house. Precisely, she was going to take for alms a scapular in exchange for four fat *reales.*

But Juli shook her head and did not want to go to the *convento.* Sister Bali, who thought she could guess the reason—Padre Camorra was called *si cabayo*³ or the stallion by another name and was very frolicsome—reassured her.

"You have nothing to fear if I go with you!" she said. "Have you not read in *Tandang Basio's* booklet given by the Curate, that young women should go to the *convento,* even without the knowledge of their elders, to report what goes on in their homes? *Aba*! That booklet was printed with permission from the Archbishop, *aba!*"

Juli, impatient and anxious to cut the conversation short, begged the old woman to go if she wished, but the *Señor Juez* remarked, belching, that the supplications of a young face could move more than those of an old one, that Heaven poured its dew on fresh flowers in more abundance than over withered ones. The metaphor was beautifully perverse.

Juli did not answer, and both women went down the stairs. In the street the young woman obstinately refused to go to the *convento,* and both returned to their barrio. Sister Bali, who felt offended by Juli's lack of confidence in her company, revenged herself by delivering a long sermon.

The truth was that the young woman could not take that step without condemning herself, aside from being condemned by men and by God! She had been made to hear several times, with or without reason, that if she made that sacrifice her father would be pardoned, and nevertheless she had refused, despite the cries of her conscience reminding her of her filial duty. And now must

she make it for Basilio, her lover? That would be to fall to
the sound of mockery and laughter from all creation!
Basilio himself would despise her; no, never! She would
hang herself or leap from some precipice first. At any rate
she was already damned for being a bad daughter.

Poor Juli! She had to suffer besides all the
recriminations of her relatives who, not being aware of
what could take place between her and Padre Camorra,
laughed at her fears. Would Padre Camorra deign to notice
a peasant, with so many in town? And the good women
cited the names of single girls, rich and beautiful, more or
less unfortunate. And, meanwhile, what if they shot
Basilio?

Juli covered her ears, stared around her as if looking
for a voice that might speak for her; looked at her
grandfather, but he was silent, his attention riveted on his
hunting spear.

That night she hardly slept at all. Dreams and
nightmares, now mournful, now bloody, danced before
her sight and she would wake often, bathed in cold sweat.
She imagined hearing shots, seeing her father, her father
who had done so much for her, fighting in the forest,
hunted like an animal because she had hesitated to save
him. And her father's figure was transformed and she
recognized Basilio, dying and looking at her reproachfully.
The unfortunate girl would rise, would pray, would weep,
invoke her mother, death, and there was a moment,
overcome by terror, in which, had it not been night, she
would have run straight to the *convento*, happen what may.

Day came and her sad presentiments, the terrors of
the shadows, were partly dissipated. Light brought her
hope. But the afternoon news was terrible; there was talk
of musketry, and the night for the young woman was

fearful. In her despair she decided to yield herself as soon as day dawned and then kill herself afterwards: anything, rather than endure such tortures!

But the dawn again brought new hope, and the young woman did not want to leave the house, nor to go to the Church. She was afraid to give in.

And so several days passed: praying and cursing, calling upon God and wishing death. The day was a respite; Juli was confident of a miracle. The reports coming from Manila, although they were magnified, said that of the prisoners, some had secured their freedom, thanks to patrons and to influences...Someone had to be sacrificed, who would it be? Juli shuddered and returned home biting her fingernails. And thus night came, during which her fears acquired double proportions and seemed to convert themselves into realities.

Juli feared to sleep, feared to slumber, because her dream was one continuous nightmare. Reproachful looks would cross her eyelids just as soon as they were closed, complaints and laments would pierce her ears. She would see her father roaming, hungry without respite or rest; she would see Basilio dying on the way, wounded by two gunshots, as she had seen in the corpse of a neighbor who was killed while the *guardia civil* escorted him. And she would see the bonds which had penetrated his flesh; she would see the blood issuing forth from his mouth and she would hear Basilio say to her: "Save me! Save me! You alone can save me!" Then a burst of laughter would resound, she would turn her eyes and would see her father looking at her with eyes full of reproach. And Juli would awaken and sit up on her mat, would draw her hand over her forehead to pull back her hair; cold sweat, like the sweat of death, would dampen her.

"Mother! Mother!" she sobbed.

And meanwhile, those who were so blithely disposing of the destinies of people, he who commanded legalized murders, he who violated justice and made use of the law to maintain force, were sleeping in peace.

At last a traveler arrived from Manila and reported how all the prisoners had been set at liberty except for Basilio, who had no protector. In Manila it was said, added the traveler, that the young man would be exiled to the Carolines, having been made to sign a petition beforehand in which he declared that he had voluntarily asked for it.[4] The traveler had seen the steamer that was going to take him there.

That news completely ended the vacillations of the young woman whose mind, besides, was already sufficiently worked up thanks to the many sleepless nights and her horrible illusions. Pale and with looks astray, she looked for Sister Balî, and in a frightened voice told her that she was ready, and asked if she could accompany her.

Sister Balî was pleased, and endeavored to reassure her, but Juli was not listening to her, and seemed only in a hurry to reach the *convento*. She had fixed herself up, put on her best clothes and even appeared to be in high spirits. She talked a great deal, although somewhat incoherently.

They set out to go. Juli was walking ahead and was impatient because her companion lingered behind. But when they were nearing town the nervous energy deserted her; little by little she became silent, lost her decisiveness, shortened her pace and then fell back. Sister Balî had to urge her.

"We are going to get there late!" she said.

Juli followed pale, with downcast eyes, not daring to raise them. She thought that the whole world was looking

at her and pointing a finger at her. An obscene name hissed
in her ears, but still she paid no heed and continued her
way. Notwithstanding, when she saw the *convento*, she
held back and began to tremble.

"Let us go back to the barrio, let us go home," she
pleaded, detaining her companion.

Sister Balî had to clutch her by the arm and to half-
drag her, soothing her and talking to her of the books of
the friars. She was not going to abandon her, she had
nothing to fear: Padre Camorra had other things in mind;
Juli was nothing but a poor peasant...

But upon arriving at the door of the parochial house,
Juli refused tenaciously to go up and she clutched at
the wall.

"No, no!" she begged, full of terror; "oh, no, no! Have
mercy...!"

"But what a fool..."

Sister Bali pushed her gently. Juli resisted, pale, her
features contorted. Her look seemed to say that she saw
death before her.

"All right! Let us go back, if you do not want to!"
finally exclaimed, irritated, the good woman who did not
believe in any real danger. Padre Camorra, despite his
reputation, would not dare do anything in front of her.

"Let them take to exile poor Basilio; let them shoot
him on the way, saying that he wanted to escape!" she
added. "When he is dead, then remorse will come. As for
myself, I owe him no favors. Of me he will not be able
to complain!"

That was the decisive stroke. Before this reproach,
with wrath, with despair, as one who kills herself, Juli
closed her eyes so as not to see the abyss into which she
was going to hurl herself, and resolutely entered the

convento. A sigh that sounded like the rattle of death escaped from her lips. Sister Balî followed, giving her warnings...

At night people spoke in hushed voices and with much mystery about various events which had taken place that afternoon.

A young woman had leapt from a window of the *convento*, falling upon some stones and killing herself. Almost at the same time another woman had rushed out of the door and run into the streets shouting and screaming like a madwoman. The prudent neighbors dared not mention names, and many mothers pinched their daughters for letting out some talk that could compromise them.

Later, but very much later, at fall of dusk, an old man came from a barrio and knocked at the door of the *convento*, which was closed and guarded by *sacristanes*. The old man knocked with his fists, with his head, emitting stifled cries, inarticulate as those of a mute, until he was thrown out by clubs and shoves. Then he made his way to the house of the *gobernadorcillo*, but was told that the *gobernadorcillo* was not in, that he was at the *convento*. He went to the *juez de paz*, but the *juez de paz* was not there either; he had been called to the *convento*; he went to the *teniente mayor* who was not in, but was in the *convento*; he went to the barracks, the *teniente* of the Guardia Civil was in the *convento*...The old man returned to his barrio crying like a baby. His sobs were heard in the night; men bit their lips, women clasped their hands and the dogs slunk into their houses fearful, their tails between their legs.

"Ah, God, ah God!" said a poor woman emaciated from fasting: "before you there are no rich, there are no poor, there are no white there are no black...You will grant us justice!"

"Yes," her husband answered her, "as long as that God they preach is not pure invention, a fraud. They are the first not to believe in Him!"

At eight o'clock in the evening, it was said that more than seven friars coming from neighboring towns gathered in the *convento* and held a *junta*. The following day Tandang Selo disappeared forever from the barrio, taking with him his hunting spear.

- 31 -
The High Official

L'Espagne et sa vertu, l'Espagne et sa grandeur
Tout s'en va!

Spain and her virtue, Spain and her grandeur
All that is lost!
–Victor Hugo

The newspapers in Manila were so preoccupied with the report of a celebrated murder committed in Europe, with the panegyrics and bombast of various preachers in the capital, with the success, each time more clamorous, of the French Operetta, that they could scarcely devote one or the other article to the misdeeds committed in the provinces by a band of *tulisanes* led by a terrible and fierce chieftain who was called *Matanglawin* or Hawkeye.[1] Only when the victim was a *convento* or a Spaniard would copious articles come out, giving fearful details and asking for a state of siege, forceful measures and so forth. So it was that they neither occupied themselves with what occurred in the town of Tiani, nor made any allusions or hints. In private circles something was bruited about, but everything was so confused, so uncertain, so inconsistent, that the name of the victim was not even known, and those who showed the greatest interest, forgot about it soon, believing there must have been some settlement with the family or offended relatives. The one thing known for certain was that Padre Camorra had to leave town and transfer to another, or to remain for some time in the *convento* in Manila.

"Poor Padre Camorra!" exclaimed Ben Zayb, passing himself off as generous. "He was so gay, he had such a good heart!"

It was true that the students had recovered their freedom, thanks to the petitions of their relatives, who did not spare expenses, donations or whatever sacrifice. The first who was seen released was Macaraig, as was to be expected; and the last, Isagani, because Padre Florentino did not reach Manila until a week after the events. Such acts of clemency earned for the Capitan General the epithets of clement and merciful, which Ben Zayb hastened to add to his long list of adjectives.

The only one who did not obtain freedom was poor Basilio—accused, furthermore, of having in his possession prohibited books.[2] We do not know whether this referred to the treatise on Legal Medicine and Toxicology by Dr. Mata, or to the various pamphlets that they found dealing with Philippine affairs, or both things together; the fact is that it was also said that he clandestinely sold prohibited works, and on the hapless fell all the weight of the scales of justice.

It was said that His Excellency had been advised:

"It is necessary that there *be* someone, so that the

prestige of authority may be saved, and let it not be said that we have made so much ado for nothing. Authority before everything. It is necessary that one should remain!

"Only one is left, one who, according to Padre Irene, was a servant of Capitan Tiago's. No one speaks for him..."

"A servant and a student?" asked His Excellency, "well, that one then, let him remain!"

"If you will permit me, Your Excellency," observed the high official, who happened to be present, "but I have been told that this boy is a student of medicine, his professors speak well of him...If he remains prisoner he loses a year, and as this year he finishes..."[3]

The intervention of the high official on behalf of Basilio, instead of doing him good, prejudiced him. Between the official and His Excellency there had been for some time some strain, certain displeasures, augmented by disputes about little things. His Excellency smiled nervously and replied:

"Really? All the more reason that he should remain a prisoner; a year longer in study, instead of doing him harm, will do him good, and be good as well for all those who afterwards fall into his hands. For one does not become a good physician from much practice. All the more reason that he should remain! And then the petty subversive reformers will say that we are not taking care of the country," added His Excellency, laughing sarcastically.

The high official realized his mistake and took to heart the cause of Basilio.

"But this young man seems to me the most innocent of them all," he replied rather timidly.

"They have taken books from him," answered the secretary.

"Yes, works on Medicine and pamphlets written by *Peninsulares*...with pages yet uncut...and what does this mean? Besides, this young man was not at the banquet in the *panciteria*, nor has he meddled in anything...As I said, he is the most innocent..."

"All the better!" exclaimed His Excellency cheerfully, "that way the punishment turns out more salutary and exemplary in that it will infuse more terror! To govern is to work that way, Señor; often one must sacrifice the good of one for the good of many...But I am doing more: from the good of one man I derive the good of all, I preserve the principle of authority so threatened, its prestige is respected and maintained. With this act of mine I correct our own errors and those of the others."

The high official made an effort to restrain himself and, ignoring the allusions, wanted to appeal by another means.

"But Your Excellency, do you not fear...the responsibility?"

"What do I have to fear?" interrupted the General impatiently, "do I not wield discretionary powers? Can I not do what gives me pleasure for a better government of these islands? What have I to fear? Can a servant, perhaps, accuse me before the tribunals and exact responsibility from me? Even though he would have the means, he would first have to pass the Ministry, and the Minister..."

He made a gesture with his hand and burst into laughter.

"The Minister who appointed me, the devil knows where he is, and he will be honored to greet me when I return! The present, that one, I let pass...and the devil take him too... The one who replaces him will find himself so hard up in his new job that he will not bother himself

with trivialities. I, my dear Señor, I have nothing more
than my conscience, I behave according to my conscience,
my conscience is satisfied, and the opinion of this one and
that matters to me two cents worth. My conscience, Señor,
my conscience!"

"Yes, my General, but the country..."

"Tut, tut, tut! The country, what have I got to do with
the country? Have I by chance contracted obligations with
her? Do I owe her my office? Was she the one who had
me elected?"

There was a moment of pause. The high official had
his head bowed. Then, as if he were making a decision, he
raised it, stared at the General fixedly and, pale, somewhat
trembling, said tiredly:

"No matter, my General, that does not matter at all!
Your Excellency has not been chosen by the Filipino people
but by Spain, all the more reason why you should treat
the Filipinos well, so that they would have nothing with
which to reproach Spain! All the more reason, my General!
Your Excellency upon coming here promised to govern
with justice, to seek the welfare..."

"And am I not doing it?" His Excellency asked
exasperatedly, taking a step. "Have I not said to you, Sir,
that I derive from the good of one the good of all? Are
you, Sir, now giving me lessons? If you, Sir, do not
understand my actions, what fault have I? Do I compel
you, perhaps, to share my responsibility?"

"Of course not!" replied the high official, drawing
himself up with pride. "Your Excellency does not compel
me, Your Excellency cannot compel *me*, *me*, to share *your*
responsibility. Mine, I understand in another manner; and
because I have it, I am going to speak since I have held
my peace for a long time. Oh, do not make those gestures,

Your Excellency, because if I have come here with this or that obligation, it does not mean that I abdicate my rights, and that I reduce myself to the part of the slave, without voice or dignity!

"I do not wish Spain to lose this beautiful empire, these eight millions of subjects, submissive and patient, who live on disillusion and hopes; but neither do I wish to soil my hands with their inhuman exploitation. I do not wish it ever to be said that, the slave-trade dismantled, Spain has continued grandly to camouflage it with her banner, perfecting it under the luxury of pompous institutions. No, Spain, to be great, has no need to be a tyrant; Spain suffices unto herself. Spain was greater when she only had her own territory wrested from the clutches of the Moor! I am also a Spaniard, but before a Spaniard, I am a man, and before Spain and above Spain, is her honor. There are the high principles of morality, the eternal principles of immutable justice! Ah, you, Sir, are astonished why I think thus, because you have no idea of the grandeur of the Spanish name, you do not have it, no. You, Sir, identify it with persons, with particular interests. For you the Spaniard can be a pirate, can be an assassin, hypocrite, deceitful, anything, just so he keeps what he has; for me the Spaniard should lose everything, empire, power, riches, all, everything, before honor!

"Ah, my Señor! we protest when we read that might is placed before right, and applaud when in practice we see hypocrisy not only twist it but also place it at its service in order to impose it...By the same token that I love Spain, I am speaking now, and I defy the frown on your brow!

"I do not wish that in the ages to come she be accused of being a stepmother of nations, vampire of peoples, tyrant of small islands, because that would be a horrible mockery of the noble purpose of our ancient kings! How do we comply with their sacred testament? They promised to these islands protection and rectitude, and we play with the lives and liberties of their inhabitants. They promised civilization and we curtail it, fearing that they may aspire to a nobler existence. They promised them light, and we blind their eyes so that they may not see our bacchanalia. They promised to teach them virtue and we foment their vices, and instead of peace, wealth and justice, anguish reigns, commerce dies, and skepticism spreads among the masses. Let us put ourselves in the place of Filipinos and ask ourselves what we would do in their case!

"Ay! in your own silence, Sir, I read the right to rise up; and if things do not improve, they will rebel some day, and with faith that justice will be on their side and with it the sympathy of all just men, of all the patriots of the world! When a people is denied light, home, liberty, justice, goods without which life is not possible and at the same time constitute the patrimony of man, those people have the right to treat those who despoil them as robbers who attack on the street. Distinctions do not matter, exceptions do not matter, there is nothing more than a deed, an expediency, an abuse of authority and all honest men who would not go on the side of the aggrieved make themselves accomplices and stain their consciences."

"Yes, I am not a soldier, and the years have passed, dousing the little fire in my blood, but as I would allow myself to be torn to pieces to defend the integrity of Spain against a foreign invader, or against the unjustified feeble wills in her provinces, so I also assure you, Sir, that I would place myself beside the oppressed Filipinos, because I would prefer to succumb for the trampled rights of humanity than to triumph with the egotistic interests of a nation, even if that nation be called as it is called, Spain!..."

"Do you know when the mail-boat leaves?" coldly asked His Excellency when the high official had finished speaking.

The high official regarded him fixedly, then dropped his head and left the palace in silence.

In the garden he found his carriage, which was waiting for him.

"Someday, when you declare yourselves independent," he said somewhat absentmindedly to the *Indio* lackey who opened the carriage door, "remember that in Spain there was no lack of hearts which beat for you and fought for your rights!"

"Where to, Señor?" replied the lackey who had not understood, and was asking where he had to go.

Two hours later the high official handed in his resignation and announced his intention of returning to Spain aboard the next mail-steamer.[4]

- 32 -

Consequences
of the Posters

In the wake of the events narrated, many mothers called
their sons to leave their studies immediately,[1] and
dedicate themselves to indolence or to agriculture.

When examinations came, suspensions abounded,
and rare was he who passed the course who had pertained
to the notorious association, to which no one returned in
involvement. Pecson, Tadeo, and Juanito Pelaez were all
suspended. The first received the *calabazas* or failures with
his clownish laughter, and promised to enter as a clerk in
whatever court. Tadeo, truant to the end, rewarded himself
with illumination by lighting a bonfire with his books.
The others did not turn out well either, and eventually
had to leave their studies, to the great satisfaction of their
mothers, who had always imagined their sons hanging if
they should come to understand what the books said. Only
Juanito Pelaez suffered the blow badly, having to leave
the classrooms for always for the store of his father, who
already associated him with his business. The truant found

the store less diverting, but his friends, after some time, saw him again with the rounded hump, the sign that he had recovered his good humor.

The wealthy Macaraig, before the disaster, had guarded very well against exposing himself, and having secured a passport by force of money, set sail with haste for Europe: it was said that his Excellency, the Capitan General, in his desire to do good for the good, and solicitous of the comfort of Filipinos, made leaving difficult for anyone who could not prove materially beforehand that he could spend and live with ease in the midst of European cities. Of those we know, the ones who fared best were Isagani and Sandoval. The first passed the course taught by Padre Fernandez and was suspended in the others; the second was able to overwhelm the body of examiners by the might of oratory. Basilio was the only one who neither passed courses, was suspended, nor left for Europe. He remained in Bilibid prison, subjected to interrogations every three days, almost the same since the beginning with nothing newer than a change of interrogators every time, for it seemed that before such culpability all succumbed or fled horrified.

And while documents were retired and dragged along, while the stamped papers multiplied like the plasters of a quack doctor on the body of a hypochondriac, Basilio was apprised in all their details of what had occurred in Tiani, of the death of Juli, and the disappearance of Tandang Selo. Sinong, the beaten-up *cochero* who had conducted him to San Diego and later found himself in Manila, visited him and put him abreast of all the latest.

In the meantime Simoun had recovered his health, at least so the newspapers said. Ben Zayb gave thanks to the "Almighty who watched over such a precious life," and

manifested the hope that the All Highest make it possible
that one day, the criminal be discovered, whose
transgression remained unpunished, thanks to the charity
of the victim, who faithfully observed the words of the
Great Martyr: "*Father, forgive them for they know not what
they do!*" These and other things besides, Ben Zayb said in
print, while by mouth he investigated if the rumor was
true that the opulent jeweler was planning to give a grand
fiesta, a banquet the likes of which had never been seen,
partly to celebrate his recovery, and partly as a farewell to
the country where his fortune had multiplied. It was
rumored, it is certain, that Simoun, having to leave with
the Capitan General whose command was expiring in May,
was making all efforts to secure from Madrid an extension;
and was advising His Excellency to launch a campaign to
have reason for staying, but it was also rumored that His
Excellency, for the first time, had disregarded the counsel
of his favorite, taking it as a question of honor not to
retain for a single day more the power that had been
conceded him, a rumor that fuelled expectation that the
said fiesta was to take place shortly. As for the rest, Simoun
remained unfathomable; he had turned even less
communicative, allowing himself to be seen less, and
smiling mysteriously when they spoke to him of the bruited
party.

"Come on, Mr. Sinbad," Ben Zayb had once told him,
"dazzle us with something, Yankee! Eeea, you owe
something to this country."

"Without a doubt!" he responded with his dry smile.

"You will throw the house out of the window, eh?"

"That is possible, except that I do not have a house..."

"You ought to have bought that of Capitan Tiago
which Señor Pelaez got for nothing."

Simoun had kept silent, and since then was occasionally seen in the store of Don Timoteo Pelaez with whom, it was said, he had associated himself. Weeks after, in the month of April, the rumor spread that Juanito, the son of Don Timoteo, was going to marry Paulita Gomez, the young woman coveted by both nationals and foreigners.

"Some men are fortunate!" said the other envious merchants; "buy a house for nothing, sell profitably his consignment of zinc; associate himself with Simoun; and marry off his son to a rich heiress, call them strokes of fortune that not all honorable men have!"

"If you only knew whence come those strokes of fortune to Señor Pelaez!"

And his tone of voice indicated what he meant.

"And also, I assure you that there will be a fiesta, and *en grande!*" he added with a tone of mystery.

It was certain, in effect, that Paulita was going to marry Juanito Pelaez. Her love for Isagani had vanished like all first loves anchored in poetry and on sentiment. The affair of the posters and imprisonment had despoiled the young man of all his charms. To whom would it have occurred to seek out danger; to wish to share the fate of his companions; to give himself up when the rest of the world was hiding itself and renouncing all complicity? It was quixoticism, madness, which no sensible person in Manila could forgive him; and Juanito had much reason to put him to ridicule, aping him in the moment he went to the civil authorities. Naturally the brilliant Paulita could no longer love a young man who so speciously understood social intercourse, and whom everyone condemned. Then she began to reflect. Juanito was smart, capable, gay, shrewd, the son of a rich merchant of Manila and a Spanish

mestizo besides, or, if Don Timoteo was to be believed, a
full-blooded Spaniard; on the other hand, Isagani was a
provincial *Indio* who dreamt of his forests full of leeches,
of doubtful parentage, with a cleric uncle who would
perhaps be an enemy of the luxury and balls of which she
was very much an *aficionada*. One fine morning she fell to
considering that she had been a great fool in preferring
him to his rival, and from then on all noted the increased
fortunes of Juanito's hunched back. Paulita complied with
the law discovered by Darwin, unconsciously but
rigorously: the female surrendering herself to the fitter
male, to the one who adapts himself to the environment
in which he lives; and to be able to live in Manila there
was no one like Pelaez, who since childhood had had at
his fingertips the grammar of survival.

Lent ended with its Holy Week, with its cortege of
processions and ceremonies, with no novelties except for
a mysterious mutiny by the artillerymen, the cause of
which was never divulged. The houses of light materials
were demolished with the aid of a troop of cavalrymen
ready to charge against the owners in case they should
rise up: there was much weeping and lamentation, but the
matter did not go beyond that. The curious, among them
Simoun, went to see those who were left without a home,
walking indifferent, saying to themselves that henceforth
they could sleep in peace.

Towards the end of April, with all fears forgotten,
Manila occupied itself only with one affair. It was the
fiesta that Don Timoteo was to give on the wedding of his
son, for whom the *General*, gracious and condescending,
had lent himself to be godfather or sponsor. It was said
that Simoun had arranged the matter. The marriage would
be celebrated two days before His Excellency's departure;

he would honor the house and bring a present for the groom. It was rumored that the jeweler would pour out cascades of diamonds, and throw out pearls by the fistful in honor of the son of his associate, and that, unable to give a fiesta in his house because of not having his own and being a bachelor, he would take advantage of the occasion to surprise the Filipino people with a heartfelt farewell. All Manila was preparing itself to be invited: never did anxiety take hold with more vigor than at the thought of not being one of those invited. People vied for the good graces of Simoun, and many a husband, compelled by their spouses, bought iron bars and zinc sheets to make friends with Don Timoteo Pelaez.

- 33 -
The Final Argument

The day came at last. Simoun, since morning, had not left his house, occupied in putting in order his weapons and his jewels. His fabulous treasure was already locked up in the great chest of steel with a canvas cover. There remained a few caskets which contained bracelets and brooches; doubtless, gifts that he expected to give away. He was leaving finally with the Capitan General, who in no way cared to prolong his command, fearful of what people might say. The malicious were insinuating that Simoun dared not stay in the country alone, that, losing his support, he would not want to expose himself to the vengeance of the many exploited and disgraced, even more so because the incoming *General* was said to be a model of rectitude and perhaps, perhaps, might make him return what he had gained. The superstitious *Indios*, on the other hand, believed that Simoun was the Devil who did not want to detach himself from his prey. The pessimists winked maliciously and said:

"The field laid waste, the locust moves on to another part."

Only a few, a very few, smiled and held their peace.

In the afternoon, Simoun had given orders to his servant that if a young man called Basilio presented himself, to make him enter at once. Then he locked himself in his room, apparently lost in deep thought. Since his illness, the jeweler's face had turned harder and gloomier. The furrow between his eyebrows had deepened much. He appeared somewhat stooped: his head no longer held erect, his body bent. He was so engrossed in his thoughts that he did not hear the knocking at the door. The raps were repeated. Simoun started:

"Come in!" he said.

It was Basilio, but *quantum mutatus*, how altered! If the change working in Simoun during the last two months was great, in the young student it was frightful. His cheeks were sunken, his clothes in disarray, his hair unkempt. The sweet melancholic look had disappeared from his eyes, which now blazed with a dark light. It could be said of him that he had died and his corpse had resurrected, horrified at what it had seen in eternity. If not the infamy, its sinister shadow extended throughout his figure. Simoun himself was startled, and felt pity for the hapless one.

Basilio, without a greeting, advanced slowly and, in a voice that made the jeweler shudder, said:

"Señor Simoun, I have been a bad son and a bad brother. I have overlooked the murder of one and the tortures of the other, and God has punished me! Now there remains in me only the will to return evil for evil, crime for crime, violence for violence!"

Simoun listened to him in silence.

"Four months ago," continued Basilio, "you spoke to

me of your plans. I refused to take part. I was wrong; you were right. Three and a half months ago when the revolution was at the point of breaking out, neither did I want to take part, and the movement has failed. In payment of my conduct I have been imprisoned and I owe my freedom only to your intervention. You were right, and now I have come to tell you: arm my hands and let the revolution break out! I am ready to serve you along with the rest of the unfortunates!"

The cloud darkening Simoun's brow suddenly vanished; a gleam of triumph shone in his eyes and, as if he had found what he was searching for, he exclaimed:

"I am right, yes, I am right! and right supports me, Justice is on my side because my cause is that of the unfortunates...Thank you, young man, thank you! You come to dissipate my doubts, to fight my vacillations..."

Simoun had risen and his face was radiant: the ardor that had animated him when, four months before, he explained to Basilio his plans in the forest of his forefathers, reappeared in his features like a red sunset after a cloudy day.

"Yes," he continued, "the movement failed, and many deserted me because they saw me crestfallen, vacillating at the supreme instant: I was holding something in my heart, I was not the master of my emotions and I still loved...Now everything is dead within me and now there is no sacred corpse whose sleep I must respect. There will be no more vacillations. You yourself, idealistic young man, a dove without bile, understand the need. You come to me and excite me to action! You have opened your eyes rather late! Between yourself and myself, we together could have combined and executed marvelous plans: I above in the high spheres sowing death amid perfumes and gold, brutalizing the corrupt and corrupting or paralyzing the few good; and you, below in the towns, among the youth, evoking life between blood and tears! Our work, instead of being bloody and barbarous, would have been holy, perfect, artistic, and with a certainty of success crowning our efforts. But no intelligence had wished to second me. Fear or weakness I encountered among the *ilustrado* classes, selfishness among the rich, ingenuousness in the youth. And only in the mountains, in the remote places, in the miserable class, I found my men. But no matter! If we cannot obtain a finished statue, polished in all its details, from the rough block that we polish, those who are to come will take charge!"

Taking the arm of Basilio, who was listening without entirely comprehending him, he led him to the laboratory where he kept his chemical products.

On one table was a great box of dark green similar to those that contain the silverware with which monarchs and the rich gift one another. Simoun opened it and revealed on a red satin lining, a lamp of a very odd form. The vessel had the shape of a pomegranate large as the head of a man, cut slightly to show the inner grains which were shaped by huge carnelians. Its rind was oxidized gold and it perfectly imitated even the corrugations of the fruit.

Simoun lifted it with much care and, removing the burner, revealed the inside of the container: the vessel was of steel, some two centimeters thick and capable of holding more than a liter. Basilio questioned him with his eyes, not comprehending.

Without going into explanations, Simoun carefully took a flask from a cabinet and showed Basilio the formula it contained. "Nitroglycerine!" murmured Basilio drawing back, and pulling back his hands instinctively. "Nitroglycerine! Dynamite!"

And, comprehending, his hair stood on end.

"Yes, nitroglycerine!" Simoun repeated slowly, smiling coldly and contemplating the crystal flask with delight. "It is somewhat more than nitroglycerine! It is concentrated tears, repressed hatred, injustices and wrongs. It is the final argument of the weak, force against force, violence against violence...A moment ago I hesitated, but you have come and have convinced me. This night the most dangerous tyrants will blow up, be pulverized, the irresponsible tyrants, those who hide themselves behind God and the State, and whose abuses remain unpunished because no one can prosecute them! This night the Philippines will hear the explosion which will turn into debris the shapeless monument whose corruption I have hastened!"

Basilio was stupefied: his lips moved involuntarily but without producing sound. He felt that his tongue was paralyzed, his throat parched. For the first time he was looking at the powerful liquid of which so much had been heard, talked about, as if it were distilled in the shadows by grim men in open war against society. Now it was in front of him, transparent and somewhat yellowish, poured with infinite caution into the womb of the artistic pomegranate. Simoun seemed to him like the genie of *A Thousand and One Nights*, who rose from the bottom of the sea and, acquiring gigantic proportions, touched the heavens with his head, made the house tremble and shook the whole city with a shrug of his shoulders. The pomegranate assumed the proportions of a colossal sphere, and the cleft, an infernal grin from which were emitted embers and flames. For the first time Basilio was overcome with terror and lost his cold-bloodedness completely.

In the meantime, Simoun screwed tight an odd and complicated apparatus, set in place the tube of crystal, the bomb, and crowned everything with a very elegant lamp shade. Then he moved away some distance to contemplate the effect, leaning his head now to one side, now to the other, to better judge its aspect and magnificence.

Noticing that Basilio was looking at him with questioning and suspicious eyes, he said:

"Tonight there will be a fiesta and this lamp will be placed in the midst of a little dining-kiosk that I have ordered made for the purpose. The lamp will give out a brilliant light so that it alone will be enough to illuminate everything; but at the end of twenty minutes the light will grow dim, and when they attempt to raise the wick, a capsule of fulminate of mercury will detonate, the pomegranate will explode and with it, the dining room in whose roof and in whose floor I have concealed sacks of powder, so that no one can be saved..."

There was a moment of silence: Simoun contemplated his apparatus; Basilio hardly breathed.

"So my assistance would be useless," observed the young man.

"No, you have another mission to perform," replied Simoun thoughtfully. "By nine the mechanism will have exploded and the detonation will have been heard in the surrounding areas, in the mountains, in the caverns. The movement that I had plotted with the artillerymen failed for lack of direction and simultaneity. This time it will not be so. At the sound of the explosion, the wretched, the oppressed, those who wander persecuted by force, will come out armed and will join Cabesang Tales in Santa Mesa to invade the city. On the other hand, the military,

whom I have made believe that the *General* will simulate
an uprising to have reasons to stay, will come forth from
their barracks disposed to fire at whomsoever I may
designate. Meanwhile, the populace, cowed and thinking
the hour of their slaughter is at hand, will panic, resigned
to die; and since they do not have arms, nor are organized,
you with some others will put yourselves at their head
and direct them to the warehouses of the Chinaman
Quiroga, where I keep my guns. Cabesang Tales and I
will link up in the city and we will take possession of it;
and you in the suburbs will occupy the bridges and will
fortify them; you will be ready to come to our aid and you
will put to the sword not only the counter-revolutionists
but also all the males who refuse to follow us to arms!"

"All?" stammered Basilio in a choked voice.

"All!" repeated Simoun in a sinister tone. "All, *Indios*,
mestizos, Chinese, Spaniards, all those whom you find
without courage, without energy...It is necessary to renew
the race. Cowardly fathers breed only slavish sons. It would
not be worth the pain to destroy and then to rebuild with
rotten materials! What? you shudder? you tremble? you
fear to sow death?

"What is death? What does a hecatomb of twenty
thousand wretches signify? Twenty thousand miseries less
and millions of unfortunates saved from birth! The most
timid ruler does not vacillate to dictate a law that may
produce misery and lingering death for thousands and
thousands of subjects, prosperous and industrious, happy
perhaps, to satisfy a caprice, an occasion, pride, and you
shudder because in one night the moral tortures of many
helots are to be ended forever, because a paralytic and
vitiated population must die to give way to another, new,
young, active, full of energy.

"What is death? Nothingness, or a dream? Can its nightmares be compared to the reality of the agonies of a whole miserable generation? It is imperative to destroy the evil, to kill the dragon, and for the people to bathe in its blood in order to make them strong and invulnerable! What other thing is the inexorable law of Nature, the law of conflict in which the weak must succumb so that the tainted species may not perpetuate itself and Creation march backwards?

"Away then with effeminate scruples! Let us follow eternal laws, assist them, and then the earth is that much more fecund, the more it is fertilized with blood; and the thrones more secure when more strongly cemented in crimes and cadavers. No more vacillation, no more doubt! What is the pain of death? The sensation of a moment, perhaps confused, perhaps agreeable like the transit from wakefulness to sleep...What is being destroyed? An evil, suffering, tenuous weeds, in order to plant in their stead other luxuriant growths. Do you call that to destroy? I call it to create, to produce, to nourish to, vivify...."

Such bloody sophisms, said with conviction and coldness, overwhelmed the young man, whose mind, weakened by more than three months of imprisonment and blinded by the passion of vengeance, was in no mood to analyze the moral basis of things. Instead of replying that the worst or most cowardly man is always somewhat more than the plant because he has a soul and an intelligence which, however foul and brutish these might be, can be redeemed; instead of replying that man has no right to dispose of the life of anyone for the benefit of another, and that the right to life resides in each individual like the right to liberty and light; instead of replying that if it is an abuse in governments to punish in an offender

the faults and crimes which they have precipitated by
negligence or stupidity, how much more so would it be in
a man, however great and however unfortunate he might
be, to visit on a poor people the faults of their governments
and their ancestors; instead of saying that God alone can
attempt such methods because he can create, God who
holds in His hands recompense, eternity and the future, to
justify His acts, and never man; instead of these arguments,
Basilio merely interposed a trite observation:

"What will the world say at the sight of such
butchery?"

"The world will applaud as usual, conceding the right
to the strongest, to the most violent!" Simoun retorted
with his cruel smile. "Europe applauded when the nations
of the West sacrificed in America millions of Indians, and
certainly not to establish nations much more moral or more
peaceful. There is the North with its egotistic liberty, its
Law of Lynch, its political deceptions; there is the South
with its restless republics, its barbarous revolutions, civil
wars, military revolutions as in its Mother Spain. Europe
applauded when powerful Portugal despoiled the
Moluccan islands; applauded when England destroyed in
the Pacific the primitive races to make room for its
emigrants.

"Europe will applaud as it applauds the end of a
drama, the end of a tragedy: the common people pay little
notice to principle, they look only at the effect. Execute
the crime well, and it will be admired, and you will win
more supporters than would virtuous acts carried to the
end with modesty and timidity."

"Exactly," rejoined the young man. "What does it
matter to me, after all, whether they applaud or censure,
when that world does not take care of the oppressed, the

poor and the weak women; what obligations have I to
keep with society when she has not kept any with me?"

"That pleases me," the beguiler said triumphantly.
Taking a revolver from a drawer, he handed it over, saying:

"At ten, wait for me in front of the church of San
Sebastian, to receive my final instructions. Ah! at nine
o'clock you should be found far, very far from Anloague
Street!"[1]

Basilio examined the gun, loaded it, and tucked it
inside the inner pocket of his coat. He took his leave with
a curt: "Till then."

- 34 -
The Wedding

Once on the streets, Basilio thought of how he could occupy himself until the fateful hour arrived; it was not later than seven. It was vacation time, and all the students were in their hometowns. Isagani was the only one who did not wish to go home, but he had disappeared since that morning and his whereabouts were not known. This was what Basilio had been told when, coming out of prison, he went to visit his friend to ask for shelter. Basilio did not know where to go; he had no money, he had nothing but the revolver. The memory of the lamp occupied his imagination; within two hours the great catastrophe would take place and, thinking of it, it seemed to him that the men who filed before his eyes, passed without heads. He had a feeling of fierce pleasure in saying to himself that, hungry and all, that night he was going to be dreaded; that from a poor student and servant, even the sun would see him as terrible and sinister, standing upon pyramids of corpses, dictating laws to all those who passed before him in their magnificent coaches.

He burst into laughter like one damned and patted the butt of the revolver; the boxes of cartridges were in his pockets.

A question occurred to him: Where would the drama begin? In his bewilderment it had not occurred to him to ask Simoun, but Simoun had told him that he should stay away from Anloague Street.

Then he had a suspicion: that afternoon, upon leaving prison he had gone to the Capitan Tiago's old house to collect his few belongings, and had found it transformed and prepared for a feast. It was the wedding of Juanito Pelaez! Simoun had spoken of a fiesta.

Just then he saw pass before him a long line of carriages filled with gentlemen and ladies conversing with animation. He thought he could see inside them large bouquets of flowers, but he did not pay them attention. The coaches travelled in the direction of Rosario Street and, encountering those that were going down the Puente de España,[1] had to halt for a while and go more slowly. In one, he saw Juanito Pelaez beside a woman dressed in white, with a transparent veil. In her he recognized Paulita Gomez.

"Paulita!" he exclaimed, surprised.

And seeing that indeed it was she in bridal attire, and with Juanito Pelaez, as if they had just come from the Church, he murmured:

"Poor Isagani! What could have happened to him?"

He thought for a while of his friend, a great and generous soul, and mentally asked himself if it would not be well to tell him of the plan, but mentally he also answered himself that Isagani would not wish to take part in such a butchery...they had not done to Isagani what they had to him.

Afterwards he thought that but for his imprisonment

he would be betrothed or a husband by then, a licentiate in Medicine living and treating patients in some corner of the province. The ghost of Juli, mangled in her fall, crossed his imagination; dark flames of hatred lighted his eyes, and again he caressed the butt of the revolver, hurting that the terrible hour had not yet come. Just then he saw Simoun come out of the door of his house with the lamp case, carefully wrapped, then enter a carriage which followed the line of those accompanying the betrothed. Basilio, so as not to lose sight of Simoun, took a good look at the *cochero* and with surprise recognized in him the unfortunate who had taken him to San Diego, Sinong, who had been battered by the Guardia Civil, the same who informed him in jail of what had happened in Tiani.

Conjecturing that Anloague Street was going to be the theater, there the young man headed, hastening his pace and getting ahead of the carriages. Indeed, everybody was headed in the direction of the old house of Capitan Tiago: there they were assembling in search of a ball, in order to be seen. Basilio smiled to himself seeing the pairs of veteran guards who were on duty. From their number he could divine the importance of the fiesta and of those invited. The house overflowed with people, pouring forth torrents of light from its windows. The hallway was carpeted and full of flowers: up there, perhaps in its old and only room, an orchestra was now playing lively airs which did not completely drown out the confused tumult of laughter, explanations and guffaws.

Don Timoteo Pelaez was reaching the pinnacle of fortune, and the reality surpassed his dreams. He was at last marrying his son to the rich heiress of the Gomezes and, thanks to the money Simoun had lent him, he had royally furnished that big house, purchased for half its value. He was giving in it a splendid fiesta, and the foremost divinities of the Manila Olympus were going to be his guests, to gild him with the light of their prestige. Since that morning, with the persistence of a song in vogue, some vague phrases that he had read in his communions had been recurring to his mind: "Now is come the happy hour! Now nears the happy moment! Soon there will be fulfilled in you the admirable words of Simoun: 'I live, not I, but the Capitan General lives in me', etc." The Capitan General godfather to his son! True, he did not assist at the wedding; Don Custodio represented him, but he would come to dine and would bring a wedding gift, a lamp which not even that of Aladdin...just between us, Simoun was giving the lamp. Timoteo, what more can you desire?

The transformation which the house of Capitan Tiago had undergone was considerable; it had been richly repapered; the smoke and smell of opium had disappeared completely. The immense sala, widened even more by the colossal mirrors that multiplied infinitely the lights of the chandeliers, was carpeted throughout: the salons of Europe had carpets, and even though the floor was brilliantly polished and of wide wooden panels, a carpet it must also have, if nothing else. Capitan Tiago's rich furniture had disappeared; in their place were other pieces, in Louis XV style; great curtains of red velvet embroidered in gold with the initials of the betrothed, and fastened by garlands of artificial orange blossoms hung at the doorways, swept the floor with their wide tassels, equally of gold. In the corners could be seen enormous vases from Japan, alternating with others from Sevres of the purest dark blue, placed on square pedestals of carved wood.

The only inappropriate items were the gaudy colored

prints which Don Timoteo had substituted for Capitan Tiago's ancient engravings and lithographs of saints. Simoun had not been able to dissuade him. The merchant did not care for oil paintings, not any that might be attributed to Filipino artists...He, to support Filipino painters, never![2] That would make him lose his peace, and perhaps his life; he knew how one had to navigate in the Philippines! The truth is that he had heard of foreign painters like Rafael, Murillo, Velazquez, but he did not know how to get in touch with them, and then they might turn out to be somewhat seditious....With prints he ran no risk; the Filipinos did not make them, they came cheaper, the effect was the same, if not better, the colors more brilliant and the execution very fine. Come! Don Timoteo knew how to comport himself in the Philippines!

The large *caida*, all adorned with flowers, was converted into a dining room: a long table in the center for thirty persons, and around, pushed against the walls, other smaller ones for two or three. Bouquets of flowers, pyramids of fruits among ribbons and lights covered the centers. The place of the groom was identified by a bouquet of roses, that of the bride by another of orange blossoms and *azucenas*. Before so much lavishness and so many flowers one could imagine that nymphs in gossamer garments and cupids with irridescent wings were going to serve nectar and ambrosia to the guests to the sound of lyres and Aeolian harps!

However, the table for the greater gods was not there. It had been set in the middle of the wide azotea in a very elegant kiosk constructed especially for the occasion. A lattice of gilded wood festooned with fragrant vines screened the interior from the eyes of the crowd without impeding the free circulation of air to maintain the freshness necessary in that season. A raised platform lifted the table above the level of the rest at which ordinary mortals were going to dine, and an arch decorated by the best artists protected the august heads from the envious gaze of the stars.

There were no more than seven covers: the dinner-ware was of solid silver, the tablecloth and napkins of the finest linen, the wines the costliest and most exquisite. Don Timoteo had sought the rarest and most expensive, and would not have hesitated at crime had he been told that the Capitan General would like to eat human flesh.

- 35 -
The Fiesta

Danzar sobre un volcan

To dance on a volcano

At seven o'clock in the evening those invited began to arrive: first the minor divinities, lowly employees, business executives, merchants, etc., with greetings more ceremonious and with graver airs at the onset, as if they had been newly learned; so much light, so much drapery, so much glassware, imposes something. Afterwards, they grew more familiar, and made feigned fists, little slaps on the belly, and some even administered familiar slaps on the neck. Some, it is true, adopted a disdainful attitude to let it be seen that they were accustomed to better things, of course, if they were not! One goddess there was who yawned, finding everything vulgar, and saying that she had *gazuza*, violent hunger; another who quarreled with her god, making a gesture with her arm to give him a slap. Don Timoteo was bowing here, there, sending out a little smile, making a movement from the waist, a step backward, a half turn, a complete turn, and so forth, such that another goddess could not do less than say to her neighbor, under cover of her fan:

"*Chica*, how exuberant the old fellow is! See how he looks like a puppet."

Then the newlyweds arrived, accompanied by Doña Victorina and the entire retinue. Congratulations, handshakes, light patronizing pats for the groom, insistent stares, lascivious, physical, for the bride on the part of the men; on the part of the women analyses of the gown, of the adornment; calculations as to her vigor, health and the like.

"Cupid and Psyché presenting themselves in Olympus!" thought Ben Zayb, and he etched the comparison in his mind, to release on the right occasion.

The groom had, in fact, the roguish look of the god of love, and with a little good will, one could take as a quiver, at best, his hump, which even the smartness of the frock coat could not altogether conceal.

Don Timoteo was beginning to feel pains in his waist, the corns on his feet were irritating him more and more. His neck was tiring, and still the *General* was not there! The greater gods, among them Padre Irene and Padre Salvi, had already arrived, it is true, but still the mightiest thunder was missing. He was uneasy, nervous, his heart was beating violently, he had desires to dispose of a necessity, but first he had to bow, smile and then he was going to leave and could not; he sat down, he rose, he did not hear what was said to him, did not say what he meant. In the meantime, an amateur god made observations about his prints, criticizing them and impressing on him the fact that they spoiled the walls.

"Spoil the walls," echoed Don Timoteo smiling, with a desire to claw him, "but they were made in Europe and they are the most expensive that I have been able to find in Manila! Spoil the walls, indeed!"

And Don Timoteo swore to himself to collect the next day on all the vales or IOUs that the critic had in his store.

Whistles were heard, the gallop of horses, at last!

"The *General!*—the Capitan General!"

Pale with emotion, Don Timoteo rose to his feet, concealing the pain of his corns, and accompanied by his son and some of the greater gods, descended to receive the Mighty Jupiter. The pain in his waist vanished in the face of the doubts which at that moment assailed him: should he put on a smile or affect seriousness? Should he extend his hand or wait till the *General* extended his to him? *Carambas!* Why had it not occurred to him to consult his great friend Simoun on the matter? To conceal his feelings he asked his son in a low voice, very shakily: "Have you prepared some speech?"

"Speeches are no longer the style, *papá*, especially in this case."

Jupiter arrived in the company of Juno, converted into a tower of artificial lights: diamonds in her hair, diamonds around her neck, on her arms, on her shoulders, on all parts. A magnificent gown of silk with a long train embroidered with embossed flowers glittered.

His Excellency literally took possession of the house as Don Timoteo, stammering, begged him to. The orchestra played the royal march and the divine couple majestically ascended the carpeted stairway.

His Excellency's graveness was not altogether affected. Perhaps for the first time since his arrival in the Islands he felt sad; a tinge of melancholy winged in his thoughts. This was the last triumph of his three years of sovereignty, and within two days, for always, he would descend from such an exalted height.

What was he leaving behind him? His Excellency did not look back, but preferred to look ahead of him, toward the future! He was taking a fortune with him; great sums deposited in the banks of Europe awaited him; he had hotels, but he had injured many, he had many enemies in the *Corte*, the high official was waiting for him there! Other *generales* had enriched themselves rapidly, as he had, and were now bankrupt. Why did he not stay longer as Simoun had advised? No, *delicadeza* before anything else. Besides, the bows were now not as profound as formerly; he noticed insistent stares and even dislike, but still he responded with affability and even attempted to smile.

"One knows that the sun is in its gloaming," observed Padre Irene within Ben Zayb's hearing. "Many now stare at it face to face."

"*Carambas*, to hell with the Curate!" he was going to say just that!

"*Chica*," murmured into the ear of her neighbor she who had called Don Timoteo a puppet, "Have you seen such a skirt?"

"Uy! the Palace curtains!"[1]

"Hold your tongue! but it is true. Well, they carry everything away. You will see how they will make an overcoat of the carpets."

"That does not prove anything but that she has ingenuity and taste!" remarked her husband, reproving his wife with a look. "Women should be thrifty."

This poor god was still hurting from the bill of the dressmaker.

"My dear! give me curtains at twelve pesos a *vara*,[2]

and you will see if I put on these rags," replied the piqued
goddess. "Jesus! You may talk when you have such
splendid predecessors!"

In the meantime, Basilio, in front of the house and
lost in the throng of the curious, was counting the persons
who were alighting from the carriages. When he saw so
many happy and trusting people, when he saw the bride
and the groom, followed by their cortege of young girls,
innocent and ingenuous, and thought that they would find
there a horrible death, he knew compassion and felt his
hatred softening.

He felt a desire to save so many innocents; he thought
to advise someone and give way to justice, but a carriage
arrived and Padre Salvi and Padre Irene got off, both
looking very much pleased, and like a passing cloud his
good intentions vanished.

"What does it matter to me," he said to himself, "let
the righteous suffer with the sinners."

And then he added, to tranquilize his scruples: "I am
not an informer, I must not abuse the confidence that has
been stored in me. I owe *him* more than I owe all of *them*;
he dug my mother's grave; those men killed her. What
have I to do with them? I did everything possible to be
good, useful; I have tried to forget and forgive; I suffered
every imposition and only asked that I be left in peace. I
bothered no one....What have they done to me? Let their
mangled bodies fly through the air! We have suffered
enough!"

Then he saw Simoun alight, carrying in his arms the
terrible lamp, saw him cross the entrance slowly with
bowed head, as if reflecting. Basilio felt his heart beating
more faintly, his feet and hands turning cold, and felt that
the jeweler's black silhouette assumed fantastic shapes

encircled in flames. Simoun paused at the foot of the
stairway, as if hesitant. Basilio held his breath. The
vacillation was momentary: Simoun raised his head,
climbed the stairway resolutely, and disappeared. It
seemed then to the student that the house was going to
blow up at any moment, and that walls, lamps, guests,
roof, windows, orchestra would be hurtling through the
air like a handful of embers amid an infernal detonation.
He looked around him and imagined seeing corpses in
place of the curious; saw them mutilated; it seemed that
the air was filling with flames, but the calmness of his
mind triumphed over that passing hallucination which
hunger abetted. He told himself:

"While he does not come down, there is no danger.
The Captain General has not yet arrived."

He sought to appear calm and, controlling the
convulsive trembling of his legs, tried to distract himself
by thinking of other things. Something was mocking him
within and he said to it:

"If you tremble now, before the supreme moment,
how will you carry yourself when you see blood flowing,
houses burning and bullets whistling?"

His Excellency arrived, but the young man paid no
attention to him. He was watching the face of Simoun,
who was one of those who had come down to receive
him, and read on the implacable features the death sentence
of all those men. New terror took hold of him. He felt
cold, he leaned against the wall, eyes fixed on the windows,
hearing alert; he wanted to guess what could happen. He
saw the crowd in the sala surrounding Simoun and
contemplating the lamp; heard varied congratulations,
exclamations of admiration; the words *dining room, debut*
repeated several times; saw the *General* smile to himself

and conjectured that the spectacle would open that same night as the jeweler had intended and, for certain, at the table at which his Excellency would dine. Simoun disappeared from view followed by a multitude of admirers.

At that supreme moment his good heart triumphed, he forgot his hatred, forgot Juli, and wanted to save the innocent; now resolved, happen what may, he crossed the street and attempted to enter. But Basilio had forgotten that he was miserably attired. The porter stopped him, questioned him rudely and, seeing his insistence, threatened him by summoning a pair of the veterans.

At that moment Simoun, slightly pale, was descending. The porter left Basilio to greet the jeweler as if a saint were passing. Basilio understood in the expression on his face that he was abandoning the fatal house for good, and that the lamp had already been lighted. *Alea jacta est;* the die was cast. Gripped by an instinct of self-preservation, he thought then of saving himself. It could occur to someone out of curiosity to move the apparatus, raise the wick and then everything would blow up and all would be buried. He could still hear Simoun, who said to the *cochero:*

"Escolta, quick!"

Terrified and fearing to hear in one moment or another the terrible explosion, Basilio made all haste to leave the damned place: his feet slipped against the pavement as if they were running but not moving; the people he met were blocking his way, and before he could take twenty steps he thought that at least five minutes had passed. Some distance away he came across a young man on his feet, head raised and looking fixedly towards the house. Basilio recognized Isagani.

"What are you doing here?" he asked. "Come!"

Isagani looked at him vaguely, smiled sadly and turned to look towards the open balconies across which he could see the bride's airy silhouette hanging on the arm of her groom, moving away languidly.

"Come, Isagani, let us get away from this house, come!" Basilio said in a hoarse voice, seizing him by the arm.

Isagani pushed him away gently and continued looking with that same sad smile on his lips.

"For God's sake! Let us get away!"

"Why should I go away? Tomorrow she will no longer be herself!"

There was so much pain in those words that Basilio forgot his own terror for a moment.

"Do you want to die?" he asked.

Isagani shrugged his shoulders and kept on looking.

Basilio tried again to drag him away.

"Isagani, Isagani! listen to me, let us not lose time! That house is mined, it will blow up any moment, through an imprudence, curiosity...Isagani; everything will perish beneath its ruins!"

"Beneath its ruins?" Isagani echoed, as if trying to comprehend without taking his eyes off the window.

"Yes, beneath its ruins. Isagani, for God's sake, come! I will explain to you later, come! Someone who has been more unfortunate than either you or me, has condemned them... Do you see that clear white light like an electric lamp, coming from the azotea? It is the lamp of death! A lamp loaded with dynamite, in a mined dining-room... It will explode and not a single rat will escape alive. Come!"

"No!" replied Isagani, shaking his head sorrowfully; "I want to stay here, I want to see her for the last time....Tomorrow it will be different!"

"Let destiny have its way!" Basilio then exclaimed, hurrying away in all haste.

Isagani saw that his friend rushed away with a precipitation that indicated real terror, and he continued gazing at the fascinating window, like the cavalier of Toggenburg waiting for his loved one to appear, of which Schiller tells us. At that moment the sala was deserted, all having gone to the dining rooms. It occurred to Isagani that Basilio's fear might be justified. He recalled his terrified countenance, he who in everything kept his blood cold; he began to reflect. A thought appeared clear to his imagination: the house was going to blow up and Paulita was in there; Paulita would die a horrible death...

At this thought he forgot everything: jealousy, sufferings, moral torments. The gallant youth thought only of his love. Without pausing to reflect, without hesitation, he ran toward the house and, thanks to his elegant attire and his decided mien, he was able to pass easily through the door.

While these short scenes were taking place on the street, in the dining room of the greater gods a piece of parchment passed from hand to hand, on which they read, written in red ink, these fateful words:

> *Mene Thecel Phares.*[3]
> Juan Crisostomo Ibarra

"Juan Crisostomo Ibarra? who is he?" asked His Excellency, handing the parchment to his neighbor.

"What a joke in very bad taste!" replied Don Custodio, "to sign the paper with the name of a *filibusterillo* dead more than ten years ago!"

"A petty subversive!"

"It is a seditious joke!"

"There being señoras....."

Padre Irene looked around for the jester and saw Padre Salvi, who was seated to the right of the Countess, turn as white as his napkin while, with eyes bulging, he contemplated the mysterious words. The scene of the sphinx came to his mind.

"What is the matter, Padre Salvi?" he asked; "Do you recognize the signature of your friend?"

Padre Salvi did not reply. He made an effort to talk, and apparently unaware of what he was doing, wiped his brow with his napkin.

"What is the matter with Your Reverence?"

"It is his same handwriting!" he answered in a low voice, hardly intelligible; "It is the handwriting of Ibarra."

And falling against the back of his chair, he let his arms drop as if he had lost all his strength.

Uneasiness turned to terror; they looked at one another without saying a single word. His Excellency wanted to rise, but fearing it would be attributed to fright, controlled himself and looked around him. There were no soldiers; the waiters serving were unknown to him.

"Let us continue eating, gentlemen," he said, "and let us not give importance to a joke."

But his voice, instead of reassuring, augmented the uneasiness; his voice was trembling.

"I suppose that this *Mene, Thecel, Phares* does not mean to say that we are to be murdered tonight?" said Don Custodio. All remained immobile.

"But they might poison us...."

The silverware dropped.

The light, meanwhile, began to dim little by little.

"The lamp is going out," remarked the General

uneasily. "Will you turn up the wick, Padre Irene?"

At that moment, with the speed of lightning a figure rushed in, overturning a chair and knocking down a servant; and in the midst of the general surprise seized the lamp, ran to the azotea and threw it into the river. Everything happened in a second; the dining room was left in darkness.

The lamp had already fallen into the water before the servants could cry: "Thief, thief!" and rush to the azotea.

"A revolver," cried one, "quick a revolver; after the thief!"

But the shape, more agile yet, had already mounted the tile balustrade and, before a light could be brought, flung itself into the river, a cutting sound being heard when it fell into the water.

- 36 -

The Predicaments
of Ben Zayb

As soon as he learned of the incident, as lights were brought in and he saw the less dignified postures of the startled gods, Ben Zayb, full of indignation and armed with the approval of the censor of the press,[1] went running to his home—a basement room which he shared with others— to write the most sublime article that would ever be read under Philippine skies. The Capitan General would leave disconsolate if he could not read in advance his exaggerated eulogies and this, Ben Zayb, who had a good heart, could not allow. He therefore sacrificed dinner and the ball and did not sleep that night.

Sonorous exclamations of horror, of indignation, imagination of a world at its end, and the stars, the eternal stars colliding with one another! Afterwards a mysterious introduction, full of allusions, innuendo...then a narration of events and the final peroration. He multiplied the turns of phrase, wrung the euphemisms to describe the fall on his back and the belated christening by sauce which His

Excellency received on the Olympian brow. He eulogized
the agility with which he recovered the vertical position,
raising his head where before had been his feet and vice
versa. He intoned a hymn to Providence for having
solicitously watched over such sacred bones, and the
paragraph turned out so well that his Excellency appeared
like a hero and fell much higher, as Victor Hugo would
have said. He was writing, erasing, adding and polishing,
such that without lacking the truth—this was his special
merit as a journalist—it would all result in an epic, grand
for the seven divinities, cowardly and low for the unknown
thief, "who had passed judgment on himself, horrified
and convinced at the same instant of the enormity of his
crime." He interpreted Padre Irene's act of placing himself
under the table as an "impulse of innate valor which the
vestments of a God of peace and meekness, worn
throughout life, had not been able to dim." Padre Irene
wanted to hurl himself against the criminal, and taking
the direct line, passed the subtabular route. In passing he
wrote of submarine tunnels, and mentioned a project of
Don Custodio's; recalled the priest's image and long
travels. The swoon of Padre Salvi was the excessive sorrow
that took possession of the virtuous Franciscan, seeing the
scanty harvest that the *Indios* were gathering from pious
sermons. The immobility and terror of their other table
companions, among them the Countess who 'supported'
(clutched at) Padre Salvi, were the serenity and
coldbloodedness of heroes, accustomed to peril in the
performance of their duties, beside whom the Roman
senators surprised by the Gaelic invaders were nervous
schoolgirls frightened of painted cockroaches.

And then, in contrast, a portrayal of the thief: "fear,
madness, bewilderment, a scowl, contorted features and

the force of the moral superiority of the race, his religious dread upon seeing there congregated such august personages!"

Coming to the point then, a long imprecation, a harangue, a denunciation against the perversion of good customs and hence the urgency to establish a permanent military tribunal, "a declaration of a state of siege within the limits of the state of siege already declared, a special legislation, repressive, energetic because it was in every way needful, it was at all points necessary, it was of imperative urgency to make the malefactors and criminals see that if the heart was generous and paternal for the submissive and obedient to the law, the hand was strong, firm, inexorable, severe and hard, for those who against all reason failed it, and who insulted the sacred institutions of the nation! Yes, gentlemen, this was demanded, not only for the welfare of these islands, not only for the welfare of all mankind, not only for the good of all of humanity, but also by the Spanish name, the honor of the Spanish name, the prestige of the Iberian people, because before all things we are Spaniards, and the flag of Spain" and so on and on.

He ended his article with this farewell:

"Go peacefully, brave warrior who with expert hand guided the destinies of this country in such calamitous epochs! Go peacefully to breathe the balmy breezes of Manzanares! We who are here shall remain like faithful sentinels to venerate your memory, to admire your wise disposition, to avenge the infamous attempt against your splendid gift, which we will find even if we have to dry up the seas! Such a precious relic will be for this country an eternal monument to your splendor, your coolness of mind, your bravery!"

Thus the article ended, rather confused, and before dawn Ben Zayb sent it to the publication already with the censor's previous authorization. And he slept as had Napoleon after having disposed of the plan of the Battle of Jena.

They woke him up at sunrise, with the sheets of copy returned along with a note from the editor saying that His Excellency had prohibited severely and absolutely any talk of the incident, and ordered a denial of the commentaries and versions that were circulating, categorizing everything as tales, exaggerated and fabulous.

For Ben Zayb that was like killing a son so handsome and so valiant, born and nurtured with such pain and fatigue. Where now to fit the proud Catilinarian, the splendid example of warlike-but-just accoutrements? And to think that within a month or two he would be leaving the Philippines and the article could not come out in Spain, because: how could he say that against the criminals of Madrid, where other ideas exist, where extenuating circumstances are sought, facts are weighed, there are juries and so forth? Articles like his were like certain venomous firewaters which are distilled in Europe, *good for Negroes*, with the difference that if the blacks did not drink them they did not harm themselves, while the articles of Ben Zayb, whether Filipinos read them or not, produced their effects.

"If only some other crime could be committed tomorrow or the day after," he said.

And at the thought of that son dead before seeing print, those frozen rosebuds, and feeling that his eyes were moistening, he got dressed to see the editor. The editor shrugged his shoulders. His Excellency had forbidden it because if it came to be divulged that seven greater gods had allowed themselves to be robbed and surprised by a nobody while they were brandishing forks and knives, that would endanger the integrity of the nation. And thus it was ordered that there should not be a search for the lamp nor the thief, and it was recommended to his successors that they should never risk dining in any particular place without being surrounded by halberdiers and guards. And since those who knew anything of the happenings that night in Don Timoteo's house were for the most part government officials and military, it was not difficult to deny the fact in public; it was a question of the integrity of the nation. At this phrase, Ben Zayb lowered his head, moved by heroism, thinking of Abraham, Guzman the Good or at the very least of Brutus and other ancient heroes of history.

Such sacrifice could not remain without recompense. The god of the press was satisfied with Abraham-Ben Zayb.

Almost at the same time the reporting angel arrived, bringing the sacrificial lamb in the form of a raid, committed on a villa by the shores of the Pasig wherein certain friars spent the hot season. That was the occasion, and Abraham-Ben Zayb praised his god.

"The bandits took more than two thousand pesos, left badly wounded a religious and two servants....The *cura* defended himself as best as he could behind a chair which shattered in his hands...."

"Wait, wait!" said Ben Zayb, taking notes. "Forty or fifty *tulisanes* treacherously...revolvers, bolos, shotguns, pistols... a lion fencing, chair...splinters...savagely wounded...ten thousand pesos..."

Enthusiastic and not content with the details, he hied himself over to the site of the occurrence, composing on the way a Homeric description of the combat. A little

harangue from the mouth of the chieftain? A contemptuous
phrase from the mouth of the religious? All the metaphors
and similes applied to His Excellency, to Padre Irene and
to Padre Salvi, his mold for the wounded religious, and
the description of the thief for each one of the malefactors.
In the imprecation he could expand further; he could talk
of religion, of faith, of charity, of the tolling of the bells, of
how much the *Indios* owed the friars—sentimentalized and
melted into phrases and lyricisms of Castelar. The young
ladies of the capital would read the article and would say:

"Ben Zayb, brave as a lion and tender as a lamb!"

When he arrived at the scene of the event, to his
great surprise, he found that the wounded priest was no
other than Padre Camorra, punished by his Provincial to
expiate in the villa of pleasure by the shores of the Pasig
his mischiefs in Tiani. He had a small wound in his hand,
a contusion on his head when he fell on his back; there
had been three robbers and they were armed only with
bolos; the amount stolen, fifty pesos.

"It cannot be!" said Ben Zayb; "Keep quiet...You do
not know what it is you say!"

"How can I not know, *puñales?*"

"Do not be silly!...There must have been more
robbers..."

"Man, you ink-slinger..."

They had a heated altercation. What mattered most
to Ben Zayb was not to throw away the article, to give
importance to the incident so that the peroration could be
published.

A whisper cut the argument. The captured robbers
had made important revelations. One of the *tulisanes* of
Matanglawin (Cabesang Tales) had made an appointment
with them to reunite with his band in Santa Mesa to sack

the convents and houses of the wealthy...A Spaniard would guide them, one tall and sunburnt, with white hair, who said he was acting on the orders of the *General,* who was a great friend. He had assured them further that the artillery and various regiments would join them; about that they should have no fear. The *tulisanes* would be pardoned, and a third part of the booty would go to them. The signal was to have been a cannon-shot, but having waited in vain, the *tulisanes* believed themselves beguiled. Some returned home, others returned to their mountains, vowing to be avenged against the Spaniard, who for the second time had failed to keep his word. They then, the captured robbers, decided to do something on their own and attacked the villa which they found close at hand, promising religiously to give two-thirds of the booty to the Spaniard of the white hair if he perchance should claim it.

The description coincided with that of Simoun; the statement was considered absurd, and to the robber was applied all kinds of tortures, including the electric machine, for that impious blasphemy. But the news of the jeweler's disappearance having called the attention of all Escolta, and sacks of powder and a great quantity of cartridges having been found in his house, the revelation had the guise of truth, and mystery gradually began to enshroud the affair, swathed in vagueness, spoken in whispers, coughed, with fearful looks, suspense, and many phrases empty of risk. Those who were in the know could hardly get over their amazement, took on long faces, turned pale, and little was lacking to make many lose their minds upon discovering certain things that had passed unperceived.

"What luck that we have been saved! Who would have thought..."

In the afternoon, Ben Zayb, his pockets loaded with revolvers and cartridges, went to visit Don Custodio, whom he found hard at work on a project against American jewelers. He whispered into the journalist's ears, in a very hushed voice and between the palms of his hands, mysterious words.

"Really?" asked Ben Zayb bringing his hand to his pockets while paling visibly.

"And wherever he may be found..."

He finished the phrase with an expressive pantomime. He raised both arms to the level of his face, with the right more bent than the left, turned the palms of his hands toward the floor, closed one eye, and making two movements of advance, "Psst! psst!" he hissed.

"And the diamonds?" Ben Zayb asked.

"If they find him..."

And he did another pantomime with the fingers of his right hand, making them rotate backward and forward, from outside in, in the movement of a fan closing, as though recovering something, somewhat in the manner of the arms of a windmill which turn, sweeping away imaginary objects toward it with dexterous sleight of hand. Ben Zayb responded with another mimicry, opening his eyes wide, arching his eyebrows and sucking air avidly as though nutritious air had just been discovered.

"Sssh!"

The Mystery

All becomes known.

Notwithstanding and despite so many precautions, the rumors reached the public, although somewhat altered and mutilated. They were the theme of comments on the following night in the household of the family of Orenda, a wealthy jewel merchant in the industrial suburb of Santa Cruz.[1] The numerous friends of the family were occupied only in it. They were not playing *tres-siete*[2] or playing the piano, and little Tinay, the youngest of all the señoritas was bored playing *chonka*[3] alone, unable to explain the interest awakened by assaults, conspiracies, sacks of gunpowder, when she had so many beautiful *sigayes* or cowries in the seven holes, which seemed to wink at one and smile with their tiny mouths half-open so that they would be carried to the mother home or *Ina*.

Isagani who, when he came, had played with her and allowed himself to be cheated beautifully, did not respond to her beckoning. Isagani was listening, somber and silent, to what Chichoy, the silversmith, was relating. Momoy, fiance of Sensia, the eldest of the Orendas, a beautiful and lively young girl, although something of a jester, had left the window where he was wont to spend the evenings in amorous conversation. This was annoying the parrot whose cage was suspended from the eaves, the family favorite for having the ability to greet everybody in the morning with marvelous phrases of love.

Capitana Loleng, the active and intelligent *capitana*, had her book of accounts open, but was not reading or writing anything in it; she was not fixing her attention on the trays, heaped with loose pearls, nor on the diamonds; that time she forgot herself and was all ears. Her husband himself, the great Capitan Toringoy, a corruption of his name Domingo, the happiest man in the suburb, without more concerns than that of dressing well, eating, loafing and gossiping, while his whole family worked and toiled, had not gone to join his group; he was listening, between fright and emotion, to the horrifying tales of the lanky Chichoy.

And they were not anything trivial. Chichoy had gone to deliver some work to Don Timoteo Pelaez, a pair of earrings for the newlyweds, at the time that they were demolishing the kiosk which the night before had served as dining room for the first authorities. Here Chichoy turned pale and his hair stood on end.

"*Naku!*" he said, "sacks of gunpowder, sacks of gunpowder underneath the flooring, on the roof, under the table, under the seats, everywhere! It was lucky that none of the workmen was smoking."

"And who put those sacks of powder there?" asked Capitana Loleng, who was brave and did not turn pale as did the enamored Momoy.

Momoy had attended the wedding, and his belated

reaction was understandable. Momoy had been near the kiosk.

"That is what no one can explain," replied Momoy. "Who would be interested in disturbing the fiesta? There could not have been more than one," said the celebrated Señor Pasta, who was visiting, "or an enemy of Don Timoteo's or a rival of Juanito's..."

The Orenda señoritas turned instinctly toward Isagani. Isagani smiled in silence.

"Hide yourself!" Capitana Loleng told him; "They may accuse you...hide!"

Isagani smiled again and said nothing.

"Don Timoteo," Chichoy continued, "did not know to whom to attribute the deed. He himself had directed the works, he and his friend Simoun and nobody else. The house was thrown into an uproar, the *teniente* of the veterans came, and after enjoining secrecy upon everybody, they sent me away. But..."

"But...but..."stammered Momoy trembling.

"Naku!" exclaimed Sensia, looking at her fiancé and trembling too at the recollection that he had been at the feast; this young man...if it had come to explode...

And she looked at her fiancé with angry eyes, and admiring his valor:

"If it had exploded..."

"No one would be left alive on all of Anloague Street!" added Capitan Toringoy, feigning courage and indifference in the presence of his family.

"I left in consternation," continued Chichoy, "thinking that if one spark, one cigarette fell, or a lamp overturned, at this present hour there would not be a general, nor Archbishop, nor any one, nor even a government employee! All those who were at the fiesta last night, pulverized!"

"Most holy Virgin! This young man…"

"*Susmariosep!*" exclaimed Capitana Loleng, "all our debtors were there; *Susmariosep!* And nearby we have a piece of property! Who could have it been?"

"Now you will know," Chichoy added in a hushed voice, "but it is necessary that you keep the secret. This afternoon I met a friend, an office clerk, and speaking of the event, he gave me the clue. He learned it from some employees…Who do you suppose had placed the sacks of powder?"

Many shrugged their shoulders; only Capitan Toringoy looked sideways at Isagani.

"The friars?"

"Quiroga the Chinaman?"

"Some student?"

"Macaraig?"

Capitan Toringoy coughed and looked at Isagani.

Chichoy shook his head and smiled.

"The jeweler Simoun!"

"Simoun!!!"

A silence, due to astonishment, followed these words. Simoun, the dark soul of the Capitan General, the very wealthy merchant to whose house they had gone to buy unset gems. Simoun who had received the Orenda girls with great courtesy and told them fine compliments! For the very reason that the account seemed absurd, it was believed. "*Credo quia absurdum*, I believe because it is absurd," said St. Augustine.

"But was not Simoun at the fiesta last night?" asked Sensia.

"Yes," said Momoy, "but now I remember! He left the house at the moment we were going to dine. He left to fetch his wedding gift."

"But was he not a friend of the *General*'s? Was he not Don Timoteo's partner?"

"Yes, he had made himself a partner in order to strike a blow and to kill all the Spaniards."

"Ya!" said Sensia; "now I see!"

"What?"

"You did not want to believe *Tía* Tentay. Simoun is the devil who has bought the souls of all the Spaniards...*Tía* Tentay said so!"

Capitana Loleng crossed herself, looked uneasily at the stones, fearing to see them turn into embers; Capitan Toringoy removed his ring that had come from Simoun.

"Simoun has disappeared without leaving a trace," added Chichoy. "The *guardia civil* are searching for him."

"Yes," said Sensia, "let them search for the devil!"

And she crossed herself. Now many things were explained: the fabulous wealth of Simoun, the peculiar odor of his house, the smell of sulfur. Binday, another Orenda señorita, ingenuous and adorable girl, recalled having seen bluish flames in the jeweler's house one afternoon when she accompanied her mother who had gone there to buy stones.

Isagani was listening attentively without saying a word.

"That is why, last night...!" stammered Momoy.

"Last night?" Sensia repeated, half curious and jealous.

Momoy was undecided, but the sight that Sensia showed dissipated his fear.

"Last night, while we were dining, there was an uproar. The lamp went out in the dining room of the *General*. They say that some unknown stole the lamp that Simoun had given as gift."

"A thief? One of the Black Hand?"

Isagani rose and started to pace.

"And they did not catch him?"

"He jumped into the river; nobody was able to see him. Some say he was a Spaniard, others, Chinese, others, *Indio*..."

"It is believed that with that lamp," added Chichoy, "the whole house was to be set on fire...the gunpowder..."

Momoy again shuddered, but having seen that Sensia had perceived his fear, tried to correct it.

"What a pity!" he exclaimed, making an effort, "what evil the thief had done. Everybody would have been killed...!"

Sensia stared at him terrified, the women crossed themselves. Capitan Toringoy, who was afraid of politics, made a move to leave. Momoy turned to Isagani.

"It is always wicked to take what does not belong to you," answered Isagani with an enigmatic smile; "if that thief had known what it was all about and had been able to reflect, surely he would not have done it!"

And he added after a brief pause:

"For nothing in this world would I wish to be in his place!"

And so they continued commenting and making conjectures. An hour later Isagani took leave of the family to go home, to stay permanently with his uncle.

- 38 -

A Trick of Fate

Matanglawin was the terror of Luzon. His band would suddenly appear in a province where it was least expected, just as it would invade another which was preparing to resist it. It would burn a sugarmill in Batangas, lay waste the crops; the following day assassinate the *juez de paz* of Tiani; another day take by surprise a town in Cavite and seize the arms in the town hall. The central provinces, from Tayabas to Pangasinan, suffered from the band's depredations, and his name reached as far as Albay in the south, and in the north, as far as Cagayan. The towns, disarmed by the mistrust of a weak government, were easy prey in his hands. At his approach the farmers abandoned their fields; the herds were decimated and a trail of blood and fire marked his passage. Matanglawin made fun of all the severe measures which were dictated against the *tulisanes*. From these, only the inhabitants of the barrios suffered; captured and maltreated if they resisted, or if they made peace with him, they were flogged and exiled by the Government, that is if the exiles arrived and did not suffer fatal accidents on the way. Thanks to this terrible alternative, many of the peasants decided to enlist in his command.

By grace of this reign of terror, commerce in the towns, already in agony, died completely. The rich dared not travel; the poor were afraid to be arrested by the *guardia civil*, who, being obliged to pursue the *tulisanes*, many times would seize the first person they found and subject him to unspeakable tortures. In its impotence, the Government put on a show of force against the persons who appeared suspect, so that by force of cruelty the people would not notice its frailty, the fear that goaded such measures.

A cordon of these unhappy suspects, six or seven, bound elbow to elbow and manacled like a cluster of human meat, was marching one afternoon along a road that skirted a mountain, conducted by ten or twelve guards armed with rifles.[1] It was extraordinarily hot. The bayonets gleamed in the sun; the barrels of the rifles were burned, and the sage leaves tucked into the helmets scarcely served to temper the effects of the deadly sun of May.

Deprived of the use of their arms and tied close to one another to conserve rope, the prisoners walked, almost all of them uncovered and unshod; those better off had handkerchiefs bound around their heads. Out of breath, miserable, covered with dust which the sweat converted to mud, they felt that their brains were melting; floating lights in space, red spots in the air. Exhaustion and dejection were painted on their faces, despair, anger, something indescribable, the look of the dying who curses, of the man who blasphemes life, himself, and God...The strongest lowered their heads, rubbed their faces against the dirty backs of those in front to wipe off the sweat that was blinding them; many were limping. If someone, falling, delayed the march, a curse would be heard and a soldier would come brandishing a branch wrenched from a tree, and oblige him to rise, striking right and left. The cordon would then run, dragging along the fallen one who would wallow in the dust and howl, begging to be killed: if perchance he succeeded in rising and getting on his feet, he would go along crying like a child and cursing the day he was born.

The human cluster would halt at times while their guards drank, and then would proceed on their way with parched mouths, darkened brains and hearts filled with curses. Thirst was the least torture for these wretches.

"Move on! you sons of *p*—," a soldier would cry, refreshed anew, hurling the insult common among the lower classes of Filipinos.

And the branch hissed and fell on any shoulder whatsoever, the nearest, at times upon a face, leaving a welt first white, then red, and later dirty, thanks to the dust of the road.

"Move on, cowards!" he yelled at times in Spanish, his voice hoarse.

"Cowards!" echoed the mountains.

And the cowards would quicken their pace under a sky of molten iron, over a road that burnt, lashed by the knotty branch that crumbled on their livid skins. The cold of Siberia would perhaps be kinder than the sun of May in the Philippines!

Nevertheless, among the soldiers there was one who looked askance at such wanton cruelties. He marched on silently, brows knitted as if disgusted. Finally, on seeing that the guard, not satisfied with the branch, was giving a kick to the prisoners who fell, he could no longer contain himself and yelled at him impatiently:

"Listen Mautang, let them move in peace!"

Mautang turned, surprised:

"And to you, what does it matter, Carolino?" he asked.

"To me nothing, but it hurts me," replied Carolino; "they are men like us."

"Obviously you are new in the business!" Mautang replied, smiling sympathetically. "How then did you treat the prisoners in the war?"

"Certainly with more consideration!" answered Carolino.

Mautang remained silent for a moment, and then apparently finding his argument, retorted coolly:

"Ah, it is because those were enemies and they were aggressors, while these...these are our countrymen!"

And drawing close, he said into Carolino's ear:

"What a simpleton you are! They are treated thus so that they may attempt to resist or to escape, and then...bang!"

Carolino did not answer.

One of the prisoners begged to be allowed to rest because he had to attend to a necessity.

"The place is dangerous!" answered the corporal, looking uneasily at the mountain. *Sulung!* forward!"

"*Sulung!*" repeated Mautang.

And the branch swished. The prisoner grimaced and looked at him with eyes of rebuke.

"You are more cruel than the Spaniard himself," said the prisoner.

Mautang replied with other blows. Almost at the same time a bullet whistled, followed by a detonation. Mautang dropped his rifle, uttered an oath and, bringing both hands to his breast, fell spinning on himself. The prisoner saw him wallowing in the dust, blood spurting from his mouth.

"Halt!" shouted the Corporal, suddenly turning very pale.

The soldiers stopped and looked around. A light wisp of smoke rose from some thickets on the height. Another bullet whistled, another bang was heard and the Corporal, wounded in the thigh, doubled over mouthing curses. The column was under attack by men who were hiding among the rocks above.

The Corporal, sullen with rage, motioned toward the bunch of prisoners and commanded:

"Fire!"

The prisoners fell upon their knees, filled with consternation. Since they could not raise their hands they begged for mercy, kissing the dust or bowing their heads: one talked of his children; another of his mother, who would be left unprotected; one promised money; another called upon God, but the muzzles were already lowered and a horrendous discharge made them silent.

Then began the firing against those up in the heights, now slowly crowned by smoke. Judging by this and by the unhurriedness of the shots, the invisible enemies could not count for more than three rifles. The guards, as they advanced and fired, hid themselves behind tree trunks, crouched and attempted to scale the heights. Pieces of rock flew, branches of trees broke off, patches of earth were torn up. The first guard who attempted to climb fell rolling, wounded by a bullet in his shoulder.

The invisible enemy had the vantage of position. The valiant guards, who did not know how to flee, were on the point of backing off, for they paused and did not care to advance. That struggle against the invisible terrified them. They saw nothing but smoke and rocks, no human voice, not a shadow: it could be said that they were fighting against a mountain.

"Come on, Carolino! Where is that *p*—marksmanship?" the Corporal shouted.

At that moment a man appeared upon a rock, making signs with his rifle.

"Fire at him!" yelled the Corporal, mouthing a dirty blasphemy. Three guards obeyed, but the man continued on his feet. He was shouting, but could not be understood.

Carolino stopped, believing he recognized something familiar in that silhouette bathed in the light of the sun. But the Corporal threatened to string him up if he did not fire. Carolino took aim and a shot was heard. The man on the rock spun around and disappeared with a cry that left Carolino stupefied.

A movement was heard in the thicket as if those who were occupying it had dispersed in all directions. The soldiers then began to advance, free of any resistance. Another man appeared over a rock brandishing a lance; the soldiers fired, and the man doubled up slowly, grabbing a branch; another shot, and he fell headlong on the rocks.

The guards climbed nimbly, fixing bayonets, ready for hand-to-hand combat. Carolino was the only one who moved sluggishly with a lost brooding look, thinking of the cry of the man upon falling, knocked down by his bullet. The first to reach the heights found a dying old man stretched out on the rock. He plunged his bayonet into the body but the old man did not even wink; he had his eyes fixed on Carolino, an indescribable look, and with a bony hand, pointed out to him something behind the boulders.

The soldiers turned and saw Carolino hideously pale,

his mouth open, in his eyes the last flash of reason. Carolino, who was no other than Tano, Cabesang Tales's son who had returned from the Carolines, recognized in the dead one his grandfather, Tandang Selo who, no longer able to speak to him, was telling him with his agonized eyes a poem of sorrow. And, already dead, he still continued to point at something behind the rocks...

- 39 -
The Final Chapter

In his solitary retreat by the shores of the sea, whose shifting surface could be seen through the open windows extending far away to lose itself in the horizon, Padre Florentino distracted his solitude, playing on his reed organ grave and melancholy airs which served as accompaniment to the repeated sonorous clamor of the waves and the murmur of the branches in the nearby woods. Long notes, full, plaintive as a prayer but without lacking vigor, would escape the old instrument; Padre Florentino, who was an accomplished musician, improvised and, because he found himself alone, gave free rein to the sadness in his heart.

Indeed, the old man was very sad. His good friend, Don Tiburcio de Espadaña, had just left, fleeing the persecution of his woman. That morning he had received a little note from the *teniente* of the *guardia civil* which said:

> "My dear Chaplain: I have just received
> from the commandant a telegram which says:
> *Spaniard hidden house Padre Florentino lame capture*
> *dead alive.* As the telegram is expressive enough,
> warn the friend so that he will not be there when
> I go to arrest him at eight o'clock tonight.
>
> Yours ever,
PEREZ
>
> Burn this letter."

"T..t..that Victorina!," Don Tiburcio stammered; "s..she
is capable of having me shot!'

Padre Florentino could not detain him: in vain he
pointed out to the latter that the word for lameness, *(cojera)*
should have been *cogera*, will catch; that the *Spaniard hidden*
could not be Don Tiburcio but the jeweler Simoun, who
two days ago had arrived, wounded and a fugitive, seeking
refuge. Don Tiburcio was not convinced. *Cojera* was to
him lame, his personal description. They were all intrigues
of Victorina's, who wanted to have him at all costs, dead
or alive, as Isagani had written from Manila. And the poor
Ulysses left the priest's house to hide in the hut of a
woodcutter.

Padre Florentino entertained no doubt that the
wanted Spaniard was the jeweler Simoun. He had arrived
mysteriously, carrying his chest himself, bleeding, gloomy
and deeply depressed. With free and cordial Filipino
hospitality, the cleric welcomed him without permitting
himself indiscretions, and since the happenings in Manila
had not yet reached his ears, the situation was not clear to
him. The only conjecture that occurred to him was that
the *General*, the jeweler's friend and protector, having left,

probably Simoun's enemies, the trampled, the injured, were
now coming out clamoring vengeance, and the interim
General was persecuting him to make him let go of the
riches he had accumulated. Hence the flight! But his
wounds, where had they come from? Had he attempted
suicide? Were they the results of personal revenge? Or
were they merely caused by an imprudence, as Simoun
had pretended? Had he received them escaping from the
force that was pursuing him?

This last conjecture appeared to him to have more
prospects of probability. The telegram recently received,
and the stubbornness which Simoun had manifested from
the beginning not to be treated by the doctor of the district,
contributed to and reinforced it. The jeweler accepted only
Don Tiburcio's care, and even then with marked mistrust.
In this case, Padre Florentino asked himself what conduct
he should observe when the *guardia civil* came to arrest
Simoun. The condition of the wounded man would not
permit movement, much less a long journey... But the
telegram said alive or dead...

Padre Florentino ceased playing and approached the
window to contemplate the sea. The deserted surface,
without a ship, without a sail, suggested nothing to him.
The islet which he could make out from a distance, spoke
to him only of his solitude and made the expanse more
solitary. The infinite is at times despairingly mute.

The old man tried to decipher the sad and ironic
smile with which Simoun received the news that he was
going to be arrested. What did that smile mean? And the
other smile, still sadder and more ironical, when he learned
that they would come at eight at night? What did that
mystery mean? Why would Simoun refuse to hide himself?

There came to his mind St. John Chrysostom's

celebrated saying defending the eunuch Eutropius: "Never
was it more opportune to say than now: Vanity of vanities,
and all is vanity."

Simoun, so rich, so powerful, so much feared only a
week ago, now more unfortunate than Eutropius, was
seeking asylum, and not at the altars of a church, but in
the miserable house of a poor *Indio* cleric, lost in the forest
on the lonely shore of the sea! Vanity of vanities and all is
vanity! And that man within a few hours would come to
be a prisoner, dragged from the bed where he lay, without
respect for his condition, without consideration for his
wounds; *alive or dead*, his enemies would claim him! How
to save him? Where could he find the moving accents of
the Bishop of Constantinople? What authority would his
poor words have, the words of an *Indio* cleric, whose own
humiliation that same Simoun in his days of glory had
appeared to applaud and encourage?

Padre Florentino no longer recalled the cold reception
accorded him by the jeweler two months before when he
appealed to him on behalf of Isagani, imprisoned by his
imprudent chivalry; he forgot the action Simoun had
deployed to precipitate the wedding of Paulita, a wedding
which had plunged Isagani into a dreaded misanthropy
which worried his uncle. Padre Florentino forgot all this
and remembered only the condition of the wounded, his
duties as a host, and he wracked his brains. Should he
conceal him to prevent the execution of justice? But if the
man concerned was himself not worried, he was smiling....

Of this the good old man was thinking, when a
servant came to advise him that the wounded man wished
to speak with him. He went to the next room, a clean and
well-ventilated place, with a flooring made of wide boards
smoothed and polished, furnished very simply with big,

heavy armchairs of ancient design, unvarnished and undecorated. There was on one end a large bed of *camagong* with four posts to support the crown of the mosquito net, and on the side a table covered with bottles, lint and bandages; a kneeler at the feet of a Christ and a small library made one suspect that it was the priest's room, ceded to his guest, according to the Filipino custom of offering to the stranger the best table, the best room and the best bed of the house. At the sight of the windows, opened wide to allow the healthful breeze of the sea and to give free entry to the echoes of its eternal lament, no one in the Philippines would have said that a sick person was to be found there, since it is the custom to close all the windows and the smallest cracks as soon as anyone caught a cold or developed a slight headache.

Padre Florentino looked toward the bed and to his great apprehension saw that the countenance of the wounded man had lost its tranquil and mocking expression. A hidden grief seemed to knit his brows; in his look could be read anxiety, and his lips were contracting in a smile of pain.

"Are you suffering, Señor Simoun?" asked the priest solicitously as he approached.

"A little, but in a short while, I shall cease to suffer," he replied, shaking his head.

Padre Florentino clasped his hands aghast, vaguely comprehending a fearful truth.

"What have you done? My God! What have you taken?" And he thrust a hand towards the bottle.

"It is useless! There is no remedy whatsoever!" he answered with a pained smile. "What did you expect I would do? Before it strikes eight...alive or dead...dead, yes, but alive, no!"

"My God, my God! What have you done?"

"Calm yourself!" the wounded man interrupted him with a gesture; "what is done is done. I should not fall alive into anyone's hand....they can drag the secret from me. Do not be upset, do not lose your head, it is useless....Listen to me! Night is coming and there is no time to lose. I must tell you my secret, I need to entrust my last will... I want you to see my life....At the supreme moment I wish to be relieved of a burden; I want to explain to myself a doubt....You who believe so much in God...I want you to tell me if there is a God!"

"But an antidote, Señor Simoun...I have apomorphine...I have ether, chloroform..."

The priest started to look for a flask; Simoun, impatient, cried out:

"It is useless...it is useless! Do not waste time. I will leave with my secret!"

The priest, bewildered, let himself fall on his kneeler, prayed at the feet of the Christ, covering his face with his hands, and afterwards rose serious and grave, as if he had received from his God all the energy, all the dignity, all the authority of the Judge of consciences. He moved a chair to the head of the sick bed and disposed himself to listen.

At the first words that Simoun whispered to him, when he told him his real name, the ancient priest drew back and looked at him in shock. The sick man smiled bitterly. Caught by surprise, the priest was not master of himself. But he soon controlled himself and, covering his face with a handkerchief, again bent himself to lend attention.

Simoun related his sorrowful story, how thirteen years earlier, he had returned from Europe, filled with hopes and pleasing illusions; he came back to marry a young woman whom he loved, disposed to do good and forgive all those who had wronged him so that they would leave him to live in peace. It was not so. A mysterious hand plunged him into the whirlwind of an uprising plotted by his enemies; name, fortune, love, future, liberty, all these he lost and he was only able to escape death thanks to the heroism of a friend. Then he swore to avenge himself. With the family wealth which had been buried in a forest, he fled, went abroad and dedicated himself to commerce. He took part in the war in Cuba, now helping a party, now another, but always profiting. There he met the *General*, then a *comandante*, whose goodwill he captured first by means of advances of money, making himself his friend afterwards, thanks to crimes whose secrets the jeweler possessed. He, by dint of money, was able to secure his appointment and once in the Philippines he made use of him as a blind instrument and pushed him to commit all kinds of injustices, taking advantage of his inextinguishable lust for gold.

The confession was long and tedious, but during it the confessor gave no further sign of surprise and rarely interrupted the sick man. Night had fallen when Padre Florentino, wiping the perspiration from his face, straightened himself, arose, and began to meditate. In the room a mysterious darkness reigned; the moonbeams, entering through the window, were filling it with vague lights and hazy reflections.

In the midst of the silence the voice of the priest sounded sad, deliberate, but consoling:

"God will forgive you, Señor...Simoun," he said. "He knows that we are fallible; He has seen what it is you have suffered, and in His permitting you to find chastisement for your faults, receiving the hand of death from the very ones whom you have instigated, we can see His infinite mercy! He has aborted your plans one by one, the best conceived, first with the death of María Clara, then by a lack of foresight, and afterwards very mysteriously...Let us bow to His will and render Him thanks!"

"According to you," the wounded man replied weakly, "His will would be that these islands..."

"Should continue in the state in which they lament?" concluded the cleric seeing the other hesitate. "I do not know, Señor; I do not read into the thoughts of the Inscrutable! I know that He has not abandoned the people who in the supreme moments have trusted in Him and made Him Judge of their oppression. I know that His arm has never failed anyone when, trampled by justice and drained of all recourse, the oppressed takes the sword and fights for his home, for his woman, for his children, for his inalienable rights that, as the German poet says, shine unshakeable and secure there in the heavens like the eternal stars themselves! No, God who is justice, cannot abandon His own cause, the cause of freedom without which no justice is possible!"

"Why then has He refused me His support?" asked the voice of the wounded man, filled with bitter reproach.

"Because you have chosen a means that He could not sanction," replied the priest in a severe voice: "The glory of saving a country is not for him who has contributed to cause its ruin. You believed that what crime and iniquity have debauched and deformed, another crime and another iniquity could purify and redeem! Fallacy! Hate does not create anything but monsters, crime, criminals. Only love brings in the end marvelous works; only virtue can save!

No, if our country is to be free one day it would not be
through vice and crime; it will not be by corrupting its
sons, deceiving some, buying others, no! Redemption
implies virtue, virtue, sacrifice, and sacrifice, love!"

"Good! I accept your explanation," answered the
wounded man, after a pause. "I have been mistaken but,
because I have been mistaken, does that God have to deny
liberty to a people and save others much more criminal
than I? What are my wrongs beside the crime of those
governing? Why does that God have to take my iniquity
more into account than the cries of so many innocents?
Why has He not wounded me and afterwards made the
people triumph? Why allow so many deserving and just
to suffer, and remain complacently unmoving in the face
of their tortures?"

"The just and the deserving must suffer so that their
ideas may be known and spread out! The vase must be
shaken or broken to spread its perfume; the rock has to be
struck to bring out the spark! There is something
providential in the persecutions of tyrants, Señor Simoun!"

"I knew it," murmured the wounded man, "and
therefore I stimulated the tyranny..."

"Yes, my friend, but it spilled more corrosive liquids
than anything else. You fomented social decay without
sowing a single idea. From that ferment of vices could
only surge revulsion, and if anything was born from night
to morning, it would be at best a mushroom, because
spontaneously only mushrooms can rise from garbage.
True, the vices of a government are fatal to it, cause its
death, but they also kill society in whose bosom they
unfold. An immoral government assumes a demoralized
people, an administration without conscience, rapacious
and servile citizens in the towns; bandits and brigands in

the mountains! Like master, like slave; like Government, like country!"

A short pause reigned.

"Then what can be done?" asked the voice of the wounded.

"To suffer and to work!"

"To suffer...to work!" repeated the wounded man with bitterness. "Ah, it is easy to say that when one does not suffer...when the work is rewarded!.....If your God demands from man such sacrifices, the man who can hardly count with the present, and doubts tomorrow; if you have seen what I have, miserable creatures, unfortunates suffering indescribable tortures for crimes they had not committed, murdered to cover other faults or incapacities; poor fathers of families dragged from their homes to work uselessly on the roads, which are destroyed each morning, and seem only meant to sink their families into misery....ah! suffer...work... is the will of God! Convince those that their murder is their salvation, that their work is the prosperity of their homes! To suffer...to work...What God is This?"

"A very just God, Señor Simoun," replied the priest. "A God who punishes our lack of faith, our vices, the little regard we have for dignity, for the civic virtues....We tolerate and make ourselves accomplices of vice; at times we applaud it. It is just, very just, that we must suffer its consequences and our children must suffer them too! He is the God of liberty, Señor Simoun, who obliges us to love Him by making the yoke heavy for us; a God of mercy, of equity who, while He punishes us improves us, and only concedes well-being to him who has deserved it with his efforts.

"The school of suffering tempers; the arena of combat

strengthens the soul. I do not mean to say that our freedom
is to be won by the blade of the sword; the sword enters
very little now in modern destinies, yes, but we must win
it, deserving it, raising the intelligence and the dignity of
the individual, loving the just, the good, the great, even
dying for it, and when a people reach that height, God
provides the weapon, and the idols fall, the tyrants fall
like a house of cards and liberty shines with the first dawn.

"Our ills we owe to ourselves, let us not toss the blame
to anyone. If Spain sees us less complacent with tyranny
and more disposed to fight and suffer for our rights, Spain
would be the first to give us liberty, because when the
fruit of conception reaches maturity, woe unto the mother
who would wish to stifle it!

"In the meantime, while the Filipino people may not
have sufficient energy to proclaim, with head high and
chest bared, their rights to social life, and to guarantee it
with their sacrifice, with their own blood; while we see
our own countrymen in private life feeling shame within
themselves, to hear roaring the voice of conscience which
rebels and protests, and in public life keep silent, to make
a chorus with him who abuses to mock the abused; while
we see them enclosed in their own selfishness, praising
the most iniquitous deeds with forced smiles, begging with
their eyes for a portion of the booty, why give them
freedom? With Spain and without Spain they would
always be the same, and perhaps, perhaps worse! Why
independence if the slaves of today will be the tyrants of
tomorrow? And they would be, without doubt, because
he loves tyranny who submits to it. Señor Simoun, while
our people may not be prepared, while they may go to
battle beguiled or forced, without a clear understanding
of what they have to do, the wisest attempts will fail and

it is better that they fail, because why commit the wife to the husband if he does not sufficiently love her, if he is not ready to die for her?"[1]

Padre Florentino felt the wounded man catching his hand and taking hold of it. He quieted, waiting for the latter to speak, but he merely felt two pressures and heard a sigh, then a profound silence reigned in the room. Only the sea, whose waves rippled with the night breeze, as if they had awakened from the heat of the day, was sending its harsh roar, its eternal song, upon landing against the jagged rocks. The moon, still unrivalled by the sun, serenely dominated the sky, and the trees of the forest, bowing down to one another, were whispering their ancient legends in mysterious murmurs which were borne on the wings of the wind.

Seeing that the wounded man said nothing, Padre Florentino, as if absorbed in a thought, murmured:

"Where are the youth who will consecrate their golden hours, their illusions, and enthusiasm for the welfare of their country? Where are they who would generously shed their blood to wash away so much shame, so much crime, so much abomination? Pure and spotless the victim has to be for the holocaust to be acceptable!...Where are you, youth who will incarnate in yourselves the vigor of life that has fled from our veins, the purity of ideas that have been soiled in our minds and the fire of enthusiasm that has been extinguished in our hearts?...We wait for you, O youth! Come, for we await you!"

And because he felt his eyes getting wet, he withdrew his hand from Simoun's, arose and approached the window to contemplate the vast expanse of the sea. He was drawn from his meditation by gentle knocks at the door. It was the servant asking if he should light the lamp.

When the priest returned to the wounded man and
saw him by the light of the lamp motionless, eyes closed,
the hand that had pressed his own, open and stretched
along the edge of the bed, he thought for a moment that
he was sleeping; but observing that he was not breathing,
touched him gently and then realized that he was dead.
He was beginning to turn cold. He knelt then and prayed.

When he arose and contemplated the corpse, in whose
visage could be read the most profound grief, the weight
of all of a worthless life which he carried far beyond death,
the old man shuddered and murmured:

"God have mercy on those who have turned away
from the path!"

And while the servants, called by him, knelt and
prayed for the dead, curiously and distractedly looking
toward the bed and repeating *requiems* and more *requiems*,
Padre Florentino removed from a cabinet the celebrated
chest of iron which contained Simoun's fabulous fortune.
He hesitated for an instant, but soon, taking determination,
he descended the stairs with it and went to the cliff where
Isagani was wont to sit to fathom the depths of the sea.

Padre Florentino looked down at his feet. Below could
be seen the dark waves of the Pacific beating on the hollows
of the cliff, producing resounding thunders, at the same
time that, pierced by a ray of the moon, waves and foam
shone as sparks of fire, as a handful of diamonds hurled
into the air by some genie from the abyss. He looked
around him. He was alone. The solitary coast was lost far
away in the vague mist which the moon dissolved until it
lost itself on the horizon. The forest murmured
unintelligible voices. The old man then, with an effort of
his herculean arms, hurled the chest into space, throwing
it into the sea. It turned many times over and descended

rapidly, tracing a slight curve, reflecting some pale rays on its polished surface. The old man saw water drops scatter, heard a loud splash and the abyss closed, swallowing up the chest. He waited for a few moments to see if the depths would disgorge anything, but the waves closed anew, as mysterious as before, without adding a ripple more to the smooth surface, as if into the immensity of the sea only a tiny pebble had fallen.

"May Nature guard you in her deep abysses among the corals and pearls of her eternal seas!" the cleric said solemnly, extending his hand. "When for a holy and sublime end men should need you, God will draw you from the breast of the waves....Meanwhile there you will do no evil, you will not distort right, you will not foment avarice...!"

Notes

Chapter 1

1. *Tabu:* A clean, polished coconut shell, the top cut off, serving as water dipper. A similarly shaped boat made trips to Laguna in Rizal's time, and was called *Batea*.

2. **Ship of State:** A warship, the Crucera Filipina, was constructed in Hong Kong under the supervision of ecclesiastical authorities. Rizal uses it to comment on the state of the Philippine ship of state (Cf. Note 18).

3. *Salambaw:* A fishing apparatus consisting of a floating bamboo platform, a tripod also of bamboo, and a net raised or lowered by pulley.

4. *Karihan:* An eatery serving Filipino dishes (*kari:* cooked food).

5. **Skipper:** According to Judge J. Camus, the ship's captain pictured by Rizal was his uncle Manuel.

6. *Tikines:* Long bamboo poles used to move river craft.

7. **Doña Victorina:** (Cf. the *Noli Me Tangere*) In real life, Doña Agustina Medel, a rich proprietess, owner of the Teatro Zorrilla.

8. **Don Custodio:** A character based on Don A.P.C., who occupied high posts in the Philippine colonial administration.

   Ben Zayb: A character based on several Spanish newspapermen who wrote in the Manila newspapers, among them J. F. del Pan, Francisco Cañamaque, M. Walls y Merino, and others.

   Padre Irene: A character said to be based on the Dean and Synodal Examiner Don E.N.

9. **Don Tiburcio de Espadaña:** In real life Señor Coca, a lame and stuttering Spaniard who married Doña Agustina Medel.

10. **Quatrefages and Virchow:** Jean Louis Quatrefages de Breau (1810-1892), a well-known French ethnologist. Rudolf Virchow (1812-1902), a German pathologist and ethnologist, father of the cellular theory.

11. **Puente del Capricho:** A bridge constructed by the Franciscan Victoriano del Moral in the town of Majayjay, Laguna in 1851. Made only of mortar and never finished, it was condemned by the Chief Architect as an unscientific work. In Majayjay it was known as *Tulay ng Pigi*, literally "Rump Bridge."

12. *Tinsin:* A plant *(Panicum stagninum)* which grows in humid places; its white porous leaves are made into a kind of pith helmet and used as wicks for coconut oil lamps.

13. **Canal:** A plan existed to open a wide canal from the Bar of Napindan to the Parañaque River, which flows into Manila Bay.

14. **Forced Labor:** Fifteen days' work without remuneration for all males was called *polo*, and could be redeemed with money.

15. **House/Hospital:** Hospital de Nuestra Sra. de Aguas Santas de Mainit, run by Royal patronage, and said to have been built by forced labor. Also in Mainit, Los Baños, Laguna, where there are hot springs, there was a vacation house for priests and civil authorities.

16. **Priests:** A predominant and well-propagated theory held that the priests were the ones who sustained the Spanish government in the Philippines and upheld the prestige of Spain.

17. **Padre Sibyla:** A Dominican, Vice-rector of the University of Sto. Tomas, said to be Padre B.N., who later became Archbishop of Manila.

18. **Carolines:** (Cf. Note 2) Because of the conflict with Germany for the possession of the Carolines, a public subscription generated hundreds of thousands of *duros* for the construction of the Crucera Filipina. Padre Payo, Dominican and Archbishop, was a negotiator who was said to have promoted construction at the Hong Kong Arsenal, where the Dominicans were stockholders. The ship was rejected by the Philippine government for reasons of instability, and was therefore a waste of money.

19. *Balut:* A fertilized duck's egg incubated 17-19 days then boiled; it is considered a native delicacy. The industry was based in Pateros and in Pasig.

Chapter 2

1. *Tampipi:* A rectangular covered basket of wicker, fiber or palm leaves, used in rural Philippines as a suitcase.

2. *Buyera:* Seller of *buyo,* the betelnut leaf *(Piper betel)* which, mixed with lime, folded and twisted, is masticated together with a slice of areca nut *(Areca catechu).*

3. *Capitan:* The term for the *gobernadorcillo,* the equivalent of what is now the town mayor.

4. **San Diego:** (Cf. the *Noli*) A town created by Rizal, believed to be based partly on Calamba and Biñan in Laguna, on Malabon in Rizal, and perhaps on Obando in Bulacan.

5. **King's profile:** *Indio* priests were rarely given parishes except those that were poor and could hardly support them, and thus where money, or the King's profile on the coin, was hardly known. They were usually assistants or *coadjutores* of Spanish priests.

6. **Fire and Water:** A popular notion held that the Spaniards were fire and the Filipinos water, action and passivity. Retana points out that fire here is synonymous to revolution.

7. **Secular priests:** A reference to the group of priests headed by Padres Pelaez, Gomez, Burgos, Zamora, Dandan, and the like.

8. **Padre Florentino:** According to Rizal himself, Padre Florentino in the novel was in real life Padre Leon Lopez, priest of his hometown, Calamba, Laguna.

9. **Events of 1872:** The Cavite uprising, in which were implicated the priests Burgos, Gomez and Zamora.

Chapter 3

1. **Hong Kong, Tenants:** Allusion is made to the riches said to have been accumulated in Hong Kong by the Dominican Order; and to the strained relations between the land tenants and the administration of the Hacienda de Calamba, which ended in a lawsuit.

2. **Sancho:** Fixed parochial fees were decreed by the Archbishop of Manila, Don Basilio Sancho de Santa Justa y Rufina, but many priests ignored them and charged higher rates.

3. **Doña Jeronima:** The cave so named is now so undermined by water action and buildings that after some years no trace of it may remain.

4. **Santa Clara:** (Cf. the *Noli*) Maria Clara, betrothed of Ibarra, was cloistered in the Santa Clara convent, run by Franciscans, and supervised by Padre Salvi.

5. **Stone Crocodile:** A legend little remembered, which the friar histories then certified as a miracle.

6. **Sugay, Sungay:** Mountains seen in the background as one enters the Laguna de Bay, leaving the Pasig River.

   Susong Dalaga: The mountain on Talim Island in the lake, named thus beause its peak resembles a maiden's breast.

7. **Kinabutasan:** A place at the mouth of the Pasig River that opens to Laguna de Bay.

8. **Father:** (Cf. the *Noli*) An allusion to Padre Damaso's order to exhume the remains of Ibarra's father and throw them into the lake.

9. **Laguna de Bay:** The lake of the town of Ba-y, of a perimeter of about 36 leagues, in the middle of which is Talim Island, and around which are the coastal towns of Rizal and Laguna provinces, including Jose Rizal's Calamba.

Chapter 4

1. **Religious Order:** The Dominicans owned the town of Calamba and many other lands. Retana points out that this chapter "has the strength of stupendous reality: here are the sufferings of many Calambeños from the friars ..." The lawsuit of Cabesang Tales alludes to the one between the land tenants of Hacienda de Calamba and the Dominican Order.

2. **Tiani, San Diego:** No such towns exist; these settings could refer to the towns of Los Baños and Calamba, as well as to Biñan, Malabon, and Obando.

3. *Cabeza de Barangay:* The chosen chief of a group of families or *barangay* in a town. *Cabezas de barangay* took charge of collecting the taxes or tributes of the families in the barangay, often covering for those who had left, had died, or were unable to pay.

4. **Son (Tano):** It was the custom and regulation at the time that all young men drafted into the military service had to have their heads shaved.

5. *Susmariosep:* A common expression, a contraction of *Jesus, Maria y Jose.*

6. **Firearms:** General Valeriano Weyler issued a decree prohibiting the use and possession of firearms, and a circular (February 1889) ordering the search and decommissioning

of firearms and ammunition in the shops of the capital, and requiring permits for their use.

7. *Panguinguera:* A player of *panguingue*, a game using Spanish cards, popular among the women.

8. **Retreat House of the Society:** A retreat house established by the Jesuits, originally an orphanage, and also called the Nunnery of St. Ignatius. Ignacia del Espiritu Santo, 20, from Binondo, and four companions set up the convent in 1684. Its rules were approved by the archbishop in 1732 and ratified by royal decree in 1761.

9. **Nun:** (Cf. the *Noli*) Maria Clara, daughter of Capitan Tiago, who entered the nunnery because she was not allowed to marry Ibarra.

10. *Tapis:* A piece of cloth, often black, simple or embroidered, worn over the skirt as part of the Filipina dress.

Chapter 5

1. **Procession:** In many places in the Philippines at the time, it was the custom to have a procession leading to the church and ending in Midnight Mass, sometimes as the climax of the *Panunuluyan*, the Christmas play about the search for an inn.

2. **Bernardo, San Mateo:** The Cave of San Mateo is in the mountain of Panitan or Panitinan of the town of San Mateo, Rizal. Folk belief says that Bernardo Carpio—a figure from Spanish folklore adapted into Philippine lore—is chained in it, slowly freeing himself. His struggles cause earthquakes, but when he is free the Philippines will also be liberated.

3. *Huepes:* Torches made of resin, pure or mixed with sawdust, enclosed in palm leaves or bamboo tubes.

Chapter 6

1. **Serve and study:** For lack of means, many young Filipinos anxious to study worked as servants, as did Apolinario Mabini, Cayetano Arellano, and many others. Those admitted to the Colegio de San Juan de Letran or to the Universidad del Sto. Tomas as servants with the privilege to study were called *capistas.*

2. **San Juan de Letran:** A college established in 1620 by a Spaniard, Don Juan Geronimo Guerrero, and supported by the State and by pious donations for primary instruction. In 1706 it was converted into a school for secondary education under the administration of the Dominican Fathers.

3. **Partisan encounter:** Rizal had a similar experience when he and three other students had an encounter with cadets of the military academy, most of them Spaniards and mestizos. He was wounded on his forehead by a stone thrown at them.

4. **Ateneo Municipal:** The Jesuit school, offering primary and secondary education, in which Rizal was a student. Retana says that the Jesuits, "much smarter than the friars, treated all the students with greater consideration, without taking into account the color of their skin. The parallelism established between this center of education and that of San Juan de Letran is ... exact."

5. **Dominican Judges:** The Dominicans then had supervision of instruction, playing the roles of judges in the examinations of the pupils studying in other schools or colleges.

Chapter 7

1. **Brother's murder:** (Cf. the *Noli*) An allusion to the killing of Crispin, Basilio's younger brother, an episode based on an actual incident.

2. **Noble spirit:** (Cf. the *Noli*) The reference is to Elias, who died to save Ibarra. Simoun dedicates himself to this "noble spirit, great soul, magnanimous heart," and Retana points out that in Elias "can well be seen Rizal's own spirit, the essence of his nationalistic ideals ..."

Chapter 8

1. *Batalan:* That part of the house contiguous to the kitchen which, in houses of bamboo and light materials, serves as balcony, but also as place for washing dishes.

2. *Salabat:* A brew of fresh ginger root, sugar and water, traditionally served at Christmas with *bibingka*.

Chapter 9

1. **Padre Clemente:** The friar lay brother of the hacienda, who at the time of the narrative was Padre F.G.

2. *Tandang Basio Macunat:* A narrative in Tagalog (1885) by the Franciscan Miguel Lucio Bustamante. It describes the peaceful life in the countryside, and the agitation in the cities, and propounds the thesis that the *Indio* needed no mentor but the friar, no companion but his carabao, since learning only led to sin.

3. **Lawsuit:** The lawsuit of the tenants against the Hacienda de

Calamba was resolved against the plaintiffs; they were dispossessed of their lands, their houses destroyed, and the lands were given to others who had asked for them.

4. *Tribunal, teniente:* The Tribunal was the municipal building; the Teniente del Barrio was the deputy of the Gobernadorcillo, or the municipal *capitan* in the barrios.

Chapter 10

1. *Bonga:* The palm *(Areca catechu)* the nuts of which are used to prepare *buyo* for chewing.

2. **Booklet:** One of eight books with different subtitles under the common title *Cuestiones de sumo interes* (questions of greatest interest) by Padre Jose Rodriguez, Augustinian.

3. *Tikbalang:* A creature of lower Philippine mythology, believed to appear in different forms, e.g. half man half horse, animal or human with disproportionately large extremities, and to have the power to disorient one and make him lose his way in the forests.

4. **Capitana Ines:** (Cf. the *Noli*) A legendary devotee of the Virgin of Antipolo, publicly proclaimed by the priests as worthy of emulation.

5. **Chinaman Quiroga:** Two Chinese (P and V) were doing business in Manila then, and enjoying favors from the Spaniards, and may have served as Rizal's models. The incidents in the *Fili*, however, are for the most part traceable to Chinaman V. The *señora* alluded to is the spouse of Governor General D.B.W.

6. **Town of Calamba:** Among the many Calamba neighbors

who suffered more or less as Cabesang Tales did, were Rizal's brother and relatives-in-law.

7. **Mariano Herbosa:** The husband of Rizal's sister Lucia, who caught cholera and died in a few hours. Because he was Rizal's brother-in-law, but on the excuse that he had not received the last sacraments, he was refused interment in the town cemetery, and buried instead on the slope of the hillock Lichiria outside of town.

Chapter 11

1. **Bosoboso:** A town outside Manila, southeast of and about three kilometers from Antipolo, now part of Rizal province. Its abundant deer and wild boar population made it a favorite hunting ground for the rich and for civil authorities.

2. **Dampalit:** A spring, which with the water coming from seven falls or *talon* in the locality, formed a river bed with crystal-clear water, to which many went to bathe.

3. **Lake of crocodiles:** A small lake of about two hectares, northeast of the city, called *Dagatan* (sea) or Crocodile Lake, and said to have a subterranean passage to Laguna de Bay. Crocodiles are no longer seen there.

4. *Tresillo:* A Spanish game of cards.

5. **Calamba:** The town in the province of Laguna where Rizal was born. The Isle of Calamba *(Pulung Calamba)* is a small island in Laguna de Bay near and facing the shores of Calamba.

6. **High official:** Rizal refers to Don J.C. y G., a man of liberal ideas, a mason of the 33rd degree, a former chief engineer

of mines, who was civil governor of Manila when Rizal returned to the country in 1887.

7. **Padre Fernandez:** It is believed that Rizal based this noble and just character on Professor M.L., professor of Chemistry, one of his teachers in higher medicine, who according to Baldomero Roxas was a perfect gentleman.

8. **Countess:** "La Condesa" was the spouse of the Director of Commerce, Don F.A.N. y G. of L., Count of Yumuri, who was in the Philippines from 1886 to 1892. He was the chief of the Department of Civil Administration, and was sent to the city as a disciplinary measure in punishment for abuses in the discharge of his duties.

9. **Schools:** In many towns, the elementary schools under the supervision of priests were in dilapidated shacks or in convent vestibules. They might consist of a table for the teacher and a few benches for the students, but without equipment or teaching aids. Governor General Weyler decreed improvements and approved funds for the buying of teaching materials, but this was hardly implemented.

10. **Teaching of Spanish:** Despite the royal decrees that Spanish should be taught to the Filipinos, there was systematic opposition from some religious orders to put them into practice. They abhorred it "by instinct," and called it "against Spain." Retana pointed out that the priests knew the indigenous languages, the other Spaniards did not, and this made them the only ones who directly understood the Filipinos. Opposing the teaching of Spanish was thus a ploy of power.

Chapter 12

1. **Padre Valerio:** Padre Valerio Kalaw Malabanan (1820-1885),

a native of Lipa, Batangas, studied philosophy at San Juan de Letran and theology at the University of Sto. Tomas, where he was a *capista*. He was the parish priest of Lipa, but resigned from his ecclesiastical responsibilities and dedicated himself to teaching, opening a school in Tanauan, Batangas (1865) which acquired great fame in the country as the Colegio del Padre Valerio.

2. *Hunkian, revisino:* Both card games, the first simple and popular among young people; the second more complicated.

3. **Puente de España:** The bridge spanning the Pasig River and joining Magallanes with Nueva Street in Binondo. It stood near where Jones Bridge now stands.

4. **Ateneo:** Called the Ateneo Municipal when Rizal was a student, it was situated at Calle Arzobispo Nos. 4, 6 and 8, and was famous for its method of teaching and its treatment of the students. It started as a school for primary education in 1859; by Royal Order of May 20, 1885, it opened a secondary level attached to the University of Sto. Tomas. Today it is the Ateneo de Manila University.

5. **Letranites:** Students of the Colegio de San Juan de Letran, which was headed by Dominicans and established at Calle Muralla No. 2, where it still stands. Founded primarily for poor children and orphans of Spanish parents, it became a Colegio in 1706 and started to receive native students and Chinese (Cf. Chapter VI, note 2).

6. **University:** The University of Sto. Tomas, founded in 1611 as the Colegio de Sto. Tomas.

7. **Escuela Municipal:** A school directed by the Madres de la Caridad (Sisters of Charity) of St. Vincent de Paul, situated in the Plaza de la Fuerza, contiguous to the Fuerza de Santiago (Fort Santiago), then later in Victoria, Intramuros.

8. **Sto. Domingo:** One of the four gates to the north of the walled city, the third coming from the west near the old convent of Sto. Domingo in Intramuros.

9. *Barbero:* He who flatters, fawns, is servile.

10. **Aduana:** The old customs house, later occupied by the old Central Bank, now assigned to the National Archives.

11. **Padre Baltazar:** Probably Padre Baltazar Font, first rector of the University of Sto. Tomas. The monument, however, was in reality for the Archbishop, Fr. Miguel Benavides, considered the founder of the University. It was constructed with university funds and private contributions, finished in 1889 and inaugurated in 1891.

12. **Professor of Natural History:** Padre Castro de Elera.

13. *Saragate:* Rogue, truant.

14. *Cuacha:* To play hooky, play truant, not attend classes.

15. *Carabineros celestiales:* This refers to the "Militia Angelica," a student association founded and organized by the Dominican fathers, Retana says, to keep "Amen" Catholic Thomasites unconditionally inclined to them.

16. *Tinamaan: Tinamaan ng lintik,* or "struck by lightning" was a common exclamation or curse.
17. *Raya:* The mark or sign placed on a class list beside the name of a student, indicating absences or faulty recitation.

Chapter 13

1. **Preparatory classes:** Courses preparatory to study for higher degrees, especially medicine.

2. *Capista:* The domestic or servant given the privilege of studying in the colleges or the University.

3. **Padre Millon:** Padre G. B. de la R., then professor in the preparatory course for medicine at the University.

4. **Ramos, Ganot:** Names of authors of textbooks on physics used in the University of Sto. Tomas.

5. **Secchi:** Angelo Secchi, S.J. was an Italian Jesuit professor of Astronomy and director of the observatory of the Roman College. He did several spectrographic and physics experiments on heavenly bodies, and wrote many treatises. When the Jesuits were expelled from Italy in 1870, he retired as director of the observatory.

6. *Camagong: (Diospyros discolor, Willd)* Ebony; a tree of hard wood, fine-grained and dark in color, much appreciated for the making of furniture and artistic objects.

7. *Per se, in quantum est superficies:* By nature, as much as it is the surface.

8. *Quae super faciem est, quia vocatur superficies facies ea quae supra videtur:* That which is on top, because surface is what is called the face that is seen on top.

9. *Bibingka:* A cake made from rice flour, sometimes with coconut milk and sugar. It may also be made from unmilled glutinous rice, or from cassava or other kinds of flour.

10. *Linintikan:* Tagalog word meaning "struck by lightning."

11. *Liber dixit ergo ita es:* The book says so, therefore it is.

12. *Soplado, sopladurias:* Corruptions of the Spanish words

chiflado (arrogant), *chifladuria* (arrogance), and used here in a tone of haughty insult.

13. *Jusito, jusito, señolia:* Pidgin Spanish meant to insult the Chinese—and the Filipinos—and their way of speaking Spanish.

14. *Sulung! Apuera la fuerta:* An aggressive and coarse way of saying "Out of here!" (*sulung* meaning to advance, to go), "Out the door!" Since the native alphabet does not have an F, it is often confused with P, and the Dominican corrupts the phrase (*Afuera de la puerta*) to mortify the Filipino student.

15. *Ñol:* Pidgin contraction of *Señor*.

16. **Philosophaster:** Fake philosopher, here used not only sarcastically, but contemptuously.

Chapter 14

1. **Lodging House:** The scene described here is typical of students' lodging houses on Sto. Tomas St. (then Postigo), where Rizal stayed while in the University. Among the lodgers this house was known as Casa Tomasina.

2. *Sipa:* A game in which a ball made of woven rattan strips is tossed by players with their feet. It is played in the Philippines and other Southeast Asian countries, and is now called *sepak takraw* in formal competitions.

3. *Bilao:* A round tray-like basket made of fine bamboo strips.

4. *Hopia:* A Chinese pastry filled with mashed beans.

5. **Acting General:** The interim general referred to was

Deputy General A.M. y D.B., who was in the Philippines from 1886-1889; he was the one who acted on the censorship of the *Noli*. The Father Provincial then seems to have been Padre J.G.

6. **School of Malolos:** Some young women of Malolos, Bulacan, sought permission to open a school at which Spanish would be taught in the evenings. It was opposed "for reasons of morality".

7. **School of Arts and Trades:** Created by Royal Decree of April 5, 1889, it was established and inaugurated on October 15, 1890, offering theoretical and practical courses. In view of difficulties in realizing its objectives, the Gobernadorcillos, principals and neighbors of the province of Bulacan elevated the problem to the governor of the province, proposing that he open a voluntary subscription for it.

8. **Decoration on the ankles:** A reference to the chain-linked iron rings (ball and chain) around the ankles of prisoners.

9. *Araña:* A vehicle pulled by two horses and guided by the owner, with a *cochero* seated behind him.

10. **Prior censorship:** No book could be printed nor introduced into the country without permission. Despite this, prohibited books entered the country clandestinely by private means or through bookstores. It is said that in the last years of the Spanish regime, even chapters of Cervantes's *Don Quixote* were suppressed by the censor.

11. **Quiroga:** Retana calls him "a perfect picture of the Chinaman V." who had in Manila a bazaar for European goods. Rumors said that it had rooms in which certain priests met with female saints. J. Alejandrino believes, however, that Quiroga was the Chinaman P. since Rizal never alluded to Chinaman V.

12. **Superior Commission of Primary Instruction:** A body which had the Governor General as president, the Archbishop of Manila as vice-president, and seven directors, one of them acting as secretary; and yet had no practical functions, these being relegated to the parish priests in the towns and provinces.

Chapter 15

1. **Señor Pasta:** Rizal seems to have pictured the well-known lawyer Don C.A. or someone similar, who, both egotistic and accommodating, never moved a finger to improve the miserable conditions of his countrymen. At the end of the chapter, however, Rizal recognizes that despite his egotism the lawyer had not completely erased the Filipino from his heart.

2. **Isagani:** The character who, in his ideas of opposition, perfectly matched the character and ideas of the author. Some believe him to be a picture of the prominent Batangueño lawyer, Don Vicente Ilustre, but others call this erroneous since the latter had no contact with Rizal.

3. **Boys in Madrid:** The Filipinos in Europe, who despite limited facilities and resources, actively campaigned for reforms in the colonial administration of the country. They sought representation in the Cortes and other liberal reforms.

4. **Servants to all the friars:** He (Señor Pasta) had been a *capista* at the University of Sto. Tomas.

Chapter 16

1. **Mexican peso affair:** A reference to the smuggling of Mexican pesos, from which the Chinese profited greatly by

transporting them to China.

2. **Lottery tickets:** Lottery reforms were decreed in August 1888, increasing the number of lottery tickets for sale. It was rumored, however, that a greater part of the tickets were exported abroad, and that because of this, premiums were collected, from which Quiroga and the Governor General's wife benefited.

3. **Port works:** The delay in the finishing of the port works. The Ministry of Works of the Port of Manila was created on January 2, 1880 to undertake the construction of a new port designed to meet specific objectives: 2% on the value of merchandise imports; 1% on that of exports; 20 centavos per peso for every ton of ship cargo from the high seas; 10 centavos per ton for coastal ships, products of free trade established on the fishing grounds; 12,000 pesos annually from the general budget; income from the sale of land reclaimed from the sea; income from the lease on those properties or of the constructions set up there.

4. **Cloth of Guadalupe:** Rizal may have been thinking of the cloth of Penelope, which she wove, unraveled and rewove as she waited for Ulysses to return from the Trojan War. He may also have been thinking of the Virgin of Guadalupe, who caused the miracle in which the peasant Diego found his cape not only filled with unseasonal fresh roses, but imprinted with the image of the Virgin. Was it association, or a slip of the pen (he wrote in longhand), as when he wrote "Francisco Gomez" instead of "Mariano Gomez" in his dedication of the *Fili?*

5. **Pigtails:** A reference to the braided queue Chinese used to wear. The newspaper of Chinese partisans was *El Comercio.*

6. **Chinese and religious ceremonies:** An allusion to the preference given to the Chinese in religious ceremonies in

Binondo district, which the natives protested. In 1886 in Binondo the Dominican priest Fr. J.H.C. decided to award the presidency of the ceremonies to the Chinese and Chinese mestizos since they had paid the most. The Filipinos, headed by Gobernadorcillo Timoteo Lanuza, protested. The case was elevated to the Governor General, who decided in favor of the natives. The priest did not agree, and was removed from his position. The case was elevated to Señor Favie, Minister of the High Seas, who ruled in favor of the priest, who much later was named bishop.

7. *Hapay:* An indigenous word meaning bankruptcy, failure in business; also prostrate, drooping.

8. **Beautiful and enchanting lady:** The Countess (Cf. Chapter XI, note 8).

Chapter 17

1. *Tabi-tabi:* A *cochero*'s cry, meaning "Make way, move aside."

2. *Camisa* and *pañuelo:* The *camisa* is the bodice of the Filipina dress, with an open neck and butterfly sleeves. The *pañuelo* is a stiff triangular scarf or fichu, carefully folded and pinned over the camisa to frame the wearer's face.

Chapter 18

1. *Why ba ...:* The dialogue in these three paragraphs is in *lengua de tienda* (market language), or pidgin Spanish spoken in a manner peculiar to Ermita, Cavite and Zamboanga.

2. **"I loved a damsel ...":** (Cf. the *Noli*) This is the Ibarra-Maria Clara story.

Chapter 19

1. *Hamok:* Amok, a state of exultation and momentary insanity that incites a person to kill.

2. *Baticuling, laniti:* Two important forest trees (*Litsea leitensis*, *Wrightia laniti* respectively) favored for sculpture because they are clean, light, white and easy to carve. Rizal used them in his work.

3. **Sibakong:** A district bounded by the streets La Coste (now Ongpin), Arranque (now T. Alonzo), Tetuan, Espeleta, etc. in Sta. Cruz, Manila.

4. *Ciriales:* Tall silver candlesticks carried by sacristans in church processions.

5. **San Fernando:** The street of San Fernando in the district of San Nicolas, Manila.

6. **Iris Street:** Calle Iris, now part of Azcarraga, running between the streets of San Pedro (Evangelista) and Alix (now Legarda).

7. **Vigilant mothers or aunts:** Well-brought-up young girls in those days never went out alone, but were always chaperoned by an elder person, usually a member of the family.

8. *Tubigan:* A children's game involving two teams crossing lines in a quadrilateral pattern usually drawn on the street with water. The game is also known as *patintero.*

9. **Castillero:** One who makes *castillos*, or towers of fireworks; a pyrotechnist.

10. **Lamayan:** Now a street in Sta. Ana, it used to be a barrio

where, it was believed, the foundry of Panday Pira was when the Spaniards arrived in Manila.

11. **Schoolmaster:** (Cf. the *Noli*) The teacher who complained of the scanty attention given by those who had the duty to teach young people in the Philippine towns.

12. **Trozo:** A Binondo barrio consisting of the principal streets San Jose (now Magdalena) and Benavides and cross streets like Salazar, Piedad, Soler, General Izquierdo (now C.M. Recto). On San Jose Rizal's family lived when they returned from Hong Kong. In Trozo the founders of the Katipunan met frequently.

Chapter 20

1. **Sociedad Económica de Amigos del Pais:** The Economic Society of Friends of the Country, founded by Governor Don Jose Basco y Vargas in 1781 by the Royal Order of August 27, 1780 for the cultural and economic development of the country. Dr. Ferdinand Blumentritt was a member till he resigned.

2. **Obras Pías:** The Obras Pías de la Misericordia was founded in 1854 to give out loans from its funds. It was governed by an administrative board composed of a president and seven members under the board directorate.

3. **Misericordia:** La Real Casa de la Misericordia or the Brotherhood of Mercy was founded on April 16, 1594, with the objective of dedicating itself to works of piety, among which were: the gathering and education of orphaned girls, the care of disabled Spaniards, the operation of a sort of monetary post office, and the establishment of lending houses to combat usury.

4. **Banco Español Filipino:** Created by decree of the Government of the islands on August 11, 1851, and approved by Royal Decree on October 17, 1854. It was managed by a board composed of two directors, two comptrollers and six council members. It is now the Bank of the Philippine Islands.

5. **Board of Health of Manila:** Called the Superior Board of Health, distinct from the Provincial Boards of Health and from the Municipal Board of Health of Manila. It had the duty to watch over public health, and was composed of a president, a vice-president, 33 members and a secretary. A member of the board was Conrad Labhart, the Austrian consul in Manila and a friend of Ferdinand Blumentritt's.

6. **Central Vaccination Board:** Established for the vaccination against viruses, with the Governor General as president and nine members, of which three had to be physicians.

7. **Kerosene lighting:** The first time it was used for illumination was in the Teatro Circulo de Bilibid (now Bilibid Viejo), but according to J. Atayde, the lamps were a failure.

8. **Antaeus:** A mythological giant, son of Neptune and the earth, who loses his Herculean strength when he does not have his feet on the ground.

9. *Kundiman, balitaw, kumintang:* Philippine songs of local origin, rhythm and flavor.

10. **Man on his knees:** A gesture that indicates keeping the *Indio* submissive and on bended knee.

11. **The English whip:** The salutary influence of the priests was claimed to be superior to the English whip, because aside from gathering souls, it was accompanied by the Spanish lash.

12. *Arroba:* A Spanish weight of 25 pounds.

13. **Epaminondas:** A Greek statesman and general, hero of Thebes, who won in the battle of Leuktra in 371 B.C. He founded the city of Megalopolis and died in a battle in the year 363 B.C.

Chapter 21

1. **Teatro de Variedades:** Formerly the Kiosko, constructed on Arroceros Street for public dances, then converted into a theater. The performance Rizal describes refers to one in August 1886 sponsored by Don Justo Martin Lunas, civil governor of Manila, of the *zarzuela Pascual Bailon,* in which the comic Valentin Fernandez and the well-known Yeyeng Fernandez "unleashed a cancan *without reservations,* so thoroughly without reservations that not a few grave gentlemen closed their eyes." Señor Lunas never again hosted another entertainment, and Archbishop of Manila P. Payo unleashed a pastoral letter against "indecorous public spectacles."

2. **Camaroncocido:** In Manila one Don N.A. y R., owner of a bookstore, was also nicknamed Camaroncocido, but Rizal's description does not fit him.

3. *Tarifa:* A book of rates or duties.

4. **M.M.:** A French shipping company called Mensajerias Maritima.

5. *Bago:* Someone new, a recent arrival in the country.

6. **Doctor K:** Dr. Don Alberto Diaz of Quintana who presented himself as a specialist in children's diseases, but dedicated

most of his time to writing in the newspaper under the pseudonym Ximeno Ximenez. He was given the nickname Herodes.

7. **Draftees:** To avoid military service, draftees availed themselves of medical certificates alleging sickness, and the doctors issuing them earned a great deal of money.

8. **Chemist S:** Don Anacleto del Rosario y Sales, Filipino.

9. **Governor of Pangasinan:** Don Carlos Peñaranda, who on May 29, 1891 issued to the Gobernadorcillos of Pangasinan the celebrated decree of salutes, in which all natives, under pain of death, must uncover themselves upon meeting any peninsular. The decree was issued scarcely two months before the publication of *El Filibusterismo*, indicating Rizal's constant communication with the Filipino propagandists and his knowledge of the happenings in the country.

Chapter 22

1. **Artillery men:** The artillery men were the only peninsular soldiers in the colony, and being Spaniards did as they wished. The veterans, however, were *Indios*, and notwithstanding their positions as security guards, were not often obeyed by the Spaniards, especially by those with official or social positions.

2. **Flowers:** An allusion to the *piropos*, or verbal flattery with which Spanish men compliment women, carried over to the Philippines, where in some cases they became gross and in bad taste.

3. **Whistles:** The blowing of whistles by the footmen or coachmen of the Captain General, announcing his arrival.

In the theater, however, a whistle indicates active disapproval.

4. **Purveyor of the Royal House:** A vulgar way of referring to the person or company supplying merchandise to Malacañang Palace.

5. *Cabezas:* The Cabezas de Barangay were in charge of the collection of taxes and tribute.

6. *Panciteria:* Among the first places for public eating in Manila were Chinese restaurants. The name is a Spanish formulation derived from *pansit*, or noodles.

Chapter 23

1. **Street of the Hospital:** The shortest way to the Convent of Sta. Clara from what was called the Plaza de Almacenes to Palacio Street, Intramuros. The hospital was the San Juan de Dios Hospital, which was then along San Juan de Dios St.

2. **Professor:** An allusion to Don Jose Lopez Irastorza.

3. **Manila censor:** The Comision Permanente de Censura was composed principally of priests who were very strict about granting approval to the works of liberal authors which Manila booksellers imported for sale. All the writings of Dr. Mata, abstracted and published by him in the folio *The Censorship of the Press in Manila* (Madrid, 1908), were absolutely condemned. The professor Rizal describes was secular; no priest would have inspired himself with Mata's famous text because he was a rationalist.

4. **Insult:** Rizal and other Filipinos deeply lamented the one-sided application of the law on censorship in the Philippines.

Publications denigrating Filipinos were permitted, but any responses were not.

Chapter 24

1. **Paseo de Ma. Cristina:** A part of what is now known as Andres Bonifacio Drive, located between the Pasig River and the battlement of San Diego.

   Malecon: That part of the actual Bonifacio Drive from San Diego Boulevard to San Luis Street, now a part of Roxas Boulevard.

2. **Sappho:** Greek poetess of Mitilene, who commited suicide for love by throwing herself into the sea.

   Polyhymnia: Muse of lyric poetry.

3. **Anda monument:** It still exists, but has been moved from the Paseo de Ma. Cristina to the rotonda where Bonifacio Drive and 13th Street cross in the Port Area.

4. **Luneta:** At that time the favorite promenade of Manila high society, made up by an oblong space between San Luis St. and P. Burgos and ending at M.H. del Pilar. It was the Bagumbayan Field on which Rizal was executed in 1896.

5. **Young men in Madrid:** The Filipinos like Marcelo H. del Pilar, Mariano Ponce, Graciano Lopez Jaena, Jose Ma. Panganiban, Eduardo de Lete, Rizal himself, and others. They worked hard to obtain political advantages for the country. One of the reasons Rizal left Madrid was the belief that in the Cortes Filipino aspirations were not being attended to.

6. **Mandaluyong:** In the town of San Felipe Neri, now

Mandaluyong City, there existed factories of brick, clay and tile.

7. **Paseo de la Sabana:** The walk from the Luneta, which is now Padre Burgos, towards the Pasig River.

Chapter 25

1. **Plaza of Vivac:** Now called Plaza de Cervantes, between Rosario and J. Luna Streets (before Anloague).

2. **The boy, the nun:** (Cf. the *Noli*) Again, the stories of Crispin and Maria Clara from the *Noli*, both based on fact.

3. *Pansit lang-lang:* A noodle dish with broth, popular in Chinese *panciterias*, with flour *(miki)* and/or mung bean *(sotanjun)* noodles, chicken, shrimps and eggs.

4. *Patis:* A fish sauce made from fermented salted shrimp or small fish; it has analogues throughout Southeast Asia.

5. *Cuapi:* A word used vulgarly to signify money.

6. **Expulsion:** The expulsion of the friars had been recommended by Simon de Anda, and again called for in a fearless exposé elevated to Governor General Don Emilio Terrero y Perinat in 1888 by the Gobernadorcillos of the districts of Manila. Don Joaquin Pardo de Tavera, at the time of Governor General La Torre, also headed a group formulating a similar plea.

7. **Remove the friar, and ...:** These two paragraphs constitute a fine satire of the then prevalent theory that the priest was everything in the colonial administration, and without him the structure would collapse.

Chapter 26

1. **Professor:** An allusion to Don Salvador Naranjo.

2. **Pasquinade:** A lampoon hung up in a public place; in the *Fili*, the putting up by students of posters judged subversive by the authorities. It is not known whether something like this actually happened in Manila, but Rizal seems to have had in mind the student strike in the Central University of Madrid which was triggered by the speech of Professor of History Don Miguel Morayta at the opening of the schoolyear 1884-85, in which he defended academic liberty and science. As a result, Morayta was excommunicated by the Bishop of Avila who later became Bishop of Toledo, followed by other excommunications. The speech, they claimed, contained "heretical propositions and errors." The Madrid students made common cause with students of the Universities of Sevilla, Barcelona, Granada, Valladolid, Oviedo, Zaragoza and Valencia, as well as the special schools, institutes and centers of private education in Spain. The event provoked the civil authorities to violence, resulting in abuses and maltreatment of the students and even of the Rector of the University, and the resignation of deans. Rizal said that many students were wounded and imprisoned, among them Filipinos. Rizal took part in this strike, and was at the point of being arrested together with Valentin Ventura, but they were able to evade their pursuers by hiding in the house of Don Miguel Morayta. Rizal relates that in one day he had to change his appearance thrice.

Chapter 27

1. **Friars and education:** Notwithstanding the Superior Board of Instruction that had been created by decree, the priests managed the teaching in and exercised supervision over educational institutions.